What they're saying...

". . . Wiley's writing continues to be descriptive and engaging. . . This timely storyline is relative and finds Jack Quinn, once again, over his head. . . ." —Dick Carter, *TATTOO 313*
Former VP of marketing, RCA Records / CEO Konica camera company

"...a hurricane, dismasted sailboat, death and a whale encounter and you have the makings of a great read...you feel like your sailing right along with him." —AC, *Eyewitness*

"The story itself is fantastic. A murder mystery set at sea. A man and a whale vs two thugs....it [has] one of the most interesting court scenes I've ever read in a book!" — In the Bookcase, *Eyewitness*

"SUPERB!! Well-written account of the Joola! This book holds so many descriptions and details of the shipwreck. I enjoyed reading it. For anyone interested in maritime history, this is definitely a must-read."
— In The Bookcase, *The Sinking of the MV Le Joola*

"Senegal, Africa, Unheard Heros. 5/5 stars.... You won't want to put it down! A true story of a disaster so enormous yet so preventable...their fight to survive in an unbelievable struggle against all odds...and how their government failed them. [A] story that will make you wonder why the rest of the world has had little news and so little interest. Get your handkerchief out." — *The Sinking of the MV Le Joola*

"Exciting & Educational. This tale is both haunting and educational.... one to sure stick with you for a long time to come."
— *The Sinking of the MV Le Joola*

Books by Pat Wiley

— Jack Quinn Series —

EYEWITNESS
a nautical murder mystery

ROUND HOUSE
a deadly side to paradise

TATTOO 313

The Sinking of the MV Le Joola
One of the worst maritime disasters in history

Sign up for notification of new releases at
PatWileyAuthor.com

A JACK QUINN NOVEL

TATTOO 313
by Pat Wiley
A Jack Quinn Novel, Book 3

First Edition

Published By
First Steps Publishing
PO Box 571
Gleneden Beach, Oregon 97388-0571
publish@firststepspublishing.com

Cover Illustration, Interior and Cover Design by Suzanne Fyhrie Parrott

ISBN
978-1-944072-33-9 (pbk/Amazon)
978-1-944072-35-3 (epub)
978-1-944072-34-6 (pbk/Ingram)

10 9 8 7 6 5 4 3 2 1

Printed in the
United States of America

To my granddaughter Caitlin -
may her love of reading stand out
as an inspiration for her generation.

CHAPTER ONE

Voices . . . a strange language . . . someone was holding my head up to give me something to drink . . . couldn't move . . . laughter when I tried to speak.

These were the dream-like memories to which Jack slowly awakened in pitch-black space. Confused, with no sense of where he was, he was shocked to find his right hand bound to a long chain with the end wrapped tight around his wrist and fastened by a padlock.

Fully awake now, he realized he was naked, lying on a foul-smelling mattress on the concrete floor of a basement. He sat up . . . his mind reeling . . . groping with reality, like waking from a nightmare, but knowing this was no dream. Then, like lightning splitting open a dark sky, a vivid memory broke through his consciousness—he remembered pulling a dart out of his leg—seeing a man in the woods grinning at him—and discerning he'd been drugged.

Crawling across the damp floor, looking for the end of the chain, he found it led to the top of a thick iron rod sticking out of a heavy cast iron dish about three feet in diameter. He tried lifting it, carefully, not wanting to make any noise. He was strong, strong enough to ward off charging linemen when he played football in college, but he couldn't lift it off the floor.

Tracing the outline of the object with his left hand, he recognized it as a mushroom anchor, the kind used in harbors for mooring boats. He guessed this one was over four hundred pounds. He might be able to drag it a bit, but knew he'd never get far.

Feeling his way around the walls, as far as the chain would let him, he surmised he was in the cellar of a small house. From dim light coming in at the end of the room, he estimated the basement was twenty to twenty-five feet long. As his eyes adjusted to the dark, he made out the shadow of a walkout where moonlight was leaking through overhead slanted metal doors.

His thoughts were interrupted when he heard the metallic sound of the doors swinging open. A moment later, a single light bulb came on illuminating someone standing on the stairs staring at him. It was Tuma, a man Jack suspected was somehow involved in the death of his best friend.

"Ah . . . you're awake Mr. Quinn! You look surprised to see me—you shouldn't be. I thought you were smart enough to know there would be consequences for meddling in my affairs," Tuma said as he walked up to Jack with a smug look on his face.

Tuma was a new businessman in town, disliked by most who met him, though no one knew much about him. They'd met only twice and Jack believed he wasn't who he claimed to be.

"You're right, I didn't think you would go this far to keep people from knowing what you're up to. But this is pretty stupid. How long do you plan on keeping me here like this?" Jack said, holding up the chain.

"Long enough to use you for an experiment. You weren't in my original plan, but sticking your nose in my business has offered me the opportunity to get rid of two problems at the same time."

"What two problems?"

"The first is you—you've become too inquisitive. I can't afford for you to stumble upon . . . ah, let's call it a "project" I'm working on. And as for my second problem, well, you'll see about that soon enough Mr. Quinn." Tuma ended his little speech with a sadistic grin.

“Are you going to share your plans with me—or am I supposed to guess?”

“In due time, Mr. Quinn—in due time,” Tuma said and started to walk out.

“How long have I been here?” Jack quickly asked.

“A couple of days, but don’t waste my time asking questions,” he answered as he continued to walk away.

“Tell me something! Why did you kill Tom? Did he stumble onto your terrorist plot?” Jack needed to keep him talking, so he’d taken a wild guess.

Tuma spun around with a surprised look on his face. “Terrorist? Who told you I was a terrorist?”

“You think I was acting alone?” Jack replied. “Well I’ll tell you something, the people I’m working with are far better than me. They know who you are and where you came from—including your terrorist friends. They won’t make the same mistakes I did.”

“Good try, Mr. Quinn, but I don’t believe a word of what you say. You remind me of a borfoot sailor who also appeared at the right time and right place for me. Now let me give you something to think about. I’m going to expedite my plans for you. We will begin tomorrow morning.”

Jack saw the anger in Tuma’s countenance as he turned around to walk out. He also saw his demonic sneer as he looked back before turning off the light and exiting the cellar.

My terrorist comment must have gotten to him, Jack surmised as he considered the confrontation. *But saying I remind him of a ‘borfoot sailor’ . . . what the hell could that mean? Maybe I didn’t hear him right, but he was clear about expediting his plans for me.* Thinking about it reminded Jack of why he suspected that his friend, Tom, didn’t kill himself and that Tuma was somehow responsible for Tom’s death. He was now sure of it—with the realization he would be next.

He had no idea what time it was, but knew it must be in the evening from the night sky he viewed when Tuma entered and exited the cellar.

With sunrise coming around six, Jack guessed he'd have no more than eight hours before they came for him. He knew Kate would be very worried by now. They'd been married long enough for her to know when to worry and when not to. She'd be calling people who would also be worried, including Max Cruz and Ray Carson.

I should've told Max where I was headed, was Jack's sobering thought, knowing he couldn't count on anyone finding him in time. Tuma's words were ominous—implying he wouldn't be alive much longer. His only chance was to find a way to escape and at the moment that looked to be nearly impossible.

This was the second time in two years that the inquisitive side of Jack led to someone trying to kill him. Max, an ex-navy seal had saved him the first time, but this time he was on his own. He had ignored the advice of Max, and detective Ray Carson, both warning him of the risks of going solo. But there was no way he could have known that prying into the death of his best friend would involve him in a terrorist plot, and ultimately a constitutional crisis unlike anything the country had ever seen.

Trying to fight off an overwhelming feeling of despair, he began reflecting on how it all began . . . ten days before . . . the night he came home from a sailing race . . . .

CHAPTER TWO

It was midnight when Jack arrived home—bone tired from 36 hours of sailing around Long Island.

"Hi, how was the race?" Kate asked as he opened the door to their bedroom.

He paused, standing there for a moment—wanting to absorb the scene. His beautiful wife had been sitting up in bed reading on her Kindle—she looked up at him with a loving smile as she welcomed him home with her question.

"Okay, came in third, not bad considering the level of competition. I'll tell you about it in the morning, too tired now," he said while undressing for bed.

"What were you reading?" he whispered after turning off the light and climbing in next to her.

"Oh . . . a book on how the balance of power has been changing amongst our three branches of government. Needed to brush up after watching the news tonight. The Secretary of Defense resigned today after President Cain fired the Chairman of the Joint Chiefs of Staff. Looks to me like he's putting only like-minded people in place. This book talks about how congress has been yielding more and more power to the presidency for over fifty years. Cain's taking advantage of that, Jack, and I think he could be a risk to our democracy."

"You're getting paranoid, Kate, but even if you're right, there are safeguards in our Constitution to prevent that. Right now, I need to sleep. I'm too tired for this, Kate. Let's just agree to disagree. We'll take this up another time," Jack said as he rolled over and pulled a pillow over his head to end the conversation.

Jack didn't totally discount what she said, but he liked the way the president was shaking everything up. He believed the country needed it. Still, he had to admit he was troubled by the man's ego. The self-aggrandizing way he did things. Kate's comments loomed large in his fatigued mind as he drifted off to sleep . . .

"Jack! Your cell phone's ringing," Kate said as she shook him awake. It took a moment before realizing he was home, not on the boat. Coming out of a deep sleep he stumbled out of bed and was surprised to see 3:00 am on the screen as he picked up the phone.

"Hello . . . " he groaned, barely half awake, but with the rising apprehension that comes from someone calling in the middle of the night.

"It's Meg, Jack . . . Tom shot himself. He's dead!"

"My God! Why, Meg? What happened?" he said, shocked by her cold hard statement. He was wide-awake now and sat down on the edge of the bed.

"I don't know why!"

"When? You mean just now?"

"No. I think about a half hour ago, that's when I heard the shot. I was sleeping. I found him on the floor in the kitchen. Didn't know he was dead. Then I saw the bullet wound in his head. I kept staring at him, not knowing what to do. I called the police and they're on their way over. Can you please come, Jack? I don't want to be alone when they get here."

Jack hesitated before answering. She wasn't crying. He didn't hear any pain or emotion in her voice. She was talking about Tom like he was a stranger—not her husband who'd just killed himself.

"Okay, Kate and I will leave as soon as we get dressed." He hung up before she could respond.

Kate was out of bed standing next to him, anxiously waiting to ask what's going on. She'd heard enough to know something awful had happened. "It's about Tom, isn't it? How bad?"

"He's dead, Kate. Meg says he shot himself and wants me to come over. Something doesn't sound right. I think you should come too. Better hurry. I'll tell you what she said when we're in the car."

Thoughts of Tom Walsh raced through Jack's mind as he dressed. How they'd met taking a course for a U.S. Coast Guard Captain's License, about both of them being in the submarine service, about Tom being ten years younger and how the friendship had grown by the unspoken knowledge they could count on each other. It all hit hard as he heard Kate say, "I can't believe he's dead!"

Jack's Mustang convertible was in their driveway so they took it to get to Tom's house, a small-winterized summer cottage in the Hayfield Point Community of New Saybrook, Connecticut.

"Did he seem depressed when you saw him the other day?" Kate asked.

"No. He kept harping on the election, trying to convince me of his conspiracy theories. He thought the president was colluding with the Russians to rig it in his favor. He'd been saying it for a while and I told him it was bullshit. I pointed out there hasn't been a shred of evidence to support collusion. Told him it was beginning to look like there's some truth to the president calling it a witch hunt.

"Tom didn't buy that. But what I'm trying to tell you is that there was nothing he said that sounded like he was depressed."

"Doesn't sound like he was, but with regard to your witch-hunt comment, I don't buy it either," Kate said,

"Not surprised you'd say that, but we haven't time to go into it now. We're here and I think that's Ray Carson in the police car pulling up."

"You're right about 'not now', but I think you have your head in the sand, not paying attention to what's going on if you really believe it's a witch-hunt," Kate said in an uncharacteristic harsh tone as Jack focused on who was in the police vehicle.

Jack ignored her, seeing it was his racquetball partner, Ray Carson, getting out of the car. Ray was recently promoted to Sergeant/Detective with the New Saybrook police. They'd been playing once a week for the past year.

Ray Carson walked towards the house, stopping short when he recognized Jack and Kate getting out of their car. "What are you doing here?" he said, as he stared at Jack with a concerned look on his face.

"I got a call twenty minutes ago that Tom Walsh, a good friend of mine, committed suicide. This is his house!" Jack said pointing to it. "Tom's wife. Meg, called me asking me to come, said she didn't want to be by herself when the police came."

"You better wait outside. I need to question her alone," Carson replied with a quick nod of his head towards Kate to acknowledge her presence as he headed inside.

Twenty minutes later, he came out and looked down to see Jack and Kate sitting on the front steps talking. He'd met Kate once before. Jack had introduced her at the racquetball court six months ago when she came to pick him up.

"My wife, Kate, Ray. I—"

"Yes, I remember. Hi Kate. Did you also know Tom Walsh?"

"Yes sir, but not as well as Jack did. We socialized with Tom and his wife a couple of times. I'm shocked—this doesn't fit what we knew about him."

Ray Carson, looking very official in his well-pressed uniform, glanced down at Jack and Kate then shook his head as he stared up at the house.

"Right! A lot of things don't add up here. Sorry, you guys can't go in yet. I called the medical examiner; this isn't an open and shut case of suicide. After talking to Mrs. Walsh, I'm going to ask for an investigation. I told her you're here, suggested she should come out and talk to you. Is there anything you can tell me now as to why he may have wanted to kill himself?"

"No, it's crazy, Ray, I saw him Thursday, two days before I left for the race around Long Island. We had a couple of beers and he seemed fine. Told me he got a raise and was looking to buy a new boat. He would've joined me in the race but had a prior commitment to visit his daughter in New Jersey."

"You said he was a good friend. Did that mean you knew him well?"

It didn't escape Jack that the tone and manner of Ray's questions were beginning to come across like he was on the job, not talking to a friend.

"Yeah, I think so. We were pretty tight."

Ray Carson was about two inches shorter than Jack, but at five ten, one eighty, he still rippled with muscles developed from college and Olympic wrestling. He'd joined the New Saybrook police department after a four-year stint in the Army. His combat experience as a Special Forces squad leader working with the poorly trained Afghan military, left an indelible effect on his character.

Two American soldiers in his squad were killed by questionable "friendly fire" from the Afghan fighters—men who Ray Carson thought he could trust and previously considered friends. He had trouble ever since trusting anyone outside of his immediate family. His promotion to sergeant/detective gave him responsibility for investigating crimes as well as his normal duties as a senior patrol officer; a dual role not that unusual in a small-town police force.

As Ray Carson listened to Jack, he thought about how little he knew him. Aside from playing racquetball together and knowing he was a freelance writer for adventure magazines, there wasn't much else he knew. The thought flashed through his mind that Jack might be like some other guys he liked and thought he knew, then found out different. He made a mental note to do a background check to see if anything would come up on him.

Jack saw the questioning look—like he was a possible suspect! *He can't get over what happened in Afghanistan.* Reading people's thoughts was a trait Jack honed during a short stint in prison when he'd been framed for a murder at sea. It was a profound learning experience. No one fared well in prison if they weren't a fast learner. His thoughts were interrupted by the medical examiner arriving as Meg Walsh came out of the house. It was good timing—the questions were becoming annoying.

"Meg's coming out, Ray, and it looks like you have a visitor. Can we save these questions for later?"

"Okay, call me if you learn anything you think I should know."

As Ray Carson walked off to meet the medical examiner, he looked back at Meg. "Why don't you go out for breakfast with these two while the coroner and I poke around inside?"

"Okay, I could use a cup of coffee," Meg said looking at Jack and Kate to see if they welcomed the idea.

"Good idea," Jack said as he reached for Meg's arm. "How about the three of us go to the Diner on Main where we can talk?"

"Can the three of us fit in that?" she said pointing to Jack's convertible.

"I'll sit in the back. I'm smaller than you and it's a tight squeeze," Kate said as she jumped in before Meg could decline to go.

Crammed in the back seat with the top down, Kate slid low to avoid the wind. She closed her eyes to picture Tom when she last saw him alive; remembering the last conversation she had with him. Tom and Meg had come over for dinner and they were talking about President Cain. Jack got upset with her for arguing with Tom and letting the conversation get out of hand. Tom had been ranting, but so was she:

"You haven't given him a chance," he'd said.

"Yeah, well voters gave Chavez, Erdogan and Putin a chance and look how well that turned out," she'd responded.

"You can't compare President Cain to those men who could never become autocrats in a democracy like ours," he'd replied, disturbed by the comparisons.

"And why not? He's doing the same thing they did, saying the press is the enemy of the people and attacking our institutions with vengeance." She'd spoke with anger in her voice and Jack had cut her off, changing the subject.

After Tom left that evening, Jack said, "I cut you off because of how you were arguing your political views—I think we can be passionate about what we believe without being angry with people who think differently than we do. You were getting angry with Tom and that's disrespectful, Kate. It's like saying, 'What's wrong with you—are you so stupid you can't understand what I'm saying!' It also risks friendship and Tom is a good friend."

Kate wasn't sorry for what she'd said. Reflecting on that evening, she just wished she hadn't gotten angry and wished it wasn't the last memory of Tom she had before he died.

Five minutes after leaving Ray, Kate and Jack were sitting across from Meg in a booth at the back of the diner. Jack again noted Meg's lack of emotion as she repeated what happened, sounding more like a witness to a petty crime than a distraught wife finding her husband dead on the floor. Her answers sounded rehearsed, same words she spoke on the phone.

Jack knew he was biased, never really liked her, thought she was a user. He recalled Tom telling him about Meg's drinking, "I'm thinking about getting a divorce," he'd said.

Meg spent too much time in bars, had that look alcoholics get, robbing her of any youthful or healthy appearance. It was hard to believe she was only thirty-five. Plain looking, she did little in the way of dress or use of cosmetics, but knew she had a sexy voice and earthy mannerisms, attributes she used to help mingle and toy with men. Looking at her now, he realized he didn't really know her, knew nothing of her past or what drove her to drink. He wondered why she was responding so unemotionally to Tom's death, concluding he should give her the benefit of the doubt, that she might be in shock.

Jack stopped ruminating when he heard Kate ask Meg, "Do you remember what Tom was doing before it happened?"

"Nothing out of the ordinary," Meg said. "We went to the Harp & Hound in Mystic for a few beers. They had a good folk group playing so we stayed 'til midnight, but I got tired, went right to bed when we got home. Tom came in the room, kissed me goodnight. Said he was going down to the harbor to check on his boat. The local weather reports were predicting violent thunderstorms during the night, he wanted to make sure it was tied up properly."

"Did you hear him come back in the house?" Kate asked, resting her hand on Meg's arm to make her feel comfortable with her questions.

"No. I think it must have been two or three hours later, cause that's when I heard the shot and found him on the kitchen floor."

Kate was surprised hearing how Meg talked about finding her husband dead on the kitchen floor—calmly describing the scene. Finally, all Kate could think of was, "Did he act or say anything in the last few days . . . anything that indicated he was troubled or not his normal self?"

"No, he seemed normal. Wasn't upset or angry, we weren't fighting or anything like that. He'd often go down to his boat at night. I never went. Those docks are dangerous to walk on—particularly at night. The pilings and dock are rotting. Some of the planks are missing and half of the dock is leaning on an angle making it dangerous to get to the boats, but none of that bothered him."

Jack had been quiet, watching Meg's body language and absorbing everything she said. Her answer reminded him of what Sergeant Carson said, "nothing is adding up," implying that nothing she said gave a hint as to why he'd kill himself."

Jack had gone fishing with Tom on numerous occasions, and was familiar with the little cove where he kept his boat. He thought it odd that Tom would have gone down there after midnight. The cove was well protected from anything except a hurricane. One of the fishermen lived on his boat and they all looked after one another.

As Meg spoke, Kate caught the disbelieving expression on Jack's face and gave him a kick under the table—a warning to watch his body language. Feeling guilty, Jack smiled, asking, "What are you going to do now, Meg? How can we help?"

"I'll have to sell the house. I can't afford it."

"Where will you go?" Jack asked, trying not to show how surprised he was that she was thinking about selling the house within hours of finding her husband dead on the floor.

"I'll stay around here. I'm working in town—part time as a waitress at Finnegan's. Maybe they'll take me on full time."

Kate, also surprised Meg was talking so soon about selling the house, was waiting for a pause in the conversation, and after seeing an opportunity she asked, "I have a question. It's really not my business, so I understand if you don't want to talk about it, but was your marriage okay? Would you have known if Tom was depressed?"

"Our marriage wasn't great. With regard to being depressed, I don't think he was, but Tom didn't talk much about himself." She paused with a hint of a smile on her face, "At least not to me. We were married less than two years. I know he had a daughter but I never met her. If I asked him anything personal, he always changed the subject. He didn't like my asking, so I stopped."

"Did you know this when you married him?"

Meg sat back in the booth and slowly looked around the diner with a blank stare on her face. There was another couple in a booth near the front but otherwise the place looked empty. She then looked down at her coffee, stirring it slowly as she spoke without looking up.

"Yeah, I knew he was divorced, had a daughter. We only knew each other for two months when we got married. I'd just started waitressing at Finnegan's. That's where we met. He'd go there some times after work. I was thirty-three, I'd never been married—we were both lonely and started sleeping together. Two months later I told him I missed a period and asked him to marry me. I was surprised he said yes." Meg looked up with a question in her eyes—waiting for a reaction from Kate regarding what she'd just told them.

"Where did you get married?" Kate asked, not buying into the baited look.

"Antigua." Meg was studying them both now as she answered the question. "We both took a week off from work so we could honeymoon there."

"What happened with the pregnancy?" Kate asked.

"I'd lied to him about missing my period—never told him, just said I miscarried."

"Do you think he knew you lied?" Jack asked.

Meg decided she'd been talking too much, "Maybe—I don't know." She then looked at her watch, "I think I'd better get back to the house, I have a lot of calls to make."

After dropping Meg back at her house and noticing the police were gone, Kate said, “I don’t get it. She was more upset when her dog died.”

“Yeah, but it’s not just that! Like Ray said—a lot of things aren’t adding up about this.”

Neither said anything for a while as they drove home, but as they pulled into their driveway Kate said, “You think she killed him?”

“I doubt it, but I don’t believe he killed himself and I don’t believe a word of her version of what happened.”

“So, what do you think we should do about it?”

“Wait and see what Ray comes up with! In the meantime, I’ll drive to the Harp & Hound in Mystic this afternoon to see if we can verify what Meg told us. I know a guy who was a part time bartender there, maybe he still is, hopefully he was there last night.”

“What’s his name? How do you know him?”

“His name is Sid Johnson, lives in Mystic, took the course for his captain’s license the same time Tom and I did. He and Tom became friends. The three of us went to the Harp & Hound to celebrate the night we passed the course. I never saw him again. Tom told me that after Johnson got his license, he got a job as first mate on the New London Ferry and that he was fired six months later for showing up drunk. He’s doing odd jobs now, like working part time at the Harp & Hound.”

Jack left after lunch, hoping to find Sid Johnson at the restaurant. On the way there, he tried to think objectively about Kate’s political views, versus his own, and of the influence their families had on them. Jack, a registered independent, leaned conservatively toward the right, similar to his middle-class parents. His conservative upbringing was also reinforced by his military experience where conservative values were the norm, unlike Kate, who came from dysfunctional parents who often ignored the responsibilities of raising their only child. Her mother would disappear for days at a time leaving her home alone to deal with her alcoholic father. Neither had any strong ideological beliefs to pass on to her.

Kate's democratic liberal views were founded on her witnessing families, including single parent mothers, struggling to get by in her working-class neighborhood. After Cain was elected, and time went by, she became increasingly troubled by Jack's middle of the road politics.

One night, after watching the news, Kate asked, "How can you remain independent? That's the same as neutral. Can't you see what's happening? Cain's three quarters through his first term and he's violated all the norms of the presidency. There's little to no middle ground left, people are choosing sides, the vast majority in both parties have closed their minds—"

"You're probably right, and that's why we're in this mess," Jack had interjected. "It's precisely why I remain independent or unaffiliated, but you're wrong to say that means I'm neutral. I'm trying to find some common ground, believing both parties want more of the same things than they're willing to admit. We need more moderates to find ways to compromise. If that doesn't happen, it won't make much difference who wins the next election—the divisiveness will continue to grow until it tears this country apart."

"You have a point, Jack, but what's going on right now reminds me of something a senator said about the challenges America is facing now, 'What can happen when we allow our human nature to be ruled by ego, tribalism, and populist leaders who ignore the norms of democracy . . . '"

Jack ended the conversation by changing the subject—still not ready to debate this with her. He didn't disagree with Kate's concerns, but he also believed that Cain's election was in no small part due to the cultural divide that had been building for decades. It reminded him of a Civil War book he'd read—about the divisiveness back then, and the rampant divisiveness that's now embodied in the collective social consciousness of America's two parties. *Will we succumb to our tribal nature,* he wondered? *Will our self-righteous beliefs overrule the democratic checks and balances we have in place?*

All these thoughts weighed on him as he drove to the Harp & Hound.

CHAPTER THREE

Jack felt good entering the Harp & Hound. He liked the feeling the place gave him—like stepping into a small country pub in Ireland where one felt relaxed chatting with friends or strangers over a pint of Guinness.

This visit, however, was strictly a search for information while looking for anyone who could verify Tom had been there the night before. It was early, no one was sitting at the bar and Sid Johnson was bartending. He looked surprised when Jack walked in.

"Hey stranger, good to see you . . . been a while. What are you doing here this early? You looking for somebody?"

"Yes, You, Sid! I was hoping you'd be working today."

"Really, what'd I do to bring you here?" Sid said as he laughed and reached out to shake Jack's hand.

"Sad news, Sid. Tom killed himself last night."

"Nooo. I just saw him about a week ago, he seemed fine. Why'd he do it? What happened?"

"I don't know why. His wife said they'd been here just hours before she found him. I came to see if you or anybody here spoke to him. I was hoping you saw him—hoping you were working last night."

"No, I wasn't. I was home. I work part time, day shift, Monday through Friday and sometimes fill in on Sunday, like today. Another guy works nights on weekends."

"Anybody around who would know if they were here last night?" Jack asked.

"I doubt it. Saturdays are very crowded. I'm the only employee who knew Tom, but . . . 'scuse me, gotta take care of business."

Sid walked away to wait on a customer who sat down at the other end of the bar. Jack understood, but was surprised when Sid stayed to strike up a conversation with the customer.

He could see him in the big mirror that ran the length of the bar. Sid had his back to the mirror, leaning on the bar with his elbow, talking to the customer with an occasional glance toward the end of the bar where Jack was sitting. Outside of downing a couple of beers with the guy, Jack realized he didn't really know him. Sid was Tom's friend and Tom never talked much about him.

The mirror allowed Jack to study the bartender chatting with the customer who was showing him photos from his wallet. Sid was pretending to be interested, but from his occasional glances towards the other end of the bar, it appeared he was just killing time to see if Jack was going to stay.

Five minutes went by before Sid came back. "Sorry can't help you, Jack—have to take care of customers," then walked back to the other end of the bar again. Jack was pissed, got up and walked out. He ignored Sid's wave goodbye as he considered what just transpired . . . *he must have been nervous hearing me say Tom was dead.*

After leaving the bar he drove to the old marina, wanting to see if any of the fishermen remembered Tom coming down at midnight to secure his boat. One of the fishermen, John Reston, known as Red from his mane of red hair, was tying up his trawler when Jack arrived. Red was huge, about six eight and looked to be close to three hundred pounds. He was rumored to be around sixty, arriving in town on his boat about ten years before to buy the bait and tackle shop that had been for sale for a couple of years. Under his ownership, it became a popular place for local fisherman to hang out.

His red hair, streaked with grey, was tied into a long ponytail in the back. He had a full beard hiding most of his craggy face.

The beard ran half way down his chest. It made him look like a caricature of the pirate, Blackbeard. His piercing blue eyes, set deep below thick protruding eyebrows, gave warning this was no man you'd want as an enemy.

Red saw Jack approaching and ignored him as he continued to tie a line from his boat to a cleat on the dock. They didn't know each other, though Jack had heard plenty of stories about the big man from Tom.

He walked up to him, saying, "Hi, I'm a friend of Tom Walsh, can I have a word with you?"

"Tom's dead," the big fisherman said as he stood up to stare down at Jack.

"I know that. But I heard Tom was here last night, sometime after midnight to secure his boat before a thunderstorm. I was wondering if anyone here saw him?"

"You say you're a friend—do you have a name?" Jack heard the sarcasm in the question.

"I'm sorry. My name is Jack Quinn. Tom and I were good friends."

"Oh . . . Tom told me about you, sorry if I sounded rude." The big fisherman held out his hand, "I'm John Reston, come onboard and we'll talk."

Jack followed him up the gangplank. It was the biggest boat tied to the old dock. It took up a third of the space available. Seeing it had a lot of lobster pots on the back, he realized it was a trawler designed for commercial fishing—not a modified pleasure craft like most of the old boats in the marina.

"Big boat," he said as he followed the fisherman up and into the Portuguese pilothouse with heavy plate glass windows slanted inward. Inside looked similar to what he'd seen on Discovery Channel's reality show, *Deadliest Catch*. The pilothouse looked down over a big high-rise bow designed for taking on heavy seas. A small cubicle behind the helm served as the dinette and chart table for the captain. Red was pointing to it, saying, "Have a seat." As they sat down, he said, "She's fifty-nine feet—a little big for the work I do these days, but I keep her because she's my home in the winter when I take her down to Florida. It's a shame about Tom. Heard you were close friends. What can I do for you?"

"Do you know Tom's wife, Meg?"

"No. But rumor has it she's a bit of a boozer."

"Well, I won't comment on that, but she called me last night to tell me about Tom." He walked the fisherman through the call and about getting to Tom's house as Ray Carson arrived.

"I know Ray." Red said.

Jack told him about his conversation with Meg and her saying Tom came down here last night to check on his boat. "That's why I'm here—wondering if you or any of the other's saw him that night?"

"Got that same question from Sergeant Ray Carson about an hour ago. He called me on my phone to tell me about Tom—that's how I knew he was dead. But to answer your question, I wasn't here so I can't say. I'm going to check with the others when I see them. I told Ray I thought it strange that someone thought he was here. Tom always tied his boat up real good since it sits in the mud at low tide. I didn't think the storms were that bad, and if they were, he knew Rusty would have checked his lines for him. You probably know Rusty. He lives on his boat, he's here every night."

"Yes, I know who he is, but never met him. I take it he's not here now?"

"No, he's not, but they'll all be here in about an hour. I'll be in my shop and Rusty usually stops by with one or two of the others before coming back here for the night. I told Ray I'd call him if I find anything out. If you want to give me your number, I'll also call you."

"Thanks that would be great," Jack said, handing him a business card.

"Happy to do that for you, we all liked Tom. Oh . . . see you're a writer. What do you write?" Red said as he looked at the card.

"Mostly stuff for adventure magazines, stories about people who have had near death experiences or survived catastrophes, also a little fiction. But none of that's has anything to do with why I'm asking about Tom. Like I said, we were close, it's hard to believe the suicide story."

"I agree, but I can't say I really knew him. I speak for all of us by saying we'd appreciate you keeping us informed and we'll do the same."

"Will do."

"Good," the big fisherman said, then he reached into a cooler by his feet pulling out two beers, "Have one with me before you go—might be good for us to get to know one another a little bit."

"Sure, I'll have one, Captain, I've got a few minutes."

"We'll get along much better if you just call me Red, everyone else does. I'm a licensed captain, but don't like formalities of any kind, they get in the way of knowing people."

Red wasn't one to hold back on what he believed. He spent the next few minutes trying to engage Jack in politics, saying, "What do you think about all those left-wing liberals trying to turn us into a communist county? And what-about our do-nothing Congress—can anyone argue they needed a little shaking up? They don't give a shit about the working people in our country—Cain does."

"Maybe he does, Red, but maybe he just talks that way to gain support for increasing the powers of the presidency. Maybe he wants the power to rule like other populist leaders do after overtaking democracies." Jack didn't really believe this, but knowing Kate did, he wanted to hear how a man like Red would respond to that argument.

Jack was surprised they were having this conversation. It was only hours ago that he'd been kicking this around in his mind; why the country was so divided, why politics had become the elephant in the room except for like-minded folks. He'd been cautious to not talk politics with others and felt a little guilty of avoiding it with Kate, but beginning to believe that saying nothing was a mistake. That it was becoming too tribal, and would only get worse if one didn't try.

Red felt uncomfortable hearing what Jack said, thinking he was talking too much like a liberal and he believed most liberals are socialists at heart, that given a chance they'd bankrupt the country. But he also believed he might be able to swing Jack to his way of thinking if he got to know him better. That was something he would like to do, but it had more to do with business than with politics. The town was threatening to take away the free dock space from the fisherman, and Red knew he was going to need everyone he could muster to help him in that fight.

"Okay, Jack, we could talk about stuff like this all day, but we hardly know each other. Here's what I'd really like to know, do you know of anybody who would've wanted to kill Tom if it wasn't suicide?"

Jack was a little disappointed Red switched the conversation back to Tom, though that's why he was here. He would've liked to probe a little more on Red's politics—why he didn't see the president as a threat to our democracy like liberals do. But Red was right, they hardly knew each other, so he answered the question about Tom.

"No, I don't. I think I knew him as well as anybody, and I don't believe he killed himself. I knew his marriage wasn't going well, it was his second, but he wasn't distraught about it. He never talked much about his first marriage other than to say it was someone he met while he was in the Navy . . . said he was away too much for either one of them to get to know each other to make it work. He had a seven-year old daughter from that marriage. He idolized her. Use to go see her twice a month."

"Did he involve his second wife in those visits? What'd you say her name was, Meg?"

"Yes, Meg. And for reasons he never really explained to me he didn't want her involved. He knew the marriage was a mistake."

"Did either have family here?"

"He didn't. He was an only child, and he told me his parents died in a car accident many years ago. With regard to Meg, nobody seems to know much about her. I asked him once about her family, where she came from and stuff like that. He laughed saying, 'We made a pact when we married, ask me no questions and I'll tell you no lies.'"

"From what you're telling me, maybe none of us knew Tom very well. I don't know anybody who would ever get married with a pact like that!" Red said with a disdainful look on his face.

"Yeah, I didn't get that either, but we were mostly on the same page with most things. He was a good kindhearted man; someone you could trust. Very liberal when it came to politics. I'm an independent, don't like labels, I vote for the person not the party. We both were in the Navy, could talk for hours about our experiences, but when it came to personal stuff, he usually changed the subject pretty quickly. Still, there was nothing in our conversations that indicated he was on the verge of killing himself."

"Okay, but you admit you know very little about his past and nothing about hers."

"Right. But I consider myself a pretty good judge of character. Like I said, Tom was a good man, had lots of friends, no enemies that I know of. I think I would've sensed if anything was going so wrong in his life that he'd be contemplating suicide."

"You're probably right about that. I didn't know him as well as you, but that doesn't mean that something couldn't have come up at the last minute, like something from his past that we know nothing about."

"True, which is why I'm more inclined to believe he was murdered."

"So, are you going to continue to play detective or let the police do that?"

"I think you know the capabilities of this town's police department as well as I do. Ray's a good cop, Red, but only recently promoted to detective. He's in a department that doesn't have a crime lab or resources for looking into something like this. I'm afraid they'll do a little bit of investigating, but quickly chalk it up to suicide."

"Okay, but what makes you qualified to do anything more?"

"I'm a freelance writer, and in the course of my career I've made some friends who I can lean on for help."

"Where you going to start?"

"Looking into where he'd been and what he was doing the last few days."

"Sounds like a good idea for a start." The big fisherman laughed. "I hope some of those friends you mentioned can help."

Jack didn't respond to that, he just smiled back, saying, "Thanks for the beer, Red. I better get going. It's my wife's birthday and I'm taking her out to dinner."

"Where you going?" Red said as he accompanied him off the boat and onto the dock.

"To Finnegan's in New London, ever been there?"

"Yes, good food, but I'd never go back."

"Why?"

"Because of that new owner. He's a mean son-of-a-bitch. Saw him fire a waitress on the spot for spilling a beer on him . . . wasn't even her fault. He ran into her as she was coming out from behind the bar. He called her a bunch of names, told her to get out and never come back. She left in tears."

"How long ago was that?" Jack asked.

"Oh, about a month ago. Shortly after Tommy Fallon sold the place. I went to see if it changed with the new guy. I didn't stay long—just long enough to see what I don't like."

"Thanks for the info. I hadn't heard about the new owner. Maybe we'll go just to see what else has changed, and thanks for the beer."

"You're welcome. Don't hesitate to call if I can help in any way. Try me at my shop if I'm not here. I'm more likely to be there these days. If you stop in after six you can probably find some of the others you're looking for. I keep it open for them. They knew Tom better than I did."

John Reston, aka. Red, offered his bear paw sized hand in a friendly goodbye. Driving away, Jack thought . . . *that's a man I might want on my side if trouble comes from my nosing around.*

On his way home he stopped at a jeweler to pick up a birthday present for Kate. He planned to give it to her after taking her out to dinner. An hour later they were on their way to Finnegan's—one of their favorite restaurants before it changed hands. He had filled her in on his visit to the Harp & Hound, and was telling her about his meeting with Red, including their political discussion, when she interrupted him—

"You know, Jack, what you just told me about your talk with Red regarding politics is upsetting. How come with him, when you've been refusing to discuss it with me?"

"I told you Red started the political talk, not me, so, please, let's not do this now. It won't be a short discussion—it touches on too many complex issues."

"Like what?"

"Like being able to look objectively at who we are, why we think the way we do, our righteous beliefs and our values regarding people who think different than us."

"Us? You mean you and I? How different you and I think. Is that what you're telling me?" Kate said and she twisted around in her seat to stare at him as he drove to the restaurant.

With one hand on the wheel, he reached over and softly touched her hand as he carefully chose his words. "Yes and no. You're far more liberal than I am, we both know that, but underneath it all I think we both have the same fundamental values. We just apply them differently to support our liberal and conservative ideologies. I think we both need to do some soul searching regarding the biases and prejudices that come with our life long tribal associations," Jack said.

"You think we're that far apart on this?"

"No. Not you and I—but the country is. I fear the divisiveness has grown to a point it's close to being beyond repair . . . it could tear the country apart, including family and friends. But I don't think we can talk about it until we come to terms with our own issues. We need to be honest with ourselves about why we see things differently. That's what I'm trying to do now. I hope you do the same."

"Okay. I'll drop it for now. That's a fair request, but I hope you agree that it's important for you and I to be able to talk about this" Kate replied with raised eyebrows implying she meant what she said.

"I agree, absolutely, so just give us a little more time so we can have a rational discussion about it."

"Fine, but don't take too long. And with regard to your comments about Tom, I don't have a good feeling about what you've learned. Maybe we should just mind our own business. Do you have any reason to believe Ray can't handle it?"

"He's smart, Kate, but he's new at this detective business, and New Saybrook isn't like New York, or other big cities that deal with murders all the time."

"You say that like you're convinced he was murdered!"

"Well, neither of us believe he intentionally killed himself. It's hard to believe it was an accident like cleaning his gun. He was too competent for that. So, yeah, the more I think about it, the more I believe he was murdered. I feel I owe it to Tom to get to the truth. Suicide is an ugly word and it would be wrong to let him disappear from our lives with everyone thinking that's what he did."

"Okay, we've been down this road before. I keep forgetting this is just the sort of thing that drives you. And truth be told, Jack, I don't believe you're doing this just to honor Tom's name. I believe you think so, but I think it's much more—like the mystery that surrounds his death. The untold story you want to uncover—a fix you go high on—this drives you as much as trying to honor his name. So please, don't try to deny or say anything to convince me otherwise, because I'm okay with it. It's part of what attracted me to you."

Jack recognized that Kate might know him better than he knew himself. He didn't agree with all of what she said, but it felt close enough that there was no point in responding. When they pulled up in front of Finnegan's he looked over at his wife and said, "This was a bad idea—let's go someplace else."

"Sure, but why?"

"Because Meg might be here. It could ruin celebrating your birthday. I just want to focus on you, everything else can wait till tomorrow."

"Okay, let's go to the Crab Shack, I'm in the mood for some seafood."

CHAPTER FOUR

It was a warm star filled night when they arrived at the Crab Shack. The restaurant had a panoramic view of the river so Kate asked for a table outside. Jack ordered a bottle of Beaujolais to begin the evening and gave her a black pearl necklace for her birthday. The week before, he'd seen her admiring the necklace in the window of a jeweler so he went back and bought it. Kate loved his gift.

Beaming with pleasure as she put it on, she looked up at him with a radiant smile, which reminded him of why he was so attracted to her the first time they met. The necklace complemented her silky black hair and soft dark facial features. She was a beautiful woman, not needing makeup to accent her looks. She was also a romantic who loved it when he bought her gifts.

"Thanks, Jack. It's beautiful. You said you wanted to concentrate on just us tonight. I assume politics is still off the table, so how about we talk about you?"

"Whoa, it's your birthday. I said I wanted to focus on you!"

"Right, which means whatever makes me happy . . . so I want to know more about your childhood. Did Tom remind you of a friend from back then? You never talk much about that time in your life." Kate had a devilish twinkle in her eye as she went on, "Just want to know more on what made you who you are."

"Okay, I'll go along with this, but only if you agree that I decide on the method of payment for answering your questions." Jack said with the most engaging smile he could muster.

"Sounds like a win-win for me, so answer my questions, Mr. Quinn."

By the time dinner was over, and they'd finished the last drop of wine, Jack had walked her through what it was like to grow up on the streets of New York, and the friends he'd made in a multi-racial, ethnically diverse, blue collar neighborhood.

"That explains why you get along with all kinds of people . . . open to points of view I sometimes find appalling," Kate said.

"Being open doesn't mean I agree with what you might call appalling, Kate. What I learned growing up is that human beings are complex and if you look hard you can find a lot of common ground with most people. The bottom line is, you and I are on the same page when it comes to character and values. But that's enough about me for one night," Jack laughingly said as he signaled the waiter for the bill.

On the way home, Kate asked him to think about staying out of the open investigation into Tom's suicide, reminding him of how much trouble he got into the last time he butted into police business.

The next day, Jack decided Kate was right about not getting involved, although he still believed Tom didn't kill himself. He decided to leave the investigation up to Ray Carson and picked out Jack London's *Sea Wolf* from his bookcase, and headed out to the back porch to relax and read for a while.

He was reading for about an hour when he remembered he hadn't looked at his e-mail for a couple of days. After getting his computer and returning to the porch he saw an e-mail from Tom, dated the day before he died. It read as follows:

Jack,

It's midnight, can't sleep. Keep thinking about something I saw the other night. Started writing this as a note to myself then decided to share it with you. It may sound a little crazy, but hear me out. I went fishing near Seldon Island the other night and saw two men step ashore from a speedboat, one carrying a shovel, the other a bag—holding it away from himself like he didn't want to be carrying it. They were looking around nervously—like they didn't want to be seen as they entered the woods. Curiosity got the better of me, went ashore to see what they were up to. It was around midnight. I saw by their flashlights they were headed toward the old stone quarry. Know those woods like the back of my hand so I cautiously followed them. By the time I got there they'd finished doing whatever they went there for, but I heard one of them say, "c'mon we need to get out of here, that fisherman might have seen us."

I raced back to where I beached my boat, about five minutes ahead of them, and motored out to begin trolling again. They got back to their boat within two minutes of my pretending to be fishing. I doubt they heard me start my engine, but it was a quiet night so it's possible. They hung around the shore watching me as I continued to troll up river. Fifteen minutes later, I was out of sight when I heard them start their engine and race away.

I tried talking to Meg about it when I got home. I said maybe I should report it to the police, that it might be drug related, but she started screaming at me, telling me I was always minding other people's business. She started shaking and looked scared, saying, "I've had it with your meddling ways."

I tried calling you the next morning, forgetting you were still sailing. I have a gut feeling there's something in Meg's past she's too scared to tell me about. She's been acting very strange lately, looked terrified when I said I might call the police. This isn't the first time she's acted this way if she thinks police will be involved in anything regarding her or us. I told you once before, I know almost nothing about her past . . . that I made a mistake marrying her. But if she is running from something, I don't want to be the one to throw her under the bus. I don't see how she possibly could have anything to do with what I saw last night but I'm going back tonight to see if I can find out what those guys were up to.

I'm telling you this, Jack, in the unlikely event I get into trouble going back there. Maybe the real reason has more to do with my needing to share with you why I have to get Meg out of my life. Writing this down has helped me see what I've known right along and been avoiding doing regarding Meg.

Give me a call after you read this, I'll buy you a beer to chat about it!

Tom

Jack laid back on the lounge to contemplate what he'd just read, concluding he was murdered. *This isn't a man talking about killing himself, this is the guy I knew who loved life, did some foolish things at times, but so have I.* The e-mail changed what he told Kate about staying out of it, it was a game changer, there was no way he could quit now. He had to call Ray, show him what Tom wrote to reinforce the need for an investigation.

Kate was late coming home from her studio in New London and she walked in saying, “I have some exciting news, Jack. How about making us some drinks so we can talk.”

He was about to answer, “so do I,” but held back when he saw how anxious she was to tell him her news.

He poured her a glass of white zinfandel and grabbed a Guinness from the refrigerator before asking, “You look really excited, what’s up?”

“I had a client walk in today who offered me ten thousand dollars for a portrait painting.”

“That’s great! Who is this person?”

“He’s the CEO of an electronics company from Silicon Valley California. He’s here on business . . . something to do with Electric Boat at the submarine base in Groton. He saw my studio and came in just as I was closing, and bought a small watercolor. He was about to leave when he saw the large oil I did of the two principal dancers from the ballet Giselle.”

“You mean the one where the guy is looking down at the girl on the bench—you got ten thousand for that?”

“No, no. He wants me to do a portrait of his wife. He asked to see more of my portraits so I gave him my portfolio to browse through. He seemed impressed, then asked how much I’d want to do a large portrait of his wife. He pointed to the Giselle painting, saying, “One about that size.”

“I said it depends; that if I did it from photographs it would be cheaper, but not nearly as good as in person, which would cost considerably more due to things like making arrangements for sittings and time lost from my studio.”

“So, did he make the offer of ten thousand, or did you set the price?”

"He did. He seemed very familiar with the process. I think he'd been talking to other artists in California. He said he'd give me thirty percent up front and pay for any travel costs to his home. My expenses would be over and above the ten thousand for the painting."

"Did you accept his offer?"

"Yes. He offered me to stay at his home. When I declined, he understood my concern, said a maid would always be present in the house for any sittings. We parted with him saying his lawyer would send me a contract in a day or two along with airline tickets. He made it clear he wanted it done before the end of the month. It's a present for his wife's birthday."

"That's great, Kate. Congratulations. But I'd like to check this guy out if you don't mind."

"No, I expected you would say that. But I have a question for you. You looked like you had something you wanted to say to me when I walked in. Am I right?"

Yes, but we can talk about it later. How about we go out and celebrate your news."

"No way, we did enough celebrating last night. So tell me, what was on your mind when I came in."

"It's about an e-mail I got from Tom. Just saw it today—hadn't turned on my computer since we got that call from Meg. I made a copy. It's there on the cocktail table. Why don't you read it while I get us another round of drinks? I think you'll want another by the time you finish."

When Jack brought back the new drinks he sat down and studied Kate's face as she read. They'd been together a little over four years and gone through things that would have destroyed most relationships. She believed he was framed two years ago when he was charged with murder and she'd risked her own life to help prove he was innocent. She understood what drove him as a freelance writer, accepted he'd be away for months at a time in pursuit of a story. She knew he was a big risk taker, worried about it, but it was part of what attracted her to him in the first place since she had a little of that chemistry in her own blood.

He saw she'd finished reading and was looking up at him. He got turned on just looking at her. Thoughts flashed through his mind of all they'd been through, that he was one lucky guy. He hoped she understood this changes what he promised.

"So, let me guess. After reading this, you're not going to stay out of it?"

"I can't, Kate, not now—you know that."

"You could, but I know you won't. Hope you understand you have to show this note to Ray."

"Of course,"

"He may not like your meddling in police business."

"Maybe, but I don't know of anything in the law that says a private citizen can't investigate on their own."

"So, what are you going to do—what's your plan?"

"I don't have a plan, but after I give Ray this letter, I'll try to find out more about Meg, where she came from—stuff like that."

"Are you going to want my help?"

"I don't think I need you now, but if you can think of something—that would be great."

"I'll do that, in the meantime don't hide anything from me because you don't want me to worry," Kate said.

"Fair enough. I don't know if I'll learn more than Ray, but I have to try. Question: after reading the e-mail, do you agree Tom didn't kill himself?"

"Yes. The e-mail seems to support that, but I wouldn't rule it out completely. You need to keep an open mind on this, Jack. Think about all the people we know, how we've often said, 'No one really knows what goes on in a marriage but the two people in it.'"

"I'll keep it in mind, but it's way back there on this one."

Kate laughed, "Okay, but with regard to my doing a portrait in California—you really don't mind if I go alone for a week or two?"

"Depends on what I find out about him. If he looks like George Clooney the deals off!"

"I'll take that for a yes," Kate said with an amused look on her face, "come to think of it he does look a little like Clooney."

The next morning Jack went to see Ray to show him the e-mail from Tom. "Mind if I make a copy of this," Ray said after reading it.

"No, not at all. But I got a question: I'm assuming you'll follow up on what Tom saw on Seldon Island, will you let me know what you find out?"

"That depends on what we find out. If anything criminal is going on up there I can't compromise an investigation. But I'll tell you what I will do, I'll call you if it isn't anything that needs to be held confidential in a police report."

"Okay, I understand that, but I want you to know I believe Tom was murdered and I'm going to look into this myself anyway I can."

"I can't stop you from doing that. I told you I was going to ask for an investigation. I did and it was conditionally approved pending the coroner's report. But whatever you do, try not to interfere with anything you see or hear I'm doing—it could screw things up."

"Like what, Ray. If you tell me what you're planning on doing it might help me stay out of your way."

"Fair enough, as long as you understand I can't tell you everything. But this e-mail tells me we need to know a lot more about Meg Walsh, and I'll look into this Seldon Island business this afternoon. That should be good enough for you. I'll go make a copy of this now." They shook hands and Jack felt satisfied Ray was seriously pursuing an investigation other than suicide.

When Jack returned home, there was a message on his answering machine from the detective saying, "Jack, this is Ray . . . give me a call tonight . . . after six on my cell. I'll be on duty till then, tied up with work."

There was a tone in Ray's voice that made Jack suspect it had to do with the investigation, that he didn't want to talk about it on duty. Jack was anxious to hear the news, but not overly concerned by the call. Not wanting to talk while on duty fit Ray's suspicious and overly cautious nature regarding his dealings with people. Jack was shocked, however, when he called Ray and heard him say, "I'm sorry, Jack, I'd called to tell you the chief has called off the investigation."

"What—that's crazy! Why? What happened since I saw you?"

"After you left, I went in to show him a copy of the e-mail. Turns out the coroner's report had come in while you and I were talking. The report confirmed Tom Walsh died by his own hands, in other words it was suicide."

"Do you believe that?"

"Doesn't matter what I believe. The chief believes the report. He thinks Tom Walsh's note to you shows they were having marital problems. And as for those two guys with a shovel, he said they could've been fishermen digging for worms. He then reminded me that if they were doing something illegal it's outside of our jurisdiction. Seldon Island is a State Park in the township of Lyme. That was embarrassing for me. I should've looked it up before I went to see him."

"Couldn't you at least pass on the information to someone who could look into it?"

"Sure I could, but think about that, Jack. All I have now is an e-mail from a man who committed suicide—that's the official position. A note that says he saw two guys with a shovel on Seldon Island; a State Park mind you. Does that sound criminal to you? The chief is already beginning to question my judgment. I'm not going to do anything to further his opinion."

Jack couldn't argue with the logic. He also knew the man was stepping out of his safety zone by saying as much as he did. Jack wanted him to know that. "Sorry Ray, I appreciate you calling, and all you said, but I can't let it change anything in terms of my pursuing this on my own."

"I didn't think it would. I hope it goes without saying that you'll call immediately if you uncover any hard evidence to open the investigation. I doubt you'll find anything, but if you do, remember you're not a cop, you have no backup organization behind you—you're not trained to deal with criminal minds."

"I'll try to remember that. Thanks again for the call. We still on for a game on Wednesday?"

"Sure, but just a game. No more conversation on this subject unless it's in an official capacity regarding something new. Is that a deal?"

"It's a deal. See you on Wednesday."

Kate was in the room during Jack's conversation with Ray, and though she heard only one side of the conversation it was clear the investigation was over and Jack was going to pursue it on his own.

"So, I take it Ray told you they're not going to investigate."

"Right. The coroner is calling it a suicide and Ray's boss is closing the investigation, which really never got started."

"Sorry, Jack, I thought the e-mail threw a monkey wrench into the suicide theory."

"Yeah, I think Ray agreed, but that was before the coroner's report came in."

"Really, you think he really believes it was suicide?"

"No, but remember what I told you about him. Ray doesn't trust many people, so he isn't going to say what he really thinks."

"So, what are you going to do now?"

"Not sure, but I think I'll take a ride up to Seldon Island tomorrow to check out the quarry."

Kate smiled, "It's about time you used the motorboat—hope it still runs. You haven't used it since you brought it to the marina over a month ago."

"I know. Ray was going to check on Meg's past before he got shut down. Do you think there's any way you might be able to do it?" Jack asked.

"Probably not, but I could ask Tony to see if there's a file on her."

Jack frowned, he didn't like the idea of Kate asking her ex-husband for a favor, but he had to admit, assuming he was still with the NYPD, he'd be a good source if Meg had a record.

"I don't like it Kate, but it's a good idea. How about starting out with a credit check. Your friend, Sue, the one that's a real estate agent, doesn't her office do credit checks for about ten bucks?"

"Yes, they do, but that's supposed to be for potential buyers. I'll ask her anyway, see if she minds. I'll only call Tony as a last resort."

Jack called the Twin Bridges Marina early the next morning to get his boat ready. As he called, he remembered it was Tom who had told him about the marina's inside boat storage. He had been considering selling his boat, hadn't been using it much. He'd told Tom, "It's too much maintenance and too much trouble going back and forth to the mooring where I keep it."

Tom had suggested he put it in dry-stack storage at Twin Bridges, saying, "It's perfect for guys like you. It's inside storage on a rack. All you have do is call an hour ahead and they take it out using a forklift truck to place it in the water." Jack had taken the advice. His boat was up on a rack and they had it in the water when he got there.

Seldon Island was about a half hour up river from the marina, the time mostly due to the numerous five-mile an hour no-wake zones he had to pass through. His boat, a twenty-two-foot Boston Whaler had a two-hundred horsepower outboard engine. He could have gotten there in less than fifteen minutes if it wasn't for the no-wake zones. He knew the river like the back of his hand. After joining the navy, his parents had retired and moved from New York to a small town about twenty miles upstream on the Connecticut river where he'd spent many hours fishing with his dad.

It felt good to be out again with the fresh air in his face as he motored into the wind. It reminded him of days like this when Tom had invited him out on his boat. Tom's boat was an old twenty-foot wooden skiff with an inboard engine and a tiny wheelhouse in the middle. With its wide beam and high freeboard, it looked like a miniature version of the trawlers that fished the Grand Banks off New England. It was surprisingly seaworthy for its size and Tom was known for taking it miles offshore to fish in the open waters around Block Island Sound.

As Jack neared Seldon Island, he remembered coming here a year ago with Tom, supposedly to fish, but suspecting his friend needed to talk. He was right. That was when Tom told him Meg was an alcoholic and talked about his marriage being a big mistake. Jack had known Tom for about two years—he'd never heard him say anything like that before.

Their friendship was based on mutual respect; similar to the friendships he had with men when he was in the Navy. Jack didn't judge a person by how much he knew about their personal life—he judged people on what he perceived from his own interactions with them and most of the time that worked. He'd been good in picking his friends.

These reflections and Tom's e-mail were running through his mind as he beached his boat on Seldon Island. He trusted Tom in that whatever those men with shovels were up to he doubted they were digging for worms. Jack knew Tom wasn't easily scared, nor did he ever show signs of paranoia. He had a sixth sense for knowing when something wasn't right.

After beaching his boat on the island, he tied it to a tree and headed for the quarry. He'd been there before, knew the island was a half mile wide, one and a half miles long, and covered in dense vegetation and trees. It was taken over as a state park after it was abandoned by a private company that quarried the land during the late 1800's for paving stones they shipped to New York City.

There was a path from the shore to the old quarry and another to the top of the island that rose to about 220 feet above sea level. It took him about ten minutes to get to the abandoned quarry. It was easy to find. Rusting machinery lay in a little clearing where the stones were processed and loaded onto rail cars that took them to barges waiting in the river. Jack was looking for any signs of digging that might have been left by the two men, but after a half hour of searching the clearing and the ground around it, he found nothing so he sat down to contemplate Tom's e-mail. From what Tom wrote it was clear the two men weren't on the island long enough to do much more than go to the quarry.

He was sitting on a log, considering what to do next, when he noticed the old rail bed that took the quarried stones down to the waiting barges. The rails were gone, but a new growth of younger trees and vegetation looked to be indicative of where the old pathway had been. He got up and worked his way towards the river hoping to see more signs of the rail bed. He hadn't gone more than fifty yards into the woods when he spotted a recently dug area covered over with leaves.

Pulling a folding shovel from his backpack he started digging. About a foot down he found the body of a small dog. It was obvious the animal had been buried recently. There were signs the body was decaying. Jack took a photo with his iPhone before covering the hole. Back on his boat, he wondered why anyone go to the trouble of burying a dog on an island.

Later that evening, Kate offered an explanation, "My guess is the dog got rabies or distemper and they couldn't afford to take it to a vet."

"So why not bury it in their backyard or take it to the dump?" Jack asked.

"Maybe they were afraid some animal would dig it up. I think you have to consider that the police might have been right in dismissing Tom's e-mail," Kate said.

"I'm not ready to do that. If it was just this dead dog I would, but you can't take it out of context with everything else Tom said in that e-mail—it was so unlike him to infer a possibility that something might happen to him."

"He prefaced that concern, 'in the unlikely event . . . ,'" Kate replied.

"I know he did, that doesn't change the gut feeling I have. It's not hard to connect the dots on a lot of what Tom wrote."

"Okay, you have been right more often than not in trusting your gut, so what are you going to do now?"

"I think I should talk to Meg again. Did you ask your friend to do a credit check?"

"Yes, she did. It came up blank—like no such person existed. You think it's time to call Tony?"

"Yeah. Go ahead. I'm being silly—I'm not really jealous," Jack said.

"Yes, it is silly. But I understand, I'd probably feel the same way—that's why I want to be sure it was okay.

"I think we have some photos of her. You might want to have them handy when you call him so—"

"I'm way ahead of you, Jack, I pulled them out."

"Not surprised. One other thing, when you talk to him—see if he's aware of any criminal activity regarding Seldon Island."

Jack decided to wait and see what Kate came up with before talking to Meg again. He was at a bit of dead end until she did, so he decided to talk to Red to see if he'd gleaned anything from the other fishermen.

Red's Bait & Tackle shop was near the old marina, about a mile north of where Red kept his boat. It was an old colonial house that had been converted into a shop. Red used upstairs as his living quarters when he was here in the summer. His wife ran the shop when he was out fishing, but in the last couple of years he was most likely to be there himself. His yard was scattered with old moorings, anchors, outboard engines and a couple of old wooden boats that no longer looked sea worthy.

When Jack arrived at Red's shop, the big man was outside in the yard talking to a couple of fishermen.

"Jack! Your ears must have been ringing. We were just talking about you," Red said.

"Uh-oh—should I leave?" he replied as he walked over to join the group.

"Not until you have a beer with us," Red said while handing him one. He informed him that Rusty, the live-aboard fisherman who had the slip next to Tom's, hadn't been seen for days.

"We were about to call you since you're looking into Tom's suicide with the police." Red said, then introduced him to the other two fishermen who had their boats at the old town dock. One was an older man that Red introduced as Arty, the other a skinny black man he called Spike.

"I was never working with or for the police, Red. I've been looking into Tom's death independent of them and I have some bad news—they've closed the investigation. The medical examiner's report said it was suicide. I'm the only one still looking into it."

"Suicide!" One of the fishermen standing next to Red exclaimed. It was the older man, Arty, shouting the word at Jack. Arty was a foot shorter than Red. He had a weather-beaten face and stared at Jack through bloodshot eyes. "Tom wouldn't have done that! He liked living too much," he said, shaking his head in disbelief.

"I take it you knew him pretty well?" Jack said.

"We weren't close friends if that's what you mean, but I knew him long enough to get a good sense of the man. So, no . . . I don't believe he would've killed himself."

"Well, I agree. I think anyone who knew him would say, 'calling it a suicide is bullshit.' I was hoping you guys would be here. Red said you might be. Wanted to ask if either of you saw Tom the night before he died?"

The two men shook their heads. "No, that's what we were talking about when you drove up, and the fact we ain't seen Rusty for days now. Red was telling us about you coming to see him, that you might want to talk to us. If Tom came down that night, nobody saw him except possibly Rusty and he ain't been around to talk to."

"Is it unusual for this Rusty fellow to disappear? Is that his real name?" Jack asked.

"All we know him by is "Rusty," Red said. "Wouldn't tell us his name, seemed embarrassed about it, so we've always called him Rusty. It's kind of hard to answer your question. As Arty said, we were just talking about him—about the last time we saw him. He usually stops over here once or twice a week, best we can remember he'd tell us if he was going someplace. What makes it hard, is that he sleeps on his boat so it's not unusual if none of us sees him for a couple of days. The longest he was ever gone was about ten days . . . told us he was leaving that time because his mother died."

"I take it he's not married. How long have you guys known him?"

"He was married, told me his wife left him." Spike said. The skinny fisherman looked like he'd been waiting for an opportunity to say something. "Rusty's a lobster fisherman. I met him three years ago and we struck up a friendship. After his wife left him, he started drinking and had to sell his house in town. That's when he started living on the boat. Had a mooring over in North Cove and had to row ashore to sell his lobsters. I told the guys about him and we invited him to join us at the town dock where we are."

"Probably off on a binge," Red said. "I wouldn't be concerned at all except he always locks his boat when he leaves and this time it's unlocked. For now, I think we just assume he forgot."

Red studied Jack for a moment before continuing, "So what does Ray say about closing the investigation? I thought he had questions about calling it suicide."

"I don't think he likes it any more than we do, but that's just my guess. He's being careful about what he says. He's new at this detective business and Chief Dunn told him the case is closed after he read the medical examiner's report. There's really nothing Ray can do, Red."

"So, what can you do now that the case is closed?"

"Same as before, keep asking people questions. Try to find out where he went that night if he didn't come down to check on his boat."

Jack almost told them about what Tom wrote and that's when it struck him. He was the only one left investigating what was now officially declared a suicide, and if he was going to play detective, he had to think like one, to know when to reveal information, and when not to. He realized, as unlikely as it seemed, that any of these three men could be complicit in what ever happened to Tom, and if so, it would be important they know as little as possible about what he was finding out.

CHAPTER FIVE

"You'll need this," Kate said walking out of the kitchen with a glass of bourbon when Jack got home. "I just got off the phone with Tony and before I tell you about it, take a look at what I've got." She handed him a contract to do a portrait for ten thousand dollars.

"When did you get this?"

"It came in overnight mail today, along with a paid round trip business class ticket to California." Kate handed him the tickets to look at with a big smile on her face.

"This says your contract starts in two days, did you know that?"

"The answer is, yes and no. If you remember, he said he would send me the contract in a day or two and that time was important. His wife is sick, he wanted the portrait for her birthday coming up this month. I forgot and didn't expect to get tickets in the mail so soon, but I feel like I'm obligated since I'd given him a verbal yes to his conditions."

"I think it's a little presumptuous, but if it's okay with you I'm fine with it."

"Did you check him out, Jack?"

"Yes—he's highly respected in the financial world, looks legit."

"Okay, I'd like to go. Can you drive me to the airport when I go?"

"Sure. Now tell me what you heard from Tony."

"Well, he says Meg's real name is Samantha Basha. Her Lebanese parents immigrated here in 1975. They settled in the Bay Ridge area of Brooklyn where there's a large Arab/Muslim community. Meg or Samantha, not sure what to call her now, was born and raised in Brooklyn and spent six months in Syria as an exchange student where she fell in love with an Arab student, named Omar Jemal."

"When did she change her name? How did Tony learn all this?"

"According to Tony, after the 9/11 attacks, the NYPD developed an intelligence network that's almost equal to anything in Washington, and closely tied to Homeland Security. He didn't know when Meg changed her name, but she obtained a false passport in 2008. Must have been shortly before she knew Tom. All Tony could say was, she gave her name as Meg Smith when she married Tom in Antigua. Tony said Antigua has very lax marriage laws, there's no way to check false identification."

"How did she manage to get false papers?"

"Tony said it was a lot easier in 2008 than now. He said the safest way to get a false passport has always been to get a new one in your country of origin using a false driver's license, birth certificate and Social Security card. He said you could get those false documents in Queens, New York for $260 back in 2008. All you had to do was ask around on Roosevelt Avenue. Investigators knew the street as the "East Coast epicenter for fake IDs." Officials believe at least ten mills operated between 103rd and 76th streets. He said with fake IDs it was easy to get a new passport back then, which is what Meg did."

"I'm surprised the fake driver's license wasn't picked up in Connecticut. I saw an article in the paper a few weeks ago about security features built into the license."

"I asked him about that. I told him about the e-mail and how paranoid Meg was about Tom talking to the police regarding anything in their lives. He said he wasn't surprised, that fake documents back in 2008 were very good for getting passports, but today, most police and state troopers have new equipment that can detect fake driver's licenses. He said Meg probably knew that."

"How did he find her real name and passport?"

"You can take credit for that, Jack. If you had quit after Ray told you the case was closed, I wouldn't have called. When I called him and sent him some photos of Meg, he said "give me an hour to check this out." He called back and told me he got a fingerprint and photo match with a woman named Samantha Basha, the woman we have always known as Meg."

"Damn. No wonder Tom was getting suspicious of her. Are they going to issue an arrest warrant for her?"

"I suspect they already have. He said to keep this to ourselves until we hear from him. Obtaining false IDs is a criminal offense, but more interesting, is that Meg's old boyfriend, Omar Jemal, is listed by our government as a key figure in Syria's ISIS terrorist network. The NYPD and Homeland security are very interested in talking to her about him."

"My God! And we thought she was boring. I never would have guessed this turn of events, but I think we're a step closer now to finding out what happened to Tom."

"Are you saying you now think she did it?" Kate asked.

"No, but I wouldn't rule that out. It's more a belief that she's mixed up in it somehow. If she did it, I don't think she would have called us. I think she would've run."

"So, Sherlock, what are you going to do now?"

"Well, I'll have to forget about talking to her, better minds than mine are taking care of that—assuming she hasn't skipped town."

"Any reason to believe she has?"

"No, but we haven't heard from her in over two days. I thought she'd call to tell us funeral arrangements," Kate said.

"You're right, you would think she would have. She also said something about needing our help regarding Tom's finances."

"That's right, so we have good reasons to call. Why don't you call her? She doesn't know we know who she really is. Just ask if she needs anything. I'm curious. It's one way to find out if she's still there or if she's already been arrested."

Jack was also curious so he called. The phone kept ringing, but he let it ring ten times before hanging up. "That's odd, I called the house phone, no answer and the answering machine never came on. Do you have her cell number?"

"Yes, it's in my directory. Here, try this number."

Jack tried her cell and got a message that the number was no longer valid.

Turning to Kate he said, "Guess what, I think she's on the run!"

An hour later, Kate got a call from Tony asking if she or Jack knew of any place Meg might be other than home. Kate had little to give him other than Finnegan's number where she worked. Tony didn't deny or confirm they'd tried to pick her up, just said it's very important they talk to her and to please call if she gets any information as to Meg's whereabouts.

The next morning Jack called Red to see if he or any of his friends had seen Meg around town. "No, I told you we don't even know what she looks like. She never came down to the docks with Tom, we wouldn't know who she was if we were standing next to her."

"Just a long shot, Red, don't tell anyone I was asking. I'll explain next time I see you. By the way, has Rusty showed up?"

"No, but it's too soon to worry. I'll get concerned if he doesn't show up next week."

"Has anyone looked in his boat to see if everything is in order?"

"Yeah, Spike peeked in but didn't go inside, said it wasn't locked, said it looked normal. Makes one think he didn't expect to be gone long, but his car is gone so maybe it was an emergency, family or something like that. He could've just rushed out forgetting to lock up. We think we should wait another week before we notify anyone that he's missing. Spike says he has a sister on Long Island, maybe we can track her down."

"Okay, but it may be more than coincidence that he disappeared around the same time of Tom's death."

"You're taking a big leap connecting Rusty to anything that happened to Tom. From what the boys tell me they hardly knew each other."

"You're probably right. I'm grasping at straws since there's so little to go on, plus most of us doubt Tom killed himself. But I didn't mean anything disparaging about Rusty. What I meant is, Rusty is the only person who might have known if Tom came down to his boat that night. If Tom did and someone was after him, Rusty might have seen or heard something that placed his life in danger."

"You got a big imagination, Jack, but if you believe Tom didn't kill himself and that he was murdered, then I guess you have to look at every possibility. I'll ask Spike to take a closer look in Rusty's cabin."

After talking to Red, Jack decided it was time to pay a visit to Finnegan's. He wanted to see for himself the changes under the new owner, and, per chance, if Meg was still working there.

Finnegan's was a favorite of the locals for as long as Jack could remember, though that was a mystery to anyone walking in for the first time. It was like stepping into an old man's bar. The bar, tables and chairs were beat up and looked like they'd been there for a hundred years. It took only a few minutes to realize that was the charm of the place, a step back in time. The walls were covered in old photographs depicting what the town looked like in the early

1900's, and the bartenders wore white shirts with black bow ties and black sleeve garters on their arms.

When Jack walked in it was early, five o'clock, so it wasn't crowded. There were two men sitting at the bar looking like they'd been there all afternoon. Three men in suits had their backs against the bar's brass rail, celebrating like they'd just closed some big business deal.

Jack sat at the bar and ordered a Guinness. He sensed something had changed, but he couldn't put his finger on it. He asked the bartender if he knew Meg and got a shake of the head with a look that said, 'not interested in talking to customers.' That's when it hit him—this was the change—Finnegan's had been known as a place where the help was always friendly. He now saw the same look on the faces of the two waitresses who were wandering around cleaning tables and trying to do anything to look busy. All three looked like they would rather be working someplace else.

While taking in the change with the help, Jack noticed a man in the back corner sitting at a table going over some paperwork. Suspecting it was the owner, but wanting to be sure, Jack called the bartender over and asked if the boss is around. Again, the bartender didn't say anything, just used his thumb to point to the man in the corner while continuing to dry some glasses with a hand towel.

Strolling over to the new owner, Jack made a direct attack on the owners obvious 'leave me alone posture.' Pulling up a chair he said, "Mr. Tuma, mind if I join you. I'm trying to locate Meg Walsh. I hear she works for you."

The new owner, Maten Tuma, looked up. "I'm busy, as should be obvious, but since you have already interrupted my work, who are you? Why are you looking for Meg Walsh?"

"My name is Jack Quinn, I was a good friend of Meg's husband, Tom, who died recently. I have some personal stuff of Tom's I want to give her," Jack said and immediately saw and felt Tuma's cold suspicious eyes boring into him.

For sure, not an Irishman, looks Caucasian, but more Eastern European than American from the look of his olive skin and oval face. Wonder why he wanted to buy an Irish bar? Jack considered this as he looked back into the eyes of the man sitting across from him.

"She worked for me, part time. Haven't seen her for over a week and don't care if I ever do again. Hired someone else to replace her. I have no idea where she is and I know nothing about her so I can't help you. I got work to do," Tuma said as he picked up some papers to look at.

"I don't know where you come from, but I'll give you a tip," Jack said as he stood up. "This is a friendly town with friendly people who loved this place and everyone that worked here. You haven't got a chance in hell of succeeding unless you learn that. I'd tell you to 'break-a-leg', but I doubt you'd have a clue to what that means." He spoke loud enough for the bartender and two waitresses to hear him and saw a hint of a smile on their faces as he walked out.

CHAPTER SIX

"Where you been?" Kate asked. She was standing in the front door watching Jack walk up to the house.

"Went to Finnegan's—wanted to see what's going on with the new owner."

"What's it like?"

"I think someone needs to check him out, someone with deep investigative capability. He puzzles me. It doesn't add up why a guy like that would buy Finnegan's.

"You want me to call Tony again?" Kate asked.

"No. I wasn't thinking of him, though that's a possibility. I was thinking more about someone like Max Cruz, the DEA guy that saved our butt's on the island of Utila two years ago. He thinks outside the box, he'll be a good guy to talk to."

Jack used the only number he had for Max, his DEA cell number. When he called a recording came on . . . the number had been discontinued, but gave him another number if he needed more information. The second number put him on with someone who wanted to know who was calling and why. Jack explained who he was and how he knew Max, but gave no reason for trying to contact Max other than being a friend. After being placed on hold for five minutes, he was told Max had retired, that he'd left to take over his father's business. He was given a phone number where Max might be reached.

Max answered immediately. "Hi Jack, I got a message a few minutes ago you might call—what have you been up to for me to deserve this call?"

"Putting my nose where it probably doesn't belong, Max, but before I say more about that, how've you been? Heard you retired—is that true?"

"Yes, about a year ago, for three good reasons. The first had to do with your friend, Angel. He married the girl of my dreams after the drug raid so I needed to get out of there. The second was my father got sick and needed help with his business. And the last was I needed a break after too many years of risking my life in a cause that we're losing. The drug business is booming—it's like any other business—it's all about supply and demand. The DEA deals only with the supply side and as long the demand remains high, the bad guys stay motivated and can easily circumvent us, particularly when Americans across the border are the biggest buyers. But that's all behind me now, so tell me about this big nose of yours—how's it got you into trouble this time?"

Max listened without saying a word. Jack told him about Tom, why he suspected it was murder, not suicide; about the bones on Seldon Island; about the local police, Sergeant Carson who was stopped from investigating the case; about Tom's wife, Meg, who disappeared; about Tuma, the new owner of Finnegan's; and how Kate's ex, an NYPD detective discovered Tom's wife had ties to a man named, Omar Jemal, an ISIS terrorist.

"This Tuma guy, the one who bought Finnegan's where Tom's wife last worked, I think he might know something about why she disappeared. That's what precipitated my trying to get in touch with you.

"I was hoping you could check on Tuma for me. I didn't know you retired. Maybe I'm crazy, Max, but my gut tells me there's a chance all this stuff could be connected to Tom's death. I needed to talk to someone like you, someone who from experience has better instincts for these things than I do."

"Well, your call is timely. You caught me at home visiting my family. My dad recovered enough for me to go back to work about six months ago, but not for the DEA. I had enough of that. I'm now working for the Homeland Security Investigative Agency. I'd be glad to help because we are interested in anybody who has or had connections to an ISIS terrorist.

"With regard to you being crazy, yeah, I think you are a little, but it's the kind of crazy I like. And Jack, with regard to those dots you're trying to connect, I've told you before—I'll always look into them all. I'd be doing the same as you. But there's a big difference when I do it. I've got back up—you don't. The same thing that local detective said, and I did when we were back on Utila. You're sticking your neck in harm's way if it turns out your friend was murdered."

"I know, Max, but Tom has a young daughter. It would be a shame if she had to live her whole life wondering why her father killed himself, left this world not caring enough to see her grow up, or not be there when she needed him. That little girl deserves to know the truth. If it was suicide, maybe I can find out why. Right now, I'm the only one that's digging around. If I quit now, it will stay as a closed case and Tom was too good a friend for me to let that happen."

"Okay, I get that, didn't believe for a moment you'd quit what you're doing. Just wanted to know if you're doing this because it's a potential story you could write."

"That never entered my mind, but if it was murder, not suicide, I'll do everything I can to let everyone who knew him know the truth."

"I believe you, and since I'm now at the DHS, that's the acronym for the Department of Homeland Security, I can probably help you more than I could've before to check out this guy you call Tuma."

"That would be great. I could use any help you can give. I have to admit I don't know much about what DHS does other than it being an intelligence agency."

"Well, I can't talk about anything classified, but I can tell you it's public knowledge DHS works closely with NSA. They track the locations of hundreds of millions of cellphones per day, allowing us to map people's movements. We also get access to communications like Google, Microsoft, Facebook, Yahoo, YouTube, Skype, and Apple. So with hundreds of millions of contact lists from personal e-mail and text messaging accounts each year, it shouldn't be hard to find out who this Tuma guy is."

"If you do this, Max, will it cause any problems for you at your new job?"

"No problem, Jack. They'll be happy to know we might have a lead on Omar Jemal, he's one of the top ten ISIS people we're after."

Jack no sooner hung up when Red called, "Been trying to get you for the last fifteen minutes. Spike just did a walk through on Rusty's boat and something ain't right. Looks like he left in a real hurry. His dinner is only half eaten, a bottle of beer only half empty, and most disturbing, he left his cell phone on his bunk."

"Doesn't sound like anyone planning to be gone for a few days," Jack said,

"No. I'd told you we weren't too concerned since he was gone before for days at a time, but I had Spike take a look since we were a little bothered by his not locking up. When you add that to the way he left the boat, you got to figure something's wrong."

"How long has he been missing now?" Jack asked.

"Been over a week. Spike found his sisters phone number, called her on Long Island. No one answered. He left a message asking her to call. I think that's all we can do until his sister calls back, unless you have some suggestions?"

"No, Red, I don't. I think you're right about waiting for his sister to call back, but do you guys know anything more about him than what you told me? "

"I don't, but it might pay for you to have a one-on-one talk with Spike sometime, you might glean something more from him."

"Do you think he'd mind if you gave me his cell number?"

"No, but I don't know it. I'll get it the next time I see him and tell him I suggested he talk to you about Rusty."

"One more thing, Red. Every time I drive down to the docks where you guys keep your boats, I see two vans parked by that old powerhouse. I thought that place was vacant. Did someone buy it?"

"It was vacant for a while, but yeah you're right, someone moved in about three months ago. I don't know who. Never seen anyone outside. Rusty told us he'd seen lights on at night. The vans are there all the time. We haven't seen anyone use them. They're all marked "Shoreline Limo Service" so I guess that's the business that rents or owns the old power plant now."

"And you say you don't you know who that is?" Jack asked.

"Right, I don't know, could be the town took it for back taxes, or might be the family who owns the boatyard up the road where all that's left is the old pilings and the big machine shop that Cappy Mudgrove rents now to make rowboats. The old power plant has been needing repair for a long time and probably got harder and harder to rent."

"Okay, Red, thanks for the update."

Kate was anxiously waiting to find out what Jack learned. "You were on the phone for a long time. What's up?"

"Well, first I called Max. He agreed to check out the new owner of Finnegan's for me. Turns out Max left the DEA and is now working for the investigative arm of Homeland Security. He was very interested about Meg knowing Omar Jemal, said the same thing Tony told you about him being high on the terrorist list. Then Red called right after I hung up with Max to tell me about a fisherman who had a boat next to Tom's, he's been missing for three days. Red said he's disappeared before, but this time it looks a little different.

"More and more it's adding up to Tom being murdered," Jack said.

"Okay, let's say it was murder. I can see a possible connection to the missing fisherman since his boat was next to Tom's, but why do you want Max to look into the new owner of Finnegan's?"

"It's just a gut feeling. I could be very wrong, but it was very clear Tuma didn't want to talk to me and I don't think it was because he was busy doing some paperwork. He knew Tom and Meg were friends of mine. It was also clear the help are all scared of him. He came across as a shrewd, cold, calculating businessman who bought the place as a front for something else."

"Wow, you got all that in just two minutes of talking to him?" Kate said with a skeptical smirk on her face.

"Red didn't like him either and don't forget we're all wondering why he bought the place knowing it was an Irish bar frequented mostly by locals."

"I don't get that either. I don't see how it all connects. It'll be interesting to see what Max comes up with."

"With guys like Tuma, Kate, I don't think I'm being overly suspicious."

"Okay, so did Red have anything else to say besides talking about the fisherman who disappeared?"

"Yeah, he did." Jack went on to tell her what he learned about the old power plant down by the docks where the fisherman and Tom kept their boats.

"You think they might have seen something that night?" Kate asked.

"Can't hurt to ask. I'll go down there in the morning and while I'm there I'll take a look at Tom's boat. I've been meaning to do that for a few days."

Jack was also wondering if he should share everything he learned about Meg with Ray Carson. The detective asked him to do that, but that was before the case was officially designated a suicide. On the other hand, Ray might be able to convince his boss to open the case if they knew about Meg's past and that the NYPD and DHS were interested in talking to her.

Kate thought it was a good idea to call Ray. "What have you got to lose, Jack? If they reopen the case, you'll get help you can use."

"Maybe, but if they do, they might also tell me to stay out of it. It's not Ray I'm worried about—it's his boss who's got a big ego and might want to personally work with the NYPD and the DHS. If that happens, I think all the emphasis will be on this ISIS terrorist who was Meg's boyfriend years ago, then Tom's murder will be secondary at best."

"You're probably right. You think there's any way you can talk to Ray off-the-record about it? Maybe he can help without getting officially involved."

"I'd be putting him in a spot. He made it clear last time we talked that the subject was closed between us. You know what happened to him in Afghanistan—he's still wary about trusting people, including me. If the chief found out he's working the case, he'd probably lose his job."

Later that afternoon, Kate said, "I'm leaving tomorrow to do the portrait commission in California. How about we pack the cooler with some wine and cheese and go to Harkness Memorial park to have a picnic? I'd like to spend some quiet time with you and forget about what happened to Tom for one night."

"Sure. Anything in particular on your mind?"

"Yes, but I'd like to save it for when we get there."

The park was a half hour drive from their house. After spreading a blanket on the cliffs overlooking Long Island Sound and opening a bottle of Pinot Noir, Jack said, "So what's on your mind?"

"You, Jack! You've become so focused on Tom you're shutting out what's happening in the world and to some extent even me. You asked me to give you some time. Well, I have and dammit, Jack, you don't know what's happening. You haven't been reading the paper or following the news. Cain's been undoing agreements on nuclear treaties, climate change, trade agreements and abandoning allies who helped us and now need our help. All isolationist actions rather than us being the leader of the free world. Add to that, his inflammatory briefings and comments are fueling the political divide at a time when he should be trying to unite us.

"You've been refusing to talk to me about it, Jack. 'Telling me it's complicated, that we need to take a hard look at the underlying reasons including our own biases.' Do you remember saying to me 'you're worried it could drive a wedge between family, friends and neighbors?' Well that's happening—I've got a bad feeling it's about to get much worse."

"Like what?"

"Look at the way he's cozying up to demagogues all over the world and surrounding himself with yes-men. I really believe Cain is looking for a way to turn us into an autocracy!

"Statements like that, Kate, are conjecture on your part, and some would say inflammatory. They don't help even if there's merit with like-minded people. As I've told you before, we need to find ways to talk about what's going on. If your comments are perceived as strongly biased by those on the other side, they will block listening to you."

"Maybe, but how would you know. You've been acting like you don't give a damn—all you care about is figuring out what happened to Tom."

"Ouch! Okay start talking—I'm all ears," Jack said.

"Republicans are tribal in believing the president's populist messages—calling the press 'Fake News' and believing FOX is the only news worth listening to, and that the FBI and all our intelligence agencies are biased against him."

"I agree he's a pathological liar and I'm troubled by his attacks on the press, Kate, but he's only hurting himself by doing that—the press is protected by the first amendment. He can't stop them and I think some of the other news media are as biased as FOX."

"You sound like—"

"Let me finish, Kate. It's not just tribal as you just commented. It's also about ideology. The president, in Republicans eyes, is fulfilling or trying to fulfill his campaign promises on health care, taxes, immigration, regulation, trade, rebuilding our military and draining the swamp in Washington. His supporters see him as a businessman, not a politician. They like most of what he's doing—shaking up the establishment. His opponents won't win by attacking him as a demagogue. His base likes his brash crude ways, believe he's paying attention to the little guys like them—the forgotten ones, who they believe the establishment has ignored. They're willing to overlook all his character flaws as long as they believe he's on their side. Add to that, the wealthy and business world love less regulation and lower taxes, so it's easy to see why he's still popular with the majority of Republicans.

"And with regard to our Republican congress, Kate, don't count on them to rein him in— it's all about staying in power. They may say in private how dismayed they are, but few are willing to oppose him—they fear his wrath and won't challenge him without the support of the people who elected them. That's the real world, Kate, if the Democrats want to stop him—the only way is at the polls."

"I hear you, Jack, but I'm having trouble reading where you actually stand on all this. I've respected and sometimes admired how you always try to see how the other side thinks—why you register as an independent, have often supported Republican candidates, saying you vote for the man, not the party, but I assumed you didn't vote for him—am I wrong on that?"

"Yes, you are wrong—I did vote for him." Jack saw the shock on her face and quickly added. "I wouldn't have if I knew then what I know now, but what I saw then was big government and the enormous growth in our national debt as the biggest threat the country was facing."

"But why didn't you tell me you voted for him?"

"First of all, you never asked. Secondly, up to the time that Tom died, we had both been so absorbed in our own careers we seldom discussed politics. And, when we did, during the campaign and after he was elected, I tried to tell you that you were so vitriol in your hatred of him that it was impossible for you to see how the other side thinks," Jack responded.

"You didn't let me finish when I brought it up last time so hear me out, Jack!" Kate was shaken from hearing him say who he voted for and was determined to make him listen.

"I'm on the side that believes he's a demagogue. I believe he will continue to have secret meetings with other demagogues like Putin. He will continue to appoint people to run our institutions who are puppets who will support him. And he won't do anything to stop our elections from being hacked in his favor, so how can we vote him out if that happens? He knows the playbook demagogues use for staying in power: 'If you tell a lie often enough, people will believe it's true.' That's what I believe, Jack, and I feel so strongly about it that it's hard for me to see how you could disagree."

"I need to put that in perspective to my own beliefs and everything we mean to each other. How about we pick this up again after you come back from California?" Jack had listened attentively, and was trying hard to convey how seriously he was taking her comments.

"That's fair. I feel better you heard me out. I understand you're trying hard to be objective. You know how much I love you, Jack, and I know you love me. We needed this conversation."

CHAPTER SEVEN

At 8 a.m. the following morning Jack drove Kate to the airport. "What will you do while I'm gone?" she asked.

"I'll take a look at Tom's boat, see if he left any clues on it. I'll also try calling anyone who might know where I can find Meg. And I want to find out who bought the old power plant. I've lots of things to look into Kate, so I'll be busy. Don't worry about me . . . give me a call tonight when you're settled in."

After dropping Kate off at the airport, Jack drove to the dock to inspect Tom's boat. He was about to go aboard when a car pulled up alongside his, a familiar looking man got out and started walking toward him. It was Maten Tuma, the new owner of Finnegan's. He was pointing a finger at him, yelling, "You can't go on that boat!"

"Says who? These docks are owned by the town," Jack said.

"No more. This parking lot and dock is now under my ownership and no one is allowed here without permission."

"Since when?" Jack said.

Tuma walked right past him onto Tom's boat and quickly snapped a lock on the cabin hatch. Turning around he said, "Since yesterday, Mr. Quinn. I purchased all this for my business," pointing to the old power plant and docks. "You're now standing on private property."

"You're the owner of all this?" Jack asked with a perplexed look on his face as he pointed to the docks, power plant and parking lot.

"Yes."

"What about the other boats here—what happens to them?"

"I've posted a notice for the boat owners. They'll have thirty days to remove their boats."

"Do you mind unlocking Tom's boat? I told you the other day he was a good friend. I have some personal stuff onboard."

"Yes, I mind. His wife can decide what to do with everything on the boat. She's missing, so I can't let anyone on until she shows up." Tuma had just climbed off Tom's boat as he said this.

Jack was pissed . . . staring hard at him as he stood three feet away, holding his arms out to block Tuma's path off the dock, "Why do you need all this—?"

"Because I have plans for this property, but that's none of your business, so get out of my way or I'll call the police!"

Jack stepped aside knowing he'd gone too far.

"Good day, Mr. Quinn," he said as he walked around him and yelled over his shoulder, "Don't be surprised if you see a fence going up tomorrow. You can tell your friends I'll leave a phone number to call when they're ready to remove their boats."

Jack drove straight to town hall to see the First Selectman. He needed to verify what Tuma said, although he suspected it was probably true. Vince Pierce, the First Selectman, considered Jack a friend; Jack had written a complimentary Op-Ed piece in the local newspaper about Pierce being a visionary for the town.

"Is the man in?" Jack asked Sherry, Vince Pierce's gal Friday and secretary.

"Yes. Let me guess—you want to talk to him about the sale of the old town docks?"

Jack smiled, nodded affirmatively, "Just found out about it ten minutes ago. Must admit, it was a big surprise."

"You're the third person who's wanted to see him about that today. He's told me to turn them away, but I think he'll make an exception in your case." She buzzed her boss to let him know why Jack wanted to see him.

The First Selectman came out a minute later to usher Jack into his office. Vince Pierce was a commanding figure. Tall, swarthy angular face, dark eyes, deep voice and a swagger to all his movements. But there was much more to this man than his looks. He was not your typical politician. He didn't mind breaking rules to get things done, and he had done a lot for the town.

After a few pleasantries the selectman said, "I know word gets around quick, but I didn't think it was public knowledge yet—how'd you hear about this deal, Jack?"

"I was down at the docks this morning. Tuma showed up to inform me I was trespassing on his property."

"That man sure lacks charm, doesn't he?"

"That doesn't bother me, what's worrisome is no one seems to know what he's up to. Why did he buy Finnegan's and why does he need a place as big as the old power plant for a business that isn't even operating yet? He implied he has big plans for the waterfront property, but no one seems to know anything about him other than he's pissing off almost everyone that meets him."

"Can't disagree with you on that, but I think people will like what he's up to when they hear it."

"What's that?"

"Well, he didn't buy the place for just his limo vans. He bought it primarily to turn it into a waterfront restaurant including the docks so people can get there by boat. He's been renting it, but just paid big bucks for the property and that's a nice addition to our Social Services kitty."

"Okay, I get that, but you know you're going to have a lot of angry fisherman on your hands."

"Yeah, but it's hard to feel sorry for them. You must know they've been down there for free for over five years and that's made a lot of boaters unhappy since dock space is at a premium in this town. I think people will be happy to learn of a new restaurant they can get to by boat instead of what's there now."

"You're probably right, Vince, but aren't you concerned about who this guy is?"

"I'm curious, Jack, but no, not concerned—at least not yet. This isn't the first time a businessman came into town and started buying up property. One of my jobs is to promote business, I can't let my personal opinion of people get in the way of doing that."

The First Selectman then looked at Jack in a compassionate way and said, "Am I right that your concern here is somehow related to your friends' suicide?"

"Yes, and if you know that then you should also know I don't believe for a moment it was suicide."

"Be careful, Jack. I heard his wife disappeared and that's a little troubling, but it's another thing to cast suspicion on anyone without hard evidence."

"I'm not looking to cast suspicion on anyone, but it's hard for me to ignore Tuma as I look into what happened to Tom that night. Tom's wife worked for him and why is he buying up all these properties? It doesn't add up to me."

"I don't know of anything else he's planning, Jack, but I'll tell you confidentially that I asked the chief to see if he had a record before we closed on the property, so I shared some of your same concerns. He came up clean, also owns a restaurant in Brooklyn, I had no reason to turn him down other than we know little about him and that's not good enough to ignore a good business deal for the town."

"It's none of my business, but can you tell me if he paid cash or took a loan out on the property?"

"I can tell you, its public information. He put twenty percent down on a bank loan. Anything else you want to know?"

"No. Thanks for the info—I much appreciate you taking time to see me."

"Thanks for coming in, Jack. I understand you questioning your friend's suicide and appreciate everything you told me. Come in anytime. It's always good to see you."

Jack left Town Hall and headed over to Red's Bait & Tackle. It was starting to rain as he arrived and Red was outside climbing into his truck so Jack quickly pulled over next to him.

Red rolled down a window and said, "I'm headed to Town Hall. The town sold the docks and I want to know why."

"I just came back from there—you'll be interested in hearing what I found out. I think we should talk, Red, before you go."

Red agreed, inviting Jack into the shop to hear what he had to say.

Ten minutes later after hearing about Jack's run in with Tuma and subsequent meeting with the First Selectman, Red said, "So the son-of-a-bitch also owns Shoreline Limo?"

"Yes, he does. Like I said, I just learned that this morning, which reminds me, how did you find out he bought the property with the old docks?"

"I got an overnight Fed Ex package in the mail this morning with a letter inside saying the property where I kept my boat had been bought by the Shoreline Limo Company and I had thirty days to remove my boat from the docks."

"Who were you going to see at Town Hall?"

"The First Selectman."

"Do you know him?"

"No. I can't change what happened, but it's about time they built some town docks for fishermen and folks who can't afford the exorbitant rates charged by the private marinas. I also want to tell him what we think about this scumbag Tuma whom they sold the property to."

"He may not see you without an appointment. Why don't you call his secretary before running down there?

"And if I were you, I'd also call our local newspaper regarding the issue of town docks. Who knows, they might be interested in running a human-interest story about how our local fishermen are being kicked out of where they are now with nowhere to go. That would give you leverage with the town"

"Good suggestions. I'm glad you caught me before I ran off half-cocked."

"Just thought you'd need some backing to drum up interest in a place for you guys. One more thing before I go—any news about Rusty?"

"Yes. His sister called Spike and said she hasn't heard from him in over ten days. He used to call her a couple times a week. You got any ideas on what we should do about that?"

"Not at the moment, but let me think on it and I'll get back to you." Jack said as he left and headed home. Back home, Jack listened to calls on his answering machine. One was from Max, wanting to talk about some interesting info he'd picked up on Tuma.

He was about to call back when his phone rang. Thinking it was probably Kate, or Max, he was caught off guard realizing it was Meg; saying in a desperate voice, "Jack! I need to talk to you. Can you come now and meet me at the Mystic Aquarium by noon?"

Jack looked at his watch—it was 11:30. If he drove fast, he could make it.

"Yes. Are you alone?"

"I am. I'll meet you in the parking lot. I know the police are looking for me so please . . . please . . . come alone. Wait to hear what I have to say before telling anybody you heard from me."

"Okay, I'm leaving," he said and hung up the phone. *Probably should call Max, but she sounded paranoid about coming alone . . . don't want to screw this up.*

Crossing the Thames River Bridge, ten minutes away from the aquarium, he was still debating whether to call Max, but decided to call later—not wanting to risk her being picked up before he spoke to her.

Arriving at the aquarium parking lot, he saw three school busses unloading teenagers, but Meg was nowhere in sight. Driving slowly around the lot he spotted her walking towards him. Pausing, she looked around quickly before jumping in. "Thanks for coming. Please drive into town. I know a good place where we can talk."

"Why all the secrecy?"

"I don't want to talk in the car. Do you mind showing me your phone? I need to be sure you're not recording me."

"God. You're really paranoid." Jack took his iPhone out of his pocket. "Look it's off, so where're we going?"

"Mystic Pizza, where we'll get a booth in the back. Do you know where it is?"

"Yes." Five minutes later they were in the restaurant sitting in a booth in the back.

After they were seated Meg said, "You know this place is famous for—"

"I'm not interested in any pleasantries. Just tell me what you wanted to see me about and why the secrecy."

"The secrecy is because my past has caught up with me. Someone is trying to kill me."

"What do you mean your past has caught up with you? Who's trying to kill you?"

"I had to change my name a few years ago. I illegally purchased a new driver's license, passport and other papers. The authorities recently found out. It was probably the police in the process of investigating Tom's death."

"Why did you change your name?"

"I'll get to that in a minute, but let me start by filling you in on all that's happened to me since I moved to Connecticut."

"When was that?"

"About two years ago, after I changed my name. Finnegan's, where I last worked, had placed an advertisement in the *New York Times* for a waitress. I applied, got the job, and then moved here where I met Tom. Things were going pretty well until Tuma bought Finnegan's."

"Yeah he's a strange duck. What do you know about him?" Jack said.

"Nothing really other than he also had a place in Brooklyn. We didn't get along. I didn't like the way he looked at me—gave me the creeps when I saw him staring at me. I hated working there after he bought the place. It also worried me a little since he said he came from the same neighborhood in Brooklyn that I did."

"You mean, he might have known who you were before you changed your name?"

"Yeah, that worried me a little. He wouldn't look me in the eyes when I talked to him.

"There were times I felt there was something familiar about him. In the end I chalked it up to my paranoia about the cops finding out about my false ID. If I'd met him before, I think I would have remembered. None of us liked him. I'd come home in a bad mood after working there. Sometimes that caused fights between Tom and me.

"Tom used to go to Finnegan's. He stopped going after Tuma bought it . . . said he ruined the place. Tom tried unsuccessfully to be friendly with him, told me he thought Tuma was a social misfit or worse. Tom didn't trust a man who wouldn't look you in the eyes when you talked to him, and he talked down to everybody."

"I met Tuma. I agree with Tom's assessment. I asked some friends of mine to check him out. I suspect he may be hiding something or there's a reason he's so unfriendly, but I can't connect him to anything that happened to you or Tom. You said someone is trying to kill you. Tell me the truth, Meg, do you really believe that?"

"Yes . . . I know someone is! The day after Tom died, the first night I was alone in the house, I woke up to the smell of gas. It was after midnight. I found the oven was turned on with the oven door open. I hadn't even made dinner that night so someone broke in while I was asleep and turned on the oven."

"Why didn't you go to the police?"

"Because I was afraid, they would find out my real name and arrest me. There's a warrant out for my arrest because of things I did years ago, turns out they found out anyway."

"How do you know that?"

"From my neighbor. I was afraid to stay in my house knowing someone broke in while I was asleep, so I stayed with her for a couple of nights. I told her I was too upset to go back to my house after Tom killed himself. I couldn't tell her about the gas—she would have wanted me to call the police. She's divorced, lives alone, and we are good friends.

"She works during the day and I was alone in her house when I saw a State Trooper pull up in front of my house. The officer kept ringing my doorbell, banging on the door. When he didn't get a response, he took out his cell phone to call someone. He looked frustrated when he hung up. After knocking a couple of more times, he got in his car and left. I'd been living in fear of this happening for years. I was lucky I was staying with my neighbor looking out the window."

"So how about telling me now why you changed your name?"

"I had an affair with a classmate when I was an exchange student when in Syria. I returned home pregnant. After corresponding with the father, we both agreed I should give the baby up for adoption. I was living in the Bay Ridge area of Brooklyn at the time with my parents. It was an Arab/Muslim community."

"What's that got to do with changing your name?"

"I'm getting to that. You'll understand better if you know what led up to it . . . more about me."

"Were you born here?"

"Yes. My parents are from Lebanon and I was born after they immigrated in 1975."

"Did you stay in contact with the father?"

"I did. I was in love with him, traveled to Syria to see him for a number of years. He kept telling me he was trying to immigrate to America. I believed him. Then on my last visit, a few years after 9/11, I discovered he was married and had four children. I was devastated when I came home—that's when I started drinking."

"Did you ever hear from him again?"

"I did, shortly before I met Tom. He wanted to renew our relationship, said Muslims can have many wives and I could be his wife in America, but we would have to keep it a secret."

"Are you a practicing Muslim?"

"I was when I first met him, but haven't been for years."

"Did he know that?"

"No, I didn't want to tell him. He asked me if I still prayed five times a day. I lied to him—knew he was very religious. I know this sounds crazy, but I was still in love with him. I actually considered marrying him knowing he had a wife in Syria. I rationalized it was okay since Muslim men are allowed to have more than one wife. I was lonely, didn't have a boyfriend. My parents had died so I thought we could spend months together if I helped him get a visa."

"Did you tell him that?"

"Yes, that's when he told me he was an important man in a Muslim organization that would one day rule the world again. He said his ties to this organization would prevent him from getting a U.S. visa, but that wouldn't stop him."

"You mean getting here illegally?"

"Yes, he didn't actually say that, but he must have meant it. I got worried hearing him say, 'we'll rule the world again,' so I asked if this organization was a terrorist group like ISIS."

"What did he say?"

"He got furious, said, 'how could you ask that? Americans are the terrorists—not us.' His tone of voice changed. I heard the bitterness in his voice as he asked me if I believed all the propaganda on the news in America.

"It was scary hearing how different he suddenly sounded . . . nothing like the boy I fell in love with years before. It was a shock, I wondered what else I didn't know about him and remembered I hadn't talked to him since I'd found out he was married.

"I told him I didn't know what to believe, that I knew Assad was an evil ruler, but bombing and be-heading innocent people was also evil. I told him I could never be part of anything like that.

"There was a silence on the phone after I said that, so I asked, 'Are you still there?' All I heard was, 'Yes,' then silence again, I could hear him breathing heavily. I was almost afraid to ask him what he was thinking, but had to. I said, 'Are you telling me you've joined ISIS?'"

"What I heard next has given me nightmares ever since. He never answered my question, but I knew it when he said, 'I shouldn't have called you . . . you're talking like a foreigner, thinking they're all innocent about what's happened here, and what they've been doing to Muslims for hundreds of years. I thought you were a believer. Forget anything I told you. If you tell anyone I called or what we talked about I promise I will kill you. I'm sorry I ever met you—you are dead to me!' then he hung up."

"Wow! Did you ever tell anyone?"

"No! I was scared to tell anyone. I couldn't sleep nights thinking about it: him being a leader of ISIS; we being lovers; he being the father of my child. I was worried that it wouldn't be long before the CIA or FBI came knocking on my door. And then what would the people in the community think when they found out I had a daughter I gave up for adoption—that an ISIS terrorist was the father?"

"Did you ever think about calling the police or FBI about information that could help them get him?"

"Sure, I did! Do you really think they could protect me? He would blame me for them coming after him. No, I didn't trust anyone to help me. I had only one thought—I had to get away. That's when I changed my name, got a new driver's license, passport, moved to Connecticut and met Tom."

"Did you ever tell Tom any of this?"

"No. I told you we both knew we married for the wrong reasons. He knew I had a past I wouldn't talk about. I knew he didn't love me—that he was lonely and felt sorry for me when we met. I thought about telling him . . . thought I could make him love me if I could stop drinking but I wasn't strong enough."

"You haven't convinced me, Meg, that someone is trying to kill you. What have you left out?"

"I got a phone call the night Tom was killed asking me if Tom was home. The caller said he was an old navy buddy, never gave me his name, said he wanted to surprise Tom, told me he hadn't seen him for ten years. Wanted to know when Tom would be back. I lied, said he'd gone to see his daughter and would be back sometime tomorrow. The truth was Tom and I had just had a big fight about my drinking, he stormed out of the house saying he was going to sleep on his boat."

"What time was that?"

"About ten in the evening. After he left, I searched the house for something to drink, but Tom had thrown everything out. I desperately needed one, but I also knew Tom was right about my drinking, so I drove down to his boat to apologize."

"Was he there?"

"No, but the boat was open, he seldom locks it. I waited awhile, thinking he might have gone for a walk or be on the boat next to his that had a light on, but I couldn't hear anyone talking. I got thirsty waiting for him, I looked in his cooler for something to drink, found a six-pack of Bud. I quickly closed the cooler, didn't want him to find me drinking, but he didn't show up. After fifteen minutes of waiting I grabbed the six-pack and left."

"Where'd you go? Back to the house?"

"No. I couldn't hold out any longer. I needed a drink, realized he must have gone back home. He would have taken it from me if I returned. I went to the boat ramp under the bridge and parked the car. I turned off the lights, drank all six beers, then fell asleep."

"Were there other cars there?"

"Yes, a couple—cars with boat trailers attached. Fishermen use that ramp when they go shad fishing at night. I parked far away from them." Meg then gave Jack a look that said stop interrupting me, so he waited for her to continue.

"When I woke up it was two in the morning. I drove home and saw Tom's car in the driveway and no lights were on. I took off my shoes and sneaked in the back door. I was about to cross the kitchen when I saw something on the floor . . . sensed something was very wrong. I turned on the light and that's when I saw it was Tom.

"It looked to me like he'd shot himself. I felt terribly guilty at first, thinking it was because of our fight, but couldn't understand it since we'd had far worse. Why would he do that? He could easily have left me—I couldn't stop him. Then, as I told you, someone tried to kill me the following night by breaking in and turning on the gas. That's when I remembered the call I got the night before from the guy saying he was Tom's navy buddy, asking if he was home. Whoever called was trying to find out if I was the only one in the house. Someone wanted to kill me—not Tom. I don't know what happened, but Tom probably caught him breaking in. They must have thought I was home alone."

"That's an incredible story. I believe you, Meg. So that's why you didn't tell the police. They might not have been so quick to chalk it up to suicide."

"Right, how would it sound if I told them about the fight we had, my drinking a six pack later on, then coming home in the middle of the night to find him dead on our kitchen floor? I couldn't prove where I'd been and it would look bad that I was drinking."

"You know I never believed it was suicide and from everything you just told me, I take it you never did either."

"That's not true Jack! I did believe it at first even though it didn't make sense. It wasn't until the second night when someone tried to kill me that I put two and two together and realized they were after me that night—not Tom."

"Where'd you go? Where have you been staying after you ran away?"

"I can't tell you that, if I did, I could get someone helping me in trouble."

"Okay, I understand, but why me? What made you decide to tell me all this—why now?"

"Because I'm scared. Whoever is after me . . . the person that is trying to kill me isn't going to give up. I don't know what to do. You were Tom's best friend. You're the only one who doesn't believe he killed himself."

Jack was in a quandary deciding how much to tell her regarding what he'd been doing. He felt sorry for her, so far she'd been honest with him, but he didn't trust she told him everything, so he said, "if you want me to help, you'll have to be completely honest with me. Is there anything else I should know—anything regarding why someone is trying to kill you?"

Meg shifted uneasily on her side of the booth, starring alternately at Jack and down at her hands before looking up and saying, "How do I know I can completely trust you?"

"Because I've been spending every minute of my time looking into who killed Tom and that includes you. I know your real name is Samantha Basha. I know your ex-boyfriend is Omar Jemal—that you met him as an exchange student—that you stayed in contact with him when you came back and that he's an ISIS terrorist our government is after.

"I also know our government is trying to find you. I could have informed them I was meeting you today, you would have been in their hands right now instead of sitting here with me. Your attempts to make sure I came alone would have looked amateurish to them. And if these reasons aren't good enough for you, I'll call them right now!"

"No, no—please don't do that Jack. I'm just so scared to trust anyone—can you tell me how you knew all this. Are you a cop?"

"No, I'm not a cop, but I've made some good connections in my profession. So, tell me what I don't know, why is someone after you?"

"It's something I did for Omar before I knew he was a terrorist. He asked me if I could get him false identification papers. I told him I'd try, knowing there were some people in my Arab neighborhood that came here illegally. Through them, I learned of people in Queens who would make false ID papers.

"I got the papers for Omar and sent them to him. It was shortly after when we had the argument—when I learned he was a terrorist, when I told him I couldn't be part of what he's doing, it was then he threatened to kill me. That's all I left out from what I said before. And that's when I got my new identity. I had to—I was the only one who knew his new name."

"You're right—it's a good reason for him wanting you dead. What's his name now?"

"The papers say Thomas Wolf."

"Wouldn't it have been better to give him an Arab name?"

"Wasn't necessary. He looked Caucasian like many Syrians do. He also was very smart in school, took English for years so he spoke it quite well."

"Okay, here's what I'm thinking. I doubt he will use the new ID you gave him since he doesn't trust you anymore, but I'll pass that information on to my friends just in case he does. In the meantime, you obviously are in danger of getting killed by him or his friends, and it's only a matter of time before they find you. You need protection, the only way you can get it is by turning yourself in to the government people who are after him."

"I don't trust they can protect me and they may put me in jail."

"Leave that to me. I think they will waive anything you did illegally if you cooperate with them. I'll find out what they'll do to protect you in exchange for you telling them everything you know about Jemal."

"How do you know they won't just use you to come after me without making such a deal?"

"You forget—you haven't told me where you're staying. I asked, but glad you didn't tell me—this way I don't have to lie to them. I won't make a deal for you unless it's what I just told you."

"Is it okay if I think about it and call you tonight?"

"Okay, but remember I won't have the same leverage to make this deal for you if our government finds you first. Trust me it won't be much longer before they do, they have ways of finding people you couldn't even imagine."

"Okay Jack. I think you're right. It's just such a big decision—I need a few hours to get my head around it. I'll call you tonight, but there's one more thing I want to ask you before you take me back to the aquarium."

"What's that?"

"Do you think Tom ever loved me? There were so many times I wanted to tell him about my past . . . times when I thought he loved me, though he never said it, but neither did I. The sad thing is, I was falling in love with him. I was so insecure I wanted to hear him say it first. When he didn't, I started drinking even more—convinced he was going to leave me."

"I don't know Meg. I know he was struggling with how to make your marriage work. Tom wasn't one to talk much about personal things. He and I were the same on that, but right now you need to focus on the danger you're in. Don't do anything stupid on your own. You need to trust me, Meg. I understand you want time to think it over, but you're running out of time. Please, for your sake, try to realize you need to cooperate. I need your answer tonight! Call me before nine."

After dropping Meg off at the aquarium Jack decided to stop at the Harp & Hound again since he was in Mystic—hoping he'd find Sid Johnson bartending. He felt Sid had brushed him off the last time he was there, he hadn't figured out why. He called first to see if Johnson was in. Disappointed in learning he wasn't, he headed home.

He had some calls to make; the first being to return Max's call about having some interesting information on Tuma. He would have to fill Max in on his visit with Meg, so he decided to wait a few hours for Meg's call.

CHAPTER EIGHT

Nine o'clock went by and Meg didn't call. Jack waited until nine thirty before trying to call her—no answer and her cell phone number was still not working. He had a sickening feeling she was on the run again. He knew he'd screwed up—should've called Max before meeting her. He dialed his number knowing this news wasn't going to go well.

Max picked up right away. "Been waiting for you to call back," he said.

"Sorry Max, would have called sooner, but I got side-tracked. You'll be very interested to hear why, but I gather from your message you've learned something new about Tuma, so if you'd like, why don't we talk about that first."

"It's what the manager running his restaurant in Brooklyn told us. He said, three months ago, when he came in to work, he found a strange typewritten note on the bar. It was a note from Tuma informing the manager that he'd left town on personal business and might be gone for several months. The manager said, Tuma informed him to send spreadsheets for all business transactions to Tuma's e-mail address, to let him know when he needed to add money to their Bank of America business account."

"Didn't the manager find this odd?" Jack asked.

"You would think so, but he told the agent interviewing him that Tuma had become more and more reclusive over the past year. That Tuma had been gradually turning over running the business to him. Tuma previously gave him signature authority at the bank to pay all bills and payroll accounts. But the note did surprise the manager. He thought Tuma should have called him. But he laughed at the suggestion the note was odd or strange behavior. He said anyone who knew his boss would've called him odd or a recluse. That it wasn't unusual for weeks to go by without him coming down to the restaurant. He said they seldom talked on the phone, but texted each other regarding business dealings, and he'd been giving Tuma updates on the restaurant business by putting spreadsheets in his mailbox once a month.

"What bothered the manager most was not knowing why he left, what was keeping him away for so long, but he felt it was none of his business to ask. But it was clear to the agent the manager liked the independence it gave him, would like it if it continued.

"Just wanted you to know, we still think there's something fishy about Tuma and we'll dig into this some more. So, tell me what you meant by saying, you got side-tracked?"

"I screwed up Max—you're not going to like this," Jack said and filled Max in on his visit with Meg, leaving nothing out of his conversation with her and the deal he thought she could get by turning herself in. He saved the part of her missing the deadline he gave her to the end.

"She insisted on a little time to think the deal over. I gave her a deadline of nine this evening, but she hasn't called. I waited till nine-thirty, hoping she would still call—she hasn't, so I called you."

"Jesus Christ, Jack . . . you made a big mistake not calling me right away. I could have put a tail on her after you dropped her off. I would've waited till after nine before picking her up." Max was clearly pissed off.

"You're right, I should have called you, but she sounded paranoid about my coming alone, and I had to rush to get there."

"Okay, I gotta' go, but if she does call, I need to know immediately . . . even if it's in the middle of the night—you owe me on this, buddy," Max said and abruptly hung up. There was a tone to Max's comments . . . warning Jack to stay tight with him on this investigation or their friendship would be on thin ice.

After talking to Max, Jack called Kate in California, wanting to hear how her portrait commission was coming along before telling her about his meeting with Meg.

"The portrait is going well. His wife is about fifty, she's strikingly beautiful—I think I'm capturing that. She sits for me most of the morning, and we have lunch together before returning for an hour sitting in the afternoon. I like her. She's a good conversationalist and I'm enjoying the whole experience. Now tell me what you've been up to."

"Meg called, wanting to see me right away. I met her in Mystic and she admitted she lied to us. What really happened is she and Tom had an argument that night, Tom left the house, she went looking for him, couldn't find him, and found him dead on the floor after she came home in the middle of the night. Said she lied about being home when it happened, didn't wake up to find him there as she first told us. She believes the murderer or murderers thought she was home alone—that they were actually after her, not Tom."

"What makes her believe that?"

"Because someone tried to kill her the following night!"

"Do you believe that?"

"Yeah, I do," Jack said and walked Kate through the entire meeting he had with Meg.

"Wow, you were right. He was murdered!"

"Yes. Tom had a pistol his father gave him. He showed it to me one night when I was at his house. He kept it in a dresser in his bedroom—said he always kept it loaded. The rest is speculation, but Meg said it was easy to get in the house, the lock on the backdoor was broken and she'd been after Tom to fix it. Meg thinks Tom must have heard someone sneaking in and got killed when he confronted them.

"He probably threatened them with the gun. They must have managed to get the gun away from him and shot him with his own gun. And remember, Kate, our small-town police department doesn't have a crime laboratory, so to our knowledge there wasn't any in-depth investigation at the crime scene, like dusting for finger prints. Not surprising the coroner called it suicide since Meg said she was home in bed, heard the shot and then found him on the floor with the gun in his hand. Her lying supported it looking like suicide."

"Jack, I'm really worried now. Have you told Max all this?"

"Yes, a few minutes before I called you. He was pissed-off, rightly so, for me not calling him before I went to see Meg. He also suspects Tuma isn't the real name of our unfriendly new businessman in town."

"What are you going to do now?"

"Well, tomorrow is Saturday when I usually play racquetball at the club with the guys. You know we play early in the morning and go out afterwards for breakfast. Both called when they heard about Tom, but I haven't seen them since. I'm going to go tomorrow. I need a little break from all this, they didn't know Tom like I did, but they liked him. I think they'll give me some honest feedback . . . "

"That's great, Jack. I've been worried—you've become obsessed looking into this. You're good at staying focused on whatever you're doing, but it shouldn't be at the expense of everything else. I don't think you've written a word since Tom died. You're right about needing a break . . . both men sound like the right guys to talk to."

Jack met with his two friends the next morning for three rounds of "cutthroat" racquetball. Later at breakfast, at the Railroad Cafe, he gave them a short summary on learning about Tom being murdered and then quickly switched the topic to politics. "I've seen the headline news . . . the war footing we're on with Iran, and subsequent demonstrations in Washington . . . but Kate thinks I've got my head in the sand regarding all that's happening because I've been so focused on looking into Tom's death. That's somewhat true, but I think Kate's become a little paranoid—she starting to compare Cain to Putin and Hitler."

Before either could respond he went on to tell them why he disagreed with Kate, then said, as he looked across the table at his racquetball partners, "I'd like to hear your take on all this. Your opinions?"

Both knew he was unaffiliated politically and respected his opinions, but it was clear to Jack, after ten minutes of listening to them, that they were on the same page as Kate. They both jumped all over him as he tried to argue some middle ground.

They told him Kate was right, he was out of touch. Said they'd been to the Women of America march in Washington and were going again to one in New York on Saturday.

"How about joining us?" they challenged him.

"I'll give it some thought," he replied. Telling them he didn't like Cain any more than they did, but didn't see how impeaching the president would help heal the divide and it could make it worse, then added, "but you're right, so is Kate, about having my head in the sand. This so called 'great divide' has gotten much worse than I realized. I'm glad we talked—I'll get back to you about Saturday."

Jack realized, after he left them, that he wasn't ready to do that. *Kate's right . . . been too focused on Tom's murder, but can't stop now, gut tells me Tom's death is connected to something bigger.*

After the meeting with his two friends, Jack started out heading home, then decided to take a little detour. The road passing the old docks was a little out of the way, but he wanted to see if Tuma had put up the security fence he talked about to stop anyone getting to the docks. When he arrived, he saw the fence blocking him from entering. He got out of his car looking around mumbling to himself. "Damn . . . it surrounds the parking for the docks . . . also around the old power plant." It was a chain link fence about eight feet high.

Looking down at the docks he noticed two poles had been installed at either end of the bulkhead with what appeared to be security cameras on top. He had little doubt that's what he was looking at, realizing they'll be able to see anyone approaching from the water as well as from land. *That's a lot of security for a limo service company, Max will be interested in this,* he noted as he walked back to his car.

He was about to drive away when he saw two men on the dock carrying a cooler getting into a small skiff tied up next to Rusty's boat. Red's boat was gone, but three of the other fishermen's boats were still there. As the men with the cooler were pulling out of the slip, Jack found himself drawn to staring at them and their boat. It was an odd feeling, made him continue to watch as they pulled away and headed upstream. Then it hit him—Tom said in his letter it was a blue hulled power boat he saw on Seldon Island that night.

The boat was too far away to get a good look at the men, but he felt sure this might be the boat and willing to bet a bundle on where they were headed. He jumped in his car and raced to the marina where he kept his twenty-foot skiff. It was less than a mile away. With tires squealing he braked to a stop in front of the marina office and ran inside.

"How quick can you get my boat in the water?" Jack asked the manger.

"Someone after you Jack?" The manager said after seeing him race up to the office.

"Long story, Carl. Can you get me ready in the next ten minutes?"

"I think so, there's one ahead of you, but let's see what we can do."

It was more like fifteen minutes, but Jack saw the blue boat about a half-mile ahead of him as he pulled out of the marina. He was surprised at first how few boats were on the water, then remembered it was Monday, the week after Labor Day. He would have to be careful not to get close.

Twenty minutes later, after going through five-mile an hour no-wake-zones, he was running wide open trying to keep them in sight. As he passed Hamburg Cove, one of the prettiest spots on the river, Jack remembered coming here years ago on his dad's sailboat. It seemed so long ago, a time when a ten-mile trip up the river was a great adventure, when war, terrorists, and partisan politics had no meaning to him. He missed those times as he followed the blue boat up the river with a growing feeling of being drawn into unknown danger.

He came around a bend in the river as the men were stepping ashore on Seldon Island. He'd closed the gap, but concerned they might recognize his boat he headed into Seldon Creek, the waterway that turned the land into an island a century before. He was now on the backside of the island, which presented a problem he hadn't anticipated, he had never tried to get to the stone quarry from this side.

The island was less than a half-mile wide where he tied up his boat in the narrow creek. There were no paths from here leading inland to the quarry. He guessed he was close to the quarry after working his way through woods covered in dense brush. *I'm making too much* noise he realized at almost the same time he saw a clearing ahead.

He'd reached the stone works and, moving silently from tree to tree, he could see one man sitting on a cooler and wondered where the other guy was. The thought entered his mind too late as he heard a pop accompanied by an agonizing bolt of pain in his buttock. It felt like he'd been shot. Reaching around, he felt a dart like projectile sticking out of him. The pain was excruciating as he pulled it out and stared at a barbed tranquilizing dart. He looked up to see the second man standing up from behind a boulder—smiling at him.

Jack started running back towards the dense undergrowth, throwing the dart away as he ran, but he didn't get more than thirty yards when he felt dizzy, along with a numbness spreading through his body. He stumbled, fell, and while attempting to get up, his legs felt like lead in a futile attempt to stand. He tried again, but could only manage a feeble movement before all resistance gave way to the sleepy unconsciousness spreading through him.

CHAPTER NINE

The impact of repeated doses of a tranquilizer drug had warped Jack's sense of time and it was a miracle it didn't kill him. He'd been trying to remember all that happened in the hours and days before waking in a dark cellar, chained to an anchor, and Tuma entering to say, "Ah . . . I see you are awake, Mr. Quinn."

Days had been compressed into minutes and all muddled together at first, but it wasn't long before it all came back to him: Coming home from a race around Long Island to hear Kate's worried thoughts about President Cain. Meg calling to say Tom killed himself, and not believing it was suicide after reading Tom's e-mail about Seldon Island. His beginning an investigation on his own when the police closed the case . . . and asking his friend, Max, to help after learning Meg's ex-boyfriend was a terrorist. He also remembered suspecting Tuma wasn't who he said he was, that he was somehow connected to Tom's death. Then meeting Meg at the aquarium in Mystic where she admitted her real name was Samantha Basha . . . and that she'd changed her name after learning her ex-boyfriend, Jemal, was now a Syrian terrorist, which is why she was now afraid for her life.

Yes, the dots were all connecting, but he needed to focus now on the ominous situation he awoke to. He couldn't stop thinking about Tuma's haunting words of using him for an experiment and his demonic sneer before turning off the light and exiting the cellar.

He realized that Tuma's men must have spotted him when he'd followed them up the river to Seldon Island. But he had no way of knowing they were on their way to a house that Tuma had rented on a small private island—the one he was in now—about one mile from Seldon Island.

And he didn't know the men he was tailing had called Tuma, telling him, "We're being followed. We used the binoculars and the guy in the boat looks like the one that's been nosing around the docks, the guy with the convertible you stopped from going on to Walsh's boat."

Nor, could Jack have known that Tuma had replied, "Good work—don't come to the house. Let's see if he'll follow you to Seldon. If he does and tries to follow you to the quarry—don't kill him. The tranquilizer gun is down below in the cutty-cabin. You'll have to use triple what we use on the dogs and then bring him to the house. When he starts to recover, keep him out by giving him a drink with the same amount you use in the dart. I probably won't be back until tomorrow so you'll have to keep doing it. I have plans for him, be careful you don't kill him!"

No, he didn't know any of that, but it didn't matter now. Remembering Tuma coming down the cellar made it obvious who was behind what happened to him. And recalling all Tuma said about the consequences of meddling in his affairs made it clear that Tuma wouldn't let him leave here alive. That became crystal clear when Jack accused him of being a terrorist, saw Tuma's angry reaction to the comment, followed by Tuma saying, "I'm going to expedite my plans for you—we will begin tomorrow morning."

Jack knew he'd made a big mistake not telling anyone where he was going before following Tuma's men up the river. There was little chance anyone would figure that out in time to save him. It was a sobering thought. He realized he had to focus all his attention now on saving himself.

It was difficult to move around the room with the heavy chain around his wrist. The chain cut into his skin if he wasn't careful to hold the weight of the chain with his free hand. He had to lift it to keep it from making a loud scraping noise across the floor. After surveying the space the best he could, Jack worked his way back to the mattress and sat down with his back against the cellar wall to assess his situation. Sitting down was painful—reminding him of the dart he pulled out of his backside.

He thought he'd been careful approaching the quarry, but they must have heard him. He also knew there were no houses on Seldon Island. That meant they must have brought him someplace else. He had no idea how long he was unconscious, but knowing they had to carry him to a boat, transport him to this house and chain him up, it meant it must have been many hours if not days ago.

There was no way he could get the chain off his wrist, it was too tight, but he was familiar with mushroom anchors, knew that they were frequently attached to chain using steel shackles. He was lucky, that's how this one was attached. The shackle was made with a removable bolt so the open end of the U-shaped shackle could be slipped through an eye on the shaft of the anchor, then through a link of the chain. The bolt was then screwed back in to lock everything together.

It was a long shot in hoping he could get the chain off the anchor, but it was the only chance he had to escape. Jack was counting on Tuma and his men having little knowledge of how anchors were attached to a chain. He worked his way over to the anchor and using his fingers, he found the shackle. He could feel the bolt that attached it to the anchor. His eyes had grown accustomed to the dark and there was just enough light slipping in through cracks around the walkout door for him to make out what he was looking at, including the shapes of objects in the room. But the bolt was rusted and there was no way he could turn it using his fingers.

Fighting off a hopeless feeling of finding any tools lying around, Jack remembered seeing a pile of junk near the walkout door when Tuma had turned on the light.

He needed to move the anchor five or ten feet and then the chain would be long enough to get over there. He knew it was difficult, but he had to try something, knowing it was naïve to believe anyone would come to rescue him. He had to get the heavy anchor up on edge and roll it if he had any chance to move it.

Using the anchor's shaft for leverage he managed to get it on edge, but his heart pounded from the noise made when he tried rolling it. He could only move it a few inches at a time and very slowly to prevent anyone from hearing it. Every time he stopped, he would hold his breath and listen for footsteps. Finally, after what seemed like an eternity, he had the anchor about ten feet closer to the walkout door— enough for him to reach the junk piled near the doorway.

The light seeping in around the walkout doors was a little better than at the back of the room. By the doorway he could make out most of the objects lying in the junk pile: He found a sledgehammer, a crowbar, two shovels, a pickaxe, a stack of burlap bags, and a toolbox. The toolbox had a hammer and three or four screwdrivers in the top, nothing of any use for getting the bolt out, but in the bottom of the toolbox he found box cutters and vice-grip pliers. He could hardly believe his luck He took them both and worked his way back to the anchor and had the bolt out of the shackle in less than a minute.

He was now free from the anchor but was still attached to fifteen feet of chain. The tools he found were useless for getting the chain off his wrist, but with the box cutters he cut one of the burlap bags into a skirt that he tied around his waist. He used another burlap to pad the chain so he could wrap the chain crosswise in loops over his shoulder without cutting into his skin. He adjusted the chain on his shoulder so he could freely move his left arm holding the box-cutter as a weapon in his left hand. That left his right arm free to hold either the crowbar or hammer in his right hand to use as his primary weapon—he chose the crowbar.

Jack liked his chances of survival far more now than when he found himself naked and chained to an anchor. He knew Tuma would never let him leave here alive. With that thought, he cautiously opened the walkout doors—ready to die fighting for his life instead of waiting to find out what Tuma had in store for him. There was no way he could have known, however, that his escaping from the cellar would expedite a planned attack on his country.

CHAPTER TEN

One year earlier, five thousand miles away, Omar Jemal woke to the sound of machine gun fire. Not surprising in Raqqa, but it sounded close, too close for a man who was well aware the U.S. government had a six-million-dollar bounty on his head.

"Check it out!" he said to Akram Ghadi, his team captain who was also wakened by the gunfire.

Ghadi was fiercely loyal—the kind of man who would take a bullet to save his leader. A commanding figure at six-foot four, two hundred twenty pounds, he moved with the grace of a leopard. He was an expert in both chemical and explosive weapons—skills Jemal needed to train terrorists for ISIS'S reach throughout the world.

"It's okay, Omar, some of our men were trying out those Russian weapons we took from the two SAA men we killed yesterday," Ghadi reported after coming back within minutes.

"Why don't they just raise a flag? Tell everyone we're here! Find out who fired those weapons."

"We still control the town, Omar. The men who fired the weapons were two new recruits and they didn't think anyone would notice where it came from."

Raqqa was under a two-stage assault. Assad's Syrian Arab Army (SAA), with support from Russia, were attacking the city on the southwest side, and the American backed Kurdish-led Syrian Democratic Forces (SDF), were liberating the surrounding countryside and attacking the city from the north.

"Our success depends on discipline, Akram. Mistakes like that lead to failure. Make sure they're punished," Jemal said as he studied himself in the bathroom mirror.

"I'll take care of it," Ghadi replied, noting his commander was now more concerned with his reflection in the mirror than the mistake by the new recruits.

Ghadi smiled, "You look great, no one could recognize you now."

"I think you're right," Jemal said as he held up a picture of his former self—comparing it to the man looking back at him in the mirror. His five-year old Syrian passport photo showed a smiling, good-looking suave faced man with a full head of jet-black hair over sensuous dark eyes, who appeared to be in his mid-thirties. A copy of the passport was the only photo the CIA had of him.

The mirror reflected a mostly bald, squinty-eyed man with a crooked smile and hooked nose who now appeared to be closer to fifty—no resemblance to the photo he held in his hand. Psychotic, oxymoronic thoughts flashed through his mind as he looked at the face staring back at him. It was a bitter pleasure to see what the plastic surgeon had accomplished—knowing it was what he asked for, but at the same time hating the result—losing the image of himself that had served him so well.

Seeing what he'd done, and believing it was key to succeeding in avenging what happened to his family, increased the bitterness in his heart as he walked out of the bathroom over to the desk where he'd stored his plans. After sitting down and reviewing everything in the folder that detailed the Jihad he envisioned, he looked up with a smug look on his face—rejoicing that all the pieces were in place to begin.

I chose well, he reflected as he looked out a window at the site he'd confiscated to run his terrorist operations. It was a junkyard, filled with rusting old cars surrounded by a chain link security fence. With the riverfront on one side and the town on its back the site provided security as well as escape routes if the coalition forces got to close.

The yard sat high on a hill overlooking the banks of the Euphrates River. Jemal had killed the owner, a Christian, when he refused to sell. He was sitting in the room that was previously the junkyard office, which he modified as his hiding place after the operation on his face. The junkyard had proved to be an ideal cover for training his men and to prepare for what would be the most important mission of his life. "You and I are going to see Baghdadi, Akram, before we depart."

"I thought you were going alone?"

"I was, but we received an encrypted message that he wants you to come. He wants you there to answer technical questions. I agree, it's better you're there for that. Tell him what you did in Mosul, it will impress him. We'll go right after our midday meal and should be back within a couple of hours. If he approves of the plan we'll leave tonight. We should have good cloud cover with the heavy rain, expect to move out as soon as it gets dark."

"The men are packed . . . they're ready. They'll be happy to get out of here," Ghadi said.

"Good, don't tell them yet, I want to do it myself—need to look into their eyes, make sure they'll remain loyal no matter what happens. One more question, have you told the others who will be in charge when we're gone?"

"Yes. They know about our replacements."

"Good."

The old junkyard office had a chair, a metal desk, and a torn vinyl couch for former customers. The office had an entry door to the yard, a second door to a small storage room and bathroom, which

Jemal had converted to a bedroom and hiding place for himself, and another door that opened into a large tin-shed building, previously used for storing automobile parts, which Jemal converted to living quarters for his men.

Ghadi was sitting on the couch nervously fidgeting with strands of his beard.

Jemal had noticed Ghadi's uneasiness after telling him he was to join him for the meeting.

"We have a couple of hours before we leave to see Baghdadi, do you have any questions before we go?" Jemal said.

"Yes, I'm anxious about meeting him, I've heard that at Mosul's Great Mosque he called on the world's Muslims to 'Obey him as Caliph,' and if he suspects your loyalty is in question— he will kill you. He's killed 320 of our jihadists who he suspected—"

"Yes, yes, that's all true, but let me tell you what you don't know." Jemal was known for his cool demeanor under crisis situations and was a cold-hearted killer, but he was becoming worried about his second-in-command coming to the meeting with Baghdadi. He was unsure how Akram Ghadi would respond to questions?

"You should be focused on why he's our leader, why he's recognized throughout the world as the head of our jihad. And why America has him on their 'Most Wanted List' with a huge price on his head." Jemal said.

"You should also think about why he's here, Akram, why he came back again when the American led forces out-numbered us fifteen to one, forcing him out of Mosul. And remember we took Raqqa back under his command—that was crucial to continue the jihad throughout the world.

"With so many attempts on his life you can't blame him for his suspicions. But his reputation on the battlefield, leading the fight against the infidels, is why he appealed to me and so many of our young jihadists— more so than Zawahiri, who did nothing after taking over Al-Qaeda when Osama bin Laden was killed. Zawahiri didn't have the fighting spirit Baghdadi has. Just think about all that . . . make him feel you're proud he's our leader."

"How much does he know about me? I'm worried he might think I was disloyal by leaving Mosul and coming here," Ghadi said.

"Don't worry about that. Remember he had to flee Mosul before you did. He knows you studied chemical engineering at the University of Mosul . . . knows you joined us when he was there . . . knows of your reputation as a fearless fighter, of your courage during the battle . . . that you stayed as long as possible."

"If he knows so much about me, why didn't he ask to see me in Mosul?"

"You should know why! He had to keep his whereabouts secret, move every day to prevent the Americans from finding him. But that doesn't mean he doesn't know a lot about you. He thought you were an excellent choice when I told him I recruited you as my second-in-command."

"I didn't know that. You're right, I need to focus on what you've said, but what about his killing so many of our own men. He—"

"Stop, Akram—you have nothing to worry about. He had to send a strong message to prevent the defections when it looked like the Americans were going to take back Mosul. He knew he needed absolute loyalty from everyone to continue the jihad. Yes, it was very harsh, but I can't fault him. I don't believe he would have done it unless he knew it was absolutely necessary," Jemal said. He didn't like Ghadi's line of questions and wouldn't have put up with it from any of his other men. It was time to stop it and give him a warning that he supported what Baghdadi had done.

"I apologize, Omar, I meant no offense. I understand. Thank you for telling me as much as you did." Akram Ghadi was no fool,

He knew he had gone too far and deferentially changed the subject. "If you don't mind, I would much appreciate hearing more about your life here in Raqqa while we still have time before we go." He knew Raqqa was Jemal's hometown and he liked to talk about it.

"No, I don't mind. I liked growing up here and going to the University of Aleppo, only ninety miles away. There were about two hundred and twenty thousand residents back then, the majority were Sunni Muslims. We lived peacefully, side-by-side with Kurds and Christian families before the civil war. Most of us resented Assad's brutal regime and most supported the Free Syrian Army (FSA) when the civil war began."

"What caused so many to start leaving Raqqa?" Ghadi asked, leaning back on the couch and feeling more relaxed now that the conversation had shifted to small talk.

"That started after the FSA lost ground to Assad's forces. When it looked like Aleppo would fall, tens of thousands of people fled here, swelling our population, but most weren't willing to fight or sacrifice for the jihad even though they hated Assad—they were cowards and fled the country when we took control of the city."

Jemal didn't tell Ghadi that he knew the citizens of Raqqa were terrified when ISIS took over. That he knew the propaganda, beheadings and hand chopping were characteristic of ISIS'S medieval law enforcement; that he didn't approve, knew why people were fleeing the city, and that he helped carry it out as a means to an end. For him, it meant becoming a force within ISIS wherein he could carry out his revenge—his jihad against America.

They left for the meeting shortly after noon, walking for a half hour through Raqqa to a pre-arranged pick up point where they would be taken to Baghdadi's headquarters. Jemal told Ghadi about the extreme precautions Baghdadi had to take to protect his whereabouts, that a panel truck modified to prevent their viewing the route would be used to pick them up and take them to the meeting today.

Akram Ghadi was from Iraq. He knew very little about Raqqa's history and took the opportunity to ask about points of interest as they walked to the pick-up point. He began cleverly asking questions that prompted Jemal to talk more about himself. They were passing the ruins of what had once been a beautiful Shiite mosque.

"Is that rubble the remains of the big mosque, Omar?" Ghadi asked as they walked past an acre of debris filled with blue and red tiles.

"Yes."

"What did it look like?" Ghadi had seen photos of it, knew the answer, but wanted to hear what Jemal would say.

"I grew up seeing the mosque as a beautiful piece of architecture, a fond childhood memory. I'm sorry it was destroyed, but I understand why—it was a symbol of Assad's regime and his Shiite sympathizers." Jemal didn't say it evoked conflicting feelings . . . reminding him of a time when he didn't hate anybody and was optimistic about his future.

"What was it like back then?"

"It was peaceful. Fifteen years earlier I was a computer-engineering student at the University of Aleppo, but I was naïve. I liked America back then, thought it was the greatest country in the world. I met an exchange student at Aleppo who came from a Muslim community in New York. She helped me with my English lessons—taught me slang words and how to speak without an accent. That was before I realized America was our enemy, before they invaded Iraq, before they bombed us, killed my family, and before I realized she was just like them—"

Omar Jemal stopped talking, realizing he was getting angry just thinking about her and it probably showed. He was hesitant to say more even though he trusted his team captain.

"What was she like when she was here? Was she your girlfriend?"

Ghadi asked with a bit of a grin. He really wanted to ask if he had slept with her but didn't want to risk being that personal.

Jemal knew what he wanted to know and couldn't resist bragging about it. "Yes, we were lovers when she was here. She wanted to marry me, but I wasn't in love with her and had no intention of ever marrying her. She got pregnant, considered abortion, but I told her "no", explained it was legal under Islamic law within the first one hundred-twenty days, but was frowned upon, so we followed my father's suggestion to put the baby up for adoption."

"Was that the only time she was here?"

"No, I kept in contact with her for years, continuing to see her on her occasional visits after I had a family. I thought she might be useful after I joined ISIS. That all changed when I learned she was a non-believer, couldn't be trusted. She believes we are the terrorists—not them."

"I also remember the peaceful times before the war, Omar. Mosul was a good place to grow up. Like you, a lot of us were naïve about America. There was a lot I didn't like about Hussein, but life was better back then. They don't know us—why we resent them sticking their nose in our problems, and how much I hate them for the bombing of the city that killed my family."

"I remember when you came to me . . . telling me about losing your family," Jemal said.

"Yes, it is very personal for me. I want revenge for my parents and two sisters who died when the Americans took back Mosul. They call civilians who get killed "collateral damage." The word has no emotional connection to them. It's not their mothers and father's or children, most of the time they don't bother to report civilians killed, just their soldiers."

"I know, talking about it reminds me of what I'd been feeling before I joined," Jemal responded.

Jemal purposely picked a path that took them past where he'd lived. He wanted to see it today knowing it was doubtful he would ever see it again.

All the talk about ISIS and why he joined, filled his thoughts with hatred as he walked through the city. It caused him to remember what happened to his family.

"That was my house, Akram," He stopped walking and was pointing to the remains of the burnt-out apartment building he grew up in. Looking at it made his blood boil.

"What happened?" Ghadi saw the tormented look on his leader's face turn into an angry fuming stare.

"I heard the Americans had targeted a van our men were using. They were miss-informed that Baghdadi was in it—unaware he'd changed his mind at the last minute. A missile fired from a drone hit the van as it passed my family's apartment building. It killed everyone in the van, but the explosion also ignited gas lines going into the building, turning the apartment into an inferno. It was a small two-story apartment complex for four families. Most were inside sleeping, no one in my family escaped. I was away on a business trip to Aleppo. I didn't learn what happened until the following morning."

"We have similar memories—we will avenge all this." Ghadi said as he looked at Jemal as not only his leader, but also as a brother who understood his pain.

"Yes. Walking pass here brings back a lot of memories. I returned to Raqqa after graduating from the University of Aleppo. Five years later, I was the owner of a successful Internet café and had a growing family. My disillusionment with America began when they invaded Iraq, more so when I realized they weren't going to overthrow Assad, and as I said before . . . it fermented into hatred when they killed my family.

"America and the West have proven to be our enemy. All this made me believe what Baghdadi was preaching—'we need to expand the jihad . . . ' I began supporting the cause by allowing them to use my Internet services for recruitment.

"This . . . " Jemal said, pointing again to the burned-out building as they began walking away, "fired me to join, and why I'm on America's most wanted list. I joined the jihad a week after my family was killed. I rose to become your leader—picked by Baghdadi—I'm proud to be known as the mastermind in outsourcing our fighters, taking the jihad to other countries.

"I think of today, Akram, as the first day of our revenge. Baghdadi will be pleased when he sees my plan." Jemal reveled in saying how successful he'd become in training the men. This is what he was thinking as they approached the pick-up point where they would be taken to Baghdadi's headquarters.

CHAPTER ELEVEN

The pick-up point for Jemal and Ghadi was at Raqqa's Food Court in the center of the city. They arrived at the prescribed time. A black minivan with a man standing by it was waiting for them. Jemal recognized him as one of Baghdadi's body guards. As they approached the van, the sliding door on the vehicle opened and another man stepped out to usher them inside accompanied by the two body guards. Black curtains covered all the windows in the rear and another large curtain partitioned the driver and front seat from the back so the passengers had no view to the outside as the driver sped away. The guards patted them down for any weapons before the guard, whom Jemal recognized, said, "Welcome." It was more than he ever said before—he was one of Baghdadi's bodyguards.

Baghdadi's headquarters was four miles away and approximately southwest from where they left. It was hidden in the cellar of a café in a small two-story shopping center. An orphanage occupied most of the upper floor of the building. It was an ideal location for ISIS headquarters. The rear of the shopping center was squeezed between a large windowless storage building by a narrow alleyway just wide enough for use as a service road.

Jemal and Ghadi were blindfolded as the van pulled up to the rear of the café. After the body guards stepped out to scan the alleyway they were taken into the kitchen in the back of the café. They couldn't see the two men with AK-47's on their laps sipping coffee at a table in the front, sizing up anyone who came in. There were tables for about a dozen people, but aside from the two men in the front there was only one other person in the café—an old man cleaning a counter in the kitchen.

Five minutes went by before the old man removed their blindfolds and signaled for Jemal and Akram to follow him. They passed a bathroom and entered a door marked "Storeroom." A bare light bulb in the storeroom revealed walls filled with coffee cans and supplies of canned food that were hard to come by in the last few months. The city, under ISIS control, had become increasingly isolated from the outside world.

The old man removed a coffee can on the back wall and knocked twice. Jemal, having been here before, recognized the sound of bars on the other side unlocking before the back wall swung open. It was a clever design. The entire wall was hinged like a door on invisible massive hinges—the locking bars tightly sealed the four sides of the wall to the mating surfaces on the inside. An observer would be hard pressed to find anything to indicate it was a false wall.

A guard on the other side motioned for Jemal and Akram to pass through onto a landing platform with steps down to a large basement. The guard frisked them again before motioning they were clear to go down. There were six men in the basement working at computer terminals and two more guards with automatic weapons watching as Jemal and Akram walked down the steps. Printers, cameras, recording equipment and other electronic media devices were lying on a long bench. A large flat screen TV was mounted on a wall over the bench. One of the guards sitting at a desk was scanning images from video cameras installed in different parts of the city and around Baghdadi's headquarters.

One of the guards pointed to a bench for the two men to sit at.

"I'm impressed," Ghadi whispered in Jemal's ear.

Jemal nodded in agreement, but didn't say anything, he'd heard rumors of listening devices installed in the room.

There were two doors in the basement, one was an old wooden door leading to sleeping quarters and a bathroom for the workers. The other, a reinforced steel door, led to Baghdadi's private office and living space. Jemal knew Baghdadi wasn't here every day, frequently moving to different safe houses in the city, he also knew it wasn't unusual for him to use disguises when he came.

Jemal had been here before. Twice to discuss the plan he'd brought today, and once shortly after it was set up as the new headquarters. He'd been called in to supervise installation of secure communications equipment needed for encrypting messages.

When Baghdadi purchased the café, he also bought the entire two-story complex the owner was renting, including a clothing store and orphanage.

Knowing the threat of air strikes would be increasing, Baghdadi, had intentionally placed his headquarters under the living space of the orphanage—coldheartedly using it as a shield. He knew it wouldn't stop Assad or the Russians if they discovered his hiding place, but he didn't think the Americans would risk killing the children.

Jemal and Ghadi waited ten minutes before the guard opened the steel door to Baghdadi's office.

Stepping in and seeing Baghdadi staring at him from behind his desk, Jemal said, "So, what do you think?" as he stopped and turned his head from side to side to show off his new face.

If Baghdadi was shocked to see the transformation, he did a good job of not showing it. "They did a good job on your face, Omar, but your voice is the same. I'd suggest cutting off your balls if I didn't think you'd be needing them," Baghdadi said, looking at Jemal and then over at Ghadi with a slight hint of a smirk on his face before motioning for the two of them to sit on an old leather couch to the right side of his desk.

Jemal was caught off guard; confused by the joke as he studied this mysterious man. There was something about the smirk on Baghdadi's heavily bearded face and the deep tone of his voice that indicated he wasn't entirely joking—like he wanted to state his authority. He was known not to joke, smile or talk to his men in a way that invited familiarity. He had managed to create a mystique about himself that was part of his appeal for recruits wanting to join ISIS.

"Thank Allah you think I need them," Jemal laughingly said as he sat down on the couch. He wanted it to be clear he took it as a joke." His retort, accompanied by a quick glance at Ghadi was intended to let his number-two man know he wasn't intimidated by the comment.

"So, you are Akram Ghadi, the bomb maker I heard about in Mosul. Tell me, would you willingly die for this man?" Baghdadi asked as he nodded his head towards Jemal.

"Yes, I would, but also for you . . . for the Jihad . . . for Allah . . . I believe the cause is just!" Akram Ghadi was no fool, understanding the hidden meaning of the question and he spoke firmly pausing to emphasize each statement of his allegiance as he spoke.

"You have the plans?" Baghdadi asked.

"I do. How about the bus? Are the tanks on it?" Jemal said.

Baghdadi nodded affirmatively. "Yes, it came in last night and the modifications went well. Here are the photos." Baghdadi handed Jemal a set of photographs showing before and after pictures of the baggage compartment of a bus that had been bringing people into Raqqa from Lebanon. There weren't many passengers coming to Raqqa anymore, and those that came knew it would probably be a one-way trip, most coming to join families or loved ones that couldn't get out. The bus usually returned empty and had to go through Damascus on its way back to Lebanon.

Jemal took his time studying the photos, holding them under a light to get a good look at the baggage compartment. "They look good. I don't see how anyone would notice it's a little shallower. I can't see any seams for the hidden compartment holding the tanks. The body shop did a great job, but how do we know they won't talk?" Jemal asked Baghdadi as he handed the photos to Ghadi to look at.

"It was done at night by two men and dead men don't talk. We had no choice. We didn't have anyone good enough and these men did it for the money—Allah would approve," Baghdadi said.

Jemal nodded in agreement, whatever compassion he'd felt for his fellow man had been erased when his family was killed. Like Baghdadi, he now saw everything as a means to an end. Both were close in age, both delusional and uncaring about the inhumane evil nature of their pursuits—believing everything they were doing was justified. But they came to their beliefs in very different ways.

Baghdadi saw himself as the rightful, Caliph, a successor of Muhammad, the unifying power to bring Islam back to the greatness that Islam enjoyed for almost eight hundred years. But the cruel, ruthless, jihad he created under ISIS; the suicide bombings that killed so many innocent women and children; the torture and beheadings of anyone suspected of opposing his regime; and the systematic destruction and attacks on everything that fell outside his personalized doctrine of a new Islamic order—all this was far removed from the teachings of Muhammad and was abhorrent to the majority of Muslims around the world.

Jemal knew on an intellectual level that Baghdadi was no true follower of Muhammad. He saw all the cruelty, but didn't care, didn't allow it to detract from the mission he was on. He saw Baghdadi's organization as his best option to achieve for what happened to his family. But he knew ISIS was fighting a losing battle in Raqqa and knew he had to act quickly.

"Let's see what you have here," Baghdadi said as he picked up the folder Jemal had handed him.

It was all there: The propane tanks filled with anthrax hidden in the modified luggage compartments of the bus; his escape to Lebanon on the bus with three hand-picked men; boarding and disguising the anthrax on a freighter departing for New York from a port in Beirut; passports for everyone; and rationale for fifty thousand U.S. dollars needed when Jemal got to America. Key to the plan was the identity theft of the reclusive wealthy restaurant owner in Brooklyn—Jemal was now a look-a-like after plastic surgery. The plans highlighted purchasing property in New Saybrook, Connecticut to set up his base of operations, and in-depth details of how the biological attack will be carried out in New York, concluding with an escape plan for Jemal and his men.

Baghdadi took his time to carefully read the report, sipping his coffee until he finished reading. "Looks like it's all here, same as you outlined previously, but I have some questions for you," he said looking directly at Akram Ghadi.

"How can you be sure anthrax will kill this many people?" he said, holding up the plan that said up to a million people might die in the attack.

"I have a degree in chemical engineering, I was also the team leader making bombs in Mosul—"

"I know all that—what do you know about anthrax. We've never used it before."

"That's true, but I studied for my master's at Baghdad University. Saddam Hussein had insisted biological weaponry be included in the school's curriculum. My thesis was on the effectiveness of anthrax as a biological weapon. I learned how difficult it is to make military grade anthrax, particularly the airborne variety and did some laboratory tests using rats. I subsequently learned that Assad's regime had developed military grade anthrax and have significant supplies of it.

"We were lucky Omar had a contact at their laboratory willing to help us, but without your support, we had no way of getting it here or hiding it in the bus," Ghadi said, acutely aware of needing to show respect for both of his superiors. He noted Baghdadi's approving nod.

"Yes, we picked up the tanks from Assad's storage facility last week. Omar's friend slipped them out at night in his pick-up truck. It was risky trusting him, but he did as promised," Baghdadi said.

"We're close friends," Jemal replied. "I wasn't worried about him. He wasn't working for Assad's people because he wanted to—he had no choice. He's more useful to us there.

"We've been friends for twenty years. When I asked for the tanks, he told me how deadly this particular strain is. It's most effective when used as an aerosol spray, far more so than the powder form—breathing it will kill most of the victims unless they get medical attention within a day or so. He took a big risk helping us, said there are many people where he works who would turn him in if they knew he was talking to us," Jemal said.

"How do we know the Americans don't have a vaccine or antidote to cure those infected?" Baghdadi asked.

"They do, but like I said, they have to get medical attention shortly after they breathe it in. The affects don't show up for a couple of days so they won't know they're sick until it's too late. By the time a lot of people get sick and authorities diagnose it as anthrax it will be too late for most. It's also unlikely they can get remedies to millions of infected people in a day or so if they somehow detect what we've done on the first day."

"What's the probability of that happening?"

"Extremely low. The poison isn't visible, has no odor and as you see from my plans the design for delivery uses vehicles with roof racks for maximum effect on the people walking the streets.

"How do you know it's still good stuff—it may have been stored for years?" Baghdadi said, directing the question at Ghadi.

"We don't know for certain, however, Omar's friend said it was made this year and anthrax is known to have a long shelf-life. I plan on running some tests on animals when we get to America. I asked for more than necessary in case it loses strength in shipping. If that happens, we should have enough to condense it to the grade we need. I know how to do that," Ghadi said.

Baghdadi turned to Jemal, "I have one more question. That American girl you screwed around with—why are you setting up your operation where she is?"

"Two reasons. First of all, I want to be far enough from New York where they have all those investigative cops walking around, but I want to be close enough to get there in a couple of hours. The second reason is in regard to my new face. I want to be sure that someone like her won't recognize me. The Americans have photos of me on the Internet and all over the place. There's also a remote possibility she gave them recordings of my voice. You know they have me high on their most wanted list. If she can't recognize me, then no one can."

"What if she does—you can't change your voice!"

"I'll be experimenting with that. The surgeon gave me some Botox to inject in my vocal cords. Say's it will make me speak softer, a little horse, and somewhat different like I'm older. He gave me needles to inject the stuff in my throat. It will only last six months, but I have enough to do it again if I need it. If I think she recognizes me—I'll kill her." What he didn't say was seeing her in his new identity would be a game for him, and of how much he hated her.

Baghdadi drummed his fingers on the desk as he studied Jemal for a minute. He then asked Ghadi to wait in the other room while he had a private discussion with Jemal, but not before giving Ghadi his blessing for a successful jihad in America.

After Ghadi left, Baghdadi said, "You have my approval to leave for America and to put in place everything necessary for the attack, but wait until you get a signal from me before executing the strike. The Americans will come after us with everything they've got if they discover we did it, and then we would have no chance of holding Raqqa. You know, however, that we might lose Raqqa, and if we do, I have contingency plans to coordinate your attack with an expansion of the jihad in other places—our timing will be crucial."

"What are your contingency plans if Raqqa falls?" Jemal said knowing Baghdadi would resent his asking, but he was worried about contingency plans if Baghdadi got killed.

"You know better than to ask me that question, Omar—better you don't know if they capture you." Baghdadi said, and a frown crossed his face as he guessed at what Jemal was really thinking.

"You're right, more important you tell me how you will signal me to go ahead with the attack," Jemal said with a smile, not wanting to leave the meeting with any bad feelings between them.

"First of all, watch the news, and don't do anything if you see we continue to hold out—be patient. You may have to wait awhile to hear from me for the right opportunity. But if we lose Raqqa, I will send you a signal from my new headquarters to go ahead."

"How will you signal me?"

"Read the obituaries in the New York Times every day. When you see an obituary for 'Ibrahim al-Samarrai', that will be the coded signal to go ahead. The date of the memorial service will be the date for the attack."

Jemal recognized the coded name as Baghdadi's real name and said, "I apologize for having to ask you, but what do I do if you are killed before I receive the coded signal?"

"I have a succession plan, Omar, stop worrying, be patient—you will get what you are looking for!"

CHAPTER TWELVE

After the meeting was over, Jemal and Ghadi were blindfolded again and dropped back at the food court. They walked slowly on their way back to the junkyard, knowing it may be the last time they saw Raqqa.

"How do you think it went?" Ghadi asked.

"Good, we got everything I asked for," Jemal said.

"We'll leave tonight. No one will stop the bus on our side. Damascus is a bit risky but all our papers say we're construction workers from Lebanon. If we get stopped, we tell them we came to Raqqa a year ago to work on reinforcing the Baath Dam fourteen miles from here. We'll say we couldn't get out when ISIS took over, but now that work on the dam has stopped they're letting us get back to our families."

"You think that will work?"

"Think positive, Akram, and pray to Allah it will. It's our best chance and Baghdadi says he got some of our agents through Damascus to Beirut with similar stories. We have to get to the bus station by nine tonight so tell the others to shave their beards. I want all three of you here in an hour to rehearse our stories, tell them to bring nothing with them but a small backpack for water, a little food, and extra clothes for the twenty-four-hour bus ride to Beirut."

An hour later, Jemal and Ghadi sat facing two of the best men selected from the fourteen fighters that had been holed up with them in the junkyard. Jemal asked the two to empty their pockets and backpacks and to show him anything personal they had on them.

Both were in their thirties, tough looking men who could easily pass as construction workers.

Jemal went through their wallets and stopped to scrutinize a photograph he found. A frown crossed his face as he put it down and turned towards the biggest man in the room, Abood Menash, a tall wide shouldered, dark complexioned man known for his cool demeanor in a fire fight.

"Abood, this photo looks like it was taken in Mosul. How are you going to explain that if we are searched and questioned in Damascus?"

"I'm sorry, I forgot it was in my wallet," Abood Menash said, looking chagrined by his mistake.

Jemal then turned towards the other fighter Ghadi had selected for the jihad. Hassan Abadi, a squat, beady eyed, bull necked man known as a merciless fighter. He also had a photographic memory which Ghadi thought would be useful for the mission.

"Hassan, is this yours?" Jemal asked, holding up an expensive Tag Heuer watch that Abadi had taken off a foreign reporter prior to beheading him.

Hassan Abadi nodded it was his—looking longingly at the watch, knowing he was about to lose it.

"How would you explain how you could afford such an expensive watch?"

"I didn't know it was that expensive, I just liked it. I didn't think anyone would notice since there's no gold on it."

"Let me do the thinking—you need to remember we can't appear, say, or do anything that will bring attention to any of us. We're all just construction workers looking forward to returning home. Study your new papers, memorize your new names and where it says you live as if they're your own. I'll do the talking like I'm the foreman of our crew. No need for any of you to say anything unless absolutely necessary. Once you get on the ship in Beirut you can relax a little, but even then, we will have to be careful. I'll talk about that some more before you get on the ship." Jemal said.

"Akram told us about the jihad in America, but how do we get there?" Hassan asked.

"Are you having second thoughts, Hassan? If you have any doubts about this jihad tell me now, Hassan!" He said this knowing it would be hard to find a better man, but Jemal needed to be sure his men were totally committed and he didn't like being questioned.

Hassan Abadi looked frightened hearing Jemal ask about his commitment. He quickly glanced at Ghadi, his team captain, and seeing a stony look on his face, blurted out, "No, I want to go. I didn't mean to question the jihad. I hadn't heard how we would get there, thought you were thinking that Akram had told us. I'm sorry if it sounded like I needed to know more. I'm ready to go. I don't have any doubts—none at all."

"Good. Both of you know there will be great risks along the way—some or all of us may get killed on this jihad. I need to know now if you want out of this mission."

"We're with you!" both men said, raising their right arms with closed fists. Ghadi was smiling—pleased his choosing had gone well.

At 8 p.m., Jemal and his team left the junkyard and headed for the bus station along with two big bodyguards who'd been sent to accompany them. The escorts were carrying AK-47's and had black bands on their arms. They needed the escort—there was a good chance patrols might stop them when seeing they'd shaved their beards.

The bus depot was deserted when they arrived. They were the only passengers who boarded the bus. The bus driver was from Raqqa. He'd gotten a large bribe to help them safely through Damascus and into Lebanon, but Jemal was nervous knowing this was the riskiest leg of the journey.

CHAPTER THIRTEEN

The first leg of the bus ride was uneventful. Going through ISIS held territory was easy since the guards were informed to let the bus through. The bus was stopped twice, however, on the route through Assad's government held territory. The story of being a construction crew returning home held up, but they had to bribe the guards to let them pass. This was expected. Jemal was aware that no one coming or leaving Raqqa got through without bribing the guards in the government held territory.

Damascus was the biggest problem. They had to get off the bus and nervously watched as guards inspected the vehicle inside and out. Fortunately, the modification to the luggage compartment went unnoticed and they were taken to a holding room in the bus terminal where their backpacks were inspected.

On the way to a waiting room, Jemal whispered, "No matter what happens here, remember to always act and talk like we're construction workers—even when we're alone. They may keep us overnight while they check our papers, assume that every place they put us will be bugged."

They were held overnight in Damascus, having to tell their stories twice to two different interrogators, but they had been prepped well and were released to continue on to Beirut. Jemal breathed a sigh of relief once they were back on the bus. He told them to hold off reveling in the victory until they crossed into Lebanon. After crossing the border, they celebrated by stopping in a restaurant to eat. The government soldiers they'd bribed had taken all their snacks.

Jemal chose a booth in the back where they could talk freely. Turning to Abadi he said, "Okay, I'll answer your question now about getting to America. If I'd told you before and we were separated in Damascus they might have tortured you, or all of us. It was better to minimize the risk. But we're in friendly territory here and you need to know of the next step of my plan when we get to Beirut. We have time now so listen carefully:

"The Port of Beirut makes a lot of money for the Lebanese government. Lucky for us, there's a lot of corrupt people working there. It's not hard to find custom agents and brokers who can be bribed—they skim off the top of what's taken in every day. It's Lebanon's biggest port."

"How will we move the tanks on board?" Abadi asked.

"I'll get to that but first you need to understand what goes on there. Corruption at the port is everywhere. Here's how it works: Goods entering or exiting through the Port of Beirut are either assigned a green or a red document by Lebanese customs agents. A green document indicates the container or goods holds no suspicious products and that the contents match what has been legally declared. All goods, crates, or containers with a green card do not undergo additional inspection and are cleared from the port after the corresponding dues are paid. We have to get that green document."

Jemal paused to take a bite of the Mahshi he ordered. A recipe of stuffed zucchini made with spiced rice, ground beef, tomatoes and herbs. Ghadi took the opportunity to say, "You guys will like what you hear next."

"This Mahshi is the best I've ever had," Jemal said as he took a mouthful of his favorite food.

He paused for a moment to chew before going on to say, "I don't want to ruin your meal, but from now on, I don't want to hear anyone use our old names again." Seeing how they all looked quickly around, he said, "It's okay, we can speak here, but you have to get used to your new names when in Beirut and on the ship. Don't forget we're a construction crew, you'll need to show your passports at the port and to get on board the boat.

"Now back to the green document we will need to get the tanks onboard. I have a contact who knows one of the custom brokers who specializes in processing transactions; one who understands we need to export goods without headaches. It happens all the time for a fee of several thousand dollars to cover taxes, bribes for customs agents and of course, a cut for the broker himself.

"It makes no difference to this guy whether the goods are gold, cement, vegetables, or in our case, propane tanks. This guy is our go-to man who can pass expensive designer clothes off as cutlery or gold as makeup."

"I heard there's equipment that can see inside crates without opening them. Don't they have that here?" Hassan asked.

"Yes, they do. The Port has advanced scanners that can do that. However, our man is one of the pros among the brokers who knows how to bribe scanner operators to get the machines to malfunction at just the right time. And brokers like this guy have a network of partners in the port's customs department to make sure everything goes smoothly.

"The tough part is getting the tanks on a ship—here's how we will do it. Our ship will be a small tanker that regularly operates from Beirut to New York. Wealthy Sunni brothers in Beirut who are sympathetic to our cause own the tanker. The boat is also regularly used for re-exporting. If goods are imported to Lebanon, the government collects customs and VAT fees. If these goods are re-exported the cargo designated for re-exportation is seldom scanned again and our broker will make sure they're not. This means we can switch something like a crate of potatoes for our tanks without anyone detecting what's in the crates."

"How do we get the tanks out of the bus?" Hassan asked.

"The bus will be taking a small detour tonight to a restaurant on the outskirts of the city where we'll have dinner. While we're eating, the tanks will be switched to a van and taken to an auto body shop where they will be painted, marked to look like ordinary propane tanks and stored there. The body shop is a front for one of our safe houses in the city and it's where the three of you will be staying until Akram hears from me.

"What about our driver? How much does he know?" Hassan asked.

"I told you don't worry about him. All he knows—the story I've told him—is that we'll be stopping at a restaurant tonight. He doesn't know we modified the large luggage compartment to store the tanks. We did it while he was in Raqqa on his last run. The compartment was very deep, our men made a hidden compartment in the back of it. It was professionally done with hidden pins for quick removal—looks just like the original compartment except somewhat smaller."

"We are lucky to have you as our leader—you think of everything. I'm looking forward to getting on that ship. I hope it's soon," Hassan said. He'd just finished the last of his meal.

"Not as soon as you'd like Hassan, it's time to tell you the rest of the plan. I'll be leaving all of you after we get to Beirut. The three of you will be holed up in the city for a while until I notify Akram it's time to leave."

Ghadi, was sitting in the booth next to Jemal. He knew this and said nothing, but his two men sitting across the table looked shocked, exclaiming loudly, "why?"

Jemal, annoyed at their outburst, held up his hand indicting for them to be quiet. "I understand you're both surprised, but you can't let that happen again. I told you 'don't do anything to bring attention to yourself or us.' Now listen carefully while I tell you the next part of the plan. We can't all go together for a lot of reasons:

"First is the risk—it's one thing to get our cargo on board, I told you how we'll do it, but it won't be that easy to get ourselves on board.

"Second, the risk of getting into America goes up with every person we add to our little group.

"Third, we're going to need someone in America to set things up for the rest of us, like where to stay and to establish a business—a front to hide why we are really there—that someone is me!"

"Can you tell us how you're going to get there?" Hassan asked.

"No, it's better you don't know. I will be contacting Akram when I get set up in America. It may take anywhere from one to six months before I can arrange to get all of you to join me. You and Abood will be staying with Akram while waiting for my instructions. He will make all the arrangements for getting you and the tanks on board.

"So, until you see me again in America, consider anything Akram asks you to do as coming from me. After we get to Beirut and I leave, he'll be making all decisions necessary for the three of you to join me. Remember you were chosen because Akram said you were the best. Our jihad depends on you—don't disappoint me," Jemal said. Jemal had told Ghadi he was going to Cuba where it would be easier for one person like himself who was fluent in English to get into America undetected, but he was prudent in telling his men only what he believed was necessary for them to know.

It was six in the evening when they arrived at the restaurant in Beirut. Moving the tanks from the bus to the van went smoothly.

The bus was parked behind the restaurant and it took less than fifteen minutes to make the switch to the van and get the tanks to the auto body shop while the others were inside eating. Two hours later, the bus driver delivered his passengers to the Beirut bus depot.

The next morning after seeing that the tanks were safely stored in the shop, Jemal gave Ghadi coded instructions for how they would stay in contact. He then headed for the city's International Airport and bought an Aeroflot ticked for Russia where he could safely head for Cuba without the Americans tracing his travel itinerary.

CHAPTER FOURTEEN

Jemal purchased a business class ticket for the four-hour flight to Moscow. Ten minutes after take-off, when the seat belt sign went off, Jemal opened his briefcase and took out the photographs he'd taken of himself after his plastic surgery. He then looked at his new counterfeit Lebanese passport photo and smiled, pleased how close he looked to Maten Tuma, the forty-five-year-old businessman from Brooklyn, NY, the man he'd been corresponding with by e-mail for the last six months.

He knew the passport wasn't good enough for getting into America, but it would get him as far as Cuba. And with Cuba being only ninety miles away, he felt it wouldn't be too difficult to get to America by bribing someone. He had plenty of money. Baghdadi had given him the fifty thousand U.S. dollars for expenses and operations in America, ten thousand of which he gave to Akram Ghadi before he left.

His thoughts quickly turned back to Meg and the mistake he'd made by getting angry with her. *I should have known she'd be upset . . . should have realized Americans think all ISIS fighters are terrorists. It was stupid, she knows too much about me.*

He put the passport and photo of himself back in his briefcase and took one out of Meg. Again, he smiled as he remembered how she unknowingly gave him a way to locate where she'd moved. As the owner of an Internet café in Raqqa, he had become very proficient in tracking where e-mails originated and blocking anyone from tracking those he sent out. He needed to get good at this in order to safely correspond with the network of fighters he'd trained and sent out of Syria.

Meg had sent him an e-mail months after their argument to let him know she'd left Brooklyn, changed her name, and moved far away so he couldn't track her down. She also warned him she would go to the FBI and tell them everything she knew about him if she learned he was trying to find her. What she didn't know, and most people don't, was that all e-mails are easily tracked to the source using software called "E-mail Tracker Pro"

Jemal and his team at the Internet café had developed their own version of Tracker Pro along with track busting software to prevent any e-mail he sent out from being tracked back to Raqqa. He knew it wasn't fool proof from hackers so he also created a coded language for messages he sent.

With the software he created, he easily tracked Meg to New Saybrook, Connecticut. Thinking of that as he put her photo back in his briefcase, an angry look crossed his face as he snapped the lid closed. No one was sitting next to him, but the stewardess saw the look- as she passed by . . . .

"Are you all right sir?"

"Yes, yes . . . I'm fine." He said as he dismissed her with a wave of his hand. *But Meg won't be when I'm done with her*, he mused to himself.

Jemal's native language was Arabic with a north Syrian dialect, but he spoke English almost as well. As a result of foreign imperialism, the Syrian Arabic language had many borrowed forms of English, French, and other languages. This made it easier for him to learn the English he'd studied as a second language since boyhood and throughout his college years. His affair with Meg, beginning when she came over as an exchange student, lasted on and off for over ten years. Meg was surprised she couldn't detect any accent other than mispronouncing some words, but he was a perfectionist, knew that pronunciation and idioms could trip him up if he ever came to America, so with her help he learned to speak like a native-born American.

The Cuban tourist visa Jemal obtained was good for thirty days. He didn't plan to stay that long—just long enough to find a way to get to America. During his recuperation from plastic surgery he worked on learning some basic Spanish, assuming that outside of Havana it might be difficult to find people who spoke any English. His plan was to find a visiting yachtsman who would take him as crew or paying passenger. He knew the risk of the maritime patrols Cuba had within their territorial limits and of the U.S. Coast Guard's, but he knew it was far less risky than joining a boat filled with refuges trying to escape the Cuban regime.

He needed to find someone who would take him alone for the right amount of money. He was convinced he had a better chance of finding that someone outside of Havana along the north coast, away from the populated areas.

After landing in Moscow and purchasing a ticket to Cuba, Jemal arrived in Havana the next morning. He then took a taxi to the resort town of Cayo Guillermo where the taxi driver dropped him off at the Iberostar Hotel. The hotel, catering to tourists, was only one mile from one of the country's best beaches, the Playa Pilar Beach where Jemal felt comfortable blending in with other tourists. The beach, named after Hemingway's cabin cruiser, PILAR, provided the setting for the climax of Hemingway's last novel, *Islands in the Stream.*

Jemal knew that U.S. and Cuba relations had softened, that yachts from the U.S., Canada, and Europe were now coming to towns like Cayo Guillermo. It was here that he hoped to find a yachtsman that he could bribe, persuade, or do whatever it took to slip him into the U.S. He'd read that yachts were often shorthanded, needed crew, or were looking to sell their boats. He'd also heard about the many places along the eastern coastline of the U.S. where there were no customs, immigration or Coast Guard stations at many of the seaside towns and villages.

Yes, this is where I'll find a way to get there, he mused as he wandered around the beach and town.

The Iberostar Hotel was full of tourists and the bar was crowded, mostly thirtyish men and women, many of whom were knocking down drinks to reinforce their confidence for the mating game. As a Muslim, Jemal, observed the no alcohol rule, as did over ninety percent of his brethren in Syria, however, he was familiar with this scene from observing the behavior of Christian friends during his college days and from watching American movies. At the end of the bar he saw an older man looking around and smiling at people in an attempt to engage someone in conversation. He was wearing a black Captain's hat, had a ring in one ear and tattoos on both arms. Jemal assumed he was a sailor and possibly just the kind of man he was looking for.

"Anyone sitting here?" Jemal asked as walked up to the tattooed patron at the bar and pointed to the stool next to him.

"Yes, you are, have a seat," the man laughingly said. "I'm Mike, Mike Ganz. What's your moniker?"

"My what? Oh, I'm Maten, Maten Tuma." Jemal said, guessing the man was using a word he'd never heard, and was annoyed at himself for showing it.

"You looked perplexed when I said 'moniker'—you're not American are you?" Mike said as he held out his hand, squeezing Jemal's hard enough to make him wince. "Sorry, I'm seventy-five, a sailor, working man so to speak and sometimes forget how strong I am." He looked pleased with himself as he said this, then added,

"Have a beer on me, been looking for someone to talk to—these young cats ain't very friendly . . . ignoring me all night, probably think I don't understand them, too old for them, but I've been there—could tell them a thing or two." He'd leaned over and whispered this in Jemal's ear as if he was telling him something in confidence.

Jemal just smiled, having already decided he didn't like this American. He thought he was an egotistical crude bastard, but reminded himself that he might be the answer to his problem.

"I'll have a Coke, thanks," Jemal replied. "I have a stomach problem, doctor told me to stop drinking alcohol," this was the standard answer he decided to give, not wanting to say he was a Muslim.

"Wow—I'd throw in the towel if I had to give up beer. Where you from? What-a-ya-do?"

"I'm from Lebanon, I'm an engineer. What do you do?" Jemal said. If this wasn't the kind of person he was looking for, then he wanted to get away from him as quickly as possible.

"Told you, I'm a sailor. Been traveling round the world on and off for last ten years. Got a forty-foot steel ketch. She's strong enough to run onto reefs without getting holed or get run down by a tanker when I'm sleeping. Happened to me once; was headed to Trinidad, it was the middle of the night and ran into a tanker while taking a nap. Bent the plates a little on the port side and broke my mast, but no leaks. Was able to hobble into port. If she wasn't steel, I wouldn't be here now—I'd be down in Davy Jones's Locker."

"I take it you're American—where you headed now?" Jemal asked.

"Beaufort, North Carolina. That's what I call home when I'm not on my boat, SALLY MAE. Named her after my wife before she left me—too much trouble to change the name."

"How long did you say you've been gone?"

"About two years . . . this time. Been island hopping all over the Caribbean and down the coast of South America. Started to run low on my loot and headed back six months ago. Always wanted to see Cuba so I got a tourist visa when things opened up. Arrived in Havana a month ago and been slowly working my way down the island."

"When you leaving?"

"Oh, I dunno. Maybe in couple a days. Been here a week, why do you ask?"

"No, particular reason, just curious how guys like you travel. Seems like a good lifestyle, Mr. Ganz." Jemal realized he'd better go slower, not wanting to scare the guy off.

"When did you get here? And call me Mike, I don't like that formal shit."

"Just arrived today, Mike. I'm only planning to stay a couple of days—got some personal stuff to take care of." Jemal hoped his response would stop further questions about why he was here.

"Wanna see my boat?"

"Sure, that would be great. When?"

"How about tomorrow? My boat is over at the marina in Cayo Guillermo—the taxi takes about twenty minutes from here. Where you staying?"

"I'm staying here. I could come about nine tomorrow if that's good for you?"

"Nine is good. How about buying me a beer?"

"Be happy to and then I have to go—it's been a long day for me and I need some rest."

After buying the sailor a beer, Jemal left and headed to the hotel's computer room for guests. He wanted to check out Ganz's homeport of Beaufort, North Carolina. He couldn't have been more pleased when he Googled it to see that it was half way up the east coast of the U.S. He thought it was perfect, *He said he's running out of money. That's good . . . just need to come up with a good reason for asking him to take me there.*

In the morning, he took a taxi to the marina where Ganz said his boat was docked. The marina was small; two concrete piers stuck out in the water with about a dozen fishing, tour boats and sailing yachts on each. Jemal was quick to notice he couldn't see any police or uniformed men patrolling the marina, nor did he see any buildings that might house customs or immigration officials. He was pleased to see that the clothes he purchased in Havana were appropriate, that he looked inconspicuous amongst a number of tourists that arrived before him who booked one of the tour boats.

It didn't take long to spot the old sailor sitting in the cockpit of his steel ketch with an American flag flying off the stern. The name SALLY MAE was printed on the stern with Beaufort, NC printed in smaller lettering below the name. Ganz's boat was berthed between two large white yachts. His was also painted white, but that's where the similarity ended. Numerous rust spots from the steel hull showed through the paint. Barnacles could be seen along the waterline and the sails rolled up on the boom looked old and dirty.

"C'mon aboard—she won't bite ya," Mike called seeing Jemal staring at his boat. He held out a hand to help him into the cockpit, but Jemal ignored it, not wanting to look like one of the tourists he saw being helped onto the tour boats. "Probably looks a little rough to you, but she's done some serious sailing for the last two years, unlike these play toys you see next to me.

"Yeah, this old gal, my SALLY MAE, is solid as a rock underneath all you were staring at—she'll still take me places I wouldn't dream of going on one of those pretty things," Mike said as he sized up his guest and then added, "You look to be in pretty good shape yourself. Ever do any sailing?"

"No, but I'd like to. Don't know anything about it. I was staring at your boat because of how different it looked from the others here and trying to figure out why. What you're telling me is that your boat is safer than these others and I get that." This was the closest Jemal could come to an apology—anything more would have felt demeaning to him.

"Hey, I like that. You don't sound like these tourists over there. Sorry, but I forgot your name and where you're from . . . had a few too many beers last night."

"Maten, Maten Tuma, I'm from Lebanon." Omar Jemal said emphasizing his new name as much for himself to remember as it was for the sailor.

"Okay, got it. You mind if I just call you Maten. I think I told you last night I'm Mike, and that's all I go by." Mike held out a fist and Jemal bumped his own into it to acknowledge that calling him "Maten" was okay. He'd remembered that Meg, his American girlfriend once told him it was a way of greeting or agreeing with someone.

"So where you headed next?" Jemal asked.

"Like I told you . . . home to Beaufort, North Carolina and I'm late for that. It's getting colder there now so I'll have to run down the inter-coastal to avoid the Nor-Easters on the outside." Mike realized his guest had no idea what he was talking, seeing the blank expression on Jemal's face, so he spent the next few minutes telling him about the inter-coastal waterway. The network of canals, inlets, bays and rivers that run the length of the Eastern Seaboard from Norfolk, Virginia, to the Florida Keys, put together so boaters could avoid the open ocean.

"When you leaving?" Jemal said.

"In a couple of days, but that's enough small talk for now—let me show you my boat."

"Good, I'd like to see what's downstairs."

"Sure, but we don't say downstairs, we call it 'below,'" Mike said as he led Jemal down to the main cabin.

Jemal was impressed to find he was standing in a small space, no more than ten feet wide by ten feet long that contained a combination stove and oven, a sink for washing dishes, a refrigeration box filled with perishable food, a retractable galley table that four people could sit at for meals, which could be converted into a bed for two people, a couch long enough to lie down on, a small desk-like table by an array of instruments that he subsequently learned was the navigation table, and an array of little cabinets stuffed with canned goods on both sides of the cabin with book shelves above them. There were also wire baskets of fruit hanging above the galley table.

"Is this typical—are most boats like this? It looks like you have everything you need to live on here for a long time."

"It's typical for an older boat this size, the newer ones are a little wider, that's called the "beam" of the boat, but this is all I need." He then showed Jemal the V-berth up forward where he slept and the little bathroom, called the "head." After the tour, Mike made a pot of coffee and they sat down at the small galley table to talk.

"I got a feeling, Maten, you didn't come to just see my boat—you look like a man that's got something on his mind. If it's about anything legal, I got all the proper papers. You mind telling me why you really came?"

Jemal studied his host for a moment or two, trying to decide if he should get right to the point . . . finally saying, "Do you ever take crew?"

Mike leaned back on his bench seat, taking a sip of his coffee as he took a hard look at Jemal before saying, "Depends, why do you ask?"

"I need to get to New York. I got a sister there I haven't seen in ten years and she's not going to live much longer." Jemal said this in what appeared to be a sorrowful tone, but on the inside, he was enjoying the real meaning of what he'd said.

"And you don't have a visa to get there!" Mike said with a smug look on his face.

"I have a Lebanese passport and a tourist visa for here in Cuba, but I can't wait to get a U.S. visa. I was told it might take a year and then there's no guarantee I'll get it, so I'm looking at other options. It's not like I'm one of those illegal Mexicans who sneak in and never leave. I don't plan to stay there long. I'll be wanting to get back to my own country."

"Listen Maten, do you have any idea of the risks someone would be taking to help you? Let's say, just hypothetically, that it was someone like me trying to get you out. If we got boarded leaving, my papers would show just me—no crew or others when I came here. I could lose my boat or worse. But the real problem is taking you into the States. If I got caught, not only would I lose my boat, but I'd go to jail and get a big fine. I'd have to have a damn good reason for risking all that, and how would anyone know you really are who you say you are. You say you're from Lebanon—you could be anybody."

Jemal hung on to every word Ganz spoke as he sat across the table talking about the risks and it sounded a bit disingenuous. He sensed by the tone and body language that he might be interested, *needs a good reason, that's what he said. He means money, but he's worried about who I am.*

"If I could find the right person, I'd pay them a thousand dollars to get me there. I understand worrying about who they'd be taking—particularly with so many people here trying to get out illegally." As Jemal said this he took out his counterfeit Lebanese passport and laid it on the table. "That's me," he said, flipping it open to show his photo and identification as Maten Tuma from Lebanon. "Like I told you, just want to see my sister."

"Thousand bucks is a little light for what you want."

"I heard it's less than twenty-four hours away–am I wrong."

"That's possible to the closest point, but no one does that. You need to find a safe place to enter, could easily take two or three days, and if you went half way down the coast, like say to Beaufort, well that's over a thousand miles—could take ten days or more depending on wind and weather."

"So how much would that cost?"

"You mean to Beaufort? Well if it was me, I'd want at least two thousand."

Jemal pretended to look surprised hearing how much the sailor wanted, he slapped his hands on the table as if it was time to leave, saying, "Well, I don't want to take up any more of your time—thanks for showing me your boat and I appreciate the information."

"Hey, what's your hurry, you haven't even finished your coffee or told me when you might want to do this. I think two-grand is reasonable, but I could probably do it for a thousand if you are ready to go now—like in the next day or two?"

"How would you answer having more than one person on your boat?"

"Did you look around here before coming on board? I'm sure you must have noticed there's no police, nobody watching the tourists who come and leave here. This isn't like Havana."

"How do you know there aren't secret police . . . men in plain clothes watching?"

"Because I been here a week, I ain't the sharpest tool in the box, but I got street smarts, I would've spotted them by now. Besides, they're not looking for one person, they're looking for a bunch slipping out at night, and the ones that do that would never try it from a port like this—they leave from little villages or uninhabited shoreline along the coast."

"What about the risks getting into the U.S. You said that worries you more. Tell me about that—what's the chance of getting caught?"

"Very low. I'll stay outside the U.S. twelve-mile limit until we decide where to get into the Intracoastal Waterway. All depends on the weather. It can be cold and stormy this time of year. If it's bad I'll go in at Fort Lauderdale, Florida where there's lots of boats going in and out—we can follow the traffic going in."

"Will the Americans inspect us coming in there?"

"No, no. They wouldn't be interested in my boat. They're looking for drug smugglers or boats packed with illegal immigrants. Boats coming in and out there are mostly pleasure boats, and mine is documented with the U.S. Coast Guard, flying the American flag on the stern. I could drop you off there and it would be a good place for you to get a bus to New York, or you could stay with me. I would continue on the Intracoastal all the way to Beaufort."

Jemal got up and walked around the boat again. "Where would I sleep?"

"See all those sail bags jammed in the back alongside the engine compartment? That's what they call a quarter berth, there's actually a mattress under all that stuff. I'll move it all someplace else and clean it up for you."

"Could we leave tonight?"

"Yes, but it would be safer in the morning—it might look suspicious leaving in the dark. And we need to get your baggage on board."

"All I got is a backpack."

"Good, do we have a deal?"

Jemal walked back to the table and sat down again. He didn't like this American, but that didn't matter since he hated all of them. It was just a question of believing whether or not he seemed capable of getting him safely into America. He looked hard into Ganz's eyes and saw the hungry look—how much he needed the money. Finally, he said, "One thousand dollars, I give it to you when you get me there."

Mike needed the money, but he didn't like Jemal any more than the man liked him, and he wasn't foolish enough to accept no money upfront. "Five hundred when you come tomorrow and the rest when we get there—that's the best I'll do." He held out his hand saying, "Okay?"

"Yes, it's okay," Jemal said as they shook hands to consummate the deal.

CHAPTER FIFTEEN

At noon the next day, the steel ketch, SALLY MAE, passed Cuba's twelve-mile zone heading towards Florida. "Well, Maten," Mike exclaimed. "We just passed the first test. If all goes well, we'll be in Fort Lauderdale in two or three days."

Jemal didn't respond. He was sitting in the cockpit staring at the horizon, feeling nauseous. Mike told him that fixing his eyes on something would help, along with the wristbands he gave him to wear. What didn't help was being laughed at for feeling seasick.

The day hadn't started well. Jamal arrived at nine as agreed, but after getting onboard and turning over the five hundred dollars down payment, Ganz insisted on him emptying his pockets and going through his backpack—telling him he had to be sure he wasn't bringing any guns or drugs on board.

When he refused, Mike said, "Then take your stinking money and get off my boat."

Jemal was surprised by the reaction, worried that he'd misjudged him—believing the American would do anything for money. He also felt superior to the man and would've had his head cut off for talking back like that if he they were in Raqqa. *Have to remember I'm not in Raqqa . . . why I'm here, this idiot is just a means to an end.*

They spoke little for the next two days with Jemal spending most of his time in his bunk or rushing topside to puke overboard. The weather had turned nasty; twenty-five knot winds turned the Gulf Stream into ten-foot, white-capped seas. But Mike was happy. The wind was behind them and they were making good time towards Fort Lauderdale.

"We should be in some time tonight, Maten, you should try to eat something—it helps to have something in your stomach to throw up." Jemal, having just thrown up again with his head hanging over the side, looked up to say something—that's when he saw the big boat with a red stripe on its side coming up behind them.

Mike, seeing the frightened look on Jemal's face, turned around to see a coast guard cutter closing fast behind him. He didn't know what they wanted, but he knew he had to think fast.

"Don't move Maten and let me do all the talking. I'll tell them you're a friend and we came from St. John's in the Caribbean—that we're returning to Beaufort and you're just seasick. If they ask how sick you are, just smile and tell them you'll be okay in a little while. We are still a little way outside the twelve-mile limit so I don't think they'll board us."

The big cutter pulled up within twenty yards of the ketch and a seaman on the bow told Mike to turn his marine radio on to channel 16. He went below and turned it on to hear, "SALLY MAE, this is the U.S. Coast Guard Cutter, Dolphin, out of Miami. We have been trying to contact you for twenty minutes. There's a big storm heading this way. Where are you headed and how's that man doing topside? Is he seasick or is it something more serious?"

"Headed to Beaufort, he's just seasick—do you think we can run around the storm?"

"No way. You'll run into it tonight if you do that. Looks like the winds will be over fifty knots, gusts higher, with seas building to twenty feet or more. Recommend you head to Fort Lauderdale, you should be able to make it before dark."

"Thanks, we'll do that—much appreciate you tipping us off about the storm."

"Keep your radio on this channel until you get in, you should be fine, but need to hear our updates on this storm." Mike thanked them again before signing off and came topside to hear the seaman, who was still standing on the bow of the cutter holding a bullhorn, asking if Jemal was okay or did he need help.

Jemal stood up, smiled, and yelled, "No, I don't need help. Thanks, I'll be okay."

The cutter stayed there for a few more minutes, the seaman standing on the bow was now conferring with an officer who had joined him. Mike pretended to play with his hand-held GPS to punch in a course for Fort Lauderdale, which he had previously entered. He then waved to the two men on the bow of the cutter but didn't breathe a sigh of relief until he saw their boat pull away to head back in the direction they came from.

"That was a close call, Maten."

"Yes, do you think they will report seeing us? Is it safe to go in to Fort Lauderdale?

"Yeah, I think we're okay, but I don't like them knowing there's two people on my boat and one who looked sick. If they reported that to the coast guard at Fort Lauderdale it's possible they might want to check if we got in safely. I think it's unlikely, but I just took a look at the charts and there's an inlet in Boca Raton about twenty miles past Fort Lauderdale. From here that's only a couple hours farther away and I think we can make it before dark. Better to play it safe and go there."

"What will we do when we get there?"

"We? There won't be any we—you're gonna get off my boat and I'm going on to Beaufort. My record for the last two years all over the Caribbean, including U.S. customs, shows only one person on my boat. Now they know there are two. If they check the record they might want to see why. You're too big a risk for me now and even bigger for you.

"How will I get to New York from there?"

"I think you can get an Amtrak train from there to New York. You got plenty of options, like the train or a bus. I will drop you off at a marina in Boca Raton and you can take a taxi from there to a train station or bus terminal."

"What if they ask for identification?"

Mike had turned off the autopilot and was standing at the helm steering the boat. Jemal had apparently been shocked out of his seasickness by the encounter with the coast guard. He was sitting in the cockpit looking up at the old man with a concerned look on his face. Mike laughed at his question.

"Look Maten, maybe that's a big problem where you come from, but you don't have to worry about that crap here. Nobody will ask for your identification at the train station or bus terminal. They will at an airport when you buy a ticket, but no place else."

"How about the police—do I have to worry about them?"

"Only if you do something stupid like get caught robbing someone or get into a fight or act strange. They don't stop people and ask for identification for no reason at all. If you see a policeman or police cars near you just act natural—like you would if you were home. Don't stare at them like you did something wrong or act like you don't belong here," Mike said and leaned forward to stare at Jemal to make the point.

"I'll need to get a hotel tonight—will they ask for identification?" Jemal said.

"Yeah, they will, but they won't care where you're from if you pay cash, particularly if you go to one of the cheaper ones. Just ask the taxi driver to take you to a motel that's somewhere between fifty and a hundred dollars. And don't forget to tip people like taxi drivers or servers at restaurants. Give them fifteen percent of the bill. They are more likely to remember you if you don't. Hey, didn't your sister tell you any of this?"

Jemal didn't like how the conversation had suddenly turned, knowing that the less anybody knew about him the better, so he got up to head below, dismissing any more talk with, "She doesn't know I'm coming. I think I need something to eat."

Hmm . . . good thing I'm getting rid of him, Mike reasoned as he watched him go below. He had been waiting for an opportunity to find out a little more about him. He didn't have a chance while the man was seasick, but reflecting on how disturbed he looked answering "the question about his sister" gave him reason to believe his passenger had lied about why he needed to get to America. The more he thought about it, the more worried he became. No more questions . . . the less I know about him the better for me if he gets caught.

The wind was driving the boat nicely, but he turned on the engine to get to maximum cruising speed—wanting to get to Boca Raton as soon as possible. The incident with the Coast Guard had unnerved him, knowing how much trouble he'd be in if he got caught transporting an illegal into the country.

Jemal was surprised to see how easy it was to enter the U.S. along the coast. They entered the Boca Inlet just before dark along with a half dozen other boats. They had to wait twenty minutes for the bridge to open leading to the Intracoastal Waterway, but he didn't see anyone checking on the boats coming or leaving the harbor.

An hour later, having safely entered the U.S., Jemal was on an Amtrak train headed to New York, and then Brooklyn where he planned to kill the real Maten Tuma and assume his identity.

On the train to New York, Jemal reflected on how it all began. The idea for the biological warfare attack germinated following a meeting he'd had with his friend, the engineer who worked for Assad's Chemical Warfare Department. The engineer knew Jemal had joined ISIS after his family was killed in a U.S. air strike, and they both blamed America for Assad remaining in power. He offered to help Jemal and two months later, six propane canisters filled with weapons grade anthrax mysteriously disappeared from one of Assad's storage facilities to support Jemal's jihad against America.

The next step in Jemal's plan fell into his lap when he met Maten Tuma's relatives on a visit to Beirut. The relatives owned a small shipping company in Beirut and were sympathetic to ISIS. The owners of the company were two brothers who were Tuma's uncles. They hated their nephew and for good reasons: Maten Tuma had immigrated to America many years before. He became a rich American and threatened to report them when he learned they were ISIS sympathizers. After Tuma's wife divorced him he became known as a selfish recluse, refusing to help anyone in the small Lebanese enclave in Brooklyn where he lived.

Jemal's interest in Tuma increased ten-fold when he learned Tuma owned a restaurant in Brooklyn and had no living relatives in America. From the uncles in Beirut, he learned that Tuma lived above the restaurant, had no friends and seldom left the building after his wife, twenty years his junior, left him for a younger man. He now spent most of his time playing on-line chess.

Using an alias, Ali Habaka, Jemal e-mailed Tuma with the intent of befriending him by becoming a frequent chess partner. It worked. Months later Jemal, came up with a plan to assume Tuma's identity.

Plastic surgery was the first step using photographs he'd hacked from Tuma's computer. Next, he convinced Tuma to have a face-to-face chess game at Tuma's Brooklyn apartment, saying he was coming to America on business. Once the meeting was set up Jemal knew he had a key part of his plan worked out for the biological warfare attack on America.

Jemal needed to move about freely in America—meaning he needed a new legitimate identity. He also knew that identity theft was hard to track. Jemal's scheme was the ultimate identity theft. He planned on killing Tuma after the plastic surgery, assuming his identity, and then setting up a base for his terrorist operation in Connecticut. Tuma was the ideal candidate. He had money that Jemal needed to set up a base of operations, he was a legitimate businessman, and a recluse, so few people cared about what he did or stayed in contact with him.

So far everything was going easy for Jemal. Entering the U.S. by sailboat had proved easier than he expected. After taking him ashore in Boca Raton, Mike assured him that getting to NY by train wouldn't be difficult, but he was still surprised to see that no one checked his identity.

He arrived in New York the next day, scouted out Maten Tuma's restaurant in Brooklyn, bought a cell phone and called to let Tuma know he was in NY for just one day and asked if he could come see him around 10 p.m. that evening. If it had been anyone else, Tuma would have said no, but he was so excited to see his online chess partner he immediately agreed. Jemal waited until the restaurant was closed before calling to say he was outside waiting to be let in. When Tuma unlocked the door, Jemal quickly stepped in while shutting the door behind him—faking shock in seeing how much they looked alike.

"My God! You could be my twin brother," Jemal exclaimed with a practiced friendly look crossing his face.

"Who are you?" Tuma said as he stepped away, obviously frightened by seeing what looked like a reflection in the mirror.

"I'm Ali . . . Ali Habaka," Jemal said using the e-mail alias he used for their chess games. "I'm as shocked as you are, but so happy we've finally met. I'm sorry I'm late. Just left a business meeting . . .

can't stay long, have to catch an early flight back but wanted to see you before I left. I bought a gift for you today—a chess set. I was hoping we would still have time for a short game."

The friendly smile, gift, and talk of playing chess worked. "I'm sorry, it's scary to see how much we look alike. I didn't mean to be rude."

"So . . . do you have time for a quick game?" Jemal said with the warmest smile he could muster.

"Yes, yes, come on up." Tuma said as he signaled Jemal to follow him up a flight of stairs to his apartment over the restaurant.

"All this just for you?" Jemal asked when they entered the richly appointed apartment. He knew the answer to his question, but wanted to be sure they were alone.

"Yes, I like living alone—you're my first visitor in a long time," Tuma said as he sat down at his kitchen table to look at the chess set Jemal had brought him. It was a fifty-dollar Chinese set, a wooden box manufactured to look hand carved. A tricky clasp held a sliding top on the box to hide the chess pieces inside.

"How do you open this?" Tuma asked as he struggled with the clasp.

"Here, let me help you," Jemal said, reaching over with his left hand to pretend to help, while simultaneously pulling a hypodermic needle out of his pocket with his right hand—which he drove deep into Tuma's neck. The needle was disguised as a pen and filled with cyanide. Tuma gasped . . . stood up . . . tried to speak . . . he starred at Jemal with a horrifying look on his face. He fell backwards onto the floor with his body shaking uncontrollably as the poison coursed through his body. He was dead within minutes, but Jemal checked his pulse to be sure.

Getting rid of the body would be more difficult since he had only a vague idea of how he was going to do it, hoping he could find a river or waterway for the purpose. Jemal knew from discussions he'd had with Tuma during chess games that Tuma had a car. He found a car parked in the back of the restaurant and stuffed the body into the trunk, along with two twenty-pound dumbbells and some rope he found in the apartment. He then went back inside to look for anything he might need to help with his taking on the identity of Maten Tuma. After finding Tuma's wallet and credit cards, he emptied out a desk that contained bank statements and financial data regarding Tuma's personal and business dealings. He put it all in a small suitcase along with some of Tuma's clothes. He would have to put on some weight, Tuma was a little heavier.

After placing the suitcase in the back seat of the car he went back to print out a note he typed on Tuma's laptop, telling the restaurant manager he would be gone for a while—that he'd get in touch with him in a couple of days. He then picked up the laptop to take with him and placed the note on the inside of the restaurant door. After taking one last look around and locking the apartment and restaurant, he got in the car heading towards Connecticut. Two hours later, on I-95 in New Haven, he exited the throughway seeing the broad expanse of Long Island Sound. Exploring the area, he found a side road to the water and a rotting bulkhead behind a factory. It was two in the morning; a dark cloudy night *perfect* he mused while looking around to make sure no one was in sight. Minutes later, he watched Tuma's remains which he'd thrown in the water with the weights tied to his body, slide below the surface.

The next steps in preparing for the attack took months to put in place. He first bought Finnegan's restaurant to establish him as a businessman in New Saybrook, Connecticut, followed by the purchase of a small island in the Connecticut River that guaranteed privacy for testing the anthrax. His final purchases were the used vans, cars, a small boat, and the old power plant, which he needed to house the men and stage the biological attack on Manhattan. The old marina with its rotting docks, was included in the purchase of the power plant. It was needed for boating back and forth to the island where they would be testing anthrax on dogs. After completing the purchases, he sent a coded message to Ghadi, waiting in Beirut, "It's time to come."

The prearranged plan was for Ghadi and the other two men, along with the canisters of anthrax, to come to America aboard the freighter owned by Tuma's uncles. They would be dropped off at night, twenty miles off the coast of Connecticut, where they would be transferred to a small boat. Jemal would arrange for the pickup after hearing from Ghadi when the freighter would arrive off the coast.

Tuma's uncles knew he was helping illegal aliens into the United States, but they didn't know, and didn't want to know, who these men were or what was in the canisters. Jemal had given them money to bribe the captain to turn off the automatic tracking equipment the Coast Guard used to track shipping coming into territorial waters.

Turning off the tracking system was of little concern. The international system used was voluntary, though most countries and all major shipping companies used it, but it wasn't unusual for some small independent companies not to comply or to have maintenance issues with their vessel's electronics. To make matters worse, most small boats and fishing vessels do not have the equipment. The Coast Guard and Homeland Security knew this was a major flaw in protecting the thousands of miles of the U.S. coastline.

After Jemal learned the men and canisters were on the way, he bribed Rusty, one of the fishermen who lived on his boat at the old marina, to do the pick up from the freighter. He instructed Ghadi to eliminate Rusty after he and his two men arrived safely at the power plant with the canisters.

The vans with Shore Line Limo painted on their sides were just decoys to mislead anyone from discovering what he and his men were up to. The power plant was needed to modify the cars he purchased for releasing the anthrax from the aerosol canisters. The cars were modified to hide the canisters under the rear seats and a feed from the canisters was installed to the roof racks to release the anthrax in aerosol form into the air.

Shortly after Jemal's men arrived in Connecticut, the cars had been modified and the testing completed on the dogs. He was ready to carry out a biological warfare attack on Manhattan. All Jemal needed now was the go-ahead from Baghdadi. He'd been reading the obituaries in the New York Times every day, looking for the coded message to carry out the attack. The men were getting anxious and couldn't understand what he was waiting for so he told Ghadi about having to wait for Baghdadi's coded message.

"I don't understand Omar, Baghdadi must know that the longer we wait the higher the risk of someone finding out what we are up to? And Raqqa was lost shortly after you left, have you had any word from him since?" Ghadi said, and it was obvious he was shaken by what Jemal told him.

"No, I'm also worried about the men, but don't tell them what I told you—they might do something crazy and we need them. But I'll tell you this, I'm thinking of going ahead with the attack if we don't hear soon. Baghdadi told me he had contingency plans, but Raqqa fell so quickly, I think he might be running from safe house to safe house. If he's in that kind of trouble, I'm not sure he can communicate with us. Let's give him another two weeks and if I don't get the message, then we'll go-ahead on our own.

“I think that would be wise, Omar, the men heard about Raqqa falling before we left to come here, they’re anxious for revenge and wondering what we are waiting for.” Ghadi said.

They didn’t have to wait two weeks. Events were about to happen that would play into Jemal’s hands beyond his wildest dreams. He was in his office at Finnegan’s when he heard on the TV, “U.S. special forces found and killed Baghdadi in Syria.”

Jemal decided not to wait any longer, he didn’t believe Baghdadi had a succession plan in place—that it was more likely ISIS was headless now. And if he was right about that, and the attack on New York was successful, if he managed to escape, then he also believed the world would see him as the new leader of ISIS. He called Ghadi, and told him the news about Baghdadi.”

Akram Ghadi was not a man who wore his emotions on his sleeve, but he was shocked, “So what do we do now, Omar? Does this mean it’s all off? I—"

“Calm down, Akram. You’re forgetting we agreed to go ahead in two weeks if we didn’t hear from him. Now that there’s no reason to wait, I’m going to New York to go over the route myself. I want to see where those detection devices you spotted are located and find the best place to meet after all of us have dispensed the anthrax.”

“Thank Allah—I’m sorry, Omar, I should have known this is what you would do. When will we leave for New York?” Ghadi asked?

“In a couple of days. I’m going to make some dry runs during rush hour tomorrow morning. When I get back, we might need a day or two to rehearse our attack and dispose of the equipment we used to test the anthrax,” Jemal said.

“You want me to tell the men now?”

“No, send them up to the house on the river. I want them well rested before we begin.”

Jemal was on his way to New York listening to Fox News praise the demise of Baghdadi when he received the call from his men that Jack Quinn was following them. This was small news compared to the previous, however, he saw it as an opportunity to solve a problem. He wasn't satisfied with just testing the anthrax on dogs, he wanted to test it on a human and now the meddlesome Jack Quinn had unknowingly offered himself as a perfect solution to that problem.

The world-wide news of Baghdadi being killed, along with the unexpected timely gift of having someone to test the anthrax on, had given Jemal reason to believe this was destiny—that he'd been chosen by Allah to lead his people to greatness again.

This was the setting on the eve of Jack's escape from the cellar—armed with a crow bar and box-cutter ready to fight for his life. Having no way of knowing what Max or Kate might be doing to find him—he knew he would have to rely solely on his own wits to escape from Tuma's clutches.

CHAPTER SIXTEEN

Kate hadn't heard from Jack for two days. Assuming he had good reasons for not calling, she left a message asking him to just let her know everything was okay and that she was anxious to hear his take on the killing of Baghdadi. She was getting close to finishing the portrait and it had been an exciting time for her, so she was anxious to tell him all about the Hansen's multimillion-dollar estate and how the portrait was coming along.

If she hadn't been so busy with the commission, she would have been more worried about him, but by the end of the third day, after repeated unanswered calls, she knew something was wrong. The problem was, who to call? They didn't have close neighbors. Their little house was situated on three acres, and in the two years since they bought it they never met the people that lived on either side of them.

She was thinking about who to call when her phone rang. It was Max asking if Jack was home.

"No, he's not, Max, and I'm out of town. Have you been trying to get in touch with him?"

"Yes, I left a couple of messages for him to call. Can you tell me where he is or how I can get in touch with him?"

"I wish I could. I haven't heard from him in three days. I'm in California working on a commission."

"I'm sorry to have bothered you. There's something I'd like to go over with him so if you hear from him please ask him to call, I'd—"

Kate interrupted him, saying, "You're not bothering me, Max. I'm actually glad you called. I'm worried about him . . . " Kate had started to cry and couldn't continue.

"Is everything alright between you two?"

"Yes, it's nothing like that. I just lost it for a minute. I'm so worried hearing you say he's not returning your calls— it confirms my fears. It's about that friend of his he told you about. Jack believes he was murdered, that it wasn't suicide. He's been chasing down every lead on his own. We usually call each other every day when we're apart."

"Do you know what his plans were before you left?"

"He was a little vague, said he had lots of things to keep him busy. I do remember he wanted to check out Tom's boat and was also going to try and find Meg, Tom's wife. I think he told you she disappeared shortly after the police said his death was a suicide. I can't remember anything more than that right now, but he told me what you knew about her and her ex-boyfriend. I told Jack he should go back to the local police and see if they would re-open the case, but he didn't want to do that."

"Knowing your husband the way I do, I wouldn't be too worried, Kate. He's very good at staying on the trail even when it's risky, but he's not stupid about it. He knows how to take care of himself."

Max wasn't so sure about the part of "taking care of himself." From what Kate told him and from what he'd learned in the last few days, he had reason to believe Jack was in way-over his head.

"I'm thinking I should fly back now," Kate replied, "but I have no idea of where to start looking for him, he'd also be upset if I did that."

"I wouldn't do that, Kate. If he's on to something, there's probably a good reason he's not calling. If it will make you feel any better, I'll try to find out what he's up to and I'll call you back." Max decided he'd better get up there now and see what's going on *much better to keep her out of this if he's in trouble.*

Max flew up that afternoon and after checking in at the Day's Inn, he looked over the notes he'd made from his discussions with Jack. Looks like Red's Bait & Tackle would be a good place to begin. Ten minutes later, he found the place using the GPS in his rental car.

"You must be Red," Max said when he walked in and found the big man sitting on a stool repairing a fishing net. Max had opened his wallet and flashed his badge, saying, "like to ask you a few questions."

"Looks like you're entitled," is all Red said as he glanced at the badge and took in the measure of the man holding it.

"I'm Max Cruz. Jack Quinn recommended I talk to you about Tom Walsh's suicide."

Red stood up and stretched out his full six foot-eight frame saying, "I can do that, but first I got a question for you. Where's Jack now? I've been trying to call him for the last three days."

"I don't know—that's the second reason why I'm here."

"Is he in trouble with the law?" Red asked.

"No, nothing like that, but he may be in trouble. When's the last time you saw him?"

"I told you, three days ago." Red went on to tell him about Jack stopping buy to tell him about the sale of the old docks and that he talked to the First Selectman about it. "That's the last time I saw him and I've been wanting to talk to him about Rusty, one of our fishermen who's missing."

"You think there's a connection?" Max asked.

"I'm no detective, but I agree with Jack about Tom not killing himself. What I wanted to tell Jack is that Rusty has a daughter he was supposed to see last week. She lives about an hour away and he never showed up. She came here looking for him. We weren't worried about Rusty at first, but now we got good reason to be."

"Why would this missing fisherman have anything to do with Tom Walsh turning up dead?"

"That's for you guys to figure out, but Rusty's boat was right next to Tom's, and Rusty disappeared the night they say Tom killed himself. Another thing that doesn't add up; Tom's wife disappeared a day or two ago, and from what you just said, it looks like Jack is missing. You gotta admit, that's a lot of people gone missing around here—kind of hard to chalk it all up to coincidence."

"I'd say it needs some looking into. By the way, where'd Jack keep his boat?"

"About a mile up the road from the old docks at Swanson's Marina."

Max spent the next half hour querying Red. By the end of the interview, it was clear they liked each other. "You going to see our police chief now and get Tom's case re-opened?" Red asked, as Max was about to leave.

"No, think I'll do a little snooping around first."

"If it was me, I'd start looking into what's going on down by the old docks." Red shouted as he watched the agent get into his car.

"That's where I'm headed now," Max shouted back as he drove away to scout out and photograph the fenced in old docks and power plant. He then drove up the road to the marina where Jack kept his boat. He introduced himself to the marina manager as a friend of Jack and asked if he'd seen him around lately.

"Yes, he was here three days ago, took his boat out and hasn't been back since."

"He didn't bring the boat back?"

"That's right. He was in a big hurry. He keeps it in a dry rack here. We ask our customers to call an hour ahead to give us time to get their boat in the water ready for them. He rushed in here without notice and asked me if we could get it in within ten minutes. He never did that before, he's a good customer, so we got it in the water for him as quick as we could—probably fifteen minutes or less. Then he jumped in and raced away."

"Was anyone with him?"

"No, but he kept looking at his watch—like he was real anxious to meet somebody."

"I take it he didn't say where he was going or why he was in a hurry?"

"No, but he wasn't really dressed for boating. He had street clothes and shoes on."

"Isn't it unusual for someone to go out like that and not return the same day?"

"They usually tell us if they're going to be gone for a few days, but not always. There are lots of homes up and down the river, so boaters could be visiting friends or heading out to Block Island."

"I get that, but from what you said about how he was dressed—"

"Look, I know what you're thinking, but it's none of our business what our customers do or where they go. I'll admit I'm surprised he hasn't returned yet, but this isn't the first time someone has done this." The marina manager then looked at Max suspiciously and said, "You said you're a friend. If he's been gone for three days, his wife must know where he is. Have you talked to her?"

Max realized his mistake, knew he'd have to be careful what he said next so he apologized, "I didn't mean to imply you should know these things. Jack and I are good friends and I'm up here on business so I thought I'd surprise him. He wasn't home so I called his wife. Turns out she's out of town, but she suggested he might be here working on his boat. That's why I'm here."

"Well, I hope you find him while you're still here."

"Thanks. I got some time to kill now, do you rent small power boats for a day?"

"No, and I don't know anyone around here that does, too much risk not knowing the river or knowing how competent people are that want to rent them. But if you just want to go sightseeing up the river, I can suggest somebody who might take you for a reasonable fee."

"Sure, got a number?"

"Red's Bait & Tackle shop, just down the road a piece. Want me to call him for you?

"No. Thanks for offering. I know where it is."

Max was about to leave when the marina manager said, "Speaking of the devil, that's Red's truck driving in now—he must have heard us talking about him."

"He keeps his boat here?" Max asked.

"Temporarily. He lost his berth down the road. It's the end of the season so I gave him a spot while he looks for a permanent home."

"Thanks for the information." Max then walked over to talk to Red for the second time that morning. "Just learned you're the man to talk to about for renting a boat for a day." Max said as Red climbed out of his truck.

Red laughed and pointing to the marina manager, he said "Did he tell you that?"

"No, not really, but he said something about 'no one around here rents boats, but you might take me out for a buck or two.'"

"Where do you want to go?"

"A place called Seldon Island that Jack told me about. Is it far?"

"No. Its about a half hour up the river from here. I'd take you, but I'm leaving for an overnighter this afternoon. I'll be back in a couple of days if you still want to go." Red said.

"Maybe, but I'd like to go today. Think any of your friends might be interested in making a couple of bucks?"

"They're all out fishing." Red said. Then seeing the disappointment on Max's face, he asked, "You got any boating experience?"

"Yeah, I was a Navy Seal. Training was pretty good with handling small boats, reading charts, and navigating to difficult places."

Red looked at Max like he was seeing him for the first time and said, "I think I can help you. I got an old twenty-foot wooden clam boat with a 150 Yamaha on it. If I give you a chart of the Connecticut River, do you think you can find Seldon Island?" He laughed as he said it. It wasn't really a question and quickly added, "Hop in my truck, Max, the boats on a creek by my place and I'll have you on the water in twenty minutes."

"I owe you big for this, Red, and I'm not talking about the daily rental of the boat. Hope I can return the favor some time," Max said as they drove back to Red's shop.

"You owe me nothing—including the boat rental. I got a steel rod in my hip from a fishing accident. Happened when I was young so I missed out serving for my country. I always admired guys like you, so I'm happy to do this."

The creek Red talked about was fifty yards from his Bait & Tackle shop and led to the river less than a quarter mile away. Red gave him a chart of the river and ten gallons of gas, which he said would be more than sufficient to get him to Seldon and back with the four-cycle Yamaha Red had on the boat.

"Any chance you have a shovel around here you can lend me?" Max asked.

"Yeah—got a couple. Mind telling me why you need one?"

"If I told you I want to dig up some dog bones, would you believe me?"

"No. I'd just think I don't have a need to know." Red said, laughing as he went to his shop and returning with a shovel and a small cooler in which he'd put a sandwich, chips, and a couple of beers.

"Here's your shovel. Also put some refreshments in here—you obviously haven't had time for lunch, and since you need a shovel, I'm thinking you'll be gone for a while. When you bring the boat back, remember to raise the engine and leave the key under the door of my shop if nobody's here."

"Thanks, Red," Max said as he started the engine and maneuvered the boat into the creek like he'd been doing it every day. It felt good to him. It had been awhile and he was looking forward to spending the day on the water. Then he remembered the only reason he was doing this was because he suspected Seldon Island was the last place Jack was headed before he disappeared.

Red said it should take about a half-hour to get to Seldon Island depending how fast he went between the five miles an hour no wake-zones. Max was surprised how beautiful the scenery was heading up the river. It was mile after mile of sparse settlements with scatterings of New England style homes, ranging from cottages to large estates nestled amidst the riverbanks. The chart Red gave him indicated it was about ten miles to Seldon Island. He counted only two marinas along the way set back in pretty little coves. One side of the river looked to be much less inhabited, long stretches of forests appeared like the foothills of a mountain range and he began thinking, *No wonder Jack loves it here . . . no industry in sight . . . it feels like a step back in time . . . a setting Mark Twain could have used for a Huckleberry Finn novel.*

The chart confirmed he was approaching Seldon Island. It didn't look like an island, but he could see the little inlet of Seldon Creek on his right. Close examination of the chart confirmed that the creek ran all the way along the backside of the island —separating the island from the mainland. Minutes before, Max passed a much smaller island in the middle of the river that he mistakenly took for Seldon Island until he saw the "Private—No Trespassing" signs along the shore.

Max was half way up the west side of Seldon Island when he found the little picnic area where Red said he should beach the boat. He took five minutes out to enjoy the lunch Red gave him. When finished, he eyed the one-gallon plastic sealer bag that was in the cooler for garbage and shoved it into his pocket, thinking it might be handy if he found anything worth taking back.

The path to the quarry began from the picnic area and was easy to find from Red's description of it. Max took the shovel and started walking, looking for any clue as to why Jack had returned here. Red had given him a brief history lesson on Seldon Island, including the stone quarry. All Max had to go on was Jack's story about Tom following two men who had snuck onto the island at night, a few nights before Tom died, and Jack following two men who he suspected were the same men, and finding the buried dog.

Finding the stone quarry wasn't hard—finding where the dog was buried took him most of the afternoon. When he did, Max knelt down to examine the remains, *Just like Jack said—they are the remains of a dog. Thought Jack was losing it telling me about finding buried dogs. Gotta admit, it looks like he was on to something . . . doesn't add up. Wonder why he thought it might connect to his friend's death?*

Max was about to shovel the dirt back when something about the carcass caught his eye—some of the bones looked like they had been eaten away, but not by an animal. He'd seen something like this before in a forensic lab, but couldn't remember what it was. His former life as a DEA agent had trained him to be exceptionally careful in handling potential evidence. He scooped up a skull with the shovel; careful not to touch it as he sealed it in the one-gallon plastic bag he'd taken from the cooler.

Before heading back, Max searched a wide swath around the quarry area looking for any sign that Jack had recently been there. Leaves on the ground from the early fall made it difficult. He was about to give up when he spotted the red tuft tailpiece of a dart lying under a fallen tree. He wouldn't have seen it if he hadn't bent over to tie a loose shoelace. He picked it up by the tailpiece and immediately recognized it as a tranquilizer dart.

The dart was .50-caliber four-inch long clear plastic cylinder, with graduated markings on it to show how much tranquilizing fluid was inserted in the cylinder. Max noted very little fluid remained, that the syringe plunger in the cylinder had been driven forward by a steel ball upon impact and the dart looked new, so he reasoned it had been recently used. *This is for big game—the kind used by park rangers. Why would anyone use something like this here . . . unless . . . yeah, unless it wasn't used on an animal?* A chill went through him realizing it might have been used on Jack.

Max took a closer look at the dart. The hypodermic needle didn't look damaged, it would have been if it had hit anything hard like as stone or tree. He was careful not to touch the cylinder, hoping there might be a fingerprint on it. He brought the dart and dog skull back to the boat, placing them in the cooler Red had loaned him. He planned to send both items to the DHS forensic lab in NYC, concluding that, it was hard to believe the items were not connected. The dog remains looked like they had a story to tell. A story that someone was desperate to keep secret—including using a tranquilizer dart on a human being.

Max felt guilty. He had warned Jack about not having back-up, knew he was a risk taker, and remembered telling him that he might be sticking his nose into something that was out of his depth—dealing with some scary people. *It sure looks like he was. I should have been with him, damn it!*

CHAPTER SEVENTEEN

Back at his hotel, Max made arrangements for the forensic lab to pick up the evidence he collected from Seldon Island. He'd just hung up with the lab when Kate called.

"I'm at the airport, Max—I'm coming back. I still haven't heard from Jack. He must be in trouble or he would have called by now. Have you found out anything? Do you have any idea what's happened or where he might be?"

"No, I haven't heard from him either. All I know is that he took his boat out and headed up river. The marina manager said he looked to be in a big hurry to get someplace, so he must be on to something and can't call. I've been in situations like that so I'm not too worried about him." Max thought it would worry her too much to tell her what he'd found on the island.

"Please don't try to protect me, Max. This isn't the first time Jack's been in serious trouble. He knows I'm strong enough to handle the truth, we know how each other thinks . . . that's why I was able to help him in the past."

Max realized he really didn't know Kate. She was making it loud and clear she wanted to be involved in searching for Jack and that she didn't want to be protected from the truth of anything negative. She was the kind of woman he admired. The kind he was hoping to find for himself, so he answered, "I hear you, Kate. I told you the truth when I said I haven't heard from him, that he was last seen heading up river on his boat. I left out a few things that I've been looking into and I'd rather discuss that when you get back here. If you need a ride from the airport, I'll pick you up and we can discuss everything then."

"Okay, I'd appreciate a ride. I have a lot of questions about what to do, so that sounds good," Kate said.

Max gave Kate his best smile when he picked her up at the airport, but she sensed from the look in his eyes that he hadn't heard from Jack.

After the usual pleasantries and thanking him for coming to pick her up, Kate said, "I take it no one has heard from him?"

"No. I haven't, but I've only been here for a day and it's not like I know this town and who he'd call besides you."

"I understand that, I was just wondering if you had learned anything that could give us a clue as to where he might be."

Max wasn't ready to tell her about his talk with the marina manager where Jack kept his boat, or borrowing a boat from Red and what he found on Seldon Island. He still didn't know her well enough to know how she'd react to all that. So all he said was, "I'm glad you flew back—I need to know much more about this town, your friends and everything you know about what Jack's been up to if I'm to be of any help."

"Of course. I thought you'd need my help. That's another reason I came back. Have you had dinner yet? If you haven't, I know a good restaurant where it's quiet and we can talk"

"Sounds good. I haven't eaten, and unless you flew back first class, I'll bet you're looking for some good food yourself."

Kate smiled, nodding in agreement. Neither said much after that other than small talk for the rest of the hour ride from the Hartford-Bradley Airport to New Saybrook Connecticut. She directed Max to Finnegan's Restaurant with two purposes in mind. First of all, they had booths, which were desirable for private conversation. Second, she wanted Max to see the place, believing as Jack did, that it made no sense as to why Tuma bought it.

After arriving at the restaurant, settling into a booth, and both ordering Bangers and Mash with cold mugs of Guinness, Max said, "How did Jack get a nice Italian girl to like beer and Irish food?"

"I like all food and I'm a firm believer in 'When in Rome, do as Romans do.' But we came here to talk, so how about we begin with, I'll tell you everything I know to help in your investigation and you tell me everything you've learned to date, no holding back on me Max. I need to know the bad news, as well as any good. I've been through what looked like hopeless situations with him before. We know how each other thinks, I have a pretty good idea how he'd react to almost any situation, so you need to be honest with me if we are going to help each other."

Max was impressed. He had listened carefully, thinking, *she reminds me of the DEA agent, Sally Kent, who briefed me on the disappearance of her CIA husband in Mexico.* That didn't turn out well for Sally Kent. Max hoped this time would be different, not wanting to be the bearer of bad news. He was impressed that Kate sensed he was holding back, *warning me if there's no quid-pro-quo, I'm on my own, and the truth is I need her help. I'll have to work with her on her terms.*

Reaching over in a friendly way to touch Kate's hand, Max said, "Okay, Kate. I wanted to wait a bit to tell you a few things, hoping to have better news, but you're right, you can best help me by being a partner in what I've learned."

"Good," Kate said, "I'm glad we understand each other. "How about we begin by you telling me anything you've learned as to why Jack hasn't called?"

"Okay, but a lot of what I'm about to tell you is speculation on my part so remember, it's too early to come to any concrete conclusions." Max went on to tell Kate how Jack hurriedly took out his boat and was last seen heading up river. He also told her about borrowing a boat from Red and finding the tranquilizer dart on Seldon Island.

"So, if he left in such a hurry you think he was trying to follow someone on the river or was late in meeting someone?" Kate asked.

"Both are possible, but I think he was heading to Seldon, having somehow learned what was going on there or maybe as you said, he was following people who were headed there," Max said.

"And the tranquilizer dart, you think they shot Jack with it?"

"It's a strong possibility if that's where he went. If I'm right, it means they didn't want to kill him and that gives us time to try to figure out where they took him." Max said.

"Jack thinks Tuma, who owns this place, is somehow mixed up in Tom's death," Kate said. "I think he's right, it's why I suggested we eat here so you could see for yourself what kind of place this is. Jack told me he asked you to investigate Tuma. Have you done that? If you have, does it make sense he would buy this place?"

"I don't know why he would buy an Irish pub, but he owned a Mediterranean restaurant in Brooklyn, so it's not like he's new to the business. So far nothing illegal has come up, but we found out some things that makes it worthwhile keeping an eye on him."

"Like what?

"He was born here; his parents came here in nineteen-seventy-two from Lebanon, they settled in Brooklyn, in the same Arab/Muslim community that Meg came from, but it's not clear if they knew each other back then. Tuma has relatives in Lebanon. His uncles own a small shipping firm in Beirut. Records show he visited there frequently after his two younger brothers disappeared in 2005. They were twins, attended NYU and were rumored to be radical supporters of Hamas in Palestine. They dropped out in the midst of their junior year and supposedly flew to Beirut for a one-month visit to relatives in Lebanon. They were never heard from again. There were unconfirmed reports that they were killed in Palestine, but our government still has them listed as suspects in Islamic terrorist organizations."

"Have you talked to Tuma," Kate asked.

"Tuma was questioned a year ago when he returned from a two week visit to Beirut. He said he'd gone again to search for his brothers, told us it was a futile search. There was no reason to doubt him at the time, however, our interest in Tuma was heightened when Jack called me, told me what he'd been looking into and asked for help. I intend to question Tuma myself, but need a little more info before I do."

"Have you talked to the New Saybrook police about Jack being missing?" Kate asked.

"No, but I'm planning to."

"When you do, ask for Sgt. Ray Carson. Jack plays racquetball with him and he's a good guy. The chief stopped the investigation into Tom's death when it was ruled a suicide, but so much has happened since. I think Ray can help you. I should tell you, I think there's a little tension between Ray Carson and his chief so you might have some trouble getting Ray on the case."

"Thanks, Kate. I'll head over there after I drop you off. Anything else you can tell me before we go."

"Yes, Jack told me about a guy he was going to see who was a friend of Tom. His name is Sid Johnson. He's a bartender at the Harp & Hound and Meg told us she and Tom had been there the night Tom died. I don't know if Jack got to see this guy, but Jack knew him and thought it was important to talk to him."

"Good information Kate. I'll check out this Sid Johnson fellow and let you know if anything comes of it."

Thanks for telling me everything, Max. As much as I don't want to believe it was Jack that got shot with the dart, I can't escape the feeling it probably was . . . that he got too close to something big and is in serious trouble."

Max didn't say anything for a moment, admiring the stoicism of this woman, finally saying, "If we're right, Kate you need to remember it was a tranquilizer dart—meaning they wanted him alive. I'll be using everything in my power to find him."

Twenty minutes later, Max dropped Kate off and was heading to Mystic. Kate had given him a couple of things to look into. He debated going to the New Saybrook Police Station first, but held off, thinking it was best to follow Jack's footsteps before he disappeared.

CHAPTER EIGHTEEN

Oh yeah, my kind of place, Max thought as he walked into the Harp & Hound. He went straight to the bar where a good-looking female bartender was pouring a beer from one of a dozen taps of craft beers. It was early afternoon, most of the lunch crowd had left, and the only people at the bar were a young couple at the end. "I'm looking for Sid Johnson, is he here?" Max said to the bartender, noting she was annoyed by his question.

"No, and I wouldn't be working here today if he was. Who are you? Why do you ask?" The bartender said as she looked Max over, obviously liking what she saw as she waited for the foam to settle in the Guinness she'd poured.

"I'm Max. I'm actually looking for a friend of mine. I was told Sid Johnson might be able to help me out."

"Do you know Sid?"

"No."

"You're lucky. He hasn't shown up here for three days, I'm standing in for him and I was supposed to be off."

"Do you know where he lives?"

"Just a minute—gotta serve this beer." Max watched as she walked away, knowing she was more interested in him than talking about Sid Johnson, but he'd have to play along to get some answers.

Two minutes later she was back, reaching her hand across the bar to him, "I'm Judy, Max. I'm not supposed to answer questions about the help, so tell me again who you are and why you want to know where Sid lives." Max saw a seductive smile cross her face as she said this.

Max decided to show his ID in order to warn her he needed answers, regardless of how he responded to her flirtations. "My friend has disappeared; he was in here talking to Sid Johnson three days ago. I'm following up on everyone he talked to that day—that's why I'm here." Max gave her his warmest smile to let her know he was also enjoying talking to her.

"This isn't the first time he's done this," Judy said. "He's an unreliable son-of-a-bitch and he's not answering his phone. I'll be happy to give you his address." She turned around, pulled a list out of the cash register and wrote something down on a note pad. "Here it is, phone number and address." She handed him the information with the same seductive smile she used before, only this time there was a bit of a question in her eyes.

"Thanks Judy. I'll see if he's there now. You got a phone number in case I have some more questions for you?" Max winked at her as he said that and got up to leave.

"Yes. My shift ends at nine tonight, hope you find him and can come back to relax a little." Max heard her giggle a little as he took the paper with her number and then walked out.

Ten minutes later Max was parked in front of Sid Johnson's apartment. It was a dilapidated two-story house across the street from a small boatyard in Mystic, CT that looked like a marine junkyard for old boats. A salty old man, who looked to be in his nineties, answered Max's knock on the front door.

"Hello, I'm looking for Sid Johnson. Does he live here?"

"Yes, upstairs, but I don't think he's in."

Max didn't flash his badge or say he was a special agent for Homeland Security. He just said, "Do you know when he might be back?"

"No idea, haven't seen him or his woman friend lately, I can usually hear them walking around up there, but if you want to leave a message for him, the stairway to his apartment is in the back. You can go there and leave a message on his door. Excuse me, but I can't talk anymore, I'm cooking," the old man said as he shut the door.

Max moved quickly around back and upstairs to Johnson's apartment while debating whether to leave a note. He was surprised, however, to see the door at the top slightly ajar. When no one answered his loud knock or asking, "Is anyone home," he pushed it wide open and stepped inside to the apartment's kitchen.

The first things he noticed was the refrigerator door wide open, two dinner plates with half eaten food on the table and a chair knocked over on the floor. He took his shoes off, remembering the old man saying he can hear when they're walking upstairs, and quietly looked around. In the bedroom he found dresser draws pulled out, an unmade bed, and an empty closet. Clear signs of panic. Something unexpected had caused them to rush from an unfinished meal and to pack; leaving in such a hurry that they didn't bother to close the refrigerator door or pick up the chair.

After leaving the apartment, Max called the New Saybrook Police to speak to Sergeant Ray Carson. He filled him in about Jack being missing and his suspicions that Jack had been shot with a tranquilizer dart on Seldon Island.

"I warned him about going alone on this. Did he tell you the investigation was closed, and that his friend's death was ruled a suicide, or that I couldn't help anymore?"

"Yes, he did Sergeant. He said you had no choice in the matter. He also told me how much he respected you, and that you would've helped if you could. But my office sees a possible connection here to a terrorist we are investigating and we'd like your cooperation. How about I come in this afternoon? I can be there in an hour."

"Can I put you on hold for a minute? I need to tell Chief Wilson what you just told me. I think he'll want to be in on this."

"Sure, and tell him I called you, that Jack Quinn gave me your number since you had been assigned to the case before it was ruled a suicide."

When Ray Carson got back on the phone he said, "The chief told me this changes everything, says he'll tell the front desk to send you in to him as soon as you get here." Max heard a resigned sigh in the Sergeant's voice as he continued, "I'm glad you guys are on the case. I think Jack's a good man, I hope he's okay."

An hour later, Max was talking to Chief Wilson who was explaining why he'd closed the investigation of what looked like a straightforward case of suicide.

The chief said, "Sergeant Carson had recently been promoted to detective and in retrospect, I probably should have put someone else on it. I think he bungled it a little, but I'll handle it personally now, and you can count on me using all the resources I have to help you."

"That's good chief, but I wouldn't be so harsh on your man. When Quinn first called me, I told him it sounded like a suicide to me and I was very reluctant to help out. I only did so because I saw a possible link to this terrorist I told you about. But I've been here for a week now and I think Quinn was on to something, my gut tells me he was right. I think his friend was probably murdered, and it's looking more and more like it's connected to some terrorist activity. I also want you to understand that it's imperative that you don't go public with this; keep it as a suicide and don't say anything about Quinn going missing. For these reasons I would like you to keep your Sergeant Carson on the case. I will want to interrogate him personally regarding everything he learned and discussed with Jack Quinn. Right now, we need to focus on finding Quinn—hopefully he's still alive."

"Okay, I don't think Carson knows more than I told you, but I'd like to be there when you talk to him."

"Sorry chief, but I don't work that way. I like to do it one on one. I find I get the most out of people when I do it that way. I'm sure you know that and would do the same if you were me." Max smiled as if to say it takes experienced professionals like themselves to know this. He saw a flash of disappointment on the chief's face, but also saw how quickly it was followed by the chief's smile in recognition of the perceived compliment.

"You're right about that, I'll call him in now. You can use my office."

"Thanks, but that's not necessary. How about showing me where he is and telling him what I want from him? I'd also like you to tell him he's back on the case so he knows, like you said, that you'll be using all the resources you have to help Homeland Security on this case." Max said this with all the authority he could muster as he got up, noting the police chief was bristling at his last remark, obviously not used to someone telling him what to do.

Five minutes later, after Chief Wilson said to Sergeant Carson what Max asked him to say, he reluctantly left the two men alone, Ray then said, "Thank you, I've been thinking about what you told me, about Jack being missing and afraid I wouldn't be allowed to help. I feel partially responsible for not doing a better job on what happened to his friend, Tom."

"Stop, Ray, no need to apologize. Jack told me you did all you could considering the circumstances. And no need to thank me for getting you back on the case. I wanted you on it because of everything Jack told me about you. You may not know it, but he respects and admires you, even though he thinks you have a little problem trusting people. So let's get back to business. If he was tranquilized, and I think he was, any idea who might have done it?"

"No sir, but I know that river very well. Unfortunately, most of it is out of my jurisdiction."

"Forget that 'sir' crap, call me Max. And from now on, Ray, I don't want to hear anything about what's out of your jurisdiction. We haven't got time to deal with that. We need to find Jack before it's too late. Let me deal with broken rules and your chief. I need you to focus one hundred percent on helping me."

"Okay, I can do that. How about I take you to Seldon Island, that's where I was going to go before the case was closed as a suicide," Ray said, thinking, *I like the way this agent handled the chief.*

"Good—I've been there, but don't know the island. Can't hurt to look again with someone who knows it. It's late now, so let's go tomorrow morning," Max said.

CHAPTER NINETEEN

Jack guessed it was after midnight when he escaped from the cellar of Tuma's island house. He stepped outside with the chain from the heavy mooring wrapped over his shoulder. He had no idea where he was, but his eyes had become used to the dark and he saw a little dock with a boat tied up to it. Recognizing the boat and the inlet across the way, he realized he was on the little island across from Hamburg Cove—a small bay on the Connecticut River. He also saw a dog kennel in the woods off to the right of the house.

Trying to quietly work his way toward the dock, he froze hearing the dogs starting to bark. When they didn't stop, he ran towards the dock in the hope of getting to the boat before anyone discovered he was gone. He got there shocked to find the boat was locked to the dock with a bicycle chain.

Jack knew there was no place to hide, that it was a small island. Seeing the lights coming on in the house and hearing the dogs continuing to bark, he knew it wouldn't be long before they discovered he'd escaped. Then he saw a canoe and knew he had to do something quickly to fool them. Stepping on to the muddy shore he made deep footprints for about twenty feet to where the canoe was stored on the bank. There was no paddle, but it didn't matter. He knew he wouldn't have gotten far before they caught him.

Sliding the canoe into the river he tipped it on its side to fill it with water. Knowing it would still float he gave it a hard push, relieved to see the strong current of the outgoing tide taking it away as he stood in the river. Retrieving the crow-bar he'd left on shore he worked his way neck deep in the water back to the dock. Struggling not to fall with the heavy chain around him he ducked under the floating end of the dock.

He was familiar with the construction; an eight-foot by eight-foot wooden platform, suspended over large blocks of flotation foam was chained to a small fixed dock that led to shore. Digging his free hand into the spaces between the blocks he searched for an open space large enough to breathe. Not finding any, and fighting not to panic with his lungs choking for air, he used the crowbar with his last bit of adrenalin fueled strength, to force an opening large enough to get his head in. A minute later he heard men coming, speaking in Arabic, as they swept the area with flashlights. He knew they'd discovered the canoe was missing; heard them shouting to each other as they raced onto the dock and sped away in the power-boat. He prayed they'd believe he'd drowned when they found the canoe filled with water.

It wasn't long before he heard the boat coming back and felt the thud of three men jumping onto the dock. He heard them arguing and stop when a fourth man began angrily shouting at them from the shore. Jack recognized the voice—it was Tuma. Through cracks in the decking he could see the flicker of their flashlights disappearing into the night. Assuming they were headed back to the house, Jack cautiously slipped out in time to see their flashlights focused on two barking dogs. They were shooting at them with what looked like a rifle but all he heard was a popping sound. That's when he realized they were being tranquilized, as he had been. He watched as they slowly stopped barking and silently fell over.

The house and dog pens looked to be around two hundred feet from shore. There was enough moonlight to watch what the men were up to, but they were far enough away to quickly slip back under the dock if they headed toward him. One man disappeared into the woods and came out a few minutes later carrying what looked like a propane tank for a barbeque grill. The others appeared to be closing up the house—hurriedly assembling suitcases and small boxes on the front porch.

Tuma was still shouting at them, and pointing to things for the men to pick up to take with them. Jack slipped back under the dock when the lights went out in the house and flashlights indicated the men had started walking down the path to the river carrying what they'd assembled on the porch.

Five minutes later, after hearing the boat racing away, Jack stumbled ashore heading up to the house hoping to find something useful to help him get off the island. The house was locked, but he easily broke in using the crowbar. He was mindful not to turn on any lights—knowing that someone in the boat might be staring back at the island, that it was possible to see a light come on from miles away as they raced away in the night. Using the light from matches he found on the kitchen table, he searched the house looking for a tool he could use to get rid of the heavy chain locked to his wrist.

Not finding anything in the house he remembered seeing what looked like a little tool shed outside. It was padlocked and again he was thankful for the crowbar he'd been carrying around. Inside he found shovels, axes, pickaxes, a wheelbarrow, all sorts of gardening tools and a large wood saw. Everything was old and rusty, obviously left by the previous owner who sold the house to Tuma. Using the wooden matches to search around he was about to leave when he saw the hacksaw hanging over the door.

An hour later, after laboriously sawing away with a dull hacksaw blade he was free of the chains. He stood up and looked around, startled to see he'd lost all track of time, morning sunrise was beginning to break through the light overcast clouds. Seeing a small fishing boat on the river slowly passing the island, he ran down to the shore yelling and waving, but he was too late. The fisherman was trolling for fish, his engine barely above idle, but he never heard him. The boat was now too far away for the fisherman to hear him, and the man was staring ahead, not looking at the island.

Jack also realized that if the fisherman did see him, how strange he must look with just a piece of burlap wrapped around him. Stranger still after all he'd been through, was the comic relief that forced him to laugh as he looked down at himself. *I look like Robinson Crusoe.* A quick search of the house revealed his caveman outfit would have to do—the men hadn't left any clothing, nor any of his own.

The morning light indicated it around six or seven o'clock. *The hell with it—doesn't matter how I look, if I hear another boat coming, I'll wave them down and tell them someone robbed me and stole my clothes . . . have to get off this island.*

CHAPTER TWENTY

Max and Ray Carson agreed to meet early at Red's place to begin their search for Jack.

Red was sitting in his shop working on an outboard engine when they arrived at seven the next morning. He looked up saying, "About time you got back on this, Ray. Rusty is still missing, so's Jack and Tom's wife. What were you guys waiting for—the Army to arrive?"

"Wasn't my call, Red."

"I'm sure it wasn't, just want you to know Rusty and Tom were good friends, I got a bad feeling about all this being connected—has the chief opened the case again on Tom?"

Max saw where this was headed, putting Ray on a spot regarding what to say about his boss. "I spoke to the chief, Red. He agreed to fully cooperate with my department and to put Sergeant Carson back on the case. I specifically asked for Ray and the chief agreed. So that's my short answer to your question. Rest assured, Ray and I will be looking into Tom's so-called 'suicide' and everything else that's happened since, including your friend Rusty being missing. Like you, I suspect it's all connected."

Red looked at Max, nodded, then turned to Ray and smiled. "You're lucky this guy showed up, but I think you know that."

"You want my boat again, Max?" Red said.

"Yes, would much appreciate that."

"Figured you might when you called last night. It's all gassed up and ready to go," Red said and walked them down to the boat.

They were on the water headed towards Seldon Island when Max said, "How well do you know Jack?"

"Not well at all, we play racquetball once a week."

Max was sitting at the helm with one hand on the wheel of the clam boat. An outboard engine hooked up to small center console for steering drove the twenty-foot old wooden boat. "That's interesting. I usually get to know a fair amount about a man when I play; like his sense of fairness, how he reacts to winning or losing, does he play only for himself or does he also enjoy the comradery of the game."

Ray didn't respond right away. He shifted uncomfortably in his seat as he saw Max looking at him—waiting for an answer. Finally, Ray said, "I take it Jack told you what happened to me in Afghanistan, seems like everyone knows that. My mistake for talking about it when I first got back."

"Yeah, Jack told me, but only because he understands that most people don't understand what guys like you went through over there. Jack's a good guy. Like I said before, he really likes you."

"It's easy to like someone, but trusting them is another matter. I learned the hard way you can't always trust the people you like. You should know that, Max. From what I heard, not many of you made it through the course. You guys are unique. You must have learned the only one you can really trust is yourself to make it through all that punishing training and all the crap you see afterwards."

"Boy have you got things mixed up about trust. Sure, getting through the training was about reaching within yourself to deal with all they threw at us, but it was also about learning how crucial it was to be a team player . . . each man trusting and doing whatever is necessary to help their buddies. Sounds like you're blaming yourself for what happened to your men. You forget you guys were put in situations where you had to trust people you didn't really know, people from another culture who you were told you have to work with. I could easily see how that could have happened to me. It's in our human nature to like people who appear to be friendly towards us."

"Yeah, I get all that, Max, but that's where I screwed up . . . as I said, confusing liking someone with trusting them."

"Oh, I get it, you're not human. You should have had the ability to read the mind of a man who pretended to be a friend. If that's true then all the spies in the world in every army going back to the Greeks and Romans, including those that worked for our own General George Washington, should have easily been discovered by the enemy. I guess those great leaders, most of whom had been deceived at one time or another by men they trusted, were all guilty like you when their men died because they mistrusted someone. C'mon Ray, I understand how bad you feel, but this is what happens in war—bad shit happens all the time. It wasn't your fault your men got killed!"

"Coming from someone like you that means a lot to me. I've had a hard time forgetting what happened."

That's understandable. I got plenty I'd like to forget, but it's not about forgetting. It's about what you learned from it. How to help the next guy, wherever you are that gets caught up in bad shit. If I had to guess, that's why you became a cop. You really want to help people and you now know more about the badasses in the world than most people so you're in a good position to become very good at it. But you won't if you don't learn to trust again—particularly friends and fellow workers who will hang tough for you if you give them a chance."

"Thanks for the sermon, Max." A broad grin broke across Ray's face as he added, "You sound more like a priest or psychologist than a Seal. Was all that included in your training? I'm not being cynical, I'm really thankful for all you said, you've given me a lot to think about."

"Good. All I said just came from my own experience. Saw too many guys come home filled with anger and hate from what they'd seen or what happened to them. It destroys them. Found out myself you got to get rid of the anger. You got to put it aside and move on or it will own you. I'm talking about the anger or hate, not the experience. Keep the experience in your trove of memories—it may help dealing with people like that in the future. I'm sure you know from our job descriptions that we're likely to deal with people like this again. These terrorists with their twisted way of thinking, killing innocent women and children —they are the scum of the earth and a threat to everything we believe in."

"So, you and Jack been friends a long time?"

"No, not that long. Met him a couple of years ago on an island off Honduras. It's a long story, but he helped me close down a drug operation when I was with the DEA. Bottom line is he's a bit of a maverick. Got himself in trouble a couple of times trying to help people, but when the shit hits the fan, he hangs tough. Problem is he's too quick to run off on his own, even gamble with his own life rather than wait for people like us to do the job. But he's got good instincts—was right about there being more to his friend's death than it being a suicide. Got to admire him for that and, yeah, I trust him—I'd want him on my team."

"That's interesting what you said about him being a maverick . . . like trying to take the law into his own hands. It's what I saw him do on this case when it got ruled a suicide. I warned him about that, about not having any backup." Having said that Ray looked pensive for a moment, and then added, "The truth is I never believed it was a suicide myself, so I feel guilty letting him run off on his own. And you're right about my problem with not trusting people—if I'd been more of a friend maybe he would have listened to me."

"Ohhh' I wouldn't go that far, Ray. I think it would be good if you two could be friends, but he is who he is, and I don't think you could have stopped him from the path he was on." Max was chuckling, "Guys like him don't change, but I like them. They make life interesting for people like you and me, so let's hope we can find him and get him out of whatever pickle he's in now."

"I'm all in, Max, but for the record we're now out of my jurisdiction. We're more than ten miles upstream and another police department has jurisdiction on this part of the river."

"Well, I don't have that problem. Homeland Security authorizes us to investigate anywhere in the country, so consider yourself covered by assisting me." Max considered the jurisdiction issue closed and was looking at a little island in the middle of the river they were approaching. "Who owns that? Looks like there's someone on the shore trying to get our attention," Max said.

"I don't know who owns it now, used to be owned by a merchant in town. Yeah, looks like he's franticly waving at us." Ray kept staring at the figure waving at them. Then, when they came within a hundred yards of the island, he turned around shouting, "Max, it's Jack!"

"I'll be damned . . . your right," Max said as he stood up to get a better look.

A few minutes later they were on the dock vigorously shaking hands with Jack who was exclaiming, "My God you have no idea how good it is to see you guys."

"Same here," Max said while taking a step back to take a good look at him. "Love your outfit. Where's your film crew—out to lunch?"

"Very funny, Max. It's all I got. But forget about how I look. We got to get back to New Saybrook as soon as possible. I'll explain it all on the way back." Jack had already jumped in the boat, yelling, "Come on, let's go!"

"So what's your best guess, any idea what they're up to?" Max said after hearing Jack's story.

"Not sure, but no question they were experimenting with the dogs and planning the same with me—don't want to sound paranoid but could be some kind of terrorist attack. That's why I thought we should get back quickly and see what's going on at the old power plant Tuma bought."

"Been thinking the same as I listened to you. If we're right, we can't wait until we get back. Ray, call your chief and tell him to get some men there ASAP. Tell him to not let anyone in or out of that plant until we get back. We should be there in half an hour. I have to make a call and see if our lab has any results on those dog bones."

Max was on hold, waiting to talk to his lab man when he heard Ray arguing with the chief. "What's the problem, Ray?"

"The chief wants to know if he should arrest anyone coming or leaving and should he break in past the gates if they're locked?"

Max grabbed the phone from Ray. "This is Max. The answers to your questions are 'yes'. Do whatever is necessary. Break in if you have to and arrest anyone there! You don't need a warrant—you'll be doing it on my authority. I don't want anyone destroying evidence. We'll be there shortly."

Max picked up his phone again to get the lab report. A minute later he hung up, but not before Jack and Ray heard him say, "Anthrax—are you sure? Okay send the data to my office and copy it to my boss with your report of why I asked for the tests."

"We heard that, Max, I take it the dog remains you gave to the lab showed evidence of anthrax?" Jack asked.

"Yes. The analysis didn't reveal any powder. They must have breathed it. Looks like it was airborne Anthrax—much more deadly than the powder."

"How is that dispensed?" Ray asked.

"In aerosol form. The lab report said what was found in the dogs was highly virile—the kind used in biological weapons."

"I think I better call the chief back and warn him of that before he goes into the building." Ray said,

"Yes, do that. Tell him to arrest anyone going in or out like we said before, but to hold off going in til we get there."

"Can I borrow your phone, Max—I need to call Kate to meet me at the power plant with some clothes?

I texted her, Jack. Told her we found you and that you're okay. Said for her to meet you at the Twin Bridges gas dock and to bring some clothes for you. I saw that we have to pass there on the way to the old power plant so it won't hold us up."

"Sounds like you're intentionally keeping me out of any action, Max."

"You got that right. First of all, you don't look that healthy after what you been through for the last couple of days, and secondly, how do you think it would look if Ray and I allowed a civilian in on a raid like this and you got hurt. No way, Jack. And besides, I seriously doubt we will find anyone there. You told us of how much of a hurry they were in to get off that island after you escaped. To me that indicates they're worried you might still be alive, so they're either now on the run, or they're on their way to commit the terrorist act they've planned."

Jack hadn't slept much in the past three days, had bags under his eyes and a three-day beard. He looked worse than he actually felt when Max dropped him off to a waiting Kate at the gas dock. Max waived to Kate and immediately sped away towards the old power plant.

"Do you feel as bad as you look?" Kate asked after they embraced and she handed him the clothes Max told her to bring.

"No, and after I tell you what I've been through for the last few days you'll understand why I feel wonderful right now." He said this as he put on the clothes she'd brought, and noted there were boaters on the dock watching with amusement.

"I think we better get to the car quickly before you get arrested for indecent exposure," Kate said as she put her arm through his and they walked off the dock. "Tell me, what's going on."

"There's evidence Tuma and his men are terrorists and right now Max is probably raiding the old power plant. If we hurry, we'll see if he catches anybody," Jack said as he grabbed her hand and ran towards the car.

The Twin Bridges Marina was less than a mile away from the old power plant. When they arrived, the police were blocking the road leading down to the plant and the old marina. Jack had just begun arguing with the police to let them through when the officer's phone rang.

It was Ray. He saw them drive up and told the officer to let them in.

"Max is inside with the chief. There's no one here and the vehicles were all gone when we got here. He wants to talk to you when he comes out about trying to identify their cars and trucks."

"Find anything inside?" Jack asked.

"No, looked like the place was cleaned out. They're still looking. Max figured you would drive over and asked me to come out. You know if anyone would have a photo of their vehicles? Max is running a check for any registered under Tuma's name."

"I doubt it, but I'll ask Red." Jack said as stepped away to make the call. He returned a minute later shaking his head. "No luck. Red said he doesn't have any and doubts the others do, but he'll ask when he sees them."

Max came back out with the chief and looked at Jack saying, “Hey, all the clothes did was make you look like you’ve been on a binge.” Turning to Kate he said, I think you should get him home. He needs some rest, there’s nothing more to do here and I’ll catch up with you guys later.”

“Good God, Max, you really believe I’ll get any rest worrying where Tuma and his men are now—probably on their way to carry out a major terrorist attack, and I haven’t even fully briefed you on what I learned,” Jack said.

“Okay, okay, calm down. But you won’t be much help now. I don’t think you have any idea how tired you are. And right now, I have more important things to do than talk to you. I have a lot of people waiting to hear from me; knowledgeable people who worry about this every day; about how to stop these guys. Meet me in an hour after you’ve gone home, cleaned up and Kate gets some food into you. I’ll be down at the New Saybrook Police Station. In the meantime, jot down everything you learned that you think may be pertinent.” Max didn’t wait for a response, he rushed off with the chief and Sgt. Ray Carson, yelling, “Come on, we got work to do.”

“He’s right, Jack, you look terrible. When’s the last time you ate or slept?” Kate asked.

“Don’t remember, but it doesn’t matter. I think every minute counts to capture those terrorists as soon as possible. Max knows that and just wants me out of the way while he reports what’s happened and gets Homeland Security going on this. A cold shower and some food might energize me a little, but I want to get back to him in an hour, so step on it so we can do that.”

“And when are you going to tell me all that happened to you. Why I haven’t heard from you for three days? I was going crazy worrying about you and flew home before I finished the commission I was working on—”

"I thought Max told you what happened."

"No, But it's obvious from all I've just seen and heard that you're all worried about a terrorist attack. All I got from him, however, was a text for me to meet you guys at the gas dock, that you were safe, to bring some clothes for you—nothing about why you'd been missing."

"I'm sorry, Kate, I guess I'm more tired than I realize," Jack said and walked her through what he'd learned from Meg; all he'd been through after being shot with a tranquilizer dart; and Max's lab report about anthrax being used to kill the dogs.

"They would have killed you if you hadn't escaped! I knew something was wrong when I hadn't heard from you. Do you think Max knows where they're headed or how they'll do it?"

"No, I don't see how he could, but I didn't have a chance to tell him all I learned from Meg. I think it may be important."

"Like what?"

"She said something about Tuma that bothered her. That there was something familiar about him, but she couldn't put her finger on it."

"Anything else?"

"Yeah, I got a good look at the guys on the Island, I think I could recognize them if Homeland Security has mug shots of them. I also heard Tuma say 'New York' several times as he was giving orders to his men. He wasn't speaking English so it really stuck out as he was speaking to them."

"You're right, Jack, you do need to get back to Max. We'll be home in five minutes. I'll make you a sandwich while you shower so you can get to the police station quickly."

CHAPTER TWENTY-ONE

Learning Jack had escaped was mind blowing to Jemal. He knew he'd been lucky so far. Still, he was unprepared, went into a rage thinking about all his planning and dreams of revenge ending in failure.

He calmed down enough to call Ghadi, who was back at the old power plant, telling him what happened. He then said, "Destroy any evidence of what we were planning, be ready to leave when we get there—we're doing it today—we can still get to New York in time to begin the attack with the morning rush hour."

Jemal knew it was naïve to believe that everything would go as intended, which is why he had meticulously thought out contingency plans for every step of the operation. Racing down the river toward the power plant, he began thinking about what he hadn't planned for. He'd been worried that Meg might run to the authorities after he failed in killing her and she went into hiding, but he didn't believe she ever recognized him. But Jemal knew that Jack's escape could be a game changer. If Jack was still alive and managed to report everything he knew, then it would only be a matter of hours before the police would be swarming all over town, raiding Jemal's old power plant and searching for him.

Jemal didn't believe in luck. He wasn't going to risk believing what his men kept saying, "He's dead—that he had drowned!" No, he knew he couldn't take that risk, instead, he accelerated the attack believing it was imperative to carry out his plan immediately.

It was five in the morning when Jemal and his men arrived back at the power plant, leaving him about a half hour to get everything together and head to New York. Ghadi was still in the process of getting rid of anything that could be traced to the attack they'd been planning. Jemal was worried they wouldn't arrive to the city in time for the commuter rush hour and was pressing them all to hurry up. He'd purchased the vans parked outside, marked, "Shoreline Limo Service" just in case something like this happened. He wanted the authorities to be looking for the vans, not the three cars he had modified to carry out the attack. He'd calculated traveling to New York from New Saybrook could take close to three hours during rush hour, leaving him little time to get rid of the evidence in the plant and to hide the vans.

Ghadi had thrown the welding equipment, copper plumbing and any material used to make the modifications into the water. He also painted over the company names on the vans, and when the men arrived with Jemal, he told them to drive them to an old dysfunctional marina abandoned years ago. The outdated marina was accessed by a dirt road less than a mile down the road. It was now a storage yard for discarded old boats, hidden from the main road by a large boatshed used during WWII. Tuma knew the boatshed and boat yard were up for sale and told Ghadi it was an ideal place to hide the vans amongst the old boats.

Jemal was counting on no one finding the vans and reporting it to the authorities before he arrived in New York, but if they did, they'd have no idea what vehicles he and his men were driving now.

Jemal was a cautious man, not one to prematurely celebrate anything, but hours later, driving the lead car on I-95 towards New York City, his pathologically warped mind realized with growing excitement that he was very close to carrying out the attack he been planning for two years. If it worked, hundreds of thousands, possibly a million Americans would die.

Arriving at the junction of the FDR drive and the 59th Street Bridge exit, woke him out of his reflections. "Yes, nothing will stop us now!" he exclaimed aloud as he headed crosstown towards midtown Manhattan.

***

Max knew everything was pointing to a biological warfare attack and worried it was already underway. He'd just called it in and had little to report in terms of where, who, or how it would be done. Sgt. Ray Carson had briefed him on what the town police knew about Tuma and his business dealings in New Saybrook, which was very little. He needed to go over it again.

"So, you're telling me there's no record of Tuma registering any vehicles in Connecticut?"

"None, Max. And no photographs that show the license plate numbers. I know that's bad news. Identity theft is as prevalent here as anywhere else in the country so—"

"Yeah, that's how he probably purchased the vans and any other vehicles he might have. Purchasing a car using someone else's identity is too easy. The FBI has been complaining about that for years. All we got is a good description of the trucks and the company names on them. I made some calls to get alerts out with the description we have, but it would have been good if we could have come up with some plates."

"I hate to give you more to worry about, but I thought I smelled paint when we broke into the plant."

"So did I, Ray. I don't think they had time to paint the entire trucks, but they could have easily painted over the company names and logos. I mentioned that in the alerts, hoping they did a sloppy job if that's what they did, and if so, it might be easy to spot."

"How lethal was the anthrax on the dogs?" Sgt. Carson asked.

"Very, it's what we call 'weapon grade.' As far as we know, it is only developed in very sophisticated laboratories. There are seventeen nations that have weapon grade anthrax, including Syria. We have to assume the terrorists are planning to use it in aerosol form using the vans, most likely in a large city like New York or Boston, but at this point we are guessing . . . we're also too late if Jack is right about when they left. They could be in New York right now."

"I wonder why they didn't they just kill Jack?" Ray asked.

"I asked myself the same question, probably because they were going to test it on him. I'm guessing they were experimenting with aerosol devices on the dogs in some sort of controlled space. Jack would have been the final experiment to get an idea of how to best dispense it."

"I'd like to think they weren't quite ready, that they still had to modify the trucks or whatever they were going to do to dispense the stuff. It's possible that Jack's escape has forced them into hiding some place around here," Ray said as he got up to look out the window of his office that he was in with Max. "Speaking of the devil, Jack just drove up. You want to talk to him alone?"

"No, but let's make this quick. We got FBI and DHS people coming here to join us—we need to make this place our center of operations for the next few days."

Max and Ray listened without comment to Jack saying he could identify the men that held him captive, and that Meg told him there was something familiar about Tuma, but what really got Max's attention was hearing him say, "I heard Tuma refer to New York twice while giving orders to his men."

“That’s great info, glad you came back, Jack. It will help narrow down the search for the trucks. I need to pass that on right away,” Max said as he got up and left the room.

“What do you make of Meg’s comment about Tuma?” Ray said after Max was gone.

“I don’t know, but I think she knows more than she told me regarding why she ran. It’s clear she’s very frightened. I know Max has people out looking for her, but I want to try myself. I think she trusts me, but didn’t believe the government would honor any deal if she turned herself in. If she learns I’m trying to track her down again I’m hoping she might try to contact me.”

“What makes you think she’d know you were looking for her?” Ray said.

“I know all her friends, the bars she frequented, the guy she was last seen with before she disappeared again. I can leave a trail that I want her to call me.”

“Sounds okay to me. Max is setting up a command post here and we will have very little time to talk to you after this so I think he will go along with you—”

“Go along with what?” Max said after overhearing Ray as he walked back in the room.

After hearing Jack repeat what he planned to do, Max said, “Good idea, but this time you’ve got to call me right away if she contacts you. I hope you’ve learned by now, you need back up. Trust us, the departments’ been through situations like this before—there’s a lot of lives at stake now and we can’t afford to have any ‘Lone Rangers’ out there making decisions on their own.”

“I told you, Max, it wasn’t intentional. I know you guys are pros. I also know my limitations; you can count on hearing from me if I learn anything significant.”

"Good. Sorry to cut this short, but I got to rush you out of here. I got to prepare for an army of FBI and DHS people arriving any moment." He got up and was about to leave when he turned around and said, "One more thing, Jack, let's all pray your escape screwed up their plans—that they're now hiding out some place—not already in New York."

***

Jemal's plan was a two-pronged attack. The cars were primary, carrying the bulk of the anthrax. He was optimistic it would work, but he knew of the many ways it could go wrong and didn't want to risk total failure. With Ghadi dispensing the anthrax in the subways there was a much higher chance of not failing completely. He believed thousands would still die, which would satisfy his revenge and hatred of America, and elevate him amongst ISIS followers to a status equal to Osama Bin Laden or greater.

The weaponized anthrax cannisters that Jemal planned for the cars were each filled under pressure in a liquid form, which would turn into a deadly atomized gas when the liquid was released into the air. The canisters looked to be identical to the propane canisters that people buy for their barbeque grills.

Installing the canisters in the cars was relatively simple. The canisters were hidden under the rear seats, which had been modified to accept three tanks in each car. The gas lines from the cannisters were run to tubular luggage racks on the cars, allowing the invisible gas to escape from the sides of the tubular racks at an optimum level. A switch under the driver's seat electronically controlled release of the gas.

The Ghadi phase of Jemal's attack created some risky technical challenges. Empty fourteen-ounce propane canisters, same as those used on camp stoves, had to be filled from one of the larger weaponized canisters. Ghadi knew how to do this but he had to devise a way to do it without venting the deadly anthrax into the air during the filling of the smaller canisters. For propane, no problem—a small amount of gas is released into the air. But venting anthrax in gas form into the air would contaminate the old power plant where they were working, risking anyone present getting infected.

Jemal had antibiotics that his friend in the Syrian storage facility gave him, which he was saving for taking on the day they carried out the attack, but he didn't want to use it for his men getting sick from filling the small canisters. Ghadi solved this problem by venting the gas into a solution of bleach and vinegar to kill the dangerous spores. He also used the bleach and vinegar to decontaminate the medical masks he was using to test anthrax on the dogs.

On the morning of Jack's escape, Jemal was in the lead car, a Ford Taurus. The other two cars, a Ford station wagon, and a Chevy Impala, were behind him with one man in each. All the cars were purchased from different used car lots using fake identity, and were modified inside the old power plant. After exiting the FDR Drive at 59th Street the terrorist's headed crosstown towards midtown Manhattan. When they arrived, Jemal called Ghadi.

"Are you there?" Jemal asked.

"Yes, the train got in about twenty minutes ago. You were right, Omar, except for this neck brace I look similar to many commuters here in their business suits, some with briefcases like mine." Ghadi had taken the train from New Saybrook to Penn Station in New York. The neck brace drew some attention to him, but it wasn't unusual to see people wearing one while recovering from a neck injury. None, however, would have suspected that the back of this harmless looking medical device was hooked to the brief case he was carrying, holding four canisters of anthrax capable of killing up to up four thousand people. He had tested the neck brace with propane to set the pressure at a level where it wouldn't make a hissing sound.

"Good, we've also arrived! Remember to meet us at the pick-up point in an hour from now. No problems so far. We can begin!" Jemal said, feeling confident nothing could stop them now.

CHAPTER TWENTY-TWO

Max was alone, sitting at Ray Carson's desk holding his head in his hands with a sinking feeling it was too late. He had just finished reading a report Homeland Security sent him on Maten Tuma. They'd discovered that the man who bought Finnegan's restaurant in New Saybrook wasn't the same Maten Tuma who owned the restaurant in Brooklyn. Search warrants obtained for both places discovered the real Maten Tuma's photographs, personal data and financial records hidden at Finnegan's restaurant, along with false identity passports of a man claiming to be Maten Tuma. Examination of the photographs by experts at DHS revealed they weren't the same man. What was most disturbing was the conclusion that someone had gone through major plastic surgery to look like the real Maten Tuma.

The report also concluded, based on interviews with employees at the Brooklyn restaurant and evidence found at the apartment above it, that the real Maten Tuma had been murdered. Adding all this to the anthrax report and what happened to Jack, convinced Max it all pointed to a major well-planned terrorist attack. He would've liked to believe Jack's escape screwed it up and forced the man masquerading as Tuma into hiding, but knew that was wishful thinking.

Three hours had gone by since they raided the empty old power plant—plenty of time to get to New York and begin the attack. The anthrax report indicating the dogs breathed in the poison, was proof the terrorists were planning an aerosol attack. If so, Max knew it would be odorless and invisible—no way for anyone to know it was happening! All he had to go on was the missing vans, but there were no reports from the helicopters, police or DHS agents who were looking for them. Who was this ringleader he wondered; a man who was willing to do anything, including extreme plastic surgery to take on the identity of another person. The fingerprints didn't match any on the wanted list of known terrorists, but DHS didn't have fingerprints for everyone on the list.

A knock on the office door interrupted his negative mood.

"C'mon in," he angrily said.

"Sorry to interrupt, I just learned something you should know about," Ray Carson said seeing the troubled look on Max's face as he walked in.

"Hey, this is your office, Ray—no problem! What have you got for me?"

"Just got a call from a carpenter who rents an old boatyard about a mile up from the power plant. Says he found three vans there this morning that have never been there before."

"Shit, let's go. I hope it doesn't mean we've been looking for the wrong vehicles all morning." Max said.

Ten minutes later they were standing by the vans and Max had scratched off the paint hiding the identity of the vans they'd been looking for. They also found a car with NY license plates.

"That looks like the car that Tuma, I mean the man we thought was Tuma, has been driving," Ray said.

"Yeah it sure does," Max said. He called in all he'd just learned to his superiors at DHS. Then turned to Ray saying, "Dammit, this character we only know as Tuma has been out-smarting us all the way. We need to get that photo of him out to every used car dealer in the state. It's critical we find out what vehicles they are driving now!"

"That'll take time and it'll probably be too late, Max."

"I know that, Ray. That's why I acted the way I did in your office—thinking it's already too late. But we still have to catch them and we don't know the extent of their plans—it may involve more than New York. We need to get everyone we can on this!"

On the way back to the police station Ray saw he had a message from the Old Lyme Police across the river. The message informed him that a surf-casting fisherman on the shoreline had discovered the body of Rusty, the missing fisherman who kept his boat at the town dock by the power plant. Ray read the message to Max.

"Why don't you check that out, Ray. I wouldn't be surprised to learn he was murdered . . . like Jack suspected, 'the dots are all starting to connect.'"

Later that evening Jack called Max. "What's happening? Can you tell me or am I now out of the loop altogether?" Jack said, knowing his question leaned heavily on their friendship.

"Off the record— we don't know if your escape forced them to hole up some place or if they went ahead with their attack. We found the vans in a boatyard about a mile from the power plant. They'd painted over the names and—"

"Oh no, Max . . . this means we're looking for the wrong vehicles."

"Right, that's what I was about to say and anything I tell you now could get me fired. The agency is in a quandary. If they gassed Manhattan with aerosol anthrax, we need to alert eight million people in the city and stock up all the hospitals with antibiotics. But we don't know for sure their target was Manhattan. There are video traffic cameras all over the city and so far, nothing has shown-up that looks unusual. They could've modified vehicles for it to come out exhaust pipes—in aerosol form it would be invisible and odorless. The lab technicians found tracks from car tires in addition to the tire tracks from the vans that we initially saw inside the power plant, so we're assuming they modified cars. They were smart—the vans were like decoys to mislead us."

"Anything else you can tell me?"

"Yeah. They found Rusty this morning. He floated up on the shore across the river. The autopsy report came in an hour ago. He was murdered."

"Anything on Meg?"

"No. I wouldn't be surprised though if she turns up dead. It's hard to believe we wouldn't have found her by now. We got divers in the river looking for any evidence they might have hurriedly thrown away and the FBI is combing through all the data they have on terrorists, trying to come up with a match on this mystery man who we now know isn't Maten Tuma.

"We need a miracle now, Jack. I'm hoping something went wrong if they did get to the city. Terrorists in Japan tried an anthrax attack some years back and it only killed a handful of people—it wasn't weapons grade. You need weapons grade material where the spores are small enough to get through the lungs, and the technology is complex to make it in aerosol form."

"What's the worst-case scenario?" Jack asked.

"If they're successful in doing everything right, then it depends on how much of this stuff they have. A hundred pounds of it could theoretically kill a million people. Aerosol anthrax is the deadliest. First symptoms are flu like, and usually the effects show up in a victim after two to five days. Antibiotics is the standard treatment for infected people, but the fatality rate could be as high as fifty percent if they are not treated immediately. So, here's the quandary we're in.

"Without knowing for sure where the attack will take place, how much of weapons grade material they might have, or when it might happen if it hasn't already, we would frighten the population to the extent that people in cities and major population areas would panic. People would be rushing to hospitals in New York, Boston, Philadelphia, Washington; people in cities all over the place clamoring for the antibiotics and there isn't enough to go around. We need more information before we go public on this."

"Thanks, Max. I appreciate you telling me."

"Much of what I just said is in the public domain if you looked for it. But not the part of how little we know, of who these terrorists are, the probability of the attack having already taken place, and our not saying anything now to avoid a panic.

"I didn't tell you because you're a friend, I told you because you have been in the thick of this since the beginning and you might remember something or get a phone call from someone like Meg. I said we're looking for a miracle or a tip, anything that will help us track these terrorists down."

Max hung up without telling Jack they had court orders to monitor cell phones of any suspect or person that might be anyway involved in the attack. From records they obtained at Finnegan's and calls made to merchants he dealt with, they obtained the cell phone number of the mystery man who had taken over Maten Tuma's identity. From the records they were able to narrow down all calls to legitimate people with cell phones except for four cases in which the phones were bought using identity theft. Unfortunately, they didn't get the court order until early this morning and all those phones indicated they'd been turned off.

Max knew how easy it was to purchase a phone using identity theft. The fact that all four suspect phones had been turned off indicated to him they had back up phones that they were using now. If that's what they'd done, then he needed their new cell phone numbers to track them down. If those phones were turned on, not only could he monitor their conversations, but he could also monitor their movement by the GPS that's built into the phones. Max also included Jack's phone in the list of those to be monitored; not because he didn't trust Jack, he did, but he did it for Jack's own safety and because he needed to know immediately if Meg called him.

CHAPTER TWENTY-THREE

After speaking to Max, Jack sat down with Kate to brainstorm what he could do to help, if anything.

"You have to be kidding. This has gone far beyond anything you can do. Max is as good as they get, and from what you just told me, the FBI and Homeland Security must be working on this twenty-four-hours a day. It wouldn't surprise me if it hasn't gone up to the president and that's what you and I should be talking about now!" Kate said.

"Last time we talked about that we agreed to give him some more time before judging him."

"No, Jack, that's what *you* decided to do . . . I told you I decided to become active in the Democratic Party and that's what I did!"

"When did you do that?"

"About a week before I went to California for the portrait commission. It was around the same time you became so totally focused on Tom's death that it became the only thing we could talk about. I'm not criticizing you for that. I understand why you did what you did, and all you have done. If it wasn't for your belief that Tom didn't kill himself, and you getting Max involved, no one would have known that it was anthrax that killed the dogs or that we had a terrorist operation based here in town.

"I'm proud of what you've done Jack, but as I've repeatedly said, you've been so focused on what you've been doing, you've had little time to discuss with me what's been going on.

"You didn't agree when I said Cain was running the country like a dictator, using executive orders and attacking our intelligence institutions in ways we've never seen before. Then it got worse when he surrounded himself with yes men and after successfully killing the terrorist, Baghdadi, he bypassed the constitutional role of Congress, by doing an arms deal with Saudi Arabia.

"What are you talking about? When did that happen?" Jack said with a puzzled look on his face.

"Oh—I'm sorry, I forgot there's no way you would have known about that," Kate said, and told him about Baghdadi being killed and all that happened while he was held captive.

"Are you telling me you disagree with killing Baghdadi," Jack asked.

"No, I think most Americans agreed with that."

"Okay, I get all that, Kate, but what's that got to do what we're facing now? I'm much more concerned that we are about to learn those terrorists who captured me are now carrying out an anthrax attack on New York City or Boston!"

Kate looked at Jack and shook her head. "I'm surprised you still don't get it. You are always talking about 'connecting the dots' when you're investigating something. Well, for me, the dots are connecting. Cain's disregard for our intelligence community, the constitution, the norms of being president, and his total control of his own party, who fear him and rationalize all his abuses of power—all points to a man who would do anything to achieve autocratic rule—"

Jack was frowning and about to interrupt, but she cut him off before he could get a word out.

"I know what you are going to say . . . 'that it can't happen here,' but I think you're wrong. It's frightening how he's divided the country, Jack. That's why I felt I had to do something, to get involved as a citizen in some way beyond just talking about it. So, I went to town hall, changed my registration from Independent back to Democrat, and before I left for California, I signed up for the next Women's Protest March scheduled for two weeks from now in Boston.

"I've been thinking about how you convinced me to switch to Independent and to give up my Democratic Party affiliations—of your argument about how divisive it's become between the two parties—about how the righteousness on each side has led to mean spirited pejorative labels attached to liberal or conservative causes and ways of thinking. I agreed with all that, and still do as evidenced by how we can't discuss politics any more with friends or family members, but it was a mistake for me to give up my Democratic Party affiliations and switch to Independent."

Kate saw Jack was about to interrupt again. "Hear me out, Jack, before you say anything." They were sitting on the porch of the little bungalow they'd bought, two years before, overlooking the marshes of South Cove on the Connecticut River. She had been staring out at the marsh as she was talking watching an osprey circle its nest. She turned to face Jack saying, "I changed back because there's no way to get really involved other than helping the opposition party. Like it or not, all the real power lies within our two-party system. I really believe we have a constitutional crisis looming on the horizon with this president. I see him as a demagogue who will destroy our democracy as we know it if left unchecked.

"I know you don't agree even though you say you don't like him. You keep saying we have a system of checks and balances that would never allow that to happen. But here's what really frightens me, if this terrorist attack kills thousands of people or more, then I believe this president, who you are so willing to give a chance to succeed, will use this attack to take on dictatorial powers that will even frighten you. It will be his way to calm the panic and to assure the nation he will prevent it from happening again. I also believe the Republican

Party now in power will do nothing to stop him. He will blame the Democrats and the liberal media for it happening; saying it wouldn't have happened if his immigration policies hadn't been held up and watered down. He will use wartime powers which might include rounding up anyone he and his cronies consider treasonable risk.

"And before you answer me, Jack, and say I sound a little paranoid, ask yourself this question: Have we ever had a president like this? Anyone who has behaved so un-presidential? Anyone that has cozied up to our enemies the way he has? Anyone who has attacked the press the way he has and calling them the enemy of the people? A president who is pathologically vengeful against anyone who crosses him? A president who's looking for ways to pardon himself and family for any crimes he might be accused of and a president that our Western Allies are afraid of because they think he's unstable? This is a seventy-year old man, who in his previous life as an oil baron left a clear trail of having no conscience when it comes to doing things that would further his power and wealth."

Kate stood up when she finished to stare out the window when she saw her man, whom she deeply loved, staring at her with a contemplative look on his face. The pregnant silence made her uncomfortable so she turned around returning his stare with, "That's all I have to say."

"That's all?" Jack said with a smile.

"That's not funny. I thought you'd have a better response than that."

"I apologize for the sarcasm, Kate, but that was quite a mouthful to absorb. I was still contemplating your point of view. You obviously have been thinking about this for a long time. As for me, you're right in implying I've been totally out of it lately, including trying to save my own ass the last few days, so forgive me if I'm not as quick as usual in responding to all you just said."

"What's your gut reaction to everything I just said?"

"I would dismiss some of it as a liberal's biased point of view. The part that worries me, however, where I agree with you, is in what you say regarding how he'll respond if this terrorist attack is successful."

"That's why I'm going to protest and why I changed my party affiliation—I wouldn't be able to look myself in the mirror if I didn't do something," Kate said.

"I get that, Kate. You know I respect people who walk the talk, but I'm not convinced yet he's as bad as you think he is. Have to say though, you've given me a lot of food for thought.

"In the meantime, I'm not finished with what I started. I'm not planning on any heroics nor am I naïve enough to believe I have anything to add along the lines of what Max or the FBI are doing—they're one hundred percent focused now on finding those guys. Max thinks Meg is probably dead, that they killed her, so he's not wasting much manpower on following that lead. I don't agree and I still think she knows more than she told me, possibly crucial to identifying the terrorists so I'm going to continue looking for her and I don't see any risk in doing it.

"My escaping changed the game. If they haven't killed her by now, then she's become unimportant—they'll forget about her and accelerate their plan for the attack. Look at it this way, Kate. This is my way of trying to do something. If I don't, I'll have trouble looking in the mirror, same as you say."

CHAPTER TWENTY-FOUR

Akram Ghadi checked his notes: Take the 1, 2 or 3 train from Penn Station uptown one stop to Times Square, then take the Shuttle S train to Grand Central. Total transit time there and back, including wait time for the trains, should be around thirty minutes allowing for two round trips before his planned rendezvous with Jemal, one and a half hours later outside Penn Station.

His briefcase contained four, fourteen-ounce canisters filled with anthrax, timed to last for the two round trips. All four were hooked up via the single gas line running up his sleeve to the back of the neck brace he was wearing. Each cylinder had to be turned off when empty before turning the next one on. To do this he had to open the briefcase in a private setting like a bathroom stall. Ghadi had made a dry run on this route days before, locating the men's subway bathrooms, and determined it would take an extra five minutes at each station, which he had factored in for his rendezvous with Jemal.

Ghadi, who had been trained as an engineer, had designed and tested the briefcase system using an inert gas. He'd also attached a miniature shutoff valve to the inside of his suit jacket, allowing him to easily turn the gas on and off by reaching into his jacket with his left hand. Jemal had informed him about biological warfare tests Homeland Security had conducted in 2016 on the New York subway system. Jemal read they'd used inert gas to evaluate monitoring systems, but had no idea if any had been installed. Ghadi's engineering background gave him some idea what they might look like. On his dry run he thought he saw devices inside and around

Penn Station that looked suspiciously like monitoring devices. He didn't see anything like that inside the trains, but knew that didn't mean anything—they could be hidden behind the ceiling grates where air is funneled through the cars by the action of passing through the tunnels.

Jemal and Ghadi were counting on the wheels of bureaucracy being too slow to develop and install monitoring systems for the trains prior to their planned attack. They limited Ghadi's briefcase weapon to being used only inside the trains when the doors closed, hoping it would reduce the chances of the anthrax being picked up by any station monitors installed.

Monitors were also a concern for Jemal's attack with the three vehicles. Ghadi had noted the monitors the day he did his dry run on the subways. He discovered portable units chained to poles along the sidewalks, along with others attached to buildings. They marked their maps, identifying where the monitors were on the routes, and planned to turn the gas off if they were within one block of the monitors to decrease the risk of detection.

The monitors were a concern since neither Jemal nor Ghadi had any way of knowing how sensitive they were, or how the monitoring system alerted authorities. If it was an automatic system sending out an alarm as soon as it detected a biological weapon, like anthrax, that would severely limit the casualties. The city would be on full alert searching for the terrorists, and it would give them time to prepare and stock the hospitals with antibiotics for anyone with the known symptoms. Many might still die, but antibiotics given early to known victims would significantly increase the chances of survival.

Jemal arrived at the corner of 60th Street and Broadway for the beginning of his deadly biological warfare attack along Broadway, all the way down to Wall Street. He had watched as the other two cars behind him turned off to begin their attack. One turned onto Park Ave and the other 5th Ave as they headed downtown toward Washington Square.

"Drive as close as you can to the sidewalks and don't forget to turn off the gas two blocks either side of the monitors marked on your maps—and start taking your antibiotics now!" Jemal said in his last call to both drivers as they turned onto their respective routes.

The attacks began half way into morning rush hour. The invisible, odorless, atomized particles of anthrax began spraying out of the cars roof racks on innocent victims walking along the sidewalks. Jemal noted there was very little wind, which reduced the risk of the anthrax reaching the monitors.

After spotting the monitors chained to poles, he called the other two cars again.

"Pay close attention to your maps. I suspect those monitors we're seeing can automatically send out an alarm. Don't panic if police approach you, shut off the spray and act calm—they won't find anything unless they pull out the back seats." Jemal had read about and seen photos of a pathogen system that could detect anthrax within three minutes. The devices looked very much like the ones he was seeing on Broadway. He hoped the precautions he'd taken to avoid them would be effective, but if they didn't and they somehow stopped his three cars before they completed the attack, he still had Ghadi, who was in the subways carrying out the briefcase attack. Thousands would still die and panic would spread across America.

Jemal estimated he had time to make a run, up and down both sides of the street of Broadway, which had two-way traffic and still have time to pick up Ghadi at Penn Station. Park Ave had two-way traffic, from 59th Street down to Washington Square for a run on both sides. The Fifth Ave route was one-way down to Washington

Square so the driver used 6th Ave to continue his attack north back to 59th Street. Since the Park Ave and 5th Ave routes were shorter than Jemal's, he told them to repeat their routes if the tanks weren't empty. The regulators on the tanks were set to last for a little over one hour.

The original plan was to return to New Saybrook after the attack. Jemal planned on using the small power boat he kept there to take them thirty miles off the coast where the tanker he used before would be waiting.

That plan was shattered when Jack escaped. Jemal didn't dare risk going back to the plant believing Jack Quinn might still be alive.

"What about our escape plan?" Ghadi had asked.

"We don't have one now—you know that. It would take weeks for the tanker to get here. I'll come up with something and let you know as soon as I do." That conversation had taken place in the morning, before Ghadi had left to take the train to Penn Station. Now as Jemal finished his southbound attack and was turning around in the Wall Street Area to head back uptown, he wondered how Ghadi was doing. The last time he heard from him he was about to enter a subway car and start his attack. It was more than half an hour ago so he called to see if it was going as planned.

"I'm back at Penn Station, Omar. The first run went okay, the subways were jammed with people— must have been over two hundred in each car. I muscled my way from end to end through each car before I got to Grand Central so I think I sprayed it over most of them. And it's not like it's going to go away, at every stop more people get on and off so the people coming on again will get exposed.

"The problem is going through the tunnels—it pushes the air in and out of the cars and possibly onto the platforms so we have to hope it doesn't trigger the monitors at the stations. Right now, I'm running around in Penn Station looking for a bathroom to change canisters. The one I planned on using is closed for maintenance so I may be ten or fifteen minutes behind schedule. By the way have you worked out our escape plan?" Ghadi asked.

"Yes, the first part is the same, the other cars come over to Broadway after they're finished to follow me down to Penn Station. That's probably going to take longer than we figured, I'm trying to coordinate that in this traffic, so you running behind is okay. Keep an eye out for our cars, jump into the first one that gets there if it's not mine.

Once the cars are together again, we'll have to get rid of them. Kennedy airport would be a good place for that," Jemal said.

"If we do that how will we get out of the airport?" Ghadi asked.

"We'll rent a car at the airport using your fake ID and driver's license. If Quinn is still alive, he can identify me, but you were at the power plant when he escaped so he has no idea you even exist. With our cars in long-term parking, they'll probably go undiscovered for a long time. It's also a good place to rent a car, there's such a high turn-over there, I doubt they'll scrutinize your fake driver's license," Jemal said.

"Where will we go after leaving Kennedy?" Ghadi asked.

"We'll be heading to see the same man that got me into the country, I'll tell you more when we get to the airport," Jemal said.

"Have you told Hassan and Abood this?"

"No, not yet. This day isn't over. I'm worried about those monitors and for them to finish the attack. All I want them to do now is follow orders!"

CHAPTER TWENTY-FIVE

Max was no longer in charge of finding the terrorists—that had moved up the chain of command at DHS. But he was still in charge of the temporary field office set up in New Saybrook, and he was now under intense pressure to find out more information regarding what the home office was unofficially referring to as the "Tuma Plot" lacking the real name of the man they were searching for and the men who were with him. Max was concerned the agency was holding back on calling it a major terrorist attack. The discovery of weapons grade anthrax was disturbing, but they said there was nothing so far to tie it to ISIS or any other foreign terrorist group.

The dilemma at DHS was how to react to Max saying this should be a "Red Alert." Max had called Chuck Morgan, his supervisor at DHS, when he discovered the old power plant was deserted and the vans gone.

"Chuck, everything we've learned and seen here points to an aerosol anthrax attack against New York. Let's look at what we know: We now know Tuma isn't who he says he is. Our suspect terrorist killed a man named Tuma to take on his identity and gain access to his wealth and reputation and he set up a phony operation here in New Saybrook by buying a restaurant, an old power plant, and a small island to cover up testing a planned aerosol anthrax attack. We also have reason to believe he killed at least two people who got in the way of his plans, and that he captured and was planning to murder Jack Quinn, the author and friend of mine who he was planning to kill if he hadn't escaped. We also know from Quinn, that Tuma kept using the words New York in addressing his men in their rush to get out of New Saybrook."

"I hear you, Max, but I think you know the country has gone to Red Alert only once, and that was in response to the Brit's telling us about a plot to blow up aircraft coming in from their country. You also know we've gone to level Orange six or seven times on a national basis, and New York has been on a constant high alert ever since 9/11. I discussed it with the director, but think about the evidence you're offering. A good deal of what you say is based on what Quinn told you—"

"Sorry to interrupt you, Chuck, but most of that is backed up by our lab tests on the dogs, which confirmed its weapon grade anthrax. Then there's the dart I found used on Quinn, the empty power plant when I raided it, the dead body of Quinn's friend, who's so called suicide turned out to be murder along with the murder of a fisherman, and solid evidence that our suspect went to great lengths to take on the identity of another man to hide his anthrax facilities in New Saybrook. Come on, Chuck you know this doesn't sound anything like a home-grown operation—this is too sophisticated a plot for that."

"Max, I would agree with you, but you're forgetting something. We have uncovered many plots since 9/11, most of which turned out to be homegrown. The agency has been criticized in the past for the accuracy of the alert system. There have been studies that show raising the threat condition has economic, physical, and psychological effects on the nation.

"The Director has a lot more to worry about than you do in making that decision. It didn't help that you first had us looking for panel trucks or vans that were subsequently found nearby. Not your fault, but now we have no idea what kind of vehicle to look for, assuming the terrorists will use vehicles, and no real evidence that the intended target is New York—just the hearsay of your friend

Quinn saying he heard those words used amongst a language he had no knowledge of. I have to tell you Max, if I was the director, I'd want a lot more evidence than you've given us before I'd declare a Red Alert in New York—it could cause panic."

"I get all that, Chuck, but how are we going to feel if we learn, four or five days from now, tens of thousands of victims are dying from anthrax? There must be something we can do to prepare for that!"

"We're working on it. New York is better prepared for that than any place else, however I'd be lying to you if I told you we weren't worried. If the attack did take place today, then we all know survival depends on getting antibiotics to victims as soon as possible. But right now, we're depending on you to get us some hard evidence so we can issue the alert with confidence that, New York has been—or is about to be attacked."

Max knew he was right, the agency couldn't risk the panic that might ensue amongst eight million people, learning they might be victims of the deadliest form of anthrax. No, they couldn't risk doing that without solid evidence. Evidence they were hoping he would provide, which he was desperately searching for now. He had agents and lab technicians inspecting every inch of the old power plant, restaurant and island Tuma had purchased. He had agents looking at every used car dealer within a hundred-fifty-mile radius for any vehicles Tuma might have purchased. He had the Connecticut Department of Motor Vehicles checking for all vehicles registered under that name. Scuba divers found copper plumbing and welding equipment that looked like it had been recently thrown into the river in front of the power plant. He'd also found paint sprayers and cans of paint, but nothing so far along the lines of what he really needed.

He needed to know who Tuma really was, the organization he belonged to, how many men they were looking for, how much weapons grade anthrax they had, and how they planned to use it on victims. He also needed more evidence as to where and when the attack did or will take place. At the moment, he had little hope that he would get any, let alone in time to save New York.

He was convinced, as Jack was, that the terrorists were headed for New York and it was probably too late to stop them. Max knew about the monitors New York had and that they weren't fully deployed or fully operational. All he could hope for now was for the system to be far enough along to detect an attack, or a miracle to give him the evidence the agency was looking for.

Ray Carson came into his office as he was pondering his conversation with his supervisor. "Hope you got something good, Ray. I need a miracle right now."

"Nothing like that, Max, but the stuff the divers recovered from the river looks like they might have been testing the anthrax using five-gallon propane cylinders. There were regulators on the canisters set for very different values than what are normally used for barbeque grills. One of the five-gallon cylinders had a little liquid anthrax in it. They also found one 14-ounce canister with slight traces of anthrax in it. So maybe they were planning to use five-gallon propane canisters each capable of holding fifteen pounds of liquid anthrax, as well some smaller fourteen ounce canisters for their attack."

"That's great news, Ray, I don't know if it's enough to convince my people to go to a Red Alert, but it sure helps." Max filled Ray in on the conversation he'd just had with his supervisor.

"So what do they need? A video recording of the planned attack before people start dying?" Ray said in a sarcastic tone.

"Yeah, something like that, but they have a point. If they send out a Red Alert and we're wrong, if it isn't New York, if the terrorists are still at large and we don't know much more than we do now—the panic could be devastating."

CHAPTER TWENTY-SIX

The following morning, a day after Jack was rescued and told Kate he believed Meg was still alive and that he would continue to look for her, he got a call from Red.

"I'm on my boat, Jack, come on down—got something to tell you."

Ten minutes later Jack was there listening to Red tell him about a phone call he got from Rusty's ex-wife. Rusty had called her trying to make amends. She said Rusty told her that a man named Tuma hired him for ten thousand dollars to pick up three men off a freighter twenty miles off shore and that Rusty sent her the money. She said that the men he picked from the freighter spoke in a foreign language. That all three men were carrying duffel bags like the kind sailors used for their clothing. That after picking up the men from the freighter, the weather turned bad and the boat began rolling in big seas causing one of the bags to slide across the deck and tear open when it got caught on a cleat. He said the men looked panicked as a propane tank, the kind used for barbeque grills, rolled out as they rushed over to get it back in the bag—"

"My God—did she say if he questioned Tuma about that?" Jack asked.

"She did. She said the man that Rusty only knew as Tuma got upset when he questioned him about a propane tank being in the bag—told him to mind his own business, that he was being paid plenty for the job."

"Why'd she call you, Red?

"Because she read in the local paper this morning that Rusty had been found dead on a beach in Old Lyme. She first started crying, talking a lot about him wanting to get back together again. But I think the real reason she called was because she wanted to know if I thought Rusty got the money doing something illegal—if she should call the police about it. Then she admitted she had already spent some of it."

"What did you say to her?" Jack asked, still stunned by this new information.

"I told her to do nothing until I called her back. To me it sure sounds like transporting illegal aliens into the country. Rusty talked like a patriot so I'd like to believe he didn't know that—but ten thousand for a night's work says he had to know he was doing something illegal. I was going to call Ray, but hate to see her get in trouble by not reporting this sooner or spending some of the money. That's why I wanted to talk to you first."

"Did Rusty tell her anything else?"

"Yeah, I don't know if it means anything but Rusty told her he saw Tuma has the number 313 tattooed on his back. She said he saw it one night when he got inquisitive about what Tuma was doing inside the old power plant. That he'd snuck up to a window in the back and saw Tuma changing his shirt inside the plant and saw the tattoo. Do you think it means anything, Jack?"

"I don't know, I'll ask Max. By the way, do you know if she's ever been in trouble with the law?"

"Not that I know of, Jack. Only met her one time when she came here looking for Rusty about a year ago. She seemed nice enough. My wife knows her from church, says she lives about five minutes from us."

"Call her, Red, tell her she's got information about men the police are looking for."

"Is that true, Jack?"

"Yes, it's very important. Max and Ray need to hear this, but I can't tell you why right now. I'd suggest you pick her up and take her down there—she probably will be scared to go by herself. I'd also tell her it'll look much better for her if she does this voluntarily, that she wouldn't want the police coming to her house."

"Okay, I'll call her now. You want to come with me?

"No, I don't know her and it might scare her off. But call me while you're on your way. I want to give Max a heads up—much better if he sees her before anyone else does."

Twenty minutes later, after Red called to say he'd just picked up Rusty's wife, Jack called Max and gave him a brief summary of his conversation with Red.

"Good, you handled it well, Jack. And thanks for the quick heads up. You're right about me seeing her first. This just might be the break we're looking for. Sounds like it will confirm my suspicion this isn't a homegrown plot—it might make a big difference on what the top guns at DHS decide on the Alert."

"One more thing Max, I'm going to run over to the Harp & Hound in Mystic to see if I can get any leads on the whereabouts of Meg."

"Go ahead if you want to, but it'll be a waste of time. We've interviewed everybody there and got nothing out of it."

"Yeah, but they just might say more to me than to cops. Know it's a long shot but I don't mind wasting my time. How about a beer later on this evening—Kate's joined the Democratic party, she's going to a meeting tonight."

"Sure, I'll call you when I'm done, I could use a break as long as you remember I can't tell you everything." Max said and hung up before Jack could reply.

At the Harp & Hound, Jack learned that Sid Johnson hadn't shown up for work for three or four days. That didn't disturb the owner since he was going to fire him. "Can't have bartenders I can't rely on," he told Jack.

"Do you know where he lives?" Jack asked.

"No, but one of my waitress's said he used to live on his boat in one of the marina's here—maybe he still does."

"Thanks." Jack said. He was about to leave when the owner added, "I think he might have hooked up with a gal that called him the last day he was working."

"When was that?" Jack said and turned around, curious to find out if it might be the same day he met with Meg.

The owner pondered the question, "I don't remember . . . then reached for something under the bar. "Here, I marked it down on the calendar because a few minutes after she called, Sid asked to leave early." Jack looked—it was the same day he met Meg, the day he told her to turn herself in!

CHAPTER TWENTY-SEVEN

Jack was familiar with the Mystic waterfront, knew there were at least seven or eight marina's there. He began his search for Sid Johnson's boat at the marinas closest to town, but suspected he'd most likely find him at one of the smaller, cheaper ones on the east side of the harbor. Turned out he was right about that, the manager at the Mystic East Yard said Johnson kept his boat there and pointed to the dock it was on.

"It's that wood, thirty-foot cabin cruiser, the last one on the end of the dock. I don't think he's there now, he works during the day, but I think his woman friend is."

"Hello Meg." Jack said when he got to the end of the dock and saw her down on her hands and knees, scrubbing the open deck of the cabin cruiser.

"How'd you find me," she said as she stopped scrubbing and looked up with a dejected look on her face.

"It wasn't hard, you're lucky it was me that did." Jack said as he stepped on board without waiting for an invitation.

"I'm sorry, Jack. I should have called you that night. I know you were trying to help me, but I didn't trust the police to protect me."

"Protect you from what?"

"I think it was Tuma who killed Tom. I've felt for a long time he isn't who he says he is—there was something scary about him from the first time I met him. I think Omar Jemal, my old boyfriend, hired him to get me."

"You made a mistake not turning yourself in. You're right about Tuma, or this man who calls himself Tuma, not being who he says he is. He's now on the run as a suspected terrorist. They have evidence he's not Tuma, evidence he had plastic surgery to look like Tuma, but he escaped before they could capture him. If you are right that he was after you, and that seems odd, then you don't have to worry about him looking for you anymore. The FBI, Homeland Security and the cops are looking for him. But they're still looking for you because of your connection with your old boyfriend. It makes you a suspect since you ran away rather than talk to them."

Jack was careful not to tell her any more than he had to in his attempt to get something out of her before calling Max. He also knew Max wouldn't want him interviewing her, but what she said about Tuma, her feeling all along he's somebody else, that was too inviting to not ask her a few questions, so he did.

"Why do you think Tuma is somehow connected to your old boyfriend?" Jack asked.

"I take it you're with the police now. What'd they do, deputize you, Jack?"

Jack laughed. "Let's just say I'm working very closely with them on this. How about answering my question?"

"It's just a gut feeling. First of all, he never looked me in the eye when talking to me, yet the other girls said they saw him staring at me with a cruel look on his face when he thought I wasn't looking. One girl even asked me if I knew him from before. I ignored all that until Tom was killed, then realized someone was after me not Tom. Remember, Jack, I told you how angry Omar got when I asked him if he was a terrorist, then you told me he was high on our terrorist list. Add all that to none of us understanding why Tuma bought Finnegan's. He seemed to hate the place—it didn't make sense. I started wondering if he ever knew Omar. I have a question for you: Do they now know who Tuma really is?"

Jack thought for a moment about how to answer her without getting himself in trouble with Max. I'll tell you this. He has the number 313 tattooed across his back."

"Oh my God—so does Omar! That's him!" Meg shrieked in a terrified voice.

"Are you sure of that, Meg?" Jack asked as she slumped over with her head in her hands.

"Yes, yes . . . it all makes sense now. There was something about the way Tuma walked, his mannerisms. His voice was softer and older but sometimes even that brought back memories of Omar. I ignored all that because of how Tuma looked—Omar was a handsome man. The plastic surgery you mentioned confirmed my own doubts of him not being who he said he was, but I didn't connect that with anything until I heard you say '313 tattooed on his back'—that's why I know Tuma is Omar!"

"Tell me what 313 means and why that's evidence he's Omar Jemal?"

"Omar had that tattoo done as a defiant act when he was a senior, a year after I met him. He's a Sunni and it's against the Sunni sect to get tattoos. But he was never very religious. He grew up with a lot of Shiite Muslims who don't have the same negative feelings about tattoos. The number 313 has a lot of meanings to Muslims, but fundamentally, 313 was the number of soldiers accompanying the Prophet in the victorious Battle of Badr in 624. Omar saw this tattoo on some of his Shiite friends and liked it. He didn't care what other Sunni's would think. He was in a rebellious mood in his senior year, so he had it done on his back."

"I thought Sunni and Shiite's hated each other?" Jack said.

"It's mostly the extremists in both sects that do, not the majority who often grew up and lived side by side with each other. It was the civil war that changed everything, when Assad's forces started murdering Sunni's. You and I talked about this, Jack, of his family being killed by an American air strike, that he blamed America for not getting rid of Assad.

"I've had a lot of time to think about all this, of how angry he was with me for calling him a terrorist, saying to me he thinks Americans are the terrorists. How naïve I was about our relationship and who he really was. I can see now, looking back, how ideologically driven he was for Muslims to reclaim the fame they had fourteen hundred years ago.

"He talked about it when he got the tattoo, even then he believed he was destined to help Muslims restored to their former glory. I have to admit, I saw there was an uncompassionate, angry part to his personality. It was always there and I was the recipient of it occasionally. But I never gave it much thought back then. I was just a young girl in love with a handsome man who talked endlessly of his dreams and I thought I wanted to be part of it."

"So there's no question in your mind now that Tuma is Omar Jemal?"

"None, absolutely none!"

"Good you need to tell all this to a friend of mine who works for Homeland Security. It could be a big help in their capturing him and a relief for you when they do." Jack picked up his cell phone and called Max.

"I found her Max. Meg is with me right now. She says Tuma is her ex-boyfriend, Omar Jemal. The ISIS terrorist you told me about—the guy high up on your most wanted list!"

CHAPTER TWENTY-EIGHT

After sending agents over to pick up Meg at the marina and interviewing her, Max called Jack to take him up on the offer to have a beer together. It was almost nine in the evening when Max arrived an hour late to Jack waiting for him in a booth at Finnegan's.

"Sorry I'm late—bad news, Jack. We found three cars early this evening at long term parking at JFK. All three had Connecticut license plates and five-gallon propane tanks under their rear seats hooked up to tubular roof racks. Technicians were rushed to the scene and detected residue of anthrax all over the roofs. Portable monitors in New York were checked and also show traces of anthrax, but never triggered an alert."

"Why?"

"We don't know, it's a new system that was rushed into service this year. We knew it wasn't fully operational and there were still bugs in the system. Doesn't matter now—it failed and everything is adding up to the attack having taken place yesterday morning like we suspected. An alert is being drafted as we speak, so I can't stay long, probably shouldn't have come, but I wanted to thank you for finding Meg. She confirmed everything she told you. It's a big help to know who we're looking for, but wish we knew that earlier."

"Meg wouldn't have known it was Jemal without knowing about the 313 tattoo Max, and we didn't find that out until this morning." Jack said.

"That's true, you're right about that. I'm just kicking myself for not getting him before this attack. Two days have gone by since the victims might have been exposed and data shows it's critical with aerosol anthrax to start treatment immediately. That means many more will die because they didn't start treatment right away."

"You can't blame yourself for that—take my beer. I've had two already, won't want this if you have to rush out of here."

"Thanks, I do have to get right back. I'll probably be very busy and hard to reach for the next couple of days, so don't take it personal if I don't answer your calls." Max took a big swig of the beer Jack gave him. "See ya," he said as he rushed out of the bar.

Kate hadn't returned from her Democratic meeting when Jack got home. He turned on the TV to watch the news, curious to see if an alert had been issued about the anthrax attack on New York. It had, and was the topic being discussed on every news channel, headlined: "Anthrax Attack on New York City." On CNN, Jack learned that the Mayor of NYC and Homeland Security were scheduled to hold a news conference at eleven that night. He also noted that news tickers about the attack ran continuously at the bottom of almost all channels warning anyone who had been in Manhattan on the day of the attack not to wait to see if they had flu like symptoms—that they needed to get antibiotics as soon as possible, that hospitals and clinics were being stocked to treat anyone that might have been exposed to the aerosol attack.

Although Jack knew how deadly an aerosol anthrax attack could be, and was aware that an attack had taken place before the news was released to the media, it still had an emotional impact on him hearing commentators, medical professionals and bio warfare experts talking about how thousands of lives could be lost by just a few pounds of the deadly material. They weren't aware that the terrorists were suspected of having sixty pounds or more of weapons grade material capable of killing hundreds of thousands of people in New York where the attack took place. There wasn't any mention of the magnitude of the attack, or as to whether the terrorist or terrorists had been apprehended.

Kate walked in as he was listening to CNN. “Have you heard what happened?” Jack asked as she walked over to the sofa where he was sitting.

“Yes, people were getting calls from home about it, they stopped the meeting and we all huddled around the television. It doesn’t sound like they know much yet, but we all left when it was announced the mayor would be holding a news conference at eleven tonight.”

“I doubt you’ll learn much from the mayor and he won’t be on for another half hour so sit down and I’ll tell you why I know a lot more than what you’ve been hearing,” Jack said as he turned off the television.

Kate listened quietly as Jack told her about his meeting with Meg and why a 313 tattoo on Tuma’s back was proof he was actually Meg’s ex- boyfriend, Omar Jemal. He also informed her about his meeting with Max an hour earlier, about the three cars found at JFK parking and about the traces of anthrax on the cars, Jack said, “So now you know the dilemma Homeland Security has regarding what to say, other than an attack took place in New York.”

“It could mean millions of people, Jack. This is going to cause a panic! Do the hospitals and clinics have enough antibiotics for that many? Are they prepared to handle this? Wouldn’t it have been better to wait until they have more information?”

“They don’t have a choice. The effectiveness of the antibiotics is directly related to how soon you take it after being exposed. Even if you start taking the medicine immediately after inhaling anthrax spores, it’s not one hundred percent effective. Max said the Agency’s director at DHS was very worried about unnecessarily causing a panic, that’s why they didn’t issue an alert the first day I was rescued.”

"Okay, I get that. But if you remember, it was something like this, some major catastrophe that my friends and I were worried about, knowing a major attack like this would take the focus off of investigating the president for colluding with foreign powers to interfere in our elections. You know he's been calling the investigations of him a "witch hunt" and trying to create distractions. This will hand it to him on a silver platter."

"This isn't the time to talk politics, or your biased view of Cain. ISIS may have conducted the worst attack this country has ever seen, far worse than 9/11. I'm turning on the TV now to hear what the mayor has to say," Jack said in an angry tone.

"Fine, you say this isn't the time to talk politics, but I have to warn you, Jack, this is going to make the politics in this country explode! So go ahead and turn on the TV—I also want to hear the Mayor speak."

CHAPTER TWENTY-NINE

The mayor tried to calm the public—saying it was possible the attack would only affect a handful of people, similar to what happened in Japan. He didn't mention the cars being found with the anthrax tanks, although he was briefed by the FBI, but he emphasized, over and over, that anyone who had flu-like symptoms must go to the nearest hospital or clinic immediately. He said they had sufficient stocks of anthrax medicine to treat everyone. He didn't have enough information to say how many people might have been affected so he ended the briefing by asking everyone to stay calm, and that he would issue updates as soon as he had more specifics as to where the attack took place in the city.

Days later, it was clear a major biological warfare attack had been carried out against the city. Emergency medical trailers, staffed by volunteer doctors coming from all over the country had to be set up to handle the overflow of victims the hospitals and clinics couldn't handle. When hundreds began dying, the president issued a major disaster declaration for the State of New York.

New York had been preparing for a biological warfare attack since 9/11, which is why hospitals and clinics were stocked with antibiotics for millions of potential victims. But so much depended on early detection and the monitoring systems, which weren't fully operational.

Footage from video cameras, pieced together from both private and public surveillance systems, revealed the route the three cars took that morning as they drove on Broadway, Park Ave and Fifth and Sixth Ave. It was estimated they covered twenty-five miles up and down those streets, exposing as many as three hundred thousand people to the anthrax spewing out of the roof racks. Traces of anthrax were also discovered in subways that ran between Penn Station and Grand Central. A frightening discovery—indicating the attack may have been carried out all over the city.

Max hadn't slept much since the night he met Jack at Finnegan's. He felt guilty not discovering sooner what Tuma was up to. He prayed that there would be minimum casualties, but the news coming in from hospitals was a sobering reality to the magnitude of the attack. The millions of people requesting throat swabs for anthrax were overwhelming medical facilities in the area. Tens of thousands were already being treated for the symptoms, more than twenty thousand would die according to early estimates.

The media was reporting horrific accounts of people dying. Videos of people on cots in overcrowded hospital hallways and the emergency trailers, revealed many victims were beginning to go into shock, shaking violently, having difficulty breathing and vomiting up blood. These victims were in stage two of being infected, which can happen within a few days of the first flu-like symptoms. Many of these victims were students heading to classes at NYU. Eighty to ninety percent in stage two would die regardless of getting any medical attention.

The fact the terrorists were still at large with the possibility more attacks could come had the entire country close to panicking. Photographs of the real Tuma, were touched up to reflect recollections of eyewitnesses who'd met Jemal in Connecticut. They were shown by media all over the world and posted in airports, post offices, and railroad and bus stations all around the country. As the death toll continued to climb, Jemal became the number one most hunted terrorist on the planet.

Everything about the attack was having a huge political impact on the country: How a major well known terrorist could have gotten into the country; why New York and other cities don't have a fully operational bio-detection system in place; and how could it be possible for a terrorist like this to escape the dragnet of all our local and national government agencies. There were right wing demonstrations demanding Congress give the president martial law power throughout the country, some of which he had already implemented to address the crisis. He did this by calling the attack on New York a "National State of Emergency" which allowed him to implement aspects of martial law in New York without calling it that.

Max came for dinner with Jack and Kate at their home the same day Congress was voting on giving the president the authority he was looking for. They were discussing the pros and cons of the president having such enormous executive power when Kate said, "In my opinion, we are already under a form of martial law. This national state of emergency declaration is bullshit. The Founders never intended standing armies policing the citizens of the United States—sadly that is exactly what we have now." Kate said this in a defiant tone, knowing Max would disagree.

"People are scared, Kate. The president had to do something with demonstrators acting like vigilantes, wanting to take matters into their own hands, which some did in killing that man who looked like Jemal," Max said, then quickly cut her off before she could respond. "And don't forget it was you that said, 'we have to do something about these demonstrators.'"

"I did, but I never envisioned giving the president such enormous power to do it—there are existing laws and means of enforcement within each state to handle what was happening."

"Maybe you're just worried about Republicans versus Democrats having the power," Max responded.

"Okay, time to change the subject," Jack said. "We could debate this issue all night, but I'd like to discuss something more important right now, like who wants another drink?"

"Your husband should have been a politician, Kate. He's right, our discussion was heading off the tracks into an area that's become dangerous to friendships and families all over the country."

"Up until recently I'd agree with that," Kate said. "But upon reflection, I think a big part of the reason partisanship has grown to such a dangerous level, is precisely because we're afraid to offend friends and family. We've become so sensitive to being politically correct that we've become afraid to discuss politics with each other regardless of the moral issues involved or potential consequences of not doing so."

Kate was angry with Jack's attempt to end the discussion and Max agreeing with him. Both saw that . . . there was a pregnant silence in the room as Jack got up and filled everyone's wine glasses. Leaning over in front of Max as he filled his glass the two men locked eyes for a moment—trying to read each other's mind. Both realized they didn't know each other that well, though a brotherly bond had formed from past encounters—knowing they had each other's back when it counted.

"Okay, you're right about why people are reluctant to talk politics today, but for a good reason, Kate," Max said. "A wartime language has grown up around how each party is seen by the other, that's what makes it dangerous to discuss the subject amongst friends or family who differ in their political beliefs. But I'll risk telling you right now I'm a Republican who voted for this president, and know it will probably offend you to hear that I still stand by my vote even though there is much about the man I dislike. So, do you still want to have this discussion?" Max said this with a warm smile on his face, hoping Kate would say no to his question.

"Yes, I do." Kate said emphatically.

"Let me jump in here," Jack said turning to face Kate as he spoke. "I think the language Max is talking about regarding how Democrats and Republicans perceive each other, well . . . that didn't happen overnight. Both parties are unrecognizable compared to fifty years ago when their ideologies were simpler and clearer as to what each offered to the country. Divisive factions and lobbies have grown so powerful, so much so, that politicians have to compromise their beliefs to win and so do the voters—both candidates were flawed—"

"Yeah, I get all that," Kate said, interrupting Jack to address Max again. "But I'm sorry, Max, it doesn't explain to me how anybody could've voted for this president knowing all his character flaws. And I think—"

"This is why people today don't want to talk politics, Kate. You're suggesting the character issue was a moral issue and therefore the Democrats were more moral than Republicans in their choice for the presidency," Max said and he was no longer smiling.

"No. I'm trying to divorce the conversation from talking about Democrat versus Republican. To me it was about the character of the two people who ran—to me it was a clear choice."

"I don't think you can divorce the candidates from their party, Kate, considering the problems we face in the country today. I'm a conservative and believe the liberal agenda has had this country on a path to bankruptcy. And when you say "character" I think you mean moral values. I think of moral values in terms of the bigger picture. I see the moral decline in our country as primarily the fault of liberal policies, so when I vote, I can't separate the candidates from their party, even if I believe the candidate I voted for has a more questionable character than the other," Max said.

"I think you and I have a different definition of morality, particularly in terms of what each party stands for," Kate said.

"We probably do and we could begin with what President Lincoln was most concerned about—it was preserving the union, not freeing the slaves, which is what liberals want everyone to believe!" Max said as he stared at Kate with a smug look.

"Okay, I'm going to jump in again—this is why I believe we need a strong independent third party to break up this divisive "Righteousness" that is tearing our country apart. The percentage of independents has been growing for years and a third party—"

"Never happen!" both Kate and Max said almost simultaneously. "Our country isn't set up for that, Jack. Congress and the electoral college favor the two-party system, and the majority of voters don't want to waste their vote on someone who can't win," Max said and Kate nodded in agreement.

Jack laughed, "Yeah, I know, I get carried away sometimes wishing things to be true. So, let's get back to what the president is doing. I think the people see this attack on New York as an act of War—that we have to mobilize with all the power we have to fight these terrorists. I think Max is right, Kate, in that the president had to do what he's done, including war like executive orders that infringe on civil liberties—the people were demanding he do something." Jack said, pausing for a moment before continuing—

"But I'm also worried, Max, about the mental state of this president. Call it whatever you want, lack of character, moral reasoning, irrational behavior or the inexplicable cozying up to our enemies for which he is being investigated—it all adds up to good reasons to be worried about giving him martial law power."

"You're ignoring what really makes our country great, Jack, no pun intended. The balance of power in our democracy that would prevent what both you and Kate are worried about. You're implying the president will use this act of war on our country to take on dictatorial powers. You're not giving the Republican Party enough credit—they would never let that happen, nor would the Supreme Court."

"I would agree with you, Max, if Congress didn't have so low an approval rating, if they hadn't reduced their voting to a simple majority, if members still met and talked to each other in congressional lunch rooms, and if the Supreme Court hadn't been stacked along party lines. The divisiveness has become so political between the two parties I think there is a legitimate concern that the party in power will put party first even when it concerns constitutional issues or the people they are supposed to be serving. That's been increasingly demonstrated in both houses of Congress and to some extent in the Supreme Court over the past few administrations," Jack said.

"So, Max, do I take it you wouldn't have a problem with this president using the military to enforce martial law throughout the country? Kate asked.

"I wouldn't like it. I'd like to believe it was necessary only as a last resort. But if that would stop another attack, if the terrorists who attacked New York are still on the loose and there's information they're part of a larger group planning more attacks, then I would support it. I think you have a problem realizing we really are at war with these terrorists. We can't stop them if we don't use all means at our disposal. I've been there, Kate, saw men die because our hands were tied by well-meaning politicians who should have left the rules of engagement to the professionals who have to engage the enemy."

"I think Kate's question was focused mostly on this president, Max, and you already answered that, but I wonder how would the military respond if the president issued martial law orders to arrest people and shut down institutions that opposed his handling of the crisis?"

"I told you why that couldn't happen and I don't believe the military would follow orders that were contrary to the constitution."

"I would like to believe that, Max, but unfortunately history tells us otherwise. During the Civil War, Lincoln continually violated the Constitution, in some cases suspending the entire Constitution that he swore to uphold," Jack said.

"How did he do that?"

"He suspended the writ of habeas corpus without the consent of congress. He shut down newspapers whose writers displayed any dissent to Union policy or spoke out against him. He raised troops without the consent of Congress. He closed courts by force. He even imprisoned citizens, newspaper owners, and elected officials without cause and without a trial."

"And you're telling me Congress and the Supreme Court okayed that?"

"Congress ratified most of Lincoln's orders except for the writ of habeas corpus, but the question on the writ, regarding whether the president had the power to do that, remained an open question until four years later when the Supreme Court said only Congress can issue martial law. The point is it happened. Lincoln ignored the constitution to address the crisis and neither Congress nor the Supreme Court overturned those orders until years later."

"Okay, but that doesn't mean it could happen again, you just said the Supreme Court overturned what Lincoln did and that would be the ruling today," Max said.

"I think you're missing the point, Max. Under Lincoln's martial law orders, more than fifteen thousand American citizens were arrested and three hundred newspapers were shut down. Ironically it was Lincoln himself who recognized the overreach taking place under martial law and it was he who took steps to rein it in—not Congress. And look at what's happened in our own time. The law says that only Congress can declare war, but beginning with President Truman almost every president since then has begun a war without Congress's approval and they've done nothing about it."

"I don't think it's fair to compare the Civil War to this crisis, Jack. That was an extreme case and required extreme measures," Max said.

"And I don't think it's fair to compare Lincoln to this president, Max." Kate said. Lincoln reined in his own power when he saw it was being abused and no one ever accused him of being a misogynist, a pathological liar or pathologically vengeful. I think Jack just showed how a president could take on un-constitutional power and how much damage could be done before any checks and balances kicked in." Shaking her head, Kate added, "I'm scared, Max, really scared this guy could screw up our democracy for good."

"Jack made some good points, food for thought as they say, but I'm an optimist, Kate. The president has placed some great ex-military people in key positions. We could argue as to his motives for doing that, but that doesn't matter to me. His National Security Advisor and Secretary of Defense are four-star generals . . . good men who I don't believe would let him abuse power to hurt this country."

"Yes, but his National Security Advisor is a lame duck, maybe you haven't heard, but the president announced today he's going to be replaced by his ambassador to the UN, who we all know is a war hawk. With regard to his Secretary of Defense, I agree he was a great choice, but rumor has it he's going to resign—that Cain wants to get rid of him too."

"Every administration goes through changes. Look, Kate, I think we've gone farther on this discussion than I thought we could without hurting our friendship so let's quit while we're still ahead. I got work to do, so thanks for the conversation, dinner and drinks," Max said as he got up and left.

Five minutes later, sitting on their back porch, Jack said, "He has a point, Kate. I, like you, wasn't thrilled to see key positions in the White House filled with military people, but they're good men who have excellent reputations. They're in good positions to stop anything crazy the president might try to do."

"I wish I had your optimism. I'm not questioning whether they were good men. I'm sure they're men our country should be proud of, but Cain is going to replace them, it's clear they haven't turned out to be yes men. I'm worried Jack, and what you said tonight just reminded me of how the checks and balances can be ignored or too slow to act . . . and everything Max said made me see how people can rationalize backing someone who supports their ideology regardless of how bad that person turns out to be."

CHAPTER-THIRTY

It was twelve-noon when Jemal and his men passed over New York's Verrazano Bridge. The GPS in the rented car indicated it would be a ten-hour drive to get to Beaufort, North Carolina. Jemal was in the passenger seat talking to the other two men in the back seat who looked tired and dejected as Jemal continued to chastise them.

"Stop telling me you think he's dead. You're both at fault he escaped. How many times do I have to tell you that finding the boat is not proof he drowned. If he's alive, and I suspect he might be, he'll go straight to the police and they'll be searching for us now. But let's thank Allah that we succeeded in executing our attack on New York. People will start dying in a few days and that's when we will know just how successful we were. If the anthrax kills thousands or more, then we can celebrate our jihad—and we'll be more famous than Osama Bin Laden. Right now, we need to focus on getting out of the country."

"You should have let me kill him—I think the animal tests showed how good the stuff worked. I don't understand why you waited—we could've done New York and Boston weeks ago." Hassan Abadi said.

"I told you, Hassan, we needed more tests to get the most effective release rate for the tanks." But Jemal knew Hassan was right; the real reason he waited was he wanted to either kill Meg or test the anthrax on her. His hatred of her had consumed him, he wanted revenge and when he couldn't find her and Jack fell into his hands, he decided to test it on him—his sick mind needed to see the effects on a human.

"So, who is this man in North Carolina that's going to help us? How's he going to do that?" Hassan said with a disrespectful tone to his voice. He knew why Jemal had waited, believed they were at risk of getting caught now because of him.

Ghadi turned on the car's radio saying, "Lets listen to the news to see if there is any talk of our attack." He knew his leader well, knew how much he hated anyone questioning his authority or judgment.

"Good idea," Jemal said, then turned around to face Hassan. "What do you think Baghdadi would have done if one of his soldiers spoke to them the way you just spoke to me? You know the answer so I'm warning you don't mistake I'd be any different if you do it again. I'll tell you my plan when I'm ready and think you need to know." Jemal turned back around and patted the gun in his pocket. *I can't trust him anymore . . . have to do something about this if I get the opportunity.*

No one said anything for the next ten minutes after hearing Jemal's warning and knowing it applied to all of them. They continued to listen to the news until finally Ghadi said, "Sounds like good news, Omar, nothing about what we did—your plan to avoid the monitors must have worked."

"Yes, let's just hope they don't find the cars before tomorrow. I plan on getting us out of the country tonight." He intentionally wasn't telling them how—wanting them to know how much they needed him to escape.

Jemal was also counting on Ganz being on his vessel when they got to Beaufort. The old sailor lived on his boat, but that was no guarantee he'd be there. He also wasn't sure how to get to the marina. Ganz had shown him a nautical map of the marina and its facilities before deciding to drop him off in Florida. He remembered it was called Town Creek and that it was a small family marina close to the town.

"What about this car—where you planning on leaving it?" Ghadi asked.

"Won't know until we get there, but wherever we leave it remind me to take the plates off it."

It was eleven in the evening when they arrived in Beaufort and discovered there were a number of marinas in the area. It was close to midnight before Jemal found the Town Creek Marina at the end of a dead-end road. He pulled into the small parking lot for customers' boats and turned the car's lights off after recognizing Ganz's boat tied up to one of the floating finger docks. It was the only boat in the marina showing a light on in the cabin.

"Okay, see that boat with the light on, that's how I got here, and that's how we're all going to escape," Jemal said to everyone in the car.

"To where?" The two men in the back of the car asked.

"Venezuela!" Jemal said, it's easy to get into and easy to get out.

Ghadi was surprised. When he heard they were headed to Beaufort he suspected the plan was to get to Cuba, not Venezuela. Jemal had told him about getting here from Cuba on a small sailboat.

"Listen close, there's only one man on board, he took me here from Cuba and I'm going to get him to take us to wherever we want to go. I'm going to offer him a lot of money to take us, but if he resists, we can't kill him—we need him since none of us knows enough how to sail or navigate."

"What do we do if he's not alone or not on board?" Ghadi asked.

"I'm going to check that out now, but before I do, here's my plan: Watch to see if I get on board his boat, if I do, wait to see if I come back up and wave to you. That will be the signal he's there alone and that I want you all to come. But after you see me wave, there's something you need to do first. We passed that small apartment complex just a hundred yards back down the road. It looked like it's still under construction. Leave the car there, take the plates off and throw them in the river. Remember to be very quiet. This place seems to be deserted at night, but there may be other people on their boats—take your shoes off before you walk onto the floating docks."

Jemal knew this was far from a perfect plan as he approached the boat. Ganz had proven to be unpredictable. There was no way to know how he'd react to taking four men on his boat. If he resisted or refused for any amount of money, then he would have to force him at gunpoint. If that happened, there was a risk of Ganz alerting authorities using the radio or some other means Jemal and his men wouldn't recognize. Yes, I must be very alert to his every move, Jemal thought as he peered through a cabin window. He smiled when he saw Ganz alone, lying on a bunk reading a magazine.

Mike was reading *Soundings*, a boating magazine that was popular along the East Coast from Maine to Florida. He had placed an advertisement in the "Boats for Sale" section and was looking at his competition since he hadn't had any response. He had sailed all over the Caribbean in the past two years, but after his Cuba adventure he was tired of living on a boat and ready to settle down, hopefully with a woman different from the ones he'd been meeting in bars. He was working again as a male nurse at a clinic in Morehead City ten miles away. If he sold the boat, he could buy a small house he'd been looking at in Beaufort. The house would be more appealing for finding a mate and visits from his eighteen-year-old daughter who he hadn't seen in three years. Hearing someone step onboard and knocking on the cabin hatch was unusual this late at night. He cautiously slid back the hatch, surprised, and not particularly pleased to see the man he only knew as Maten Tuma from Lebanon.

"What the hell . . . what are you doing here and how did you find me?" Mike exclaimed.

"Can I come down below and tell you, I think you'll like what I have to say."

Seeing the hesitation and worried look on Ganz's face, Jemal didn't wait for him to respond. He smiled as he slid back the hatch leading into the cabin and stepped inside saying, "I want to make you an offer I think you wouldn't want to refuse."

"Make it quick, it's late and I'm tired, but if it's about money to take you some place I'm not interested." Ganz had got over his initial shock and wanted to sound tough, but a little fear entered his gut when his visitor didn't wait for his answer and entered with a twisted smile on his face.

"I have ten thousand dollars with me for you to take me and three other men to Venezuela, but we have to leave tonight."

"Why tonight and who are these men?"

"They are Lebanese like me. They have been living here illegally for ten years and have been caught up in the deportation executive orders for anyone who came here illegally."

"I thought that was for Mexicans?"

"No, it was for anyone who came illegally. They have to get out with the money they saved—they're afraid it will be taken from them if they get arrested. Homeland Security agents came to my sister's house looking for them today."

"Why Venezuela?"

"It has very porous borders and much easier for us to get home from there."

"Venezuela is far—let me look at the maps."

Five minutes later after taking out the nautical maps with Jemal looking over his shoulder, Ganz said, "It's too far, over two-thousand-mile sail. Could take us two to three weeks to get there and I don't have provisions for that."

"I saw on your maps that Cuba is on the way, couldn't we stop there and get provisioned?" Jemal asked.

"Probably, but that's at least ten days from here and I barely have enough food for me on board for ten days."

"We can get by—we're used to that sort of thing."

"You never answered how you found me."

"It was easy. When we left Cuba, we were originally planning to come here. You told me all about the place, showed me a photo of the marina before we changed plans and dropped me off at Boca Raton. You said you lived on the boat—so I took a chance I could find you and you'd be here tonight."

"Give me a moment to think about it, ten thousand is a lot of money and I could use it, but the risks are great. If I got caught, I could lose everything, the Coast Guard will take my boat and I have it up for sale," Mike replied as he sat down next to the locker where he kept a pistol. What Jemal said was reason enough to refuse . . . he sensed the danger . . . *don't trust him . . . remember how relieved I was to get rid of him last time* . . . he knew he'd be crazy to take him anyplace for even a million bucks, but had to be careful how he answered him.

"Okay, I'll do it, but I can't leave tonight. I have to notify my boss at the hospital and my daughter that I'll be gone for a while. I also have to pay my bill here at the marina or they'll notify the police and Coast Guard that I've skipped town. Come back tomorrow at the same time and I'll have the boat provisioned and ready to go."

"No. We have to leave now—I told you there are government agents on our tail and we can't risk hanging around here for another day," Jemal said not realizing or caring about the angry way he said it.

"Well I'm sorry about that, but tonight is out of the question," Mike said as his hand reached for the locker handle.

Jemal was wearing a light windbreaker that hid the gun in his waistband. In one motion he pulled the gun out and with a deft kick knocked Ganz's hand away from the locker.

"I was hoping we could do this the easy way, but now you have forced me to make it clear—you will take all of us to Venezuela and we will leave tonight. If you refuse or try to notify anyone in any way, you will find my men far more ruthless than I am. You will pray to die before they are through with you."

Jemal opened the locker and took out the gun.

"If you were smart you would have waited for a better opportunity to get this." Jemal then stood in the hatch-way and waved to his men—the signal they were waiting for.

CHAPTER THIRTY-ONE

The Department of Homeland Security and the White House began holding daily news briefings when it was corroborated that people in New York were dying from anthrax. America's worst fears were confirmed when the death toll quickly climbed to five thousand—panic spread like wildfire that more cities might be attacked.

The attack on New York was headline news around the world. Five thousand dead within five days of the attack and thousands more critically ill in hospitals. The cable channels were talking about it twenty-four hours a day. No news of the terrorist's whereabouts was contributing to the fear rising around the nation. It seemed inconceivable they could have escaped the dragnet of FBI, CIA, Homeland Security, and the myriad of other state and local police agencies looking for them all over the country.

When the number of victims reached ten thousand, the president issued another executive order that amounted to martial law from Maine to Florida—federalizing the troops to help search for the terrorists. The president popularity, that had been falling before the attack, began rising again. He was getting big support blaming the media, Congress and what he described as inept government agencies in not preventing the attack and letting them get away.

Jack and Kate were at home watching CNN news when the martial law announcement was made. Pundits immediately questioned whether the president could take over the National Guard from the Governors, however, legal analysts said he could, citing changes made to Federal Law in 1956 that gave the president the power in times of crisis.

"I told you this could happen—that he was waiting for the right opportunity," Kate said.

"You did, but you're still jumping to conclusions. He had to do something and this doesn't mean we now have a dictatorship."

"It could be the first step—he now has military control over a large segment of the National Guard."

"Yes, but you don't—"

Jack was interrupted by his cell phone ringing and saw it was Max.

Kate knew it was something very important when she heard Jack say, "Okay, I'll fly down tomorrow morning. I can make lunch if I take the shuttle."

"What's up? What did you mean you'll 'fly down tomorrow?' Where are you going?"

"D.C. Max said the Secretary of the DHS, that's the acronym for the Department of Homeland Security, wants to have a press conference with me tomorrow."

"Why you?"

"I don't know, but it has something to do with being captured and escaping from the terrorists. He said they would tell me all about it when I get there. We will have to finish our conversation at another time, Kate. I need to start packing."

"They probably want you there to tell the public everything you know about the terrorists," Kate said.

"Maybe, but I think the Secretary will be disappointed to learn I don't know anything more than I've already told them."

"How long you staying?"

"I don't know. He said it could be a couple of days, said there's a lot of people who want to talk to me."

"Okay, this actually works out well. I got a call this morning regarding the California commission I left unfinished. I said I'd try to get back there in the next couple of days. I think it'll take two or three days more at the most," Kate said.

Jack was at thirty thousand feet on his way to Washington, D.C. when he remembered they didn't finish the conversation about martial law and Kate's concern it could lead to a dictatorship. He always believed that what happened in Nazi Germany couldn't happen here.

He wondered how the Founding Fathers would react to seeing how much more powerful the presidency had become since their time. They clearly wanted only Congress to have the power to declare war unlike the Korean, Vietnam and Iraq conflicts, which were in reality as much a war as anything in the past. And now, because of changes Congress made in 1956, this president could take over the National Guard to address a crisis. A presidential power specifically limited in the past to putting down rebellions or enforcing constitutional rights if state authorities fail to do so.

Jack wondered if Kate was right. Had all these changes, being executed through executive orders, tipped the power of the presidency to the point they could override our democracy? So much depended on the character of the man in office and he had to admit this president had very worrisome character flaws. He had a gut feeling this meeting with the Secretary of the DHS might challenge his own values and beliefs. It was a reminder to remain true to himself, that the Secretary or even the president put his pants on in the morning same as he did.

The next morning, Jack arrived at the DHS temporary headquarters in Washington, D.C.'s Nebraska Avenue Complex, a former naval facility across from American University. Max was waiting for him and ushered him into Secretary George Thompson's large office at noon.

"Nice to meet you, Jack, I've been looking forward to meeting you from the briefings I've received from Max," Thompson said.

"I also appreciate this opportunity to meet you, but you may be disappointed. I think Max knows all there is regarding my involvement in this crisis."

"That's not the major reason I asked you to come. Take a seat over by the table where lunch is set up, we can eat while we talk. I invited Max to join us, but he said he's told me all I need to know for this meeting," the Secretary said and looked over at Max.

Max took leave following the Secretary's comment and Jack wondered if he was really invited to stay.

"Let me start by saying we all owe you our gratitude in risking your life to investigate these terrorists. What you did was a very gutsy one man show."

"Thanks, but I didn't suspect they were terrorists until after I was captured. For me this all began because I didn't believe my best friend committed suicide even though the police report said he did. I believed he was murdered and that's what I was looking into. I had no idea he was killed by terrorists. I was frustrated knowing it made no sense he committed suicide and wanted to set the record straight."

"I read all that in Max's report, including your background as a reporter turned writer.

Max also told me about your helping him out on a drug raid a few years ago. I haven't read your books but you obviously have a good nose for detective work. Is that why you get drawn into these affairs? Why you are such a risk taker? Is it grist for your writing?" The Secretary, who was a big athletic looking man in his early fifties, said this in a very measured way with steady eyes on Jack. There was nothing accusatory in tone or facial expression, but the emphasis on every word let Jack know it was a very serious question.

"No, I don't think of myself as a good amateur detective, nor do I seek out that work. What happened with Max on the drug operation fell into my lap and I just told you how I inadvertently got involved in this terrorist operation, however, I don't shy from these things if I believe I can help. My writing does involve a lot of armchair detective work and at times research in the field, all of which I enjoy. I also have a generous dose of adventurous spirit in me, so I have a habit of jumping at opportunities if they come my way. Does that answer your question?" Jack said in a manner that let the Secretary know he wouldn't appreciate any more personal queries.

"Yes, it does and your answer is a perfect segue for my telling you the real reason I asked you to come today. The president is aware of how you became involved in this terrorist attack. He was impressed with how you escaped. He likes heroes and thinks you're a hero, even went so far to say that the attack wouldn't have happened if we had more people like you in the agency—"

Jack was embarrassed and started to protest, but the Secretary held up his hand, saying, "Hear me out. The president wants you by my side when I talk to the press tomorrow. We think the public needs to hear your story. Hear first-hand what they were intending to do to you, so they understand it could happen to any one of them. There's a minority, as I'm sure you're well aware, that's protesting how he's responding to the attack. They think he's acting like a dictator. They can't see that what he's doing is trying to capture the terrorists before they carry out another attack," the Secretary said.

"This makes no sense to me. I'm no hero. I'd be flattered if I had a higher opinion of the president's intellect or if I still believed he could be good for our country. I doubt he would still want me if he knew I'm registered as an independent and my wife is a very active liberal in the Democratic Party. I admit I voted for him knowing all his character flaws but hoped the presidency would change the man—"

This time it was Jack holding up his hand to stop the director from interrupting. "It may be too early to judge, but I was thinking about him on the way here, particularly about extending martial law throughout the eastern seaboard and his taking over the National Guard. It really worries me. Where does it end? I'm concerned we're headed down a slippery slope."

"I'm not going to debate that with you, it has nothing to do with my immediate problem of capturing the terrorists before they attack us somewhere else, which is why you are here."

"So, everything I just said should make it easy for you to tell him, 'It would be a mistake for me to say anything at your press conference tomorrow!'"

"I was going to do that after I met you today, but listening to you talk has changed my mind. You don't sound like the kind of man that would say anything contrary to your values. You're not being asked to defend his policies, so what have you got to lose by saying a few words tomorrow? All you have to do is tell the truth about what happened to you. Describe these terrorists the best you can. Who knows, it might help to spot them or scare them out of wherever they're hiding. Give it a shot, Jack."

"Okay. If that's all you want—I can do that."

"Good. I would like a copy of what you will say so I can make sure it doesn't conflict with my own remarks. That's standard policy here, have it ready by nine o'clock tomorrow morning and leave it with my secretary.

"One more thing, Jack. Can you stay a couple of days? I would like you to talk to my people regarding all you know about these terrorists and what happened to you. We have Max's report, but there's nothing like hearing it first-hand. The attack happened over a week ago and we haven't a clue where they are now. No one is more frustrated than we are. Every little bit of information you have, regardless of whether you think it's important or not, may be helpful in apprehending them."

"I understand that and will be happy to talk to anyone here."

"Thanks. I will speak first at the press briefing to address questions on what we are doing to capture the terrorists. I'll let you speak last to leave them with something optimistic to write and talk about other than we haven't captured them yet.

"It was a pleasure meeting you, Jack. I've made a note to myself to read one of your books. My secretary, Donna, will be your contact person from now on regarding hotel arrangements, any meetings here, and handling your expenses."

CHAPTER THIRTY-TWO

When Jack left Thompsons' office and approached Donna, Thompson's personal secretary, she was on the phone. She smiled and nodded approvingly when she hung up, "Congratulations I hear your meeting went well, the Secretary said you will be staying a few days. I'll book you at the Marriott Courtyard. It's close by. Keep all your receipts for airfare, taxis, restaurants and anything else associated with this visit and we will reimburse you before you leave. I'll put together a schedule of briefings the Secretary would like you to attend this afternoon and tomorrow. Max is waiting for you in his office and will be your escort for the briefings. My assistant will take you to his office."

After Jack got to Max's office, he spent fifteen minutes filling him in and telling him what he agreed to.

"So, are you ready for the cameras?" Max said.

"You kidding me? I've never done this before. Still not sure it's a good idea. You know I don't like Cain, don't want to do anything that will help empower him, but the Secretary made some good points. I couldn't refuse if it will help capture the bastards and he didn't ask me to say anything I don't believe. I was also surprised he still wanted me to talk after hearing what I said about the president."

"Yeah, so am I. He's a tough read, a bit of an enigma. He's very ambitious, but at the same time, I don't think he's just a yes man like some of the recent Cabinet appointments.

"He asked me a lot of questions about your writing, mostly what you write about, how close your fiction is to reality. I told him I've only read one of your books and thought it was a thinly veiled piece of fiction close to the truth regarding how you got involved with me on a Caribbean drug raid when I was working for the DEA," Max said.

"He said you filled him in on that. What time is the press briefing tomorrow?"

"Not sure, Jack. Donna will let you know as soon as she hears, but I think she's trying to set it up for around noon."

"Do you have any idea what he will say? Or what he expects from me other than telling my story?"

"A big 'No' to the first part of your question, but with regard to you, I think he's looking for two things: I think he's hoping that putting you on camera will scare the terrorists, show them you're alive, didn't drown, and force them to make a mistake by worrying about how much you know. But I think he also believes that having you, a survivor of terrorism, speaking alongside him from Homeland Security Headquarters will help public support for what the president is doing."

"That's why I first said 'no.' I have no intention of letting him use me that way. I only agreed to tell about what happened to me, nothing else."

"Are you having second thoughts of speaking tomorrow?"

"Some. I'm still trying to absorb what your boss told me. That crap about the president thinking of me as a hero, escaping the way I did. That really bothers me."

"Why?"

"Because look what he thinks about men who fought in Vietnam who were captured and tortured for five years—he says they're not heroes because they were captured. As for me, I was only held for a few days and my escape didn't stop the attack on New York! It's ridiculous for him to hold me up as a hero. I'm worried he will use me as an example to defend his irrational cruel attacks on real heroes who suffered so much in that war."

"Might be an opportunity to correct that, Jack. I think you have to look at the bigger picture."

"I'm not a politician, Max. But you're right I could make a few remarks along those lines. The problem is I don't think it would matter what I say, he'll lie about it and use it to his advantage like he does everything else. I think he's degraded what the presidency is all about. He said things that has given rise to white supremacists and his attacks on Liberals, Muslims, Mexicans or anyone who disagrees with him is dividing the country in ways that could cause irreparable damage to our democracy. And there's nothing conservative about his policies. He hasn't lowered the debt—it's rising faster under him than it did under his predecessor. I voted for him, Max, but I wouldn't have if I'd seen the direction he's taking the country."

"I don't like some of the things he's done or said, Jack, and I'd like to see him act more presidential, but I don't see how you can judge him so harshly. How would history have judged our past presidents if it only judged them on their popularity? People voted for him hoping a straight-talking non-politician, would shake things up."

"Well he's sure doing that, Max, and that's the only reason I voted for him. I knew it was a risky bet. You say it's too early to judge, but he's had ample opportunity to show his true colors and I don't like what I see."

"One of the things I like about you, Jack, is that you walk the talk, but I hope you're not planning to try and say all that tomorrow. The Secretary will cut you off if you go off script. It's one thing to comment about not believing you're a hero, but I think you'd be making a big mistake to use this as an opportunity to attack the president, and truthfully I'd feel obligated to warn the Secretary."

"No, I wasn't planning on doing that, but if he goes off script and tries using my remarks in a political way to support the president, I'll respond."

"Okay, that's fair. I don't think any of this will happen. Right now, we have a meeting to go to with some of my colleagues—mostly good guys by the way. They're all smarting from the criticism we're getting about letting the terrorists get away, so be kind to them, they're just looking for anything that might be worth looking into. Remember you're the only witness to see some of the things the terrorists were up to."

"Thanks for the tip, I'll try to remember that."

It was a long afternoon. Three different meetings with different specialists, grilling him about everything he knew about Jemal and his men. It was six o'clock before he got to the hotel. He made himself a drink from the mini-bar with two little bottles of Jack Daniels and began writing what he wanted to say at the briefing.

After finishing his briefing notes, he called Kate, still ambivalent as to whether he should speak at the briefing when the country was so divided over the executive orders extending martial law to include coastal states from Maine to Florida.

"I hope you know how anxious I've been to hear how it went, and why he wanted to see you," Kate said. "I haven't called you, thinking you would call me as soon as you got out," she said and he could hear the hurt in her voice.

"I left just a little while ago and needed a little time to sort out my thoughts before calling you. Neither of us could have ever guessed why the Secretary wanted to see me. He wants me to join him in a press conference he's having with reporters tomorrow regarding the search for the terrorists. After he talks, he wants me to make a speech, to talk about my capture and escape. He said the president sees me as a hero."

"Are you serious?"

"Dead serious, Kate."

"Why?"

"Good question." Jack summarized his meeting with the Secretary, including his negative thoughts about the president. "My immediate reaction was to say 'no.' I said I didn't want to be used, but the Secretary made some good points about how it might help lead to capturing the terrorists. I'm torn, Kate, this martial law business has me very concerned as you are. I don't want to say anything that will look like I support what he's doing, but it would have been wrong to not agree after considering his argument. I think you know me too well to think I would take it for some sort of an ego trip."

"I agree, you had to say yes, but like you, I hope you're not being used. Cain is good at twisting things around in his favor. I don't know, Jack, it kind of feels like my husband is joining the enemy's camp. I know it's wrong to think that way, it's probably my righteous mind. I wish I could tell you I feel good about you doing this, but I don't."

CHAPTER THIRTY-THREE

Kate's words kept invading Jack's thoughts as he worked on writing his story. He knew she was right to be worried. He wasn't comfortable knowing it was the president's idea for him to do this. He also had to consider that his speaking would prompt questions from the press. He had to prepare for questions like: 'Do you think the terrorists are Syrian, Iranian or homegrown? Or did they say anything that would indicate they are planning to attack other cities?' He'd have to be careful with his answers, be clear, leaving no room for misleading interpretations. Max was also right, it would be wrong to think of this as an opportunity to go off script and attack the president, however, as he told Kate, he wasn't going to be shy about speaking his mind if it looked like he'd been set up to support the president.

What, he wondered, did the president hope to get out of this? The facts were straightforward—he was captured and managed to escape. Would putting a face to the man who escaped give the president more leverage to justify his irrational comments about who he thinks are heroes, and who are not? Jack didn't think so, it had to be more than that. Then it struck him. The president had declared martial law amongst the eastern states after the attack on New York, and used some of the same words that Lincoln used to justify martial law during the Civil War. He was also considering internment for any Muslims deemed by the government to be a threat to public safety.

Jack worried he was going to be used by the president as the public face of what the terrorists could do to any citizen, thus giving further justification for the president to do much more in the name of public safety. Jack was planning to talk about how he became suspicious of Tuma. The man now identified as Omar Jemal, the radical Muslim terrorist who was the architect of the attack on New York. Would the president use Jacks testimony of being suspicious of Tuma, as an example of why fellow Americans need to be watchdogs on their Muslim neighbors? *Yes, I believe he would*, Jack thought as he reflected on the president's previous attacks on Muslims and Mexicans.

It had been a wild ride for the country so far. The president never stopped campaigning. He'd been constantly working his base into believing the Democrats and liberal press were the enemy of the people. Sadly, he was succeeding in creating a war-like atmosphere between the two parties. His Republican Congress had passed only one major piece of legislation, but the economy was hot, a major factor in his keeping Republicans in the Senate and House in line, regardless of serious questions about his abuse of power and character flaws. His character flaws were manifested everyday by his pathological lying regarding anything that diminished his image of himself, however, that never seemed to affect the support of his base.

Cain's support amongst the majority of Americans never rose to fifty percent, primarily because he was the most polarizing president the country had ever seen. He had broken all the norms of the presidency by his fondness for oligarchs and dictators, tirades against anyone who disagreed with him, isolationists policies that created distrust by foreign leaders, disregard for the emoluments clause, and his mocking of the constitution by believing it gave him the power to do whatsoever he wanted to do as president. It was all this, and his disregard for foreign intervention in our elections that worried most Americans. The killing of Baghdadi had improved his ratings significantly, but President Cain wasn't a risk taker. He was a man who would do anything to assure he would win.

He needed a fix, a major distraction or incident to help his approval ratings, and to assure he'd win his next term. Nothing could have helped the president more than the terrorist attack on New York and the day by day worry of the terrorists still at large. His tweets fueled the growing panic throughout the country. It played perfectly into his skills of inciting large crowds and using social media to further the fear; to make people believe that he was the only one who could save the country from the Muslim terrorists who he had warned would do this. He was on a path of convincing the public he needed to take drastic steps to stop them before it got far worse.

The attack on New York had given the president the rationale he needed for issuing executive orders to implement martial law from Maine to Florida. When, days later, it looked like the terrorists could be anywhere, the president addressed the nation again, threatening to extend martial law throughout the country. He said the attack on New York amounted to war against the United States by radical Muslims, some of whom he said had infiltrated our country. He said it demanded a response similar to what Lincoln did when he issued martial law orders including the suspension of habeas corpus in order to save the union.

The attack on New York succeeded in changing the conversation about ongoing investigations of his presidency, but it heightened his war with the press. Daily headlines now were about National Guard troops arresting thousands of innocent Muslims in the search for the terrorists, and accusations of the president using dictatorial tactics that went against everything our democracy stands for. The president said the press was interfering with his attempts to apprehend the terrorists and if they didn't stop, he would shut them down.

This was the situation on the eve of Jacks scheduled talk with the Secretary of Homeland Security. He was in his hotel room discussing it with Kate using a face time connection on their iPhones.

"So, have you decided what you will do?" Kate asked holding up a newspaper headlined with, "President Threatens to Shut Down Press."

"Yes, I'll tell my story. I think I have to, since it might aid in capturing the terrorists, but I'll be careful to phrase everything I say in a manner that can't be interpreted in support of internment or being watchdog on our neighbors. With regard to his threats to shut down the press, I can't say anything about that. The Secretary wants a copy of what I'm going to say tomorrow morning."

"And you still think our checks and balances are working? What will it take, Jack? Men in uniform banging on our front door?"

"I think you forget there's a chain of command those orders go through, like the Secretary of Defense who has already indicated he wouldn't go along with shutting down the press. And then there are the governors of the states, some of whom said they would defy the martial law orders that usurped their command of their National Guard Troops if there was any attempt to shut down the news media. There's also the judicial motions that have started working their way through the courts challenging the constitutionality of the presidents martial law actions and the manner in which congress approved it."

"I'm aware of all that, Jack, but look how his approval rating is improving. More than fifty percent of the public agreed that drastic action is needed. They're conflicted regarding martial law, somewhat fearful what it could lead to, but most believing it's a temporary action necessary to apprehend the terrorists."

"That poll was taken before his comment about shutting down the press," Jack said.

"Okay, I hear your argument for going to the press conference. I agree it might be an opportunity to counter what the president has said about heroes, but I'm worried that you and I are still not on the same page regarding Cain," Kate said before they ended their video call.

The following morning, Jack gave a copy of his talk to Donna, Thompson's secretary.

Donna called him fifteen minutes later saying, "If you're still in the building, the Secretary would like to see you now, Mr. Quinn."

"Did he say why?"

"I think you can assume it's about what you gave me this morning."

"Thank you, I'll be there in five minutes."

When Jack arrived, the Secretary was discussing what Jack wrote with an assistant whom he introduced as Bob Steele, his communications director.

"This all looks fine, Jack, accept you're too humble. I think you could say something more about how you suspected this man you knew as Tuma to not be whom he said he was. I think Bob can help you with that. I'd like you to work with him the rest of the morning to help polish what you are planning to say. It's important that the public, and the terrorists if they hear this, get the message that we know a lot more about these terrorists than they think we do." The Secretary, an experienced speaker, was gesturing with his hands as he spoke. He was pointing to Jack and smiling in a complimentary way when he critiqued that Jack could emphasize that he suspected Tuma was not who he said he was.

"I think that's a mistake, sir. I don't want to mislead anybody regarding what I know and don't know. What I gave you is what I'm comfortable saying, including 'I'm no hero.' If that isn't good enough, you might want to reconsider having me talk."

Bob Steele, the communication director, turned angrily toward Jack, "That doesn't sound like—"

"No, Jack, I do want you to speak," the Secretary said. "I respect your need to be comfortable with what you say," and he dismissed his communication director from saying anything more with a wave of his hand. "All I ask is you give it some thought! We're on at one this afternoon. Talk to Donna on your way out. Let her know where you will be and she will send someone to accompany you to the press conference."

Jack headed off to see Max after talking to Donna, who said the meeting would be in the pressroom of the Nebraska complex, and that her assistant would pick him up at Max's office about fifteen minutes before the meeting. After filling Max in on his little confrontation with the Secretary, Jack said, "Am I right in assuming you had no idea they would attempt to wordsmith what I should say?"

"No, he never discussed anything like this with me, but I'm not surprised, nor should you be. He's got to worry that what you say today will be played over and over by the press if this doesn't go right. What I'm surprised about is that he still wants you to talk after what you said to him yesterday and this morning. He's taking a big risk on you, knowing you're no fan of the president."

"I had the same thought, Max. I wondered if I'm missing something, but he seems like a straight shooter."

"He's well liked here. I don't think you have anything to worry about. Are you ready for this press conference?"

"I think so. What I have to say should take less than five minutes, unless the press has a lot of questions."

When Donna's assistant called to say it was time to go and brought him to the waiting area behind the press-room, the Secretary was already there and said, "Well, Jack, are you ready for this? I assume you are sticking with what you gave me since I haven't heard back from you," he said this with a friendly smile and patted Jack on the shoulder indicating it was okay.

"Yes, I'm as ready as one can be for someone who hasn't done this before. I appreciate you letting me do this my way."

"Okay let's go," the Secretary said after introducing Jack to his small entourage of assistants and leading the way to the pressroom.

There were about thirty reporters waiting for the Secretary to speak. When Jack followed the Secretary into the room, he saw a number of the reporters staring at him and murmuring to each other, obviously recognizing his face from news photos from a week ago.

The Secretary began with, "I know you're all here to question me about the terrorists, wanting to know what we know about them, and what we're doing to hunt them down. But first, let me introduce you to Jack Quinn, the man the terrorists held prisoner in a cellar, from which he managed to escape and identify the terrorists to the authorities.

"The president has rightly called Jack a hero. If it wasn't for his escape, the anthrax attack on New York would have been far worse and other cities attacked— millions might have died. Jack Quinn has generously agreed to come here today to say a few words to you and the citizens of our great country about his capture and escape from the terrorists."

Jack was caught off guard when the Secretary said, "Jack, c'mon over," as he gestured for him to come to the podium, saying in an affected southern drawl, "I'm going to let him speak first, don't want you all to have to wait to hear his story."

Walking up to the podium, Jack realized why the Secretary wasn't overly worried about not letting them wordsmith his story. They'd told him he would speak after the Secretary gave the press briefing. He must have switched me to speak first after I wouldn't let them change what I wrote, *Okay, time to pull the gloves off.*

"Let me begin by saying, I would like to thank the honorable Secretary for asking me to speak today. It gives me an opportunity to clear some things up.

First is the idea that I'm some sort of hero. Nothing could be further from the truth. I was captured because I tried probing into the suspicious death of my best friend, which led to following some men I thought might be involved. They caught me because I bungled it. I'm not a detective! I should have asked trained professionals to do what I was trying to do.

"I also want to clear up any misguided reports that I was investigating a man, or men, who I suspected were terrorists. That's absolutely not true. But I did suspect that a man, whom I only knew as Tuma, might be involved or responsible for the death of my friend. We now know that the man I knew as Tuma was actually, Omar Jemal, the terrorist who led the attack on New York, but I was surprised to learn that! I never suspected he was a known terrorist with a high price on his head when I began the investigation that led to me being captured by the terrorists.

"With regard to my escaping, I knew there was no chance anyone was coming to rescue me. No one knew where I'd gone the day I was captured and it was clear they were planning to kill me. I had nothing to lose by trying to escape. I was also lucky to be familiar with the area where I was being held captive, and familiar with the hardware used to prevent me from escaping. I was being held in the cellar of the only house on a small island in the middle of the Connecticut River. They had chained me to an old mooring, the kind used to secure boats in harbors. When I was a teenager, I worked weekends at a marina so I knew how these moorings were put together which was crucial in helping me escape."

Jack was choosing his words carefully so they couldn't be spun by the Secretary or the president to support drastic actions against Muslims, including rumors the president was considering internment. He tried to go quickly through the rest of his escape regarding the terrorists being upstairs above him, of no one guarding him in the cellar, how they had foolishly left some small rusting old tools in a corner he was able to reach by moving the heavy mooring, of how dogs on the island alerted the terrorists to his escape, and how he hid under a dock after flooding a canoe to make it look like he drowned in the river.

The reporters, anxious for details, didn't wait for him to finish and began asking questions. When a CNN reporter asked if he thought what he knew about the terrorists would help capture them, he hesitated before answering—remembering it was a stated reason he'd been asked to speak today and the only reason he'd agreed.

"I hope so, I spent most of yesterday telling the people here everything I know about them, both prior to and after I was captured."

"That's something we would all like to hear," two other reporters shouted out simultaneously.

"I understand, but I've been asked to refer any questions like that to the Secretary who is in a far better position than I am to decide how to best use the intelligence we have on our enemies."

Jack's answer was both factual and inflated. He had agreed that his interviews with DHS personnel should be considered confidential, but he'd just implied he knew more about the terrorists than he actually did—that was intentional. It was the Secretary's idea that his speaking might worry the terrorists, force them to make a mistake, so he gave the Secretary what he'd asked for, believing that in no way could it be spun into supporting the president's policies. But he was worried the Secretary might be anxious by now to cut him off as he was leaving little room to spin the story.

"Look," Jack said. "I know you guys have a lot more questions, most of which I doubt I'm qualified to answer, so let me summarize by repeating 'I'm no hero.' I wasn't captured while fighting for my country, tortured for years while locked in a cell where men were under surveillance with no possible way of escaping. Those are the men who deserve to be called heroes.

"And finally, with regard to any questions of my probing into the suspicious death of my friend, I'm thankful it contributed to identifying the terrorists and hopefully their capture, but that was sheer luck. I'm not clairvoyant, had no idea, or evidence the man I was suspicious of, was a terrorist! That never dawned on me. It's true I didn't like him, he wasn't a popular figure in my community, but it's also true I knew almost nothing about him. It's worrisome to think I could have been very wrong—attempting an investigation on my own against an innocent, ambitious businessman. That's another reason why I don't like being called a hero. We don't have to look far back in history to see what happens when a country becomes so divided that people become suspicious of their neighbors.

"That's all I have to say today. My five minutes are up and I'm sure you are all anxious to get on to the briefing with the Secretary," Jack walked away from the podium ignoring a chorus of questions being shouted from the reporters.

The Secretary had a hint of a smile on his face as he looked at Jack on his way up to speak. Jack took it as acknowledgement he had turned the tables on him, but the speaker was a pro; with a booming voice and the palms of his hands stretched out towards the reporters still shouting questions at Jack, he quickly quieted them. "Hold it guys! He's right, it's my job to address questions of intelligence concerning the terrorists.

"I'll tell you though—he's too humble about his role in following them, maybe he didn't know they were terrorists, but he knew they were badasses and he took a big risk in trying to find out what they were up to. We need more people like him. We live in a dangerous world where there are radicals amongst us capable of causing great harm with the technology available today."

That was as far as the Secretary dared to go in spinning what Jack said. He'd been caught off-guard, knew he'd get some heat for not rebutting more, but he was a conservative Republican who was also conflicted about the more extreme measures the president was considering.

The press briefing was over ten minutes later. The Secretary had walked the reporters through the extensive army of FBI, CIA Coast Guard, National Guard and police departments throughout the country who were searching for the terrorists. Over a week had gone by, and with more than twelve thousand dead it was estimated that number would more than double. Doctors had flown in from all over the country to help with the sick.

The Secretary didn't have any good news to report about apprehending the terrorists.

They'd found the cars used in the attack, but had no idea where the terrorists were or might have fled to. He didn't want to have this briefing with so little good news to report. But he agreed with the president that they couldn't delay updating the public any longer. He'd also reluctantly agreed to bringing Jack into the briefing on the premise it might help defray the lack of good news, but he never anticipated being upstaged by him. He cut it short when they started asking questions, implied by Jack, about extreme measures the president was rumored to be considering.

"I don't address rumors. My job right now is to track down the evil men who carried out the attack on New York and to bring them to justice. I'm as frustrated as everyone else we haven't done that yet, but I'm confident we have everything in place to make it happen any moment now." After thanking everyone for coming, the Secretary walked off the stage knowing he would shortly receive an unpleasant call from the White House.

Before heading home to Connecticut, Jack spent the rest of the afternoon doing the briefings he was asked to do, and then a few minutes saying goodbye to Max, who seeing him coming greeted him in his office singing, "You picked a fine time to leave me Lucile . . . " They both broke into laughter and then Max added, "for the record, I don't agree with everything you said, but I admire you for saying it."

"Thanks, Max, that means a lot coming from you. I'm going home today. I finished the briefings and I think I wore out my welcome around here."

"With some maybe, but from the feedback I'm getting you also made some friends."

When Jack arrived home it was close to midnight. He'd called Kate when he got in and they were on the phone for an hour talking about his speaking at the HSA press briefing. Kate had been listening to cable news commentary all evening and said, "You were good, Jack, the pundits I listened to all liked what you said."

The following morning, Jack received a call from Bob Grant, the Executive Editor of the *New York Times*, who after a short introduction got right to the point of the call, "We were very impressed with your performance yesterday and wondered if you might be interested in doing some contract work for us."

"Sounds interesting, what kind of work are you talking about?" Jack said trying to hide his elation of being offered a job with the *Times.*

"Right now, the government doesn't seem to have a clue as to where these terrorists are, or what they're up to. If they do, they are not telling us. We think there is more to this story than just finding the terrorists and bringing them to justice, that there's political implications to finding them, assuming that they do. Think of what we would like you to do as a continuation of your private investigations, which wound up playing such a significant role in what we know about the attack on New York. We think you have all the earmarks of a creative investigative reporter. You know this story is still playing out and we believe you're the right man for the job."

"Okay, you've piqued my interest, but I'd have to know a lot more before I'd commit."

"Of course, how about coming in to see us sometime this week."

"I can do that. You caught me at a good time. I live in Connecticut, as you surely know, and I'm about two hours from Manhattan. I can come tomorrow if that works for you."

"It does, we'll do lunch. My secretary will send you an e-mail for directions to my office."

After hanging up, Jack sat back in his lounge chair to contemplate the call. He'd been relaxing on his back porch, reading an article in the *Hartford Current* about a recent quote by the president, "Drastic action was needed to stop the terrorists from attacking other cities."

The quote had Jack thinking about Kate's warning regarding the president using the attack to his political advantage and of comments by political pundits about the president's blatant lying, that he'd say or do anything to stay in power. And now this phone call with Bob Grant implying the attack has political implications that are worrisome.

Yes, Jack thought, *the president should be trying to calm the nation, instead of dividing us by blaming democrats for creating an environment for this to happen . . . and implying all Muslims are to be feared . . .*

After the call from Bob Grant, Jack contemplated what Kate had been repeatedly telling him about having his head in the sand regarding President Cain, that there's no middle ground left, *She's right I can't continue to remain independent. It's time to choose whose side I'm on.* He saw the call from Bob Grant as providence—that he'd be a fool to pass it up—a chance to contribute in his own way with the backing of the *Times.* He was anxious to tell Kate about the call, but decided to hold off saying anything until he knew more about the proposed assignment and had a firm offer. He left the next morning to meet with the Executive Editor of the most influential newspaper in the country.

It was not unusual for the *Times* to hire freelance writers, or stringers as they are sometimes called for one-time assignments. But Jack suspected that few were offered the sweetheart deal he was being offered as he sat across from Bob Grant in the company's private dining room.

They had just finished talking about Jack's time as a cub reporter, his published books, his experience with the terrorists, and the proposed assignment. Grant made it clear that his comment on the phone about "political implications" was at the heart of what the assignment was all about. He said, "We at the *Times*, think the government is holding back, that they know more than they are telling us. This crisis gave the president what he needs to support his autocratic way of governing, which flies in the face of our constitution, including extreme measures he's rumored to be planning to find the terrorists."

Grant went on to say they'd received information that implies the terrorists may have already been caught, but nothing they could substantiate.

"If these were normal times, Jack, I don't think any of us would have taken accusations like that seriously. But as you know, these are not 'normal times.' Cain has broken all the norms of being president. I sincerely hope it's not true, that he hasn't gone so far as to use this crisis for his personal benefit. But it's not inconceivable, that's why, while we still have a free press, we must investigate the possibility these accusations are true. And that brings me to you. I was very impressed by how you handled the Secretary at that press conference the other day. You're obviously quick on your feet and have convictions that are in harmony with us here. With all your involvement with the terrorists to date, with your contacts at DHS, and your creative investigative skills, we believe you're the right man for the job.

"I have no problem with the money you're offering me—it's the timeline. What happens if I haven't uncovered anything worth writing about at the end of three months?"

"Depends. If it looks like you are on the trail of something good, we'll extend the contract. If not, you will have just made the equivalent of what we pay our best investigative reporters, including expenses, and we get nothing. We're willing to take that gamble. Sometimes we just have to trust our gut, don't we, Jack," Grant said with a confidence that communicated he believed they were both cut from the same piece of cloth.

"Okay, I'm in," Jack said as he reached across the table to shake hands on the deal.

"Good and I wish you luck—you'll need it. I have no misconceptions of how tough of an assignment this is. My administrative assistant will introduce you to my staff this afternoon, people who you can rely on for help if the need arises, but I want you to communicate directly with me on this assignment. My secretary will advise you on any staff meetings I might want you to attend and progress reports needed."

Jack spent the rest of the afternoon being introduced to people in the newsroom and going over the contract with their lawyer. The lawyer said he could start as early as tomorrow after it was signed, but advised him to take the contract home and go over it carefully, including the rules on freelance contractors who are held to the same ethical and reporting standards as full-time employees. Jack was anxious to sign it, but took his advice and headed back to Connecticut.

He called Kate while driving home to tell her he was offered and accepted an assignment with the *Times*. She was still in California working on the portrait. She couldn't talk long and though she was excited for him, she asked the same questions he'd been asking himself. "What makes them think you can do this, Jack? How are you going to go about investigating what's happened to the terrorists?"

"I don't know," Jack said, "but I'm going to sign the contract tomorrow and start by flying to Washington to talk to Max about it. I doubt the terrorists are still here if they haven't already been captured as Bob Grant suspects. I think the president's rage over them not being captured and trying to worry everyone about an attack on another city, is an attempt to justify the martial law he's implemented and possibly further his dictatorial powers.

"I also think it's extremely unlikely the terrorists could carry out a second attack if they're still here—my escape made them accelerate their plans, give up their staging area and destroy equipment they left behind. They could be anywhere now, trying to get out by crossing at the southern border, or flown out with fake passports, or by boat anywhere along the coast from Maine to Florida. I tried putting myself in their shoes and my guess, if they're not already in custody, is they'll focus on the boat option somewhere along the coast."

CHAPTER THIRTY- FOUR

Jemal was unaware that Ganz had plotted a devious course towards Cuba after Jemal insisted they go far offshore to avoid Coast Guard patrols and other boats. They'd left five days before and were still three hundred miles from Cuba.

Mike had taught him some basics about sailing when he took him from Cuba to the States, but Jemal still knew little about navigating, not realizing Ganz had picked a course about seventy miles offshore in the middle of the Gulf Stream, where they were sailing against a three-knot current and making only fifty to seventy-five miles a day. That gave Mike time needed to try to figure out how to survive. He soon realized that bad weather, which sailors normally dread, was coming to help him out.

"You shouldn't have destroyed the marine radio and flares Maten, the weather is getting worse, the barometer reading tells me there's a major storm brewing. I could've used the radio to find out where it's headed so we could avoid it."

Mike still only knew Jemal, as Maten Tuma. He had no idea who he really was or the three men with him. He hadn't seen the photos of Jemal on TV that came out two days after the attack, they were at sea by then, but when he was forced at gunpoint in the middle of the night to take them, he knew they would kill him when he was no longer useful.

Mike also thought it odd they kept listening to the news on his little clock radio, *They all gather around when he listens, like they're waiting to hear something . . . they give me the feeling they've done something terrible . . . I'll be blamed for whatever it is by bringing him from Cuba.* An overwhelming guilty feeling came over him as he reflected on what he'd done.

"You left me no choice, Mike. I couldn't risk you trying to radio or signal someone for help. If you'd have done it the easy way, and willingly helped us, you could have made a lot of money instead of being forced to do it. As for the storm, you told me this boat is made for that."

"Yes, but this storm is going to be really bad. I've never seen barometer readings this low. It was foolish of you to destroy the EPIRB. It's an emergency beacon that would have only gone off if we started sinking. I got a bad feeling we're hours away from sailing into a hurricane. There are high thin gray clouds streaking across the sky and I smell salt in the air. Yeah, I said she's made for storms, but not hurricanes. I'm going to break out the storm boards for the windows so tell your men that—I'm not looking for a weapon, just stuff to keep us alive."

"You think he's right?" Ghadi asked as he and Jemal watched Ganz go below. "I mean about the hurricane and this boat not made for it?"

"No, I think he's just trying to scare us so he can change course and head for shore. We'll have to watch him real close—he knows we can't let him live. But we need him now, none of us are good enough yet to sail this boat. I've been watching everything he does and I suspect he's purposely making it go slower."

Four hours later, Jemal was concerned that Ganz might be right, but he still didn't trust him. The wind was howling through the rigging as the boat rolled and lurched into fifteen-foot seas. All his men were sea sick below, puking their guts out into buckets. He was beginning to feel sick himself, but stayed topside with Ganz in an attempt to learn everything he could about handling the boat in a storm.

"I have to reduce sail or we'll get knocked over!" Ganz yelled into the wind as he tied on a safety line and started to move forward.

"No, it will slow us down, let's wait and see what happens," Jemal said.

"Are you crazy? If I wait any longer it will be too late—too dangerous to reduce sail! I have to do it now!" He turned back around and went forward, knowing they needed him even more than before. He took down the main, rigged a storm trysail on the mast, furled the headsail and reefed the staysail. He debated taking down all sails and running under bare poles, but decided he still had time for that if the storm got worse. He knew hurricane conditions were approaching, but miscalculated how quickly it would happen.

It wasn't long before the wind was gusting to over seventy knots and the seas had grown to thirty-footers. Foam tops were ripping off, skipping over the waves into horizontal streaks of salt laden water that stung the face. The autopilot failed and Ganz was no longer trying to steer a course. He'd tied himself to the helm and was trying to keep the boat from capsizing by angling the bow into steeper and steeper curling waves that were breaking over the deck and turning the boat dangerously sideways to the mountainous seas. Jemal had gone below, feeling more seasick by the minute and fearful of falling overboard as the boat began rolling heavily on its side.

It was midnight when Mike saw what looked like a low dark cloud bank behind a series of thirty-foot breaking waves, which he was angling the boat into. Then, seeing the dark mass dip down and rise again, he suddenly realized, with a sickening feeling of fear and awe, that he was staring at a rogue wave—a monstrous wall of water curling and coming straight towards him as it rose to almost twice the size of the others.

As he stared at the wave, the cabin hatch opened and Jemal came rushing out with vomit gushing from his mouth. Mike saw him like he was the devil incarnate appearing at a moment in his life when he could erase the evil he represented and appease his conscience. He turned the wheel hard over for the boat to face broadside to the wave—assuring it would capsize and flood with the open hatch. Jemal was too seasick to see the wave towering over them as he lurched to vomit over the gunwales.

The steel vessel capsized, flooded and the mast broke off as the boat rolled three hundred and sixty degrees. Jemal had rushed topside without a life preserver and was thrown overboard by the initial impact. Mike, tied to the helm, survived the capsizing and saw him franticly waving and yelling for help as the boat drifted away. Jemal was quickly hidden from sight in the troughs of huge seas that were about to claim him. He'd never learned to swim and hopelessly clawed at the surface of the water as his body slipped into the depths below.

Mike was taken aback to find himself alive and the boat still floating. In his selfless moment to intentionally capsize the boat, he'd forgotten he'd been tied to the helm. He was unhurt other than swallowing some seawater and amazed to find himself still alive. He wondered what happened to the others when the boat capsized. Ghadi had been in the u-shaped dinette area that had been made up into a bunk. His two men were in the forward berth trying to get some sleep after hours of constant seasickness.

When the boat capsized, Ghadi was thrown across the cabin and broke his back on the chart table. The two men in the forward cabin were desperately trying to open the glass hatch above them, not realizing it was held down by storm boards. The broken mast was now banging into the hull in the tangle of wires that attached it to the boat. The cabin, flooded by the open hatch, was now three feet deep in water. Ganz, believing the boat couldn't remain afloat much longer, untied himself from the helm and threw the four-man life raft overboard. It opened on impact with the sea as it was designed to do, and trailed behind the boat, tethered to the stern by a short line, looking very small as it bobbed around in the storm.

Looking around at the raging seas, Ganz knew his chances of survival in the raft were poor. That his best chance was to stay with the boat as long as possible. He didn't hear or see the two men who had given up on escaping from the forward berth come up behind him. All he knew was the feeling of his head exploding as he fell into the cockpit from the blow of a winch handle. He never saw them jump into the raft to take their chances with the little four-foot diameter inflatable, rather than staying with the boat. It was a fatal decision—there was no way for them to know the raft would be flipped upside down by the hurricane force winds and huge seas, or that the forty-foot steel boat would still be afloat two days later when spotted by a Coast Guard plane.

CHAPTER THIRTY-FIVE

"So I went over the contract carefully, Kate, before signing it. I faxed them a copy and put the original in the mail before flying to Washington for my meeting with Max, tonight," Jack said. He'd waited 'till six California time before calling her, not wanting to interrupt her finishing the portrait.

"That's great, Jack. I can't tell you how happy I am that you finally realized you had to choose sides. The woman I'm painting had recorded your talk at the press conference and we watched it again the following day. I felt proud to be your wife. This martial law business, however, scares the hell out of me, Jack. I was watching TV when you called. Have you seen or heard what the president did today?"

"No, I was planning on watching the news after calling you."

"Well, he extended martial law throughout the country as he'd previously threatened to do. He deputized the military to be a civilian police force until the terrorists are caught, and he suspended the writ of habeas corpus for anyone they arrest. He cited the National Emergency Act as his authority for doing so. They're reporting thousands have been brought in for questioning; mostly Muslims, the majority from the New York tri-state area, but there are reports of others from all over. House to house searches, supposedly looking for the terrorists is the rationale being used to round up undocumented workers. My friends in Connecticut say it's difficult to know the extent of this since no search warrants are required and no one knows who will be next. Reporters can't get information from the police or their sources since it's the military carrying out orders."

"I share your concern, Kate, but if the terrorists were captured, as Bob Grant suspects, all this would end quickly when it becomes public knowledge . . . rationale for these draconian actions would be gone. But Max thinks Tuma, or Jemal as we know him, got out of the country, and who knows what this president will do if he finds that out.

"This may not make any sense to you, Kate, and may be delusional on my part, but I have a feeling I was destined to take this job. It was investigating Tom's murder that brought me to this point. I couldn't have guessed it would all lead to my working for the *Times.*

"I think Bob Grant is right; that what I've learned to date through my contacts with people like Meg, Max and others as I carried out my solo investigation, including being held captive by the terrorists, may give me a leg up in investigating what's going on now. I know it sounds presumptuous, considering the thousands of professionals who are searching for them, but often it's someone thinking outside the box, or the unexpected informant, or an amateur stumbling on evidence that breaks a case wide open. I have no idea what will come out of this, but accepting challenges is part of who I am, and this time I have backing—people I can count on for help."

"That's a mouthful for me to contemplate, Jack, and as always, I'll be worrying about your penchant for ignoring risks, but I have to admit, I feel better this time knowing you're not doing this alone, that you have the backing of the *Time's.*"

"Okay, I've gotta go now, Max is meeting me downstairs by the bar, but I'll call you again later if it's not too late." Jack hung up, but not before hearing Kate say she loved him in a manner that conveyed she was behind him all the way on this.

Max was in the bar talking to a beautiful redhead with a southern accent when Jack walked in. "Sorry I'm late, Max, but looks like you didn't miss me at all. I'm hungry and can go get a hamburger if you'd prefer to join me later," Jack said trying to give Max an out if he wanted it.

"No, no this is Sally Flynn, she's an old friend. We bumped into each other here by chance," Max said and then introduced Jack.

Sally Flynn laughed as she shook his hand. "Max was evasive when he said he was meeting a friend and I asked who it was and what you do. Do you also work for the government, Jack? You don't mind if I call you Jack, do you?"

Before Jack could answer, Max said, "Sally I'm sure he doesn't mind, but like I told you, we have some important business to discuss, so we'll have to postpone our chat for another time."

"Wow, must be really important, nice meeting you Jack," Sally said as she laughed again and walked out of the bar.

"Sorry about that, Jack, she's a reporter for the Washington Post, very aggressive as you can see, so I had to be rude to get rid of her."

"Thanks, a reporter is the last person I needed to talk to tonight. How do you know her?"

"When I was working for the DEA, she tracked me down in Honduras for an interview on that drug bust that went down so badly. We dated a few times, but she thinks of men as nothing more than a means to further her career."

"You said it was a chance run in. You think it was just coincidence?"

"Not sure, Jack. She said she heard some senators were meeting here to discuss the martial law issue over a round of drinks, but they never showed up. How about we move over to a booth, order some grub and start talking about why I wanted to see you."

"Good idea," Jack said. After they were seated, he held up a cautioning hand to stop Max from saying why he wanted to see him. "Before you say anything, Max, I need to tell you the *New York Times* has hired me."

"You're kidding!" Max said as he sat back staring at Jack with a stunned look.

"No, I'm not. They called me the morning after the press briefing, offered me a freelance contract to write a story about the terrorists, focusing on trying to find out what's happened to them—like have they really escaped—or have they been captured as the editor of the *Times* suspects."

"That does change things. It raises the possibility that our conversations might wind up in the news and it wouldn't take long before someone figured out where you're getting your information."

"I understand why you say that, but I'd like to think you know me well enough to know I'd never betray anything you asked me to hold in confidence."

"Yeah, I believe you mean that, Jack, but what if I knew something that was at the heart of what you will be investigating—something that could cause a constitutional crisis if leaked to the press, lead to riots, or worse, civil war across the country. Would you, a reporter now for the *Times,* be torn, believing you had to do what you felt is morally right, even if it meant betraying a confidence and our friendship?"

"If a situation as you just described actually occurred, I would ask you, might even beg you, to release me from the confidence in question. But if you refused, I would honor the confidence entirely as originally agreed to. I understand, Max, that my moral perceptions do not entitle me to play God—that my righteous reasoning might belie the truth of any given situation or what's in question."

Max crossed his arms, studying Jack for a moment before closing his eyes deep in thought. Jack respected the silence wondering what he would do if the situation was reversed. It was obvious Max had some new information about the terrorists, troubling his conscious regarding what to do with it, including the possibility of being the source of it being leaked.

"How long have we known each other, Jack?" Max said as he looked up. It was clear he had made a decision.

"About four years."

"Right! More than enough time to know if we can trust each other—no matter what. So, here's the deal. I'm going to tell you something in confidence, very relevant to your assignment, and you and I will debate what's best to do with the information. But you must agree that I have the final say regarding what you do with anything I tell you in confidence."

It was Jack's turn to be silent for a moment, to reflect on the implications of what Max said before agreeing to his conditions. "Okay sounds very fair, except for the remote possibility I may stumble across the same information through other means. If that happens and you agree I didn't use what you told me, then I'd be free to use what I discover on my own anyway I want."

"That's reasonable and a very remote possibility. If we were lawyers, I'm sure we'd both think of many more conditions and exceptions, but this agreement is based on mutual trust so I'm fine with your exception."

Jack nodded in agreement and reached across the table to shake hands on their deal.

"Okay, now that we've dealt with that issue, I can go on with what I started to tell you before you warned me you're now a reporter for the *Times*." Max shook his head and chuckled to himself regarding what they agreed to before going on.

"I'm going to tell you a story that clearly falls into the 'in-confidence category' so you can't print it, at least for now. I want to hear how you might use this information to carry out your investigation and then we can talk about if any or all of it needs to be made public. Here's the story:

"A Coast Guard plane spotted a sailboat boat dismasted in a storm and saw a man onboard signaling for help. A cutter was deployed for rescue and found two men onboard. One was a man named Mike Ganz, the owner of the vessel, and the same man who was signaling for help. A second man was below with a broken back from the boat capsizing.

"Ganz had an incredible story to tell. Said he was forced by four men to take them to Venezuela via Cuba, at gunpoint. This same four have been identified as the terrorists—their rented car was found in a construction site outside a marina and Ganz's boat went missing the same day as the attack on New York. The man with the broken back was later identified as Akram Ghadi, one of the terrorists. His fingerprints on the rented car matched fingerprints on the cars we found in Kennedy airport.

"Ganz claimed he recognized one of them, but didn't know he was Omar Jemal. He said he never saw the news or photos of Jemal before they commandeered his boat. He said he'd met Jemal in Cuba, months before, where Ganz said he stopped for supplies on his way back to the States after two years sailing in the Caribbean. He said Jemal, had introduced himself as Maten Tuma when they met in Cuba, had paid him to take him as a passenger to the U.S. on his boat. Ganz claims he'd showed him a U.S. passport, but there are holes in Ganz's story."

"You said Ganz claimed there were four men who forced him at gunpoint to take them to Cuba, but you also said there were only two men onboard when the Coast Guard came to rescue. What happened to the other three terrorists?" Jack asked.

"I was just getting to that. Our guys took Ghadi, the guy with a broken back, to a military hospital where he was positively identified from fingerprints found on the car that was rented from JFK and that matched the cars used in the attack. Under questioning he confessed there were four of them, including their leader, Jemal, who had masterminded the attack on New York."

"What happened to Jemal and the other two?"

"Ganz said the boat was caught in a terrible storm, said he intentionally put the boat broadside to a rogue wave to try and kill his captors. The boat rolled over and was dismasted. He said the man he knew only as Tuma was seasick, had just come up when the boat capsized and was thrown overboard and that Tuma didn't have a life jacket on. Ganz said he saw him franticly waving for help as the boat drifted away. Ganz said 'the other two saw me preparing the life raft, snuck up behind me and knocked me unconscious with a winch handle and took the raft for themselves.' His head was bandaged, Jack, and it was confirmed in the hospital he'd suffered a concussion, but he's being held for further questioning because of holes in his story about his relationship with Jemal. With regard to the other two, the Coast Guard found the life raft floating with nobody in it two days ago."

"So Jemal is dead."

"He has to be. We checked and there was a cyclonic storm the night he said they capsized. There were winds of hurricane force and both the boat and life raft were found over one hundred miles offshore. So even if Ganz is lying about Jemal being washed overboard in the capsize and he was actually in the life raft with the other two, there's no way he could have survived. "That's great news, Max. It eliminates any reason for continuing the search for the terrorists."

"You would think so, but the White House was informed of everything I just told you and we were told to say nothing until they confirm it," Max said.

"What's to confirm? From all you just told me, Jemal has to be dead. You have a witness, Ganz, and one of the terrorists in the hospital. It's insane to believe anyone could've survived for days in storm tossed seas a hundred miles offshore, without a life raft or life jacket."

"We agree, but the White House hasn't had a press conference to announce the news. Nor have they said anything to relieve everyone that the terrorists are no longer on the loose. You're right, Jack. This makes no sense, that's why I wanted to discuss it with you."

"You said, 'We agree,' how many people know about this?" Jack asked.

"That's not an easy answer. There's the Coast Guard crew in the cutter that boarded Ganz's boat. They talked to Ganz and the injured man. It's doubtful the boarding crew learned enough to suspect he was one of the terrorists. He wasn't interrogated until we confirmed who he was by fingerprint matching his prints with those on the car. He didn't confess until shown the overwhelming evidence we had tying him to Jemal and the cars used in the attack. And remember what I just told you, 'Ganz didn't know Tuma was actually Omar Jemal and Ganz wasn't interrogated until he was turned over to DHS,'" Max said.

"I understand that, but how about the boarding crew, didn't they talk to Ganz?" Jack asked.

"Very little, remember he had a serious head injury—a concussion. The Coast Guard Chief in charge of the boarding party said Ganz told him about the man thrown overboard when the boat capsized, and of the two men who left in the raft, but Ganz didn't give him any names. It wasn't until later, when he was interrogated, that Ganz told us about Maten Tuma and we informed him that Tuma and Jemal were the same man," Max said.

"I don't know, Max, you said Ganz did tell the boarding crew that four men commandeered his boat at gun point. With the whole nation worried about the terrorists still on the loose, wouldn't you think that the Coast Guard men involved in the rescue might suspect that the four men Ganz talked about might be the terrorists?"

"Yes, some probably did. But Coast Guard men are no different than the military in knowing they can get in trouble by talking about operations they are involved in, so there's little chance they would go talk to some reporter about their suspicions without proof to back up anything they might say.

"Okay, but how about people like you and others in Homeland Security who have been involved in tracking down the terrorists?"

"Good question. As far as I know, there are only six of us who know the whole story of what happened to the terrorists. There are a few others who know bits and pieces, but not enough to put the story together."

"Who are the six, Max?"

"Secretary Thompson, three senior management officers in charge of the investigation, myself, and Ghadi's interrogator. This was a classified investigation so all of us are bound by the confidentiality of our security clearances. I'm sure you're aware Jack, I could go to jail for all I've just told you, and wouldn't have done it if I didn't trust you would honor our agreement."

"I know that, Max, I'm honored you place that much trust in me. Let's go back to the question of why all this is being kept secret. If, as you say, the Secretary informed President Cain, then one can only assume it's the president who doesn't want this news to be made public. The only reasons I can think of for him doing this is because he either doesn't believe you guys, same as he doesn't believe his own intelligence people, or, and this might sound like paranoia to you, maybe he has some diabolical reason for wanting to keep martial law in place."

"Maybe," Max said with a pensive look on his face. He was contemplating how to respond.

Staring hard into Jack's eyes, he replied, "I think it's time we leveled with each other, Jack, on some things we've avoided talking about. First I need another drink, something stronger, like a Jameson. How about you," he asked as he signaled the waitress to come over.

"Make it two when she comes," Jack said as he sat back to let Max begin the conversation.

"We've avoided politics as everyone seems to do these days when we know we're not on the same page. We tried it before with Kate in the room and it ended with us all agreeing to disagree and knowing the friendship was too important to sacrifice for our political views. It also clarified for me what I suspected, that Kate was a very liberal Democrat and you, an independent, who reluctantly voted for this president, and, now sorry you did. As for me, I'm sure you both came away believing I was a very conservative Republican."

"That's a pretty accurate assessment," Jack said as he continued to listen.

"Yes, but that was then and this is now, when we're facing issues that are too important to not talk about. You and I find ourselves involved far beyond anything we could've imagined. I think it's crucial we put all political niceties aside and talk about how we really see it, and what if anything we can do about it," Max said.

Jack thought for a moment, what Max just said before answering. "Okay, how about starting with why you voted for this president and I'll do the same. I suspect we are probably closer today on this than six months ago, but it will be a good segue into what we really need to talk about."

"We could spend a week on why we are who we are, Jack, why we vote a certain way, and we'd just scratch the surface, but I'll sum it up for you this way. I'm very conservative and make no apologies for who I voted. Does that mean I turn a blind eye to character flaws when I pull the lever, I don't like to, but yes, I admit I do and so do most people regardless of party affiliation. It's all about winning, Jack."

"You think winning is more important than who or what is best for the country?"

"I think they are one and the same. You've heard me say my reasons for being a conservative Republican is based on things like, concerns about big government, the decline of our education system, the growth of social programs we can't afford, and a military that can protect us from the terrorists and regimes that want to destroy us. That to me is what's best for our country and why winning is so important."

"You make a good point, Max. That's probably as good an explanation as any why most Republicans voted for the man, but for independents like me, it was a much harder decision."

"How so?"

"Because I think most independents share the moderate views of both parties and hope their vote can sway the outcome one way or the other."

"That doesn't explain why you and so many others voted for him?"

"No, just why it was hard. For me, and I think many others, it was all about feeling demoralized by the choice, that there was a need to shake things up, that helping a populist would show the strength of independents. I didn't really think he could win, but once he did, I hoped the presidency would humble the man and that it would be a wake-up call to the Democratic Party."

Max laughed, "Well, it sure didn't do either. That brings us back to what I started to talk about. When the president extended his martial law orders last week to include all states it shook a lot of us up in the department. We didn't have any information to support that. And now, with his deputizing the military as a civilian police force and suspending habeas corpus, many of us are worried that these executive orders are more about solidifying his power and to dampen dissent before the election, rather than his claim they were necessary to protect the country from more attacks. We have knowledge, beyond reasonable doubt, that all the terrorists are accounted for—three dead and one in the hospital as I told you."

"Question, Max: The discovery of the car and the boat the terrorists hijacked, was that the result of martial law and searches by the National Guard?"

"No, the owner of the marina suspected foul play. He knew Captain Ganz wouldn't have left without notifying him. The marina owner called the local police when a few days went by without hearing from him. That's when they found the car and fingerprints that matched the cars at Kennedy."

"You said it was two days ago that Secretary Thompson notified the White House about this—are you sure about that?"

"Yes, I was the point man for the department, coordinating support amongst the agencies. When the Secretary was informed about finding the boat, and what happened to the terrorists, he held a meeting with the same people I told you about a minute ago to assess the news before notifying the White House. All way above my pay grade. I was invited to the meeting because I'd been the point man. There was mutual agreement that we had verified what happened to the terrorists from the information gathered by the Coast Guard, FBI and our own people. The director thanked us and said, 'I need to inform the White House of this good news immediately.'"

"How do you know he did?"

"Because my boss saw the communique sent to the White House and reminded me that everything I heard at that meeting was classified."

"Do you know him well, I mean the Secretary?"

"No, I would have never been on this case if it wasn't for you asking for my help. Neither of us had any idea the guy you wanted me to investigate was one of the top ten terrorists in the world. My job was way down the rung, so there's no reason I would've met the Secretary if this case didn't fall into my lap the way it did. The first time was the day after the attack in a strategy meeting with a bunch of other people, the second time when I was asked to bring you in to meet him, and then the other day in the meeting I just told you about."

"What do you think of him?"

"He's a business man, took over from a military guy. He's lucky in that we have a lot of long-term professionals in the department who are good at what they do. Other than that, what I know about him is the same as you. It's a political job; he got it because he's been a big supporter of the president. I hear they're real tight—talk a lot. Why do you ask?"

"Just wondering, like you, why he didn't go to the press with the news about the terrorists," Jack said.

"I take it you're speculating the president stopped him?"

"It's all supposition, Max. All I can tell you is that there's a lot of people who believe he needed something like this to insure his re-election.

"I don't know, Jack, I don't like the man, some of us are worried that might be true, but I still find it hard to believe he would knowingly go that far. It's also possible he still doesn't trust his own intelligence people."

"C'mon, Max. You got fingerprints, the car, a confession from one of the terrorists. If he doesn't believe all that then he's delusional, and either way it says he'll do anything to stay in power."

"Possibly, but now we're getting into politics, and if we're not on the same page it affects many things we see differently, conceivably even things I told you tonight," Max said this with raised eyebrows implying it was more a question than a statement.

"I'm a little ahead of you on President Cain. I've given up on him. I really hoped he would change. I'm an independent, Max, but now I see him as a threat to our democracy. The democrats have a point—we've impeached presidents for doing far less. So yes, we probably see things differently, but rest assured, I would never let my politics affect anything you and I agreed to."

"I didn't think you would, Jack, but even the best of friends can have misunderstandings on what they say to each other and what was meant to be, as they say, off-the-record."

"Then let me make it clear. I consider everything you told me tonight regarding the terrorists as confidential. I'll go a step further. To me it means I will not discuss the information you shared with me tonight with anyone without your approval—including my wife." Jack knew he could trust Kate with anything he told her, but also knew Max didn't know her well enough to believe that himself.

"Thanks—we're good on this Jack, so let's move on. I'm sure you've figured out by now that I wouldn't have shared this information with you if I didn't have some of the same concerns as you have regarding Cain. But you're right, I haven't moved as far as you have on him, which is one of the reasons why I won't approve you using any of it until I'm convinced it's the right thing to do."

"You just said it's 'one of the reasons,' what's the other?"

"The other is you will need more than me to quote—that's the real world. Without someone or something else to back up what I told you, the story will get dismissed as fake news by Cain and his friends at Fox," Max said.

"It's promising to know you're keeping an open mind, but that's a tall order knowing I can't use anything you told me to find another source to verify the story."

"I think the first step, Jack, is for you to spend a little time thinking about how you would proceed with this new information at hand, then get back to me with your plans as soon as possible."

"That's fair, and thanks, Max. I hope I can prove worthy of your sharing this with me."

CHAPTER THIRTY-SIX

"How was your first day with the *Times*?" Kate asked. She'd called twice, before Jack decided what to say to her about his meeting with Max.

"You had dinner with Max? Did you tell him about your new Job?"

"I briefed him on it. He was a little taken back believing he would have to be careful now with anything we talked about. We worked that out—"

"Sorry to interrupt, but how did you do that?"

"We mutually agreed to treat anything either one of us tells the other in-confidence as if it's classified data." Jack was trying to avoid saying "that excludes telling anyone including you."

"I would've thought that was understood without saying it." Kate said in a questioning tone.

"Yeah, but he was shocked to hear I'm now working for the *Times* so you can't blame him for being overly cautious. But let's put that all aside for now. This assignment is beginning to feel like "Mission Impossible" any bright ideas how I might proceed," Jack was trying hard to change the subject.

"Are you kidding me? It sounded impossible when you took the job, but all I heard was they thought you were the best qualified person to do it." The emphases in Kate's words were clear. He changed the subject, asking questions about the portrait commission and the woman in it.

After talking to Kate, Jack reflected on all he learned from Max. He wanted to start his investigation by finding everything out he could about the sailor, Mike Ganz, as well as talking to the Coast Guard, but he needed to find a way to do it without violating his agreement with Max. *Yeah it would have to look like I learned about this Ganz guy on my own.*

Reflecting on what Max told had him, made Jack start to think about all he knew going back to being chained in the cellar, a time when he only knew Jemal as Maten Tuma. He'd been truthful in telling Max and others at the DHS everything he knew, but he had a nagging feeling he'd forgotten something . . . .

He closed his eyes and began reflecting on being chained in the cellar. Sometime later, as he relived all those moments, including Jemal entering and implying he would die soon in an experiment . . . a buried memory of what Jemal said to him came back "you remind me of a borfoot sailor who also appeared at the right time and place for me" Jemal's comment didn't make sense to Jack at the time. It was also overshadowed by Jemal's following comment about "expediting his plans for him"—implying he was going to kill him.

Jack played the forgotten memory over and over in his mind. Trying to connect the meaning of . . . "a borfoot sailor" with . . . "the right time and place for me," and that's when he realized that when Jemal used the word "borfoot" he probably mispronounced the word and was talking about a "place" That's when it struck him, he might have meant "Beaufort" not "borfoot." Beaufort is the name of town's in North Carolina and South Carolina, both of which are located on the Intracoastal Waterway, through which sailors pass to avoid open ocean passages along the East Coast. Jack was familiar with both having sailed the intracoastal some years back.

Yes, Jemal meant Beaufort . . . what he said now makes sense, Jack thought and realized he now had a great lead for investigating where Jemal might have gone to try to get out of the country. More important it didn't violate his agreement with Max. The location of Ganz's marina and where the car was found never came up in his conversation with Max. Jack suspected that was intentional and reason to suspect there might be a lot more Max didn't tell him.

He called Max to let him know about his memory recall, and what he now believed was Jemal's mispronunciation of "Beaufort." He wanted Max's approval that it didn't violate their agreement before heading to Beaufort.

"No, it's quite a coincidence you remembering that so soon after our talk, but I agree—don't see how anything I told you could have tipped you off to what you intend to do now. Would much appreciate, though, you keeping me in the loop on anything you learn there."

"Will do, Max."

For the first time since he'd signed the contract with the *Times,* Jack felt good. *Yeah, maybe they were right about asking me to do this.* A few minutes later, he called Kate to tell her he was leaving for North Carolina in the morning.

"I told you the portrait was almost completed and I'd be coming home tomorrow—what happened? I thought you were almost finished in Washington?" Kate said, and he detected the hurt in her tone.

"I am, but I remembered something today that might help in my investigation. I need to check it out and it's too complicated to explain on the phone. I should be back home in a couple of days." He hung up after some small talk to avoid saying anything more. He knew Kate wasn't fooled—that she knew he was avoiding talking about what he was up to, that he would tell her eventually.

Since Beaufort, North Carolina was closer to D.C. than South Carolina by a couple hundred miles Jack decided to head to North

Carolina first. He left early in the morning for the three-hundred-and-fifty-mile drive and arrived at noon to visit seven marinas he found on the internet. It was his lucky day. Within minutes of arriving at the third marina he was talking to the proprietor and learned that a boat went missing the same day as the attack on New York, and that a man named Mike Ganz owned the boat.

"You're the third person this week to come and talk to me. The first was a man from the FBI and the second was someone from Homeland Security," the proprietor said and then requested ID Jack used what the *Times* gave him.

"Hey, you're the guy I saw on TV, the one who escaped from the terrorists!"

"Yes, that's me. The *Times* hired me knowing I'm a writer. They're suspicious the government knows more about these terrorists than they're telling us—they're grasping at straws by hiring guys like me to help with their own investigation." Jack was intentionally trying to diminish, in the proprietor's mind, the idea he had any knowledge about the terrorists beyond what was reported in the news.

"Yeah, but you wouldn't be here if you didn't believe like I do that the FBI were here because of the terrorist attack on New York.

"Why, were they inquiring about this man Ganz who you say had a boat in your marina?" Jack asked.

"They said the Coast Guard discovered Ganz's boat dismasted in a storm offshore. They found him onboard with a head injury and took him to a hospital. He was subsequently identified as a possible suspect in an on-going criminal investigation they weren't at liberty to tell me about. I told them I was aware of a car with no license plates being found at a construction site just outside my marina, and that it had been towed away.

"I asked if all this had anything to do with the terrorist attack on New York, but they said they couldn't comment on their investigations—that like all investigations of this kind it would be improper for them to reveal what it's all about and I shouldn't jump to conclusions based on anything they told me."

"But you think it is related to the attack on New York?"

"Like I said, I thought it might be, and now you, a reporter for the *Times* coming here is making it look more and more to be true. Why did you ask me if a sailor or boat was missing from this marina—there was nothing in the news about a boat being dismasted in a storm and rescued by the Coast Guard. How did you know to come here?"

"I didn't know. I decided to focus my investigation on how the terrorists might try to escape. Aside from being a writer, I've done a lot of sailing in my life and decided to focus my investigation on the possibility they would have tried to escape somewhere along the coast. Then I got lucky, because Beaufort came up on my radar yesterday while reflecting on what happened to me after a conversation I had with an anonymous source. I was in Washington D.C. so I decided to check it out and your marina was one I was planning to go to."

"Your anonymous source was probably one of the other boaters here who knew Ganz's boat was gone and of the FBI coming here."

Jack ignored the comment, kept a poker face, and said, "So did the FBI say where Ganz is now or if anyone else was on his boat?"

"No, to both questions. That's another reason I'm suspicious, as you are, that Ganz being missing is related to the terrorists."

Jack again felt it important to distance himself from conclusions anyone here was espousing. He had to constantly remind himself he was on the job now so he changed the subject, "I, for one, would like to know much more about this Captain Ganz. Did he strike you as the kind of person who would get involved with terrorists?"

"No, he didn't, not to me or anyone here. He went out of his way to let you know he was a conservative Republican. He rented dock space from me periodically over the past ten years. Came back about four or five months ago after sailing the Caribbean for two years. He was talking about selling his boat so he could buy a house in town. That's all I know about him other than he was divorced, and had an eighteen-year-old daughter.

"Did he leave a note or speak to anyone here about where he was going?"

"No, and that's not unusual, most boats here are seasonal customers and often are gone for a week or two, but I spoke to him the morning before he was gone and he didn't say anything about leaving, he would have if he was, that's why I called the police a few days later."

Jack was stymied. He left the proprietor of the marina feeling good about having identified the place where Ganz kept his boat—all information developed on his own, but he still didn't have an independent means for writing about the terrorists who were dead and the one who'd been captured. Max would want more to approve of him printing the story.

Reflecting on the list of names who Max said, "did know, or might know . . . " brought to mind the Coast Guard rescue crew who talked to Ganz and the injured terrorist. *Yes, a good next move*, he thought and Googled the nearest Coast Guard station. Station Fort Macon came up, just ten miles away in Atlantic Beach, NC—a twenty-minute drive from Beaufort. He booked the Sand Piper Hotel there, about two miles from the station knowing this was going to take some time. He then called Kate to let her know he wasn't coming home tonight.

After checking in at the Sand Piper, Jack asked the clerk at the front desk for directions to the Coast Guard station and a recommendation for a good local bar close by. His first stop was the

Coast Guard station that the clerk said was only two miles away in Fort Macon State Park. He was surprised to see the park partially surrounds the Coast Guard Station with the main gate located directly across from the park office. He caught a glimpse of a big cutter docked there and later learned it was the USCG RICHARD SNYDER that had recently been assigned to the station. What he didn't know, and was soon to learn, was that this cutter, a new one hundred fifty-eight-foot boat, was the same vessel deployed for rescue to the SALLY MAE, Ganz's dismasted sailboat.

The Tipsy Mermaid, recommended by the clerk, turned out to be just what Jack was looking for—a small beach bar frequented by locals who might have knowledge of any recent Coast Guard rescue operations. Jack went straight to the bar where a half dozen men were drinking and struck up a conversation with a pretty blonde barmaid in her thirties, who introduced herself as Tess. He told her he was a freelance writer looking for someone who might have knowledge of any recent Coast Guard rescue operations. "My names, Jack," he said and handed her one of his freelance cards.

"Jack Quinn . . . hmm, not the same man captured by the terrorists?" she asked, as she looked at the card with an amused smile crossing her face, which could have passed for a younger version of Dolly Parton. She then looked up with wide eyes exclaiming, "Oh my God you are him—I saw you on TV!"

"Guilty," Jack said and began laughing along with the man at the bar next to him who overheard the exchange and was amused by her reaction.

"So, why are you here? Why asking about this Coast Guard station? This is Bo Carter, by the way, who's laughing at my expense." Tess had regained her composure and was now a little annoyed with herself for reacting like a teenager.

"I'm looking for those guys that captured me. I have a score to settle with them," Jack said in the most facetious way he could muster, knowing he had an audience now from Tess's outburst.

"That's funny, but doesn't answer 'why here?'" Bo Carter said in a friendly manner, but overlaid by a warning in the way he asked the question. If Jack didn't explain, his acceptance here would be short-lived amongst the regulars who had nothing to do but drink and gossip of happenings about town. He needed to establish some rapport with them, to have them accept him into their circle before asking questions.

The man staring back at him waiting for an answer had a wry smile set into his rugged weathered face. He looked to be in his forties. Dressed in Levi's and a tank top, he appeared to be an inch or two under six feet as he leaned on the bar with a forearm, marked by a fading blue anchor tattoo. The tattoo, a deep tan, and the weathered face were implicit of a life outdoors. *Likely a fisherman or sailor,* Jack thought. He had a good sense of men and intuited this was a no-nonsense guy, thinking he'd better be honest and stay as close to the truth as he could.

"That's a fair question deserving a direct answer," Jack said. "My coming here came about in a roundabout way so I'd appreciate you bearing with me if it sounds like I'm avoiding your question, I'm not. If you saw me on TV as Tess here did, then you know I'm a freelance writer and was captured by the terrorists and escaped. I'm the only person who knows what they look like, except for their leader, whose photo is all over the news as they search for them. And it's no secret the government has everyone worried they might still be in the country.

"As for me, I don't believe that," Jack said and noted he had their attention so he continued. "I've sailed all my life and know how porous our coastline is. I've sailed past here on the intracoastal, on my way to Florida so I know how easy it is to come and go if one wanted to avoid customs and immigration. So, based on a hunch the terrorists might have tried to escape from around here, I began an investigation on my own by visiting marinas to see if there were any missing boats in the days after the terrorist attack—"

Jack saw the skeptical look on Carter's face as he interrupted Jack to say, "I would think someone from the FBI, CIA or Homeland security would have already done that?"

"Yes, they have, so hear me out!" Jack said. "I know this sounds like I'm grasping at straws, but earlier today I was at the Town Creek Marina in Beaufort and discovered a sailboat from there was missing the day after the attack, which brings me to the main reason I'm here. The proprietor of the marina told me a boat, owned by a live-aboard sailor named Mike Ganz, had gone missing the day of the attack, and that the FBI questioned him about this sailor who they said the Coast Guard rescued after his boat was dismasted in a storm."

"Was he alone?" Carter asked, who was now looking at Jack in a new light.

"No, the FBI told the proprietor there was another man onboard, injured in the capsize and that he spoke very little English. They also said both men are being held for questioning in a criminal investigation."

"Okay, Quinn, let me guess. You think this criminal investigation has something to do with the terrorist attack, that the FBI isn't telling us the whole story and you shot over here from Beaufort to see if you could learn something from us locals."

"That's about right, except I'm also assuming the Coast Guard rescue operation was carried out from here—by that new big cutter at Fort Macon. If I'm right then I'm hoping to find someone from the cutter to talk to, like a crew member that boarded Ganz's boat and talked to Ganz before he was taken into custody."

Bo Carter stared at Jack for a moment then turned around as if he was looking for something. He was . . . and turned back to whisper, "Come with me, there's an empty table in the corner, it's the only spot in here where we can have a quiet private conversation."

"Thanks for suggesting this, I was beginning to get uncomfortable answering all your questions at the bar," Jack said after getting seated and ordering another round of beer.

"Yeah, I noticed. So was I. But I need to know some more about you before I tell you why I dragged you over here for some private talk. First of all, you say you are a freelance writer, does that mean anything I say to you, or anyone else here says to you, might be reported in the news tomorrow?"

No, I'm not an employee of a magazine, newspaper or TV station. What I do, I do mostly on my own, but sometimes I do contract work for the news media. Most news outlets hire contract workers or freelancers like me from time to time on special assignments. The contracts vary in nature, meaning in some the media controls and owns everything that is produced in the assignment, and others the freelancer controls the assignment and owns all subsequent rights to it after completing the assignment."

"Are you under contract now?"

"After I did that briefing Tess was talking about, I was approached by one of the major newspapers in the country and offered a contract assignment to look into what happened to the terrorists. I accepted, first of all because I was essentially still doing it on my own and this offered the opportunity to cover my expenses and make some money, but the main reason I said "yes" is because they agreed to all my terms and conditions. I have total control over the assignment and what is published—they don't even know I'm here.

The only say they have is that it has to meet their ethical standards, and that's a good thing," Jack said.

"What if I told you I might know someone who was involved in the rescue you referred to? Could you give that someone a guarantee you won't publish anything he said unless he approves?"

"Yes."

"Who did you sign the contract with?"

"That I can't tell you. I agreed I wouldn't reveal to anyone who I signed with. It's in there to protect what they are doing from their competition. I'm sure you're not the competition they have in mind, but still, I have to honor what I agreed to as I would with anything we agree to."

"Okay, I don't have a problem with that, but I can't speak for the person I have in mind. Give me one of those cards you gave Tess and I'll try to get back to you tonight."

"Thanks, I really appreciate your help," Jack said as he reached over to shake his hand. Seeing he was about to get up and leave, he quickly added, "From the way Tess introduced you, I assume you live here. Are you a native of this area, Bo?" Jack had sat back, crossed his arms across his chest and asked the question with the warmest smile he could muster. He was letting Carter know he was very comfortable in his company and wouldn't mind knowing a little more about him.

"Yes, I was born in Atlantic Beach, just a short distance from Fort Macon Park and the Coast Guard station. Spent a lot of time as a kid playing at the park and watching the sailors come and go from the station. I couldn't wait to be one of them and joined up when I was eighteen. Did my twenty and retired four years ago. This place was up for sale and I bought it the day after I got home."

"That's my story, Jack. What's yours? How'd you get to be a freelance writer?" Carter said as he sat back smiling with his arms crossed to let Jack know that's all he's was going to get out of him for now and it was his turn to get a little personal.

Jack laughed. "So, you own the place. I'll be dammed—you are one cool guy. Okay, my turn." Jack told him a little about his navy experience, about being a cub reporter, freelancing, and two of the books he wrote, but spoke mostly about how the murder of his best friend inadvertently led to his capture and escape from the terrorists.

Bo Carter was a good listener, and liked what he heard, "Okay, I've heard enough not to worry about you being one of those reporters who would sell his mother for a story. You can count on me calling you later."

Jack left the Tipsy Mermaid feeling good about his first day on the job. He'd identified Beaufort, and the marina that Max left out of the story, and now the owner of a local tavern is holding out the possibility of introducing him to a Coast Guard crewman who was involved in the rescue of Ganz and one of the terrorists. After getting a quick bite to eat he went back to his hotel to wait for Bo Carter's call.

The call came at nine. "Jack, we will meet you at the Tipsy Mermaid at seven tomorrow morning. There's a door on the left side of the building that goes to my office. Knock and I'll let you in. He has to be back on the ship by eight so you'll only have forty-five minutes to talk—see you in the morning," Carter said and hung up.

A minute later, Kate called, "Hi, is this the missing persons bureau? I'd like to report my husband has disappeared, I think he has Alzheimer's and can't remember where he lives, his phone number or even my name."

"Sorry Kate, I've been tied up all day and forgot to call. The good news is I've had a great day and lots of progress on this assignment I took on for the *Times*," Jack said, and filled her in on his memory recall, his visit to the Beaufort marina and with Bo Carter.

"Sounds promising. When do you think you might come home?"

"No idea right now, I'll follow this trail to where ever it leads me, but if I had to guess, sometime next week."

"Did you listen to the news today about the internment camps?"

"I overheard people talking about it, but was so busy I put off listening to the news 'till tonight—how about you filling me in?"

"Cain is scaring everyone about the terrorists. Implying, since they still haven't been captured, that they could attack again at any moment. He says we are at war with the Muslims and accused the National Guard of being soft on executing his orders to round them up. They have been ordered to step-up the pace. Entire families are now being sent to internment camps. The election is less than six months away and now his approval rating is hovering over fifty percent since the attack on New York and his issuing these executive orders. I knew he was waiting for an opportunity like this—it appeals to his base," Kate said.

"Do you think he'll try to string this out to gain support for canceling or delaying the election?"

"He knows how difficult that would be to do, Jack, even Lincoln didn't attempt that during the civil war. No, he doesn't have to do anything like that now that his approval rating is over fifty percent. I think it's more about taking on as much executive power as possible, believing it will enable him to do anything he wants to remain as president. I know your head is all around this assignment, trying to track these guys down, but you have to promise me something, stay tuned-in to what's happening, Jack, it's much worse than you think."

"Like what? What don't I know?" Jack asked.

"Cain is succeeding in splitting the country in two with his rallies and tweets. This is much worse than the Women's Protest March in D.C. when a dozen people were killed. Millions are protesting around the country regarding the round-up of Muslims and the internment camps. Thirty Muslims have been killed by neo-nazi groups and twenty protestors have died so far in clashes with Cain's supporters. It's going to get worse. Cain has ordered a ban on all protest marches and given the National Guard Troops authority to shoot, if necessary, to enforce his orders."

"I know, Kate, sorry to cut you off, but I do know, that's why I'm so focused on tracking the terrorist's down. I told you the editor at the *Times* suspect they might have been captured. If that's true, and it can be proven, that would be a game changer.

"Yes, but you're running out of time, Jack. If the government has captured them, they will do everything they can to prevent anyone from finding that out. It doesn't sound like you're anywhere closer to doing that!"

Jack wished he could tell her everything to make her feel better, but he knew it would be wrong to violate the deal he made with Max. And even if he did, he needed far more than he had now to prove obstruction by the White House. *Yeah, clever these people, they can arrest and detain guys like Ganz, or even me if I'm not careful.* He knew they'd keep anyone from knowing about it as long as habeas corpus was suspended. He also knew time wasn't on his side and that he'd be at a dead end if nothing came out of his meeting with Carter's Coast Guard friend.

CHAPTER THIRTY-SEVEN

"So, Bo tells me, you belong to a fake news organization, but can't say which one," Jake Johnson said after being introduced the next morning to Jack in Bo Carter's' office.

"I take that as a compliment since in the lexicon of our president, he always substitutes Fake News for any genuine criticism. And for the record, I don't belong to any news organization, what Bo is referring to is a temporary assignment contract in which I have total control of the story line—they can either accept or reject it," Jack said in the same friendly tone Jake Johnson's spoke.

"Okay, that agrees with what Bo told me so let's not waste any more time. I think Bo told you I have to be onboard in an hour and I need time to change into uniform so let's sit down and get started.

"Can I record this interview?" Jack asked and took out a small digital recorder he had in his pocket.

"Yes, but under one condition. I want Bo to hold the recorder. I may want him to erase all or part of it when we're done—it all depends on how this goes and what agreements we come to regarding my knowledge of a recent rescue operation."

Jack nodded okay and handed Carter the recorder. He had no choice. Johnson was no fool, knew his career could be at risk by talking to someone in the news media, which was most likely the reason he didn't show up in uniform. Jack noted he walked with a bit of a swagger as the three of them went over to sit at the little table Carter had in his office. Deep blue eyes set in a patrician face gave him an authoritarian look that matched the measured way he spoke.

"I think I have a pretty good idea of what you're looking for, so I'll save some time by telling you what you need to know about me. I'm an MCPO that's a Master Chief Petty Officer in the Coast Guard. My rank is E9 and I have nineteen years in the service. I was on the cutter, RICHARD SNYDER, when we were deployed to a disabled sailboat called the SALLY MAE. More important to what you're looking for, I led the rescue with three other men using an auxiliary craft launched from the SNYDER. I was the first to talk to Captain Ganz, the owner of the boat—he had quite a story to tell."

Chief Johnson walked him through his boarding the disabled boat and of Ganz saying four men forced him at gunpoint to take them to Venezuela via Cuba, and of Ganz describing the storm and capsizing, and why three of the men must have drowned, including their leader, and that one man was down below with a broken back. It supported everything Max told him, claiming Ganz met the leader of the four men months earlier and took him as a paying customer to the states, and that he'd never seen the other three before they had boarded his boat. But there were some significant differences from what Max knew.

The Chief didn't know he had boarded a boat the terrorists used to try to escape after the attack on New York—he thought he was just rescuing a sailor whose boat was damaged in a storm. He didn't know that Ghadi, the man on board with the broken back, was one of the terrorists or that Ghadi's fingerprints were found on one of the cars used in the attack. He didn't know these things when he spoke to Ganz, but his suspicions were aroused when he talked to Ganz and later when he was interviewed by special agents from Immigration and Customs Enforcement (ICE) who work for Homeland Security. They wanted to know everything Ganz told him.

"When Ganz told you about the four men who hijacked his boat, did he describe them?"

"No, all he said about them was their leader had the number 313 tattooed across his back, then made a little nervous laugh, said it made him suspect they were drug dealers."

Holy cow! "He said 313," this proves Jemal is dead. Jack could barely contain his excitement as he continued to question the chief.

"Did you suspect they might be the terrorists for which there was a nationwide hunt?"

"It crossed my mind, I asked Ganz that. He looked shocked—said he didn't know about any attack on New York, repeated he thought they were drug dealers. He seemed very rattled by my telling him about the terrorists. Asked me when it happened. When I told him, he suddenly changed the subject and started talking about his head injury hurting and needing medical attention."

"I told all this to our captain when I brought Ganz and the other guy back to the boat. He must have radioed this ahead because a helicopter came out to pick them up off our cutter. They took Ganz and the other guy into custody and that's when they asked me to not repeat anything he told me.

"What do you think now—do you think the men on Ganz's boat were the terrorists?"

"I can't prove it—I've just told you all that I know. But my gut tells me I'm right, otherwise I wouldn't be here talking to you.

"Well I can tell you with absolute certainty you are right, and here's why: Omar Jemal, the leader and architect of the attack on New York had the number 313 tattooed on his back, the same man Ganz told you had that number on his back and drowned when the boat capsized, and that number, by the way, is—"

"How do you know all this?" the chief blurted out.

Jack told him about Meg and how she knew and told him.

"There's much more, Chief. I know someone in government who knows the whole story—knows that Ganz and Ghadi are being held in custody—knows that Jemal and Ghadi's fingerprints were all over a car found near the Town Creek marina where they left from in Ganz's boat and that Ghadi has confessed," Jack said.

"I'm confused, if your friend knows all this, and you, why hasn't the government said so instead of continuing this manhunt and scaring the hell out everyone with talk about the possibility of another attack?"

"Fair question, and sadly I think it's because there wouldn't be any more justification for marshal law, suspension of habeas corpus and internment of Muslims."

"Are you suggesting the president is doing this intentionally—to keep these executive orders in place?"

"Yes, I do believe it's intentional, but I'd leave it to a psychiatrist as to why. We all have seen how he doesn't believe and attacks our intelligence agencies. I suppose it's possible he doesn't believe Jemal is dead since we don't have a body, but you know as well as I there's no way a person could survive being thrown overboard in the middle of a hurricane, hundreds of miles from shore," Jack said as the chief nodded in agreement.

"So why haven't you gone public with this, sounds like you have enough to print this story now."

"You would think so, but I agreed to not print a word unless I could verify it all myself. I believe my friend is worried his story would be labeled fake news and his superiors wouldn't back him. What you told me today of Ganz saying he saw 313 on the back of his captor, that verifies it was Jemal who drowned, and verifies everything my friend told me. I needed that to print it, and believe me, it will be headline news if you give me the okay to use what's on that recorder."

"I'll do that if your government source, this friend who you say knows the terrorists were on Ganz's boat, knows what happened to them, is also willing to go public with the information he has, and you agree to include his testimony in the story you print. I need to know he will stick his neck out as far I will. There's a much better chance this won't get dismissed, as your friend said, if there's two of us—two independent sources. I have a lot more to lose than you, Mr. Quinn, and I assume so does he. We could lose our pensions and possibly be arrested for insurrection under the current executive orders that now exist."

"You're right, but remember I was captured and escaped from the terrorists, that fact, and the fact the president called me a hero, which I'm not, gives a lot more weight to my credibility and your stories, which will be penned by me. I'm not naïve, however, of the risks you both will be taking. You make a good point, it's a fair request. I will call him tonight and tell him your conditions, I know this man well, I feel confident he will agree," Jack said.

"The reason you gave Carter for not saying what major newspaper you're working for is no longer valid. You now have my story if you meet my terms, and one of my terms is the name of the major newspaper that gave you this assignment, and how they will publish the story. I'd be stupid to go ahead without you telling me that!"

"It's *The New York Times*. It will be published as headline news on the front page followed by my article that will reflect your story as quoted to me, and confirmed by my government source, also quoted to me. I will use your names and describe both of you to the extent necessary to reflect the unique validity of your stories.

"Okay—I think we understand each other, but I want you to know why I came here this morning willing to talk to you. I consider myself a patriot, a conservative Republican who worries what the liberal left would do if they come into power. This was very hard for me, I wrestled with talking to you all night, the only other person I talked to about this is Bo, both of us have been increasingly worried about Cain, but never thought he would go this far.

"I'm sickened, knowing what I know, over protestors on both sides getting killed because Cain's been fanning fear and instilling distrust of our neighbors by promoting the idea the terrorists are still amongst us. Bo convinced me I should hear you out. Everything I knew pointed to my believing the men Ganz called drug dealers were actually the terrorists, and if that were true then what Cain was doing was incomprehensible. But I had no proof of that until today. I'm glad I agreed talk to you.

"I have to get back to the base, so here's my phone number. You can call me anytime up to eleven this evening. If your man says 'yes,' I'll want to meet him, hear it first hand, so the two of us can agree on what you'll print in your story. Bo can set the meeting up for the four of us."

Jack called Max right after Chief Johnson left. "I didn't think you could do it," Max said. "Good detective work, Jack. I'll tell you now this is what I hoped for, someone like him to back up what I told you, because he's right, two independent sources make it much harder to call it 'Fake News.' You can tell him, 'Yes,' I'll meet with him. How could I not? I have my military pension and can go back to my dad's farm if Homeland Security fires me. Nineteen years you say he's got in? He could lose it all with just one year to go."

"Can you come here, Max, I don't think it would be easy for him to go to Washington and it might scare him off if the meeting wasn't held on his turf."

"Sure, let me know when and where. I can drive there tomorrow if that works for everyone. Why don't you call him now—let's get this rolling."

Back at his hotel, Jack called the Chief to tell him Max agreed. Jack was relieved to hear him say, "Okay, tell him we'll meet late tomorrow afternoon. Bo will call you to let you know when and where," he hung up without saying anything more.

Jack was writing a draft of the story he envisioned for the *Times* when Carter called. "The chief said it's a go and asked me to set up a meeting with your friend tomorrow. What time will he get here?"

"He's driving from D.C. and expects to get here tomorrow early in the afternoon."

"Good. He wants to do this on my boat, away from the eyes and ears of any nosey people, wants to make it look like we are going fishing. Atlantic Beach is a small town where it's easy to notice what others are up to. I have a thirty-foot Grady-White tied up in front of the Tipsy Mermaid, I occasionally use it to take customers on a tour of the inlet and around Fort Macon. Meet us on the dock at four o'clock"

"We'll be there," Jack replied and went back to writing the draft. Now that it looked like he had all the pieces in place, he started thinking about how the story will be perceived by the public and the rest of the media. He hadn't thought about it beyond knowing it would be headline news. Seeing the words unfold on his laptop woke him to the profound impact the story would have on the current political situation—realizing this could be history in the making.

Kate calling him brought him back to dealing with what to tell her. He wanted to tell her everything that happened since he arrived here, about his meeting tomorrow with Max and the chief, a meeting he believed would lead to headline news that will shock the nation. Yes, he wanted to tell her all that, but he didn't trust discussing it on the phone, as paranoid as that felt. He wasn't taking any chances with the explosive story at his fingertips. He also didn't want to jinx the outcome by talking about it too soon.

"Still can't say much, Kate. But I'm optimistic the *Times* will be happy they gave me this assignment."

"You've done it?"

"I said 'I'm optimistic' and that's all I'm going to say now. Either way I should be home in a day or two. I miss you and look forward to hearing all about the portrait you did."

"Clever you. Changing the subject again, but I can wait until you come home, knowing you must have good reasons for clamming up." They chatted some more, mostly she talking about Cain, and about how thirteen more protestors were killed outside a rally in Los Angeles the president held to gain support for the internment and marshal law he'd put in effect. He was still claiming they're necessary policies to expedite finding the terrorists.

Max arrived the next day barely in time for the meeting. They were in his car and Jack was asking how to address Chief Johnson. "Just continue to call him "Chief" Max said. "That's what I'd do. He's used to everyone calling him that. That's what most of the guys called me and I kind of liked it when I was in the service."

"I thought you were a Warrant Officer?" Jack said as they pulled into the parking lot of the Tipsy Mermaid.

"I was for the last five years, that's when they addressed me as "Sir." The truth be told, I liked it much better when they addressed me more informally like, 'Hey Chief how about we go out for a few beers tonight?'"

"Okay, got the message. We're here and I see them waiting out on the dock."

After a quick round of introductions, Bo Carter hustled everyone onboard, handed out beers and started talking like a tour guide as he pulled away from the dock. Ten minutes later after cruising under the causeway bridge, he dropped anchor in the inlet off Fort Macon State Park. The twin outboards were noisy so no one said much on the way there except for hearing Carter shout out points of interest about the area. Once the boat was secured, he invited them to the main cabin where Jack opened up the meeting.

"Chief, I'd like to tell you a little about Max, all I told you before was that he worked for the government. That's all I could tell you since I was honoring an agreement with him in which he had approval of what I disclosed. That all changed after I told him about you and what we discussed yesterday and as you know that's why he's here today.

"Before the two of you start talking, let me tell how I know him." He went on to tell the chief about Max being an ex-navy Seal, working five years for the DEA and now for Homeland Security. Also, about Max helping him trying to find the people who killed his best friend, and neither of them knowing they were the same people who carried out the attack on New York.

"I met Max on a Caribbean island where I was writing a story and he was working for the DEA on a drug bust. He saved my life when I got carried away with a false sense of my own capabilities in helping with the drug bust. I'm telling you all this because I'm sure he thinks of himself as a patriot, same as you do, so I know how hard this is for both of you to allow me to quote and publish the truth about what happened to the terrorists that attacked New York, particularly when you know it contradicts everything the president is saying.

"I believe being a patriot goes beyond being willing to give your life for our country. I'm sure you know every word you say will be scrutinized and some will accuse you of spreading fake news.

"I think patriotism also means being willing to fight for the soul of our country and everything it stands for in the first amendment of the Bill of Rights. After thinking about what I'm asking you both to do, I looked up what Madison said—I think it's most relevant to what's happening today so I printed it out to read it to you," Jack saw they both nodded in anticipation so he went ahead with what Madison argued . . .

"Madison said a republic like the United States is founded on the principle, 'the people, not the government, possess the absolute sovereignty. In order to hold public offices responsible in a republic, people must be able freely to discuss public officials and their policies. If office holders have violated the people's trust, they should not be able to shield themselves from criticism by restricting the press.'"

"That is a direct quote of Madison defending the Bill of Rights and I think it speaks volumes to what is going on today and why I believe it is so important for us to publish the truth of what happened to the terrorists. It's inconceivable from everything you two have told me that the president doesn't know the truth of what has happened. His lying to us while people were being interned and killed in protests, violates the public trust he was given when he was elected. I emphasize those words because I believe they precisely define what Madison was worried about when he defended the First Amendment the way he did. I think he had people like you in mind, true patriots willing to stand by their conscience when constitutional crises arise, like the abuse of power that we're facing now."

There was a silence in the cabin for a long moment before the chief spoke up. "I'd like to speak to Max alone—give us a couple of minutes," the chief said and it sounded more like an order than a request.

Jack and Bo Carter left and grabbed a couple more beers when they sat down by the stern. "What do you think, Bo, is the chief having second thoughts?"

"No, I don't think so. But I think he's rightly worried about how all this will impact his life. I told you, this is a small town—mostly conservative I might add and they don't like liberal newspapers like *The New York Times.*

"Would you do it if you were him?"

"I think so, but talk is cheap when you're not standing in the other person's shoes. This has been bugging him ever since the rescue, he tried talking to his skipper and was told, 'There must be a reason—it's not up to us to question their actions—and I'd suggest you keep your thoughts to yourself.' That's what the chief was told and it was hard for him. He's a good man, Jack, he wants to do the right thing."

Max came out a few minutes later, "We're done, come back in."

Chief Johnson looked like a big load was just taken off his shoulders. "I asked you two to leave because Max is the only one here that knows what I'm up against. I'm still active duty and I'm not authorized to talk to the news media about rescue operations and there's the problem of my skipper warning me to keep my mouth shut. I'm not bowing out, Jack, but Max has a suggestion—"

"Let me take it from here, Chief. I told you, Jack, he has much more to lose than I do. I've got my retirement and truthfully it should never have come down to this. Coast Guard Command and Homeland Security should have broken this news—they're holding one of the terrorists and know the others are dead. The chief shouldn't have to take it on the chin because the big boys are afraid to stand up to the president. Accordingly, here's my suggestion:

"Your article should be based on everything I told you. The chief just told me in detail everything he learned in talking to Ganz, so as far as I'm concerned, I just interviewed him. And for the record, I'm a special agent in the DHS investigating the attack on New York. I came here to interview Chief Johnson because I knew he was the first person to speak to Ganz. No one can question that it was in my authority to do this, and I didn't need the permission of the ship's captain to do it. Now this is what I want you to do, Jack. The article you plan to publish should reference everything I told you about the terrorists being dead except for the one in custody and also include my interviewing Chief Johnson today to verify what he knew about the rescue as well as what he learned from talking to Ganz when he boarded the boat. In other words, there's no need for you to quote or reference him other than through what he told me. With regard to my interviewing him, he had no choice. Why would he refuse telling the truth about a rescue operation to a special agent from the DHS. That should override any regulations or protocols regarding him not talking about Coast Guard rescue operations.

"As for me, I'll quit when this is over or before that if they try to stop me from testifying about what you publish in the *Times*. You still have everything you need. This shouldn't change the impact of your article. It will include the fact the chief backed up my story in my interview with him. The difference is the chief won't risk his retirement as he might if it read like his quotes to a reporter, but you can quote me, I don't care if my people don't like it!"

"I like it Max, and I think we're done here. You both make me feel good again about our country. I think it's fair to say there'll be fireworks when this hits the newsstands." Jack thanked everyone and headed to the airport. He wanted to fly to New York that night so he could be at the *Times* office first thing in the morning.

"Here it is," Jack said as he handed the article to Bob Grant. He sat down and took a deep breath as he watched the Executive Editor of *The New York Times* read what he and Max mutually agreed should be published. He had called Max the night before from the Madison Hotel in New York and they'd gone over every word Jack wrote.

Bob Grant looked up when he was finished and said," Do you have any idea how explosive this is? This is the Smoking Gun the congressional investigators were looking for. Do you have tapes to back this up?"

"Yes, I went over all of it last night with Max on the phone, he allowed me to tape our conversation. He knew I would need that and I have it here," Jack said holding up a small digital recorder.

CHAPTER THIRTY-EIGHT

DHS AGENT SAYS PRESIDENT
IS LYING ABOUT TERRORISTS,
KNOWS ALL DEAD BUT ONE HELD CAPTIVE

This was the headline in the *Times* the morning after Jack met with Bob Grant. The article following the headline showed it "bylined by Jack Quinn—the freelance writer who was captured and escaped from the terrorists," and it revealed everything Max told Jack, and Chief Johnson told Max.

Within hours, the story was on every news channel in the country. All except the most conservative saying, "If this story is true it goes beyond obstruction of justice. People on both sides have been killed protesting and supporting the president's executive orders to find the terrorists. Blood is on the hands of those who perpetrated the lie."

White House aides were unreachable for comment until later that evening when they released a statement saying "There's no proof their leader is dead, no body found and no proof there were only four." Cain tweeted essentially the same message and asked for the DHS agent, Max Cruz, to be arrested for lies that could cause insurrection. But this time was different. Few Republican congressman were coming to the president's defense, and the Secretary of Homeland Security had made himself unavailable for comment.

Jack's article had legs that were impossible to ignore. Max was a DHS agent, a highly decorated ex-navy Seal, and former DEA agent with an impeccable record. Chief Johnson, it turned out, had been awarded the Coast Guard Distinguished Service Medal by the former Secretary of the DHS. For the first time since Cain had been elected his base was quiet. His lying was never a problem for his supporters as long as he attacked the media, liberals, political opponents or anyone he thought he could effectively bully. But these men were seen as patriots by the majority of Americans—their credibility was beyond question and the facts appeared to be indisputable.

Cain had been caught in a lie that was far south of any respectable person's moral compass. There had been cries for his impeachment before this. His demagoguery, alienating our allies, suspect collusion with the Russians, and charges of obstruction of justice had liberals clamoring for impeachment, but with the economy running well, and unemployment low, impeachment had no chance of being passed by congress.

The New York Times headline article, however, was a game changer. What Jack wrote was as explosive as Bob Grant thought it would be. Public opinion for impeachment shifted almost overnight from under forty percent to over sixty-five percent and was growing every day. It was the smoking gun investigators needed to get people to testify against the president and if they refused, subpoenas were quickly granted. Legal scholars had always recognized that impeachment was more of a political process than a legal one—it would only happen if the people wanted it and not before.

The people were clamoring for it now. This was the climate throughout the country when Jack and Kate met with Max in Washington D.C. Jack, and after Max, Chief Johnson and the Secretary of Homeland Security had testified before the House Judiciary Committee.

"It's been a while since I've seen you Max, how's life on the farm?" Jack asked knowing he'd quit the DHS the day the *Times* published the article. They were at his apartment in Georgetown, five miles from the Capital

"Loving it, the only thing missing is a woman—you have any single girlfriends, Kate?"

"Yes, but they're Democrats. Are you thinking of switching over?"

"No, what I wrote about Cain does not reflect any change in my politics, but I'm very liberal when it comes to women," Max replied, with a broad grin.

"Speaking of politics, what's your take on impeachment, do you think congressional Republicans will stand behind it or fold at the last minute?" Jack asked, it was a pointed question that reflected his own skepticism of Congress holding firm.

"I think it will pass, Jack, and here's why: I don't know many Republicans who really liked Cain, and probably for the same reasons Democrats don't. But as I told you before, regardless of his troubling faults, it is all about winning to protect our ideological beliefs, liberal vs conservative principles that divide our two parties. But this time he crossed the line—millions protesting and fighting over a lie—a lie that caused close to a hundred to die and many more injured.

"So yes, I think he will be impeached and partly because I think people like myself were subconsciously looking for a reason to get rid of him."

"The next election is less than a year away, you think the Republicans can win with the vice president you have now," Kate asked.

"I think there's still time to pick a strong candidate. Look what's going on with the Democrats—you have ten candidates running and no clear winner has emerged yet. The vice president will run, but he's weak. He will have to compete for the ticket, similar to the

Democrats. It's an opportunity to restore the Republican Party to its conservative roots to field candidates we can be proud of. I look forward to those debates."

"How do you explain the fact that over eighty percent of Republicans supported Cain prior to this? Why wasn't it clear how big a risk he was to our democracy?" asked Kate.

"I think I answered that Kate, but it was better said by Jonathan Haidt in his book, *The Righteous Mind,* when he talked about how good people are divided by politics and religion . . . how our morality is shaped by our social agendas and defending our tribes. I know I was guilty of much of what he implied as I think we all were.

"I have a question for you, Kate. If the situation was reversed with the economy being healthy, with legislation passed that created free college for everyone, but at the expense of ignoring the national debt, and your president was guilty of what Cain did—acting like a demagogue—alienating our allies and so on, do you really think the democrats would have rushed to impeach him?"

"I'd like to believe they would, it's hard to imagine anyone being like Cain, but you make a good point, Max, about the tribalism. I'm just thankful Republicans are waking up to the risk Cain poses. The Senate votes tomorrow, I'm praying they impeach him," Kate said.

"Cain knows he's in big trouble, knows they have the votes—but wants us to believe he didn't do anything wrong. He's been tweeting all day that he has knowledge of there being more than four terrorists, that they are still out there amongst us. What he's doing now is what he does best, trying to deflect, trying to sow doubt about his guilt. But I've been told by reliable sources he knows he's finished. He will resign before the vote, hoping he can get a deal to be pardoned by the vice president—same as what happened with Nixon," Max said.

"That would be best for the country, wouldn't it," Jack said, "Fastest way for the country to heal and both sides could focus on the upcoming election. I think you're right, the Republicans might field a large number of candidates—they have as many factions within the party as the Democrats. And you know what, I think Max is right, it could lead to healthy debates for both parties and could bring them back to their roots, but recognize they have to compromise for America to compete in this fast-changing world.

"I'm starting to feel hopeful," Kate responded. "The Republicans may field some good candidates, but they're going to get attacked hard for their silence during the craziness of Cain's presidency. The Democrats are going to be in a good position for this next election."

"Only if they nominate a moderate," Max was shaking his head negatively as he looked at Kate and spoke. "The country has had enough of someone trying to impose big changes on us. The far-left Democrats may have some worthy goals, but they scare people. Millions and millions worry their taxes will sky rocket and changes will be imposed on them that they don't want, which they see as socialism. That scares them as much as how Cain disappointed them. I'm hopeful, Kate, but not for the same reasons you are."

"Max has a point, Kate, and I too am hopeful. I think all of us are looking for a new tomorrow—wanting to put this all behind us. A world where America has found its soul again."

The End

ABOUT THE AUTHOR

Following a successful career in the aerospace industry, Pat Wiley studied at the New School for creative writing. After attending workshops with Stuart Dybeck and William Kitteridge, and writing a series of short stories, he wrote, *Sinking of the MV Le JOOLA*, a non-fiction narrative of one of the worst maritime disasters in history. Jim Wade, the former Executive Editor and Vice President of Crown Publishing, praised the book. *Eyewitness, a nautical murder mystery*, was Wiley's first novel. It follows the exploits of freelance writer, Jack Quinn. *Round House, a deadly side to paradise*, is the second in the Jack Quinn novels.

Wiley spent three years in the navy as a submariner, worked as an electrical engineer on aerospace projects and as a contractor on highly classified projects for the DOD. His outside interests have included teaching sailing and boat building to disadvantaged children at a maritime school; working as a volunteer at an orphanage in Africa; rock climbing in the U.S. and Canada; long distance, solo, blue water sailing; and he and his wife sailing thousands of miles for two years, on their forty-foot sloop from Chesapeake Bay to South America.

Pat Wiley and his wife, an accomplished painter and sculptor, are now living in Flat Rock, North Carolina. On most days he writes four to five hours a day and spends afternoons doing research and reading. An avid outdoorsman, he trains for hikes in the mountains by swimming for an hour in a pool, five days a week. But he is still lured by the sea, where he returns for a month each year to focus on his next writing project. Books like *Moby Dick* inspire him to search for a story that will mesmerize readers as he constantly works on honing his writing skills.

PatWileyAuthor.com

CPSIA information can be obtained
at www.ICGtesting.com
Printed in the USA
LVHW081643250121
677447LV00028B/237

9 781944 072346